Praise for *If the Shoe Fits*

"A sexy, sparkly story, with witty dialogue and likable characters… a fun, lively read."

—*Booklist*

"The romantic tension entices the reader from the very first page and never flags."

—*Publishers Weekly*

"Both flirty and intense, and combining a luxury fashion setting with the English aristocracy, this love story will elicit many a contented sigh among romance fans."

—*Kirkus*

"The characters were both charming and realistic, and I was only sad when the novel ended. I want more!"

—*Laura's Reviews*

"If you're looking for a book that pulls you in and doesn't let you go, look no further… With great supporting characters, a fast-paced tempo, ever-changing dynamics, and a steamy romance… I found myself laughing out loud!"

—*My Book Addiction and More Reviews*

"Megan Mulry has cleverly crafted an unforgettable tale of substance that proves that love will always prevail… a rollicking, laugh-out-loud, feel-good novel that will leave you with a smile on your face."

—*Harlequin Junkie*

"If you like Kinsella and Cabot, you'll adore Megan Mulry!"

—*Talk Supe*

Praise for *USA Today* bestseller *A Royal Pain*

## An NPR Best Book of 2012

"This book is a romantic, fantastic, enchanting treat. If you ever had the dream of marrying a British nobleman, don't miss *A Royal Pain!*"

—Eloisa James, *New York Times* bestselling
author of *The Ugly Duchess*

"A light and breezy read... Filled with clever characters, witty banter, and steamy sex, readers won't be able to put it down."

—*RT Book Reviews*, 4½ stars

"Though the premise may be that of a fairy tale, the very human characters keep the plot fresh, funny, and engaging, with Mulry's lavish descriptions of fashion an added bonus."

—*Booklist*

"This delectable story... is all about second chances and every girl's secret fantasy of marrying the perfect guy... A charming book worth reading again and again."

—*Publishers Weekly*, starred review

"Great characters, and their troubles are explored in a natural, entertaining way."

—*Long and Short Reviews*

"A little bit *Bridget Jones* mixed with a little bit *Pride and Prejudice* with a side of steamy interludes! I can't recommend this book enough. You'll cheer for Max and Bronte!"

—*Anglotopia*

# R is for Rebel

## MEGAN MULRY

sourcebooks
landmark

Published by Sourcebooks Landmark, an imprint of Sourcebooks, Inc.
P.O. Box 4410, Naperville, Illinois 60567-4410
(630) 961-3900
Fax: (630) 961-2168
www.sourcebooks.com

Library of Congress Cataloging-in-Publication Data

Mulry, Megan.
  R is for rebel / Megan Mulry.
      pages cm
  (trade paper : alk. paper) 1. Young women—Fiction. 2. Royal houses—Great Britain—Fiction. I. Title.
  PS3613.U4556R5 2014
  813'.6–dc23
                              2013028276

Printed and bound in the United States of America.
VP 10 9 8 7 6 5 4 3 2 1

The caveman plus sweet-little-thing theory is long past. It was a theory insulting to the best qualities of both.

—Vita Sackville-West

# Part One

# Chapter 1

"So, ARE YOU STILL a lesbian or not?" Max asked, out of pure curiosity.

Abby almost spit her mouthful of scotch directly into her older brother's face. Instead, she swallowed loudly and asked, "What does that even mean?"

"You know what I mean. I'm not trying to pigeonhole you or be small-minded or anything—I'm just ill equipped to understand the parameters."

"Do you love your wife?"

"What kind of question is that? Of course I love my wife. I'm mad about her. What does that have to do with anything?"

"Everything. It has to do with everything." Abby tried not to get too fired up, but when Max acted like an ass, it was sort of her sisterly responsibility to set him straight. "Look. I loved Tully. I'll probably always love her. She was everything to me for almost ten years—I can't very well dismiss that as some sort of *passing phase*. But, to be perfectly honest, I never really thought of ours as a primarily gay relationship. I think it's difficult to explain."

"Try me." He lifted one eyebrow in challenge.

"Especially to one's older brother." She quirked her eyebrow up in a mirror image of his, then settled a little deeper into the comfortable deck chair. "Okay. And this is only for you, by the way. I'm not trying to be some bisexual standard-bearer in *The Guardian* weekend section, all right?"

Max smiled. "All right."

uppose I understand what you're asking and my answer
ere is no answer. Or maybe, I don't think your need to know
d force me into some weird cultural-box answer. Lesbian, bi-
al, pansexual. I mean, *please*. I'm not going to label myself to
ake you feel better."

Taking a deep breath, Max continued. "I only meant... do you
think you're going to start dating? Do you like anyone?"

There was someone, but she wasn't about to admit that to
Max when she could barely admit it to herself. "That's not what
you were asking and you know it. But obviously you're going to
badger me until I give you some sort of data on this. You're such
a statistics nerd."

"True enough. Go on."

Abigail sighed. She didn't resent it as much as she ought. Max
was kind of forcing her to pinpoint what had been rolling around in
her brain for the past six months anyway. "Tully was the best. She
was... look, you know her. She's glorious. She really was *all that*.
Beautiful, caring, sexy. I loved Tully... the person." Abby's voice
went a bit quieter. "But it wore out, somehow."

"I get it."

Abby straightened a bit and took a deep breath. "No time for
being maudlin at the end of such a splendid weekend. Devon and
Sarah's wedding was lovely, didn't you think?"

"It's not maudlin." He ignored her attempt to steer the conversation away from herself. "You don't always need to be the one
who buoys everyone up, you know? I think it's amazing how much
you loved Tully, but that you're strong enough to want to strive for
something... more. You're brave, Abs. You're an adventurer."

She shrugged. She didn't have the heart to tell him she was starting to feel like a bit of a coward where a certain man was concerned.

"So." Max took a sip of his scotch. "If I were to set you up on a
blind date, hypothetically, of course, would it be with a boy or a girl?"

"Max!" Abby laughed. "Enough! When I find out, I'll let you know, how about that?"

"Oh fine. I'm not trying to pry—"

"Of course you are! It's what big brothers do, remember?"

"All right. I admit it. I'm prying you open with a crowbar. You just seem out of sorts lately. You're usually so outgoing and involved in all your... *things*..."

"Oh, dear Max. You're adorable. I'm an activist. There's a word for all my *things*."

"I know, I know." He waved one hand as if *activist* was a word that didn't really count... a retrofitted word. "Abigail the Activist."

Lady Abigail Elizabeth Margaret Victoria Catherine Heyworth, fourth child of the eighteenth Duke of Northrop, sister to her filial inquisitor, the nineteenth Duke of Northrop, felt the weight of all those powerful, regal names pressing down on her. "I'm sick of monikers," she added with a touch of defeat.

"Well, if nothing else, *that* I understand entirely," Max added with bitter enthusiasm. "When Bronte really wants to set me off, she insists on calling me 'your grace' or refers to me in the third person as 'the duke' when it's only the two of us in the room, like, 'Is the duke in a bad mood?' or 'What does the duke want for dinner?' She knows it's the worst possible taunt. No one wants to be a moniker. Sorry, Abs."

"That's all right. I know what you were asking. Maybe I'm just trying to avoid having to really think about it. I feel like I've been Abigail-the-lesbian-younger-sister for so many years, especially in Mother's eyes, it might be easier to maintain the role."

"As long as you also maintain that Mother is often cruel and senseless, then go right ahead. Otherwise, just be you. We all revel in your independence and free will, especially those of us who are more tethered to tradition through no fault of our own."

"Are you complaining about being a fucking duke again?" Bronte's cheerful, flat American accent cut through the hot Caribbean night air as she stepped out onto the misshapen deck that extended at a precarious angle overlooking the moonlit bay.

Abby looked up and smiled at her fabulous, if brash, sister-in-law, and watched as Bronte settled happily into Max's lap. Her long, straight chestnut hair hung over one shoulder (and Max gave her a quick kiss on the other) as she looped her hand around the back of his neck.

"Even worse," Max drawled, "I asked Abby if she was *still* a lesbian, and *then* I started complaining about being a duke."

"You didn't! Oh, Abby, he's so dim sometimes! I'm trying to be patient, but…" She gave him a kiss on the cheek and turned back to her sister-in-law. "He's not as smart as he is handsome."

"In any case," Abby said, looking pointedly at her brother, "and regardless of what Mother would euphemistically refer to as *my choices*—I need a plan for when we get back to England. It's been great of you two to weave me into the fabric of your happy little family at Dunlear for the past few months, but I have to start a life of my own at some point. I don't even know where I want to live, let alone what I'm going to do."

Bronte spoke with quick efficiency. "I'd offer you a job at the agency in a second—I think you could sell steak to a vegan, with all that enthusiasm and fire—but advertising would probably be tantamount to heresy as far as your moral compass is concerned. What do you want to do?"

"Damned if I know… something that does good?" Abby's voice sounded unsure, then she barked a laugh. "What a toff I sound like!"

"Well, aren't you?" Bronte asked.

"Ha!" Max laughed. "Yeah, Abs, aren't you a toff?"

"Very funny. You two are beastly. I'm not the one living in a castle."

"Really?" Max pushed. "Last time I checked, you were living with us in said castle."

"I'm not living with you! I'm staying… with you… for a while."

"Right." Max smiled and took another sip. "After six months, staying is also known as living."

"Enough!" But Abby laughed because he was right. "I'm going to be staying in London a lot more once we get back."

"At Mother's? In Mayfair?" Max asked with another taunting smile.

"That was low." Abby smiled and took a long swallow of scotch.

"Well? If it looks like a toff and quacks like a toff?"

Bronte burst out laughing. "That's so fucking true!"

Abby tried to keep a straight face. "I am *not* a toff… moving on. Do you two want to help me get on with my life or not?"

Bronte clapped her hands together, as if embarking on a new adventure. "Yes! What should Abigail be?"

Max watched as the two women discussed the various ideas for Abby's future, enjoying their easy camaraderie and the warmth of Bronte in his lap.

"I didn't love being removed from civilization," Abby mused.

"What do you mean?" Bronte asked.

"Well, all those times Tully and I were away—working on the organic farms in New Zealand or helping build the wells in Kenya or living in the caravan at Findhorn—I loved all the work, the physical labor and having something real to show for our efforts, but I kept thinking, not always, mind you, but often enough, that all I really wanted to do was walk out my front door at two in the morning and get a pint at some crowded pub off of Leicester Square and smoke a few cigs and laugh at some dirty jokes. But then I felt guilty that I wasn't *satisfied* with the simple life and all of the good we were doing. I see now that a lot of that was due to what was, well, disintegrating between Tully and me. I think I want to be in a city for a while and work with an organization that's really hands-on, with people. I still sound like a toff, don't I?"

Max smiled as Bronte launched in.

"No! I know exactly what you mean. You need to talk to my friend Cammie; she's the head of an organization in New York that funds one-woman projects. You would love her—"

"You are impossible," Max mumbled.

"What?" Bronte turned to her husband in mock innocence.

"Don't pay her any mind, Abby, she's the world's worst matchmaker."

"The last thing I want is to be set up on a date, Bron!"

"No! Nothing so transparent," Max said. "She would hardly try something as easy as meddling in your *love* life; she will orchestrate your *whole* life! Just wait, she'll have names and numbers and emails flying your way within a day."

Bronte conceded, "He's right, of course, but there's nothing wrong with that as far as I'm concerned. I just want the best for everyone." But she looked a tiny bit sheepish.

"And you know what is best for everyone, I presume?" Max said as he gave her a little pinch on the behind.

She leapt from his lap and laughed. "Well! At least I don't fucking ask people if they're still lesbians!" She looked at Abby and continued, "You'll get years of payback on that one, Ab. Years! And"—she turned back to Max—"as for you in particular, yes, I do know what's best." She leaned over his chair and kissed him briefly on the lips. "I finally got Wolf to sleep and I'm about to nod off myself. So, stop pestering your poor sister and come fulfill your husbandly *ducal* duties."

Max looked over at his sister and gave her a guilty shrug. "You heard the lady, Abs. I have duties. Are you going to turn in? Do you want me to stay up with you? Sorry about all the gender-labeling nonsense before."

"No need to apologize, Max. I know you're only trying to fit me into your neat spreadsheet view of the world. The duke needs order in his life." She winked at her brother. "I'm going to turn in soon, you should go."

He crossed the deck and gave her a quick kiss on the c
turned back to Bronte, putting his arm around his wife's
they headed back into the villa.

Abby stood up and looked out over the bay below. She
never been here before, but the island of Bequia had completely ca
tured her imagination. Her other brother, Devon, had been marrie
earlier that day on the small, crescent-shaped beach at the base of the
steep hill below. The villas—if you could even call them something
that sounded so posh—had been constructed about fifty years ago
by a friend of the family of Devon's new wife, Sarah James. The
entire complex was called Moonhole. The name suited. Especially
as it neared midnight and the full moon shone down, the free-form
curves and prehistoric feel of the buildings evoking a strange lunar
landscape. Trees grew into and out of windows that had no screens
or glass. Many of the homes had no doors, limited running water,
and occasional electricity, yet they still managed to exude a feeling of
quiet dignity. Abby was in heaven. It felt raw and beautiful.

She thought about her mother's favorite quotation from Coco
Chanel: "Elegance is refusal." And, in that sense, Moonhole was
pure elegance. It relied on nothing; it refused everything extraneous.
Its existence was a study in simplicity. Abby took a deep breath,
savoring the unfamiliar warmth of the scented night air.

Calm.

And then she felt a slight shiver of recognition. When she
opened her eyes, she saw Eliot Cranbrook on the narrow beach
below, walking under the bright Caribbean moonlight.

She took the last slow sip of her watered-down scotch and
stared. Her stomach churned in a slow roll of emotion that was an
unfamiliar mix of fear, anticipation, hope, and lust. Somehow over
the past few months, she and Eliot had become a very unlikely pair
of fast friends. She was a hippie: rebellious, erratic, joyful. He was a
capitalist: driven, successful, precise. They loved the same bottles of

   e same dirty jokes, the same stupid action films. He was
   ally great older brother.

   oby frowned at the realization that she already had two of
   e, and she really didn't need another. Added to that, the mere
   at of Eliot lately was making her feel all sorts of things that had
  othing to do with brotherly love.

He must have felt her eyes upon him, even from this distance, because he turned swiftly to look up the steep slope. The quick smile that came to his face had the unexpected effect of warming Abby's skin from the roots of her unwieldy mane of black wavy hair to the tips of her unpolished toenails. He made a pantomime gesture, pointing to himself and then up to the villa. She shook her head *no* and pointed at herself and then the beach. He made a quick drinking motion. She smiled and raised her glass then pointed at him. He nodded enthusiastically then raised his clasped hands in an exaggerated display of victory.

She turned back into the villa and tiptoed across the bare stone floor toward the kitchen area. She took a plain jam-jar drinking glass off the open driftwood shelf, unscrewed the bottle and poured in a healthy few inches of Oban, then did the same into her glass. She was not one for overthinking much—in fact, her mother often accused her of shooting first and aiming later—but something about walking down those uneven, mismatched steps to the beach below was giving her pause.

Max's joking aside, the past few months living at Dunlear Castle had been a wonderfully restorative transition. After ten years of boarding school, university, and traveling the world with all of her possessions strapped to her back and her dearest Tully at her side, Abby had returned to her childhood home last summer.

After their marriage, Max and Bronte had settled into the comparatively small family wing at the western end of the castle. Over a year later, they still spent the better part of the workweek in town, but Bronte had set up a small satellite office of her advertising agency at Dunlear for the ever more frequent stays that stretched into the week. Abigail spent most of her days riding, working on the grounds of the estate, and adoring her new nephew, Wolf.

Almost since the first moment she'd met him, she felt that the two of them had been born under the same mischievous star. She had never connected with a baby before—she'd always thought they were wailing, complaining bundles that offered little in return for their constant demands—but this particular monster held her in his thrall. Max constantly joked that, between Bronte and Abby's endless attentions, his son's nanny was the highest paid person on the planet in terms of actual hours spent doing her job: to wit, zero hours.

Abigail and Wolf bonded immediately the weekend of his christening last May. Abby had arrived at Dunlear late (as usual) in the midst of a blustery spring storm, her wild appearance the perfect reflection of the internal tumult from her recent breakup with her long-term girlfriend, Tulliver St. John, better known to all as the lovely Tully.

Come to think of it, she met both of the new men in her life that night, there in the warm drawing room: the baby, Lord Heyworth, heir to the dukedom, better known as Wolf, and the impossibly tall, sandy-haired, broad-shouldered American businessman, Eliot Cranbrook.

At the time, Wolf had given her a long, glassy, drooly look, as if to say: *Yes, I am the new best thing around here. Take it or leave it.*

Eliot had given Abby a long approving look, as if to say: *I'll take it.*

She had loved them both instantly.

Abby tended to love things with an all-encompassing immediacy and a complete absence of ambiguity. Her mother claimed she lacked discernment. Abby preferred to think that she lived her life completely open to all of its possibilities. She didn't waste her time worrying about imaginary consequences to things that might never happen. She didn't allow the (usually cruel) thoughts of others to cloud her own optimism or dictate her behavior.

She loved baby Wolf's honest egomania: he *was* the new best thing, after all.

She loved Eliot's open humor, how he exuded confidence without a hint of arrogance. He was just as likely to laugh at himself as he was to poke fun at others. Abby had come to think of him as *solid*.

As a teenager, it had never occurred to Abby to categorically dismiss the idea of being with a man. Far from it: she was nothing if not open-minded. She just had never *wanted* a man the way she had *wanted* Tully. Then, after all their years together, Abby had simply stopped looking at men *that way* and foolishly assumed that was the end of that. Some part of her mind rationalized: Abby loves only Tully, ergo Abby loves only women.

Such a pity when we discover our core belief is as solid as spun sugar.

When the possibility of a *physical* attachment to Eliot started crossing her mind, Abby kept dismissing it as postbreakup nerves or shallow curiosity of "the other" or something equally dismissible.

Except lately.

Lately, the possibility seemed to be crossing her mind like the running commentary at the bottom of the BBC News. Unavoidable. "This just in: Eliot Cranbrook has entered the drawing room wearing perfectly faded blue jeans, a long-sleeved black T-shirt, and a pair of mirrored sunglasses that make him look like Daniel Craig on a very good day... Breaking now: Riding bareback behind Eliot Cranbrook on horseback now illegal in four counties... Alert the media: Eliot Cranbrook smells like saddle soap and fresh-baked bread and autumn."

Worse than the physical pull—which, let's not mince words, was quite lovely—Abby's feelings for Eliot were becoming rather *menacing*, and that was just not on. She was a lover of life, pure and simple. She didn't go in for menace. She loved riding out onto the grounds of Dunlear at five in the morning in late winter, watching the hoarfrost disappear as the low mist began to burn off and the horse's steady breathing played an earthy symphony. She planted trees with the gardeners on the estate. She dug ditches. She did *not* fret.

When she'd fallen in love with Tully, it had been a whirl of mutual desire and joy. Tender, sweet, passionate for many, many years. Abby was not a second-guesser by nature. Forward momentum, water over the gills, and all that.

Odd then, that she was standing in the middle of a rusticated stone building in the middle of the Caribbean at midnight with a glass of scotch in each hand, suddenly paralyzed by a whispering fear. Abigail was just beginning to realize that for someone who had always seen herself as a wild thing, she had been, up until now, rather tame in the emotional risk department. She was unaccustomed to the dips and spikes of adrenaline that accompanied nearly all of her thoughts about Eliot. For a decade, Abby had been in a loving, ardent relationship and had never once had a single moment of this creeping feeling of terror.

Her feelings for Eliot felt dangerous.

The irony wasn't lost on her. Abby's ostensibly wild life with Tully suddenly felt like a misty morning, while a fling with the ostensibly conservative, buttoned-up Eliot Cranbrook felt like a monsoon.

Was Eliot going to kiss her? Did she want to make the first move? Did she want him to? Maybe just out of curiosity?

She hated herself a little when she thought of it like that, reducing Eliot to a curiosity. Then she swept away the small guilt with the probably more insulting thought that he wouldn't much mind how she reduced him if it involved even half of what she had in mind after the kissing.

The sound of a single, soft, muffled laugh coming from Max and Bronte's room finally shook Abby from her thoughts and she made her way through the overgrown bougainvillea hedge and carefully down the mismatched stairs. Her rubber flip-flops made a little slap against the heel of each foot as she proceeded, turning this way to avoid a large palm frond, and then ducking under a riotous pink hibiscus that was dropping its nightly blooms. She stepped out onto the sand and saw the outline of Eliot's strong shoulders and the soft waves of the moonlit sea beyond his silhouette. She kicked off her flip-flops and felt the powdery sand beneath her feet; the faint scent of night jasmine came from somewhere off to her left.

Her stomach did that slow-motion flip-and-roll again, and her mind embarked on a string of obsessive if-then scenarios: *If he turns to look at me over his right shoulder, then he will be a terrible kisser; if he turns toward me over his left shoulder, then he will kiss better than, well, than anything I could imagine; if he puts his hands in his pockets, then...*

It's just stupid Eliot, she tried to convince herself, but her nerve endings seemed to have a very different opinion. *Just look at him!* her libido screamed. *He's everything delicious!* Abby had to confess that over the past few months, she had fallen into the very sexist and en-joyable habit of Objectifying Eliot-the-Man. It was wrong... but he was so easy to objectify, she rationalized. Those dark, dark blue eyes: sparkling, humorous, dreamy. That leonine hair: caramel brown for the most part, with those golden threads in the sunshine, thick and grab-able, like riding bareback and using the horse's mane to hold on. Those damned shoulders: like a Bavarian lumberjack from a bloody fairy tale. Everything about him exuded strength. Whatever needed taking care of, Eliot would take care of it.

Handily.

She wanted to get her hands on him. She wanted to mess him up a little.

Who knows how long she stood there staring at (yearning for) his muscled back, thinking giddily that this was going to be the first time she kissed *a man*. She felt simultaneously—incongruously—way too old to be thinking such a silly thought, and way too young to actually do it... with someone like him. Eliot was a proper grown-up. Abigail didn't know what that made her.

He had turned around during that reverie and had walked up to where she stood at the base of the stairs. She never did notice if he turned to his left or right or if his hands were in his pockets or out when he came toward her up the beach. Eliot took the glass of scotch out of her left hand and brought it to his lips. His eyes stayed on hers, closing slightly when the liquid slid down his throat. She stared at his neck.

"Mmmm." Then with a slight raising-glass gesture said, "Thanks for that." He gave her a pat-pat on the upper arm, a typical big-brotherly move that she had recently come to despise, and, without thinking—or deciding to be done with thinking—Abby grabbed his wrist as he started to pull it away.

She was barely an inch over five feet tall—a sweet little thing, as her father used to say—though she was well accustomed to physical labor and her grip was strong. Eliot was several inches over six feet, ten years older than she was, and she felt the pulse in his wrist quicken beneath her hold. He could have crushed her, but she felt like she was the one crushing him. The night was clear, silent, thick. Their breathing filled her ears: his was becoming shredded, dry; hers was burning her nostrils.

"What is it, Abigail?" His voice was sure and powerful, but somehow deferential and kind.

He always called her by her full name, never Abby, or Abs, or Ab, like the rest of her family. She always thought of herself as Abby. It was almost like he was talking to someone else when he spoke to her. At first she thought it was because he was older and patronizing and domineering and formal and traditional and every other chauvinist epithet she could think of, but lately she had taken to actually looking at his mouth and eyes when he said her full name, and she saw how he took his time rolling the syllables over his lips, as if he wanted to prolong his own pleasure. Or maybe hers.

# Chapter 2

MOVING HIS HAND SLOWLY, with her grip still tight around his wrist, Eliot took a small strand of her black wavy hair between his index finger and thumb, rubbing the silky threads together, as if handling the finest skeins of silk at one of his fabric factories. His voice was raspy when he spoke. "This is probably a really bad idea."

Eliot Cranbrook had spent the past six months forcibly dismissing the possibility of ever having this woman in his bed. Initially, he'd heeded Bronte's warning about Abigail Heyworth's disinterest in the male species. For a while—even now, if he was honest—it didn't really matter to him if they ended up in bed; he loved being around her—adored her spark, her laughter, her wit, her fire—whether it was a sexual relationship or not. Of course she was beautiful in that wild, untouched way that he hardly ever saw on the runways in Milan or Paris. But the two of them were also becoming really good friends, and he didn't tend to have the time or inclination to make really good friends lately. Or maybe never had.

Whenever someone at a party would say something entirely ridiculous and he thought he was the only one who heard it, he would look up quickly and see the spark of shared amusement in Abigail's eyes, raise his glass in silent recognition, and look forward to the time that they usually spent going over the night's foibles. Lately, though, Eliot was slipping. He was starting to *want* her. He wavered between wanting to seduce her and wanting to preserve the status quo. The seduction would be a quick fix, for both of them; he knew they'd share the same pleasures in bed as they did when he silently raised a glass at a party. They were intimate on some level already. Eliot had spent way too much time—alone—conjuring how the sound of Abigail's voice would change as it slipped into a lower register in the midst of sexual anticipation or the cry of laughing joy that he knew would accompany her climax.

On the surface, that scenario was all well and good. Easily taken care of, as it were. But there was another more treacherous thread of longing that had begun to weave into his thoughts about Abigail. He thought she might be the all-encompassing, soul-fulfilling woman of his dreams. The fact that he had never contemplated, much less uttered, words like *all-encompassing* or *soul-fulfilling*, especially when it came to a woman, had forced Eliot to concede that the quick-fix theory was rapidly losing traction.

For someone who bought and sold companies with quick assurance, diving into a proper relationship with Lady Abigail Heyworth made Eliot completely insecure. He couldn't even imagine how the two of them would talk about it. He smiled as he thought of even using the word *relationship* in a sentence and having Abigail reply in her throaty, plummy, aristocratic impersonation of her mother, "Oh *gawd*! Not a relationship!"

On a good day, Eliot's life looked like this: Late thirties. Totally satisfied with work. Focused. A success. On a bad day, it looked like this: Pushing forty. A slave to work. Obsessed with business to the exclusion of anything else. An emotional void.

Intellectually, he knew it would be impossible for any one person to make up for all the missed exits on the emotional highway he'd been speeding along. For nearly two decades, he'd dedicated himself to his career. It was highly unlikely an impish, backpacking sprite still in her twenties was the right woman for that big a job. Their day-to-day lives had about as much in common as the proverbial fish and bicycle. She was the fish; he was the bicycle. In her world, he served no purpose whatsoever. She was fast and fleet. He was mechanical and well oiled.

She looked up at him expectantly. "Do you think you might kiss me, Eliot?"

He saw how her cheeks flushed and he listened to the simmering eagerness in her voice. There he was, methodically rubbing her hair between his fingers, but his mind was engaged in some sort of fierce battle. He never would have predicted she'd have to prod him, but he hesitated.

She was suddenly embarrassed. "I mean, not if you don't want to—"

His eyes refocused on hers and the strength of that look stopped her words.

"Oh. I want to." But he didn't make a move.

A part of him wanted to toss everything else aside. That part of him didn't care if he was only going to have her tonight, or if he had to start taking random trips to Ugandan refugee camps or organic farms in Australia, or if future visits with Sarah and Devon would be made awkward by this type of flippant transgression. That part of him wanted to satisfy this insane curiosity once and for all. She was just a slip of a girl, after all. He could have any runway model in Paris, any young thing in Milan. Abigail was simply an itch he could scratch. Perhaps the time for chivalrous restraint had passed.

But in that moment, he realized he wanted a lot more than a roll-around on the beach and a string of casual meetings here and there. His mother's words rang in his ears: "Begin as you mean to go on."

And he meant to *have* Abigail Heyworth. Not just the flitting, curious, eager imp gripping his wrist right now, but rather the whole woman.

He tucked the strand of hair carefully away, letting his fingers trace the tender, satiny clamshell edge of her ear as he did so, then— her hold on his wrist still half-guiding and half-restraining his movement—he finally touched the pale, perfect length of her neck with the pad of his thumb. He felt a jolt course through him, then a thick tension settled low in his abdomen: raw desire.

Her grip tightened on his wrist, as if to protest.

"You're not going to kiss me, are you?"

He let his hand come away from her neck and she released his wrist.

"I just don't think it's a good idea. We're such good friends—"

"Are you taking the piss? I thought—" Abigail's face flushed hot with embarrassment. Then fury. "You're totally into it. I can tell, Eliot. I'm not an idiot. Jesus, just now when you touched my neck, I felt it from my hair follicles to the tips of my toes. And so did you. What are you doing? Are you trying to turn this into some stupid game?"

"You know I don't go in for stupid games, Abigail." He stayed calm, watching her carefully.

"I know! That's why this is so infuriating!"

He took another sip of his scotch.

"Damn it!" But she was starting to laugh through her anger. "Don't just stand there and drink your scotch as if we're running through the postmortem on the wedding. Speaking of which—oh my *gawd*!—did you see Sarah's stepmother? What was she wearing?"

Eliot smiled and put his arm around Abigail's shoulder, guiding them both closer to the edge of the gently lapping surf and away from all that messy passion. "In the fashion industry, we call it an atrocity."

Abby burst out laughing and Eliot smiled wider, as he always did when she gave him the full-blown guffaw. He was relieved he'd averted a full declaration of his feelings, but it was going to come flying out sooner or later. He needed to tread very carefully so he didn't scare her right the hell off. Hell, he was already scaring himself and he had ten years on her.

"Oh, everyone thinks you are so *good*, Eliot, but you really are just as cruel as the rest of us." The humor faded from her voice and she sighed as she looked at the sea. "We were supposed to have some wild sex on the beach or something, darling. What am I going to do with you now?"

*You're going to marry me*, he thought. "You'll think of something."

"You're right. I probably will." She exhaled and looked up at him with a crooked smile. "But I was really looking forward to my first real *man* kiss. You're sure you don't want to step up to the challenge?"

She was still half-joking, but he could see the fizz of desire just below the surface of her levity. And it only made him more convinced that he did not want to be her *first* man kiss. He wanted to be her *last* man kiss. He also wanted Abigail Heyworth to want *him* specifically. He wanted her to want *Eliot*. He hoped it wasn't a form of egotism on his part, that need to feel known by her—to be wanted—with all of his goodness and cruelty rolled up together in the bargain.

"I'm not sure you're ready for the overwhelming magnetism and power that a kiss from Eliot Cranbrook would provide." He kept it light. "You need to be prepared for that kind of supremacy."

She started laughing again then began air punching and jumping around like a boxer. "Have to get in shape, is that it, darling?"

God, when she flippantly called him *darling* like that, it was almost more debilitating than her eager vitality and exuberance. "Yes, *darling*. Lip exercises. Tongue rolls. Jaw stretches. I want you in top condition."

She dropped her arms and looked up at him with a dramatic show of wide-eyed innocence. "You want me, Eliot?"

God damn her. "You know I do, Abigail."

"You're a nutter, you know that? I basically just told you, you can have me and you said no."

"I wouldn't say that's exactly what happened."

"You're impossible." She grabbed his hand and they continued walking along beneath the star-filled Caribbean sky. She squeezed his hand. "But I like you anyway."

"I like you too, Abigail."

"Oh, come on then." She was swinging his arm as they walked. "What's the worst that could happen? Let's have a pash."

"I don't even know what that means. And a lot could happen!" Eliot laughed. "A lot of *the worst* can happen!" He squeezed her hand in his to get her attention. "What if you don't want to be friends anymore? I know it sounds juvenile, but there it is."

"Oh, fine, if you're going to go all slushy on me, then I suppose you're right. Friends for now."

He was so tempted to pull her hard up against him and let his hands finally grip the sweet round curve of hips and ass he'd been admiring for months—on horseback, in a bikini, as he helped push her chair into the dinner table—but he refrained with the icy realization that his lust was the last thing that would win her. Really win her. Clearly, she was the one who was in it for a quick fix, a remedy he was no longer interested in providing.

And then he was spontaneously joyful. *He would win her.* It was a practical idea he could actually implement. He excelled at implementing. He might be accommodating and obliging and peacemaking and kind, but he also knew how to compete, and he would simply set his mind to it. And then do it. He was a closer. Eliot knew how to win things. He took over companies and rooted out corporate spies, so he would simply apply himself: he could make this woman come around. His world was rife with beautiful women—models, designers, lawyers—but this was the first time that he'd felt this wave of spirited aggression.

He had a plan.

He gave her the coach-like pat-pat on her upper back—a gesture he knew she was coming to loathe—and followed it up with an equally infuriating platonic kiss on the cheek. "Off to bed with you, then." His smile was genuine; she despised when he was patronizing.

This was going to be delectable. She was going to fight it, but eventually she was going to be his. Entirely. Maybe not right away, but eventually. And he was a very patient man.

"We should probably get you back up to Moonhole," he said, pulling her back toward the way they'd come.

"Are you dismissing me?" she asked, peeved.

"No... *let's hang out*," he said, with a silly accent from a silly movie they both loved.

"You're being weird."

"No, I'm not. I just don't want to spend the rest of the night wringing our hands and gnashing our teeth about *the future* like a couple of tenth graders in a John Hughes movie when it's a beautiful evening under a beautiful sky."

"Let's sit for a while, then," Abigail suggested.

"Okay."

She sat cross-legged in the sand and tucked her lightweight, Indian cotton skirt around her knees, then patted her lap. "Come here."

He looked at her skeptically.

"Can't I at least touch you a little since you won't kiss me?"

"Fine. Twist my arm." Eliot smiled and sat down on the sand in front of her, then rested his head in her lap, looking up at the night sky framed by the turn of her jaw. "I'm all for touching... and talking."

She smiled and set her scotch glass in the sand. "What do you want to talk about?" she asked, beginning to massage his neck and scalp.

"God, that feels good." His eyes slid shut, then he opened them slightly to enjoy the look of her while she petted him. "Anything. You can talk about anything. Read me a laundry list... I love the sound of your voice... which is particularly promising since I will soon be spending hours talking to you on the phone, wherever you might be, and enjoying the sound of your prim little British expressions."

"Eliot, I don't have a cell phone. You know that."

"That's being remedied as we speak. I had my assistant send one from Miami. It should be in your room tomorrow first thing."

She laughed at his arrogance. "I can well afford a phone, Eliot. I choose not to have a phone."

"I know. Free spirit and all that. You don't have to answer it if you don't want to. Just think of it as the tin can with the string that connects your bedroom to mine across the backyard of our houses. I'm the lecherous boy-next-door who stares into your bedroom window at night."

She tugged on his hair.

"Ow." Even though he balked, he liked the way she handled him.

"But then Mother will call me," she said, "and Max will call me, and Devon will call and take up the whole answering machine."

"No, they won't."

"What do you mean? Of course, they will. Why do you think I've spent the last ten years at the four corners of the globe? *Without* a cell phone. My family can be quite meddlesome." But she smiled, and Eliot thought it might be from the realization that it was her family's love that was meddling and that might not be such a bad thing. He smiled at the thought of how uncomfortable all that love was going to make her. He was going to love her up like mad.

She stopped rubbing his scalp when she saw the look on his face.

"Why are you all stiff again?" he asked.

"Because you scare the hell out of me when you look like that, Eliot."

"Not possible. I'm putty in your hands."

"That's what's so terrifying. You are supposed to be an intimidating CEO and a pompous ass, and then I'm supposed to flick you out of my mind without a second thought. It's disturbing."

He started laughing again. "You sound like my mother," Eliot said as his cheer subsided. "She tells me I am far too accommodating, far too much of a peacemaker. I'm a bastard in business, if that helps, but I don't really go in for disturbing people in my private life. You, on the other hand, were aptly named, oh fiery daughter of Nabucco…"

She couldn't help but smile at the idea of Abigail the Warrior and Eliot the Peacemaker trying to find their way in this world.

"I know what you're saying, or implying, but face it…" Abby shook her head again. "You ride around in chauffeur-driven limousines in Danieli suits and I drive a beat-up Morris Minor and buy my clothes at the Oxfam shop. We're not a good pair. We should just fool around and get it out of our systems."

"The fact that you know my suits are Danieli proves that your beat-up Morris Minor is really an heirloom and your Oxfam rags are utter affectations."

"Not utter affectations!"

He raised a skeptical brow.

"All right, I might be *slightly* affected," she conceded. "But the fact that you are the *chairman* of Danieli-Fauchard and I have chosen to abandon the absurdity of my mother's—and yours, I daresay—*haute couture* world might be *germane*."

"I love when you use big words." He moved his head deeper into her lap to remind her to start rubbing him again.

She resumed stroking his neck and proceeded with her litany of their potential relationship pitfalls. "You're too old."

"Well, that can't be helped and it's just plain mean of you to point it out."

She held his head firmly between her palms. "You're impossible, Eliot Cranbrook!"

"So are you. That's why I got you the phone."

"All right. Tell me more about this magic phone that doesn't take calls from my mother."

Eliot smiled. "It'll be delivered to Moonhole tomorrow morning. Take it or not. I had it programmed so it only receives calls from one number. *My* number. That's what I meant when I said no one from your nosy family was going to be bothering you on it. Answer it or not, I just want you to know when I'm thinking of you. And, to make it even creepier, I put in the GPS tracker, so if you have it with you and turned on, I'll know where you are. If you want privacy, just turn it off."

It was bordering on stalking, but he could tell that her treacherous, lusty side loved the idea that he had already been plotting a concerted pursuit.

She looked down into his face with a little pout of disappointment. "Maybe you're right about leaving the *us* discussion behind for now."

"Is that what this is?" He smiled up at her. "An *us* discussion? There's an *us*?" By that point, she could tell he was making fun of her.

"Get up, you big beast." She gave his shoulders a final squeeze and then they stood up.

They walked along the beach in a companionable silence for a few minutes, until Abby broke the quiet. "Since we don't seem to be seeing eye to eye on the whole sex-on-the-beach idea, how about you talk to me about my future. What do you think I'd be good at, Eliot?"

"You'd probably turn a pretty profit with that whole sex-on-the-beach business idea—"

She gave him a swift kick to the back of his calf by swinging her left leg behind her right.

"Ow!"

"I just told you I'd give it to you for free, you rotter!" she cried.

"Very bad financial model—"

"Stop it, you!" She was laughing in frustration, but he could tell she was also relieved to feel like he was back to being plain old joking Eliot.

"All right. Fine." He sighed in mock resignation. "I'll quit teasing and go back to being your Good Friend Eliot. What would Abigail be good at? She's fetching, charming, a defender of the weak. She's pure of heart, kind, democratic, not afraid to get dirty. She sits a horse perfectly, despises pretension—"

"Enough!" She laughed again. "I'm none of that. I'm a haphazard, hodgepodge, mishmash of a woman. My CV looks like a brainstorming session for an unreliable teenager: farmer, well-digger, eco-warrior." She sighed and whispered, "Heiress."

"Beautiful. Graceful," he added gently.

————

Abigail hated how much she loved hearing those weighty, timeless compliments fall so effortlessly from this man's lips. She knew she should have been more wary of the businessman whose life was a capitalist study in the commoditization of said Beauty and Grace. But still. She melted a little when he said them to her. About her.

"You're not helping," she said.

"All right. I'll try again. Why don't we work our way back from what you *don't* want to do… just blurt out yes or no. Let's see. Nine-to-five office job?"

"No."

"London?"

"Maybe."

"New York?"

"I think no, but maybe for the right job."

"Paris?"

"Yes."

"Geneva?" His voice rose an octave in hopeful inquiry.

"Eliot! I'm not moving to Geneva just because you live there!"

"Well, why not? There are worse reasons."

"All right, maybe Geneva… there are more NGOs there per

capita than anywhere else… I guess The Hague might have more, but it just sounds so boring. Amsterdam and Barcelona sound like fun."

"Okay, so we've narrowed it down to Geneva—"

She kicked him lightly on the back of his leg again.

"Okay, so we've narrowed it down to someplace urban and fun in Europe. Barcelona, Geneva, Paris, London. I get it. Now about the nuts and bolts. Are you definitely committed to all this enviro-nonsense?"

She pulled her hand out of his grasp and turned to set herself directly in front of him. "See? That!" She poked her right index finger into his chest. "It's not nonsense, and yes, I'm committed to it."

He grabbed her accusatory hand and brought it to his lips; he gave her a courtly kiss on her knuckles. "I apologize, Abigail."

She rolled her eyes and tried to pull her hand away.

"Please forgive me," he added sincerely.

"Well, that was pretty nice, as apologies go, so I suppose I'll forgive you. But as you Americans like to say, knock it off with the dismissive eco-talk. You sound like Max on a very bad day."

He twined her fingers through his and they resumed walking along the abandoned beach. Eliot started in again. "Okay, something really important and meaningful, that will save the world."

She laughed despite herself. "I get it. Yes, I would like to do something that helps people. I don't intend on being Mother Teresa or anything. And to be perfectly honest, I'm not sure environmental lobbying is really my strongpoint. I'm more interested in advocating for women's rights or children or something a bit more to do with humans…" She turned to look up at him. "I sound ridiculous."

"No you don't. I know what you mean. It's your life. Pick something that actually drives you to distraction, a wrong that you find so patently egregious, that seems so outrageously and flagrantly inconceivable, that you absolutely must do something about it."

"You're not such a brick after all." She smiled through the

words, then her voice fell into a serious dip. "I was just reading an article about a girl who was buried up to her neck by her own father and left to die under the chicken coop behind her house. For kissing a boy. Imagine if she had kissed a girl?" Abby tried to make light of it in a perverse way, but her insides sort of curdled at the insanity. Eliot draped his arm across her shoulder and gave her a supportive squeeze. Her throat tightened and she felt a thick pressure behind her eyes.

"It's okay, Abigail." Eliot leaned in and kissed the top of her head. "You know what you want to do."

"I suppose I do. I'm just afraid. And guilty."

"Guilty? What could you possibly be guilty of?"

"It's ridiculous I suppose, but here I am, bucking against my mother's euphemistic criticism of my relationship with Tully, against a maternal raised eyebrow for goodness' sake, and these women are fighting for their lives, having to run away or be tortured. Who am I to offer my silly, meaningless assistance?"

"I'm not coming to this pity party. Get to London, or Geneva, or wherever and get your ass in gear, Abigail. You've spent enough time, as you say, gallivanting, and now you need to get down to the very real business of helping people. Do you want to work for a large organization? Do you want to volunteer on the ground? Do you want to start something yourself?"

"I don't know... I need help. I have so much... so many resources at my disposal, it's shameful—"

"Abigail." Eliot's voice was impatient.

"All right, whatever, I'll leave the rich-guilt at the door—for now—but I mean, I don't really know where to begin."

"I know you think I'm a capitalist tool and all that, but Danieli-Fauchard is already involved with several women's rights organizations. As preposterous as it might sound to you, the history of fashion and women's rights are happily intertwined. Why don't you meet with a couple of our contacts in London? I won't make any heavy-handed phone calls or anything. Have Bronte call if you want. She probably knows everybody already anyway."

"You trying to keep an eye on me?" she asked, trying to bristle, but feeling like maybe that would be quite all right.

"I think I'm still fantasizing about you moving to Geneva, but yes, I would settle for an eye." He kissed her on the head again and she was starting to wonder why he wasn't kissing her on the lips. Her body flushed at the thought.

Then she understood. He wasn't going to settle for anything that had a whiff of a fling. Now she really was in a pretty pickle. On the one hand, she wanted him to rip her to bits right there on the beach, leave her in a heaving, satisfied heap, clothes torn, muscles pulled. Utterly satiated. On the other hand, she now understood that she would have to, if not initiate, at least encourage any future ripping, shredding, or heaving. There was no way he was going to let her have him in pieces, but she wasn't sure she was after the whole emotional kit.

Eliot must have felt it too, somehow. He let go of her with an abrupt start.

"I think we'd better call it a night, Abigail," he said, breathless, with a strange lack of conviction.

She looked at him, both of them awash in that strange mix of desire and fear. "You're probably right. Will you walk me back to my place?"

"Of course."

He took her hand with pragmatic efficiency. Whatever sizzling desire had coursed through them moments before had been tucked away and his hand was nothing more than the top of a cane or a stair railing: a device. She took it nonetheless. Gratefully. He led as they walked up the uneven steps that rose from the beach to the villas on the cliff above.

When the path was wide enough, she walked beside him, feeling the heat of his body, the rich smell of him wafting over and through her. A stray branch of bougainvillea scraped against her bare upper arm. She welcomed the sharp scratch against her tender skin, something, anything, to make her wake up and out of this stupor. A cut. A pinch.

They didn't speak again until they were standing outside the arched, doorless entryway to the villa Abigail was sharing with Max and his little family.

"Do you want to come in?" Abby asked.

"I probably shouldn't. I've got to leave really early for Miami." He looked down at her. "Hey, why don't you come?"

"What?"

"Never mind."

"Why would I come to Miami?"

"You're right. It was a stupid idea. I just thought we might have fun. I'm not looking forward to being alone."

"I'm sure you won't be alone," Abigail said.

"You know what I mean." He couldn't bring himself to tell her flat out that he was already missing her and she was still standing right in front of him. "Just send me a text or call me when you're ready to see me again, and I'll see what I can do." He leaned in and gave her an achingly tender kiss at the base of her neck, followed by a wisp of a kiss across her lips, a brush really. Abigail leaned in for more, but he had already pulled away. "That's all for now, I'm afraid."

Abigail felt herself twitch between her legs. *Why?* her body screamed. *Why is that all for now?* But she merely stood there staring up at his beautiful face, his hair mussed, his top button unbuttoned, a bit of sand on his shoulder, and knew he was right. That was all there could be for now. He wanted everything. And she had no idea what she wanted.

She let her palm rest on his cheek, met his eyes, then turned into the villa and listened as his steps retreated back down toward the sea, and from there, alone, to his hotel down the beach.

As promised, the sweet housekeeper from Moonhole had shown up with a tentative knock at seven in the morning, holding a small white bag from the "Mistah Eliot" for the "Lady Abigail." An hour later, she still hadn't removed the late-model iPhone from its trim white box. Instead, she tossed it unopened (with a contrived lack of interest), into her rucksack, slung the whole pack over one shoulder, and joined Max, Bronte, and Wolf out on the porch of their villa. It was still early Sunday morning, the Caribbean sun bright and warm.

"All ready?" Max asked.

"I think I've got everything," Abby answered.

They took a taxi to the small harbor town of Port Elizabeth, then a water taxi over to Mustique, where Abigail's mother (more commonly known as Sylvia, Dowager Duchess of Northrop) was staying at a *proper* villa that was, at least partially, closer to her idea of an acceptable place to stay. Abigail's newlywed brother, Devon, and his wife, Sarah James, were staying on in Bequia for their honeymoon, not returning to London for another two weeks, at the very least.

Ten o'clock Sunday morning, the dowager duchess, along with Abigail, Max, Bronte, and Wolf, were all wedged into the relative luxury of Sylvia's private jet. It was not *her* jet, per se, but the one-sixth time-share of a jet that she rarely made use of, except on occasions such as these that would require inconvenient plane changes on obscure third-world tarmacs. Abigail and her mother faced each other across the aisle in the first group of four seats and left Max, Bronte, and the baby to spread out in the four seats toward the rear of the very narrow fuselage.

After what she was now ruefully telling herself was the Seduction-That-Wasn't and a fitful few hours with her cheek burning a hole in the cool cotton pillowcase at her villa in Moonhole, Abigail fell easily asleep once the small plane reached cruising altitude. There wasn't much to distract her, since her mother had very little to say to Max and even less to say to Bronte. Somewhere along the line, those three had fallen out of the habit of normal communication, though Wolf was turning out to be a happy bridge of sorts.

Abigail, unlike her older brother, was beginning to see her mother as a separate adult, rather than the brisk, unloving matriarch of her childhood. She wasn't sure if they would ever share a genuine affinity for one another, but in the meantime, Abby was grateful for the thaw. Lately, when she visited London, she often stayed at her mother's (very large) townhouse in Mayfair, Northrop House. Abigail had assumed those visits would be few and uptight. As it turned out, her widowed mother was grateful for the company, and often made an effort to free up her schedule on the occasions that brought Abigail to town.

Their interests were diametrically opposed (Sylvia's grand passions included clothes, shoes, and interior decoration), but lately Abigail had the feeling that her mother was actually trying to cross the generational (or, more accurately, profound philosophical) divide that separated mother and daughter. Almost by accident, they had fallen into the habit of attending the BBC lunchtime concerts at Wigmore Hall on Mondays.

Music was a passion they shared. Her mother was rarely moved by much of anything at all, a fact that Abby found almost frightening, especially because she herself seemed to feel everything around her with an unavoidable poignancy. But music seemed to affect the duchess. During concerts, Abigail had taken to stealing the occasional surreptitious glance at her mother: only then could she see a glimpse of a real woman, a real person, free of agendas and social constraints. Sylvia's entire life had been a series of short- and long-term goals and, in due course, accomplishments. Lady Abigail, in one of her more deeply engrained—and perhaps self-defeating—acts of parental defiance, had always made a point of avoiding goals and accomplishments at every opportunity.

Abigail awoke somewhere above the Atlantic Ocean, her neck bent at an uncomfortable angle. Her mother was quietly working on a piece of Bargello needlepoint that Abigail thought looked familiar, from twenty years ago.

"How long have you been working on that, Mother?"

"I think I got the pattern when I was pregnant with you."

"Why haven't you ever finished it?" Abigail asked with a small laugh.

"This way I always know I'll have something to do on lengthy plane trips. I don't really need another pillow, I just need something to occupy my time while I'm traveling."

Abigail covered her mouth as she yawned and looked out the small oval window to the sparkling sea far below.

Miami.

Just… Miami.

She let her eyes close for a few seconds as she remembered Eliot's invitation for her to join him in Florida.

"Did you see that nice Eliot after the wedding?"

# Chapter 3

DAMN MOTHERS. THEY ALWAYS knew what you were thinking. Abigail almost gave in to a momentary desire to lie, just to protect her privacy, but that seemed petty somehow. And Eliot, well, her heart bounded forward a bit when she thought of Eliot and there was nothing petty about it. A lie would have been some small show of disrespect to him. "I did actually."

"Actually?" Her mother's needle paused in midjab, halfway through the colorful canvas pattern.

"You know what I mean. Yes, Mother, I saw Eliot again later last night. He stopped to say good-bye."

"Well, you'll see him again, I'm sure."

"You're sure?" Abigail parried.

Her mother laughed with unfamiliar levity. "I'm surprised you didn't prevaricate when I asked."

"I know you've thought the worst of me, *lo these many years*," Abigail said with a genuine smile and a theatrical tremor to her voice, "but it was never for lying… in fact, I recall a time when you wished I would lie, at least a little, when your friends would ask if I was seeing anyone and you would cringe in anticipatory dread."

The duchess had returned her attention to her needlepoint and her lips were firmly shut.

Abigail forged ahead. Perhaps long plane rides were just the thing for hammering out age-old family squabbles. It was impossible for anyone to storm off and abandon the conversation (and live).

"Mother?"

"Yes, dear." Eyes still bent on her work.

Abigail sighed and looked out the window. Did she care what her mother thought of Eliot? Of course, she was so used to her mother's disapproval that her approval in this case might prove more off-putting. "What do you think of Eliot?"

That stayed her hand for a moment. The Dowager Duchess of Northrop seemed to disappear for a few moments, and a mere mother took a long look at her youngest daughter—the daughter better known as her folly—and then the mother was gone. She chose her words with a touch of spite. "Since when do you care what I think?"

"Forget it—"

"No. That was wrong of me. I'm, well, I'm taken aback. Let me think."

Abigail thought her mother might have just apologized, but that would have been, if not impossible, highly unlikely.

Sylvia continued thoughtfully, her hands resting delicately in her lap amid the folds of yarns and canvas. "You have hamstrung me, Abigail."

"What do you mean?"

"If I say I like him, that will make him far less appealing to you, I fear. If I say I don't like him, that might endear him to you, but I would be a liar." Her mother's smile was bittersweet.

"Let's forget about the perverse nature of how your opinion may or may not color my response, and just, you know, discuss him in the abstract. Do you find him charming, intelligent, garrulous, what?"

Sylvia's smile widened. "I find him to be simply divine, Abigail." She glanced down the aisle to make sure Bronte, Max, and Wolf were all still asleep, then continued when she was assured of their privacy. "I know children are always horrified to hear their parents talk about their marital intimacy or whatever you all are calling it these days, but Eliot reminds me of your father in some ways—"

"Great…" Abigail crossed her arms and rolled her eyes.

"You don't have to turn everything into a sordid, postfeminist, Oedipal thesis topic, Abigail!" Sylvia kept the volume of her voice low, but the power behind her words hit Abigail like a quick slap of a riding crop.

"Go on, then."

"Never mind. You just go on living under the happy misapprehension that I disapprove of your *lifestyle*." The older woman gestured in a circular motion with her free hand, as if said lifestyle was of very little consequence.

"It's not a misapprehension, Mother." Now it was Abigail's turn to tighten the timbre of her voice. "You basically ignored me for much of my childhood then treated me with cool disdain in early adulthood. And now that I'm no longer living with a woman"—her mother looked away, as she always did when mention of her relationship with Tully came up—"you've suddenly taken an interest. *Why?* I cannot have misapprehended my entire life."

The silence spread, an uncomfortable, palpable void. Maybe long-avoided discussions between mothers and daughters in cramped planes were not such a good idea after all. Then her mother looked at her, really looked at her, and Abigail saw the depth of her pain and confusion.

"What is it, Mother?" she asked with quiet sympathy.

Her mother's jaw flexed then relaxed; her mouth opened to speak, then closed. Abigail let her take her time.

"You're right, of course. I was never cut out to be a mother. I just wasn't made for it. My mother trained me, quite literally, to be the wife of an aristocrat, and that's what I was. I only—" She turned away from her daughter's hard gaze, then regrouped and looked at her again. "I only did what had been done for generations. After your sister Claire was born, I thought I might be maternal. I wanted to hold her, I craved the feel of her skin, the smell of her milky neck, the silk of her hair…" Her voice trailed off as if recounting a dream, then firmed. "But it just wasn't *done*. And I was so young. And my mother kept telling me that my husband must always be my priority; children had nannies and governesses and tutors, but a man only had one wife. I believed her, and was more than happy to oblige. I adored your father. *That* you never had cause to misapprehend, I hope?"

Abigail shook her head with a guilty acknowledgment. "No, that was never in doubt," she said, then forced herself to stuff the immature barb that, in the midst of all that love for her husband, the woman might have spared a few drops of kindness for her desperate children.

"And then when you took up with Tully, I thought you were beyond me. I thought I didn't know you." Abigail opened her mouth to protest, but her mother raised one hand to still her. "Let me clarify. I mean that I realized I never knew you to begin with, not that your choice to be with Tully made me think I no longer knew you. So then it became easier to reside in that little stereotype with which Max and Bronte and you are so happy to define me. Bigot or whatever. But it's not that. Would I choose Eliot over Tully for you?" Sylvia's laugh was low and jovial. "Yes! But not for those silly, narrow reasons you think: male, female, what have you—" Sylvia paused suddenly to contemplate how to go on, then said, "But because Eliot makes you soar. You laugh and sparkle and it's just, well, it's quite lovely to see. For the past ten years, I've watched you and Tully getting along together. Sweet. And I almost cried at the hypocrisy of the semantics. You were supposed to be *out*, but I had the terrible feeling that you were very much *in*."

Abigail felt a sharp pain at the back of her throat and the pressure of unshed tears at the back of her eyeballs. Maybe having an honest discussion with her mother was a very bad idea indeed. Maybe it was easier to keep her in that little bigot box. Because the truth of everything she said was going to be much harder to process than years of closely held righteous indignation. Abigail's voice was nearly a whisper: "Why didn't you ever say that to me before now?"

"Would you have heard me?"

"Probably not."

"It would have just sounded like I was picking on Tully, and you know I think she's quite charming. Besides, there wasn't Eliot before now. Who was I to tell you Tully wasn't right for you? You would have cried foul immediately. All that narrow-minded, old-fashioned dowager duchess nonsense. I couldn't bear it." She smiled and Abigail saw the glimmer of kindness, that maybe they could be friends. Starting from now. She was just some woman who had loved her husband and was a terribly inattentive mother, but was observant, and patient. Abigail smiled back at her.

"So anyway," her mother continued in a lighter tone, picking up her needlepoint again, "Eliot Cranbrook is divine. All that brawny American outside, and all that sophisticated, continental je ne sais quoi inside. But I'm just an old widow. What do I know?" She raised one eyebrow in silent challenge.

"Quite a lot, I think."

"So do you have plans to see him again?"

"No. We just sort of left it up in the air."

"How dreadful."

Abigail burst out laughing, then her voice dripped with a spot-on impersonation of aristocratic sarcasm. "It is, *rawther*! No balls, or routs, or tea dances; no Almack's or carriage rides on Rotten Row; no ices at Gunter's! How will I *ever* be thrown into his path, Mother dear? Perhaps you and I will have to take a trip to the continent? A grand tour!"

"Oh! What a fabulous idea!"

"I was joking, Mother. I need to get a life, not go on a grand tour with a *dowager*." Abby looked back out the small window at the cloud formations.

"You don't get to call me *dowager*, only I get to call me *dowager*." Her mother pointed her needle in Abigail's direction to drive home the small but salient point. "But, oh darling, let's go to Paris, at least for a long weekend. I'm sure there are lots of *activists* there for you to mingle with. They're known for their revolutions, after all. And we could visit Sarah's grandmother, and eat at La Tour d'Argent, and shop—"

Abigail rolled her eyes in mock horror.

"Very well," her mother continued, a touch of exasperation coloring her voice. "I shall shop in the mornings while you look into do-gooder type things that engage you, then we can hear music in the evenings. And perhaps Eliot will happen by."

Abigail smiled despite herself. She very much liked the idea of Eliot happening by.

---

Eliot found Miami in July an enervating, infernal haze. After five days of bucolic serenity on the islands, floating in the orbit of the ethereal Abigail Heyworth, everything in South Beach seemed too bright and too loud. He usually spent his time in Miami enjoying the larger-than-life music, food, cars, and women. He usually loved the Cuban restaurants in the smaller neighborhoods; he usually loved the cool drama of the Delano or the Setai; he usually loved the packed-at-three-in-the-morning bars and clubs.

But this visit was just annoying. He was not accustomed to this feeling of missing something. Okay, missing someone. He wanted Abigail Heyworth in his pocket.

He was only in town for two days, and he felt like there were a million other places he needed to be; he hadn't been at his head office in Geneva in almost a week and he knew the pile was mounting there. He had agreed to come to Miami since he was already going to be in the Caribbean for Sarah and Devon's wedding, otherwise he would have relegated the meetings to his North American team. He was working on a deal in Milan that would solidify Danieli-Fauchard's ownership of the top five luxury fabric mills in the world. He would much rather be working on that.

He would much rather be curled up on a beach or a couch with Abigail.

He tried to shake off that last thought.

It was Monday morning and he'd only left her Saturday night... very late... technically Sunday morning. But still, it was way too soon to be wondering where she was and what she was doing. He was regressing. He pulled his cell phone out of his side pocket and checked his emails and texts. He had held off texting or calling her; for all he knew, she had thrown the cell phone into the ocean. On the other hand, he had shown his cards—she must know he was crazy about her—so what was the point in holding back now? He tapped a few keys and pulled up her number, then texted a quick note:

thinking of you

*Nothing wrong with that*, he thought to himself, trying to assuage his feelings of immaturity and, he hated to admit, longing. He was longing to be with her. The pathetic part was that he wasn't even able to relegate the longing to a purely ache. He was actually longing just for Abigail... he wanted to sit across the dinner table, ride across a field, watch a movie, take a drive... with Abigail. If it were possible to punch himself in the stomach or slap himself across his own face, he might have done it. He needed to snap out of it.

Eliot was alone in an elevator, riding up to the twenty-seventh floor of a glass box high-rise in Miami Beach. He normally avoided photo shoots, but since he was already in town, he had decided to check in on the most exorbitantly paid model who was the face of

Danieli-Fauchard's top female fragrance line. He had accepted long ago that a recognizable face sold more products than high-quality fabrics or excellent craftsmanship ever would, but it still rankled.

The amount of money the company paid these models was nothing more than a necessary evil, as far as he was concerned. After the elevator doors opened, he turned down the corridor to the right, following the booming sound of techno-hip-hop blaring from the well-known photographer's studio. Benjamin Willard was one of the most respected photographers of the past forty years, his black-and-white portraits held in the permanent collections of the Whitney, LACMA, MoMA, and the Pompidou in Paris. Eliot stood unnoticed for a few minutes as Willard barked random phrases at the impossibly beautiful Russian model.

Despite what Eliot considered a healthy disdain for some of the spoiled, neurotic models he had dealt with, he had to admit Dina Vorobyova was beyond reproach. Given the importance of her role in launching the fragrance that was the first ever to have the eponymous Fauchard name, Eliot had been closely involved in the year-long search that had to be based on far more than a pretty face. The idea was that she would be a part of the brand for years to come: she needed bones, staying power, an absence of frivolity when it came to her work habits and her personal life.

On the other hand, the brand was intensely feminine, light, delicate. She needed to exude a soft, accessible sexiness.

Eliot watched from the door as Dina transformed her expressions with the slightest twitch of her eye, a flexing of her jaw, a softening of her brow. He had to hand it to her.

She caught a glimpse of him and waved her hands in front of her face to let Willard know to stop shooting, and she grabbed at the flimsy, chiffon fabric that was coiled around her body, barely concealing her (real) breasts and her fantastic curves. She had offered herself to Eliot so many times that it had become an ongoing joke between them. She ran barefoot across the crowded studio, skipping over heavy black extension cords and lighting equipment, then threw herself into Eliot's arms.

Eliot marveled at the way such a full-formed woman could feel so weightless in his arms. It was as if she was all smooth skin and curves… and air.

"Oh, my darling Eliot! You came to see me!"

After she kissed him on both cheeks, her light hands still caressing the back of his neck, Eliot held her a few inches away. He looked at her immaculate skin, her perfectly twinkling eyes, but with the detachment of a connoisseur judging a piece of art.

She pouted up at him, her Russian accent a seductive purr. "You are no fun, Eliot. I can see you are judging me, like you would judge a fabric or a dress."

He smiled to let her know she was right. "You're one of my best investments, Dina. Of course I must reassess your value every now and then."

"You're a cruel man. If you didn't pay me so much, I would quit, then you wouldn't be my boss and I could show you my best work. This silly rule of not sleeping with your colleagues." She waved her hand dismissively. "It is so small-minded and American of you…"

Eliot knew that Dina had probably had to sleep with half the men in her small, dismal hometown outside of Samara in order to make her way to the runways of Milan, and that she was ultimately grateful that Eliot was not one more sexual line item on her to-do list, but he kept up the charade nonetheless. She had an ego that needed massaging as much as the next girl, despite (or because of) the hard won confidence and ambition she had built up around herself.

"You know I welcome the expiration of your contract as much as you do." He winked. "But since, thanks to your fierce legal wrangling, it is still over ten years away, perhaps you will release me into the arms of other women?"

She smiled and let her arms fall away from his neck. "I suppose I must throw you back, then."

Benjamin Willard had snapped a few random shots of the two of them in their embrace. From the artist's aesthetic perspective, Dina and Eliot were almost too beautiful to be interesting. Willard had made his place in the art world by seeing the obscure, by teasing out the nearly grotesque, and showing the transformative beauty of the human face. Eliot and Dina were both over six feet tall, exuding an almost palpable health, vitality, and confidence. Willard mused that they were too magnificent together… Olympian gods who would only instill jealousy in the rest of the mere mortals. Willard tilted his hand and looked at the digital screen on the back of his camera, scrolling back to the first image of Dina and Eliot, and paused to contemplate the gleam in Eliot's eye. Willard zoomed in on the small screen, taking a closer look at the particular expression that played across the man's face, then he looked up from the image to the man himself.

*Well, well, well. The usually transparent Eliot seemed to have a new secret.*

Willard walked across the cluttered studio and reached out to shake Eliot's hand. Dina was making her way back to the white backdrop to resume the photo shoot.

"How's it going, Cranbrook?"

Eliot smiled at Ben's use of his last name in greeting and then replied, "Very well, sir."

Ben Willard was well into his sixties, and Eliot had had to kiss his ass for months to get him to take on the Fauchard campaign. All that crap about being an artist and not wanting to sully his reputation with all that dirty commercial work. Eliot offered him complete artistic license, final approval of Dina, and enough cash over the next ten years to ensure the financial security of generations of Willards to come. The artist finally caved—or rose to the occasion, depending on your perspective—and a solid professional relationship had easily grown into a friendship built on mutual respect and humor. But Eliot continued to treat him like the old, demanding, pain in the ass that he was, just for the hell of it. "How are you holding up under the strain, old man?"

"Maybe better than you, I think."

"Why's that?"

"Just a little something around the eyes is giving you away." The older man's hand gestured toward Eliot's face, as if considering the angles.

Eliot shook his head. "Am I so transparent?"

"Aaah, so there is something... or, I daresay, someone?"

"I should know better than to show my face around you... much better to catch up by phone and avoid these probing interrogations."

"That bad, eh?"

"I haven't been this distracted by a woman since, well, since ever, I suppose."

Willard turned to one of his studio assistants and told her to get the lighting back up and prepare Dina to continue shooting, then returned his attention to Eliot. "Six months ago, I thought you were finding the shoe maven distracting..."

"I might have, but she was immune to my charms... thankfully, as it turns out. This one is something else altogether." Eliot shook his head and unconsciously rubbed his thumb across the tips of his fingers, refeeling the texture of her hair.

Willard's smile was broad and knowing. "Let me guess... she's... unusual?"

"Oh, Ben, it's going to be such a battle."

"You of all people can ply her with luxurious inducements, no?"

"Alas, I think I'm falling for the only woman on the planet who has an ingrained resentment of the entire luxury goods market."

Ben Willard slapped his young friend on the arm and barked a laugh. "Oh, this is rich!" Then he turned back to his craft.

Eliot spent the morning and part of the afternoon hanging around the studio, enjoying the buzz and whir of creative energy that fueled everyone there. The young studio assistant, a lovely redhead who couldn't have been more than twenty-two, tried to catch his eye more than once. He shook his head to let her know his answer was no, as much as to laugh at this crazy world of his. He certainly wasn't above the casual sexual encounter, but suddenly he seemed to have lost his taste for it.

Things were going to go very badly for him if he failed to bring Abigail to her knees… the metaphor led immediately to the delectable possibility of Abigail on her knees, and loving being there, wanting to be there as much as he would adore her being there. He tried to resent the rapidity with which the mere thought of her burned right through him, but it was unavoidable.

At best, he could stifle it.

He pushed himself roughly from the edge of the work table he'd been leaning against, called a farewell salute to Ben and Dina, and headed back out to the hallway. It was about 2:30 in the afternoon and the heat assaulted him as soon as he exited onto the street; his cell phone vibrated and buzzed about seventeen times. Apparently he had been in a no-cell-reception zone up there in the ether. He paused on the sidewalk to glance at several emails from his assistant in Geneva and others from the negotiators in Milan, then switched over to his texts and felt an involuntary flush of pleasure at what he saw from Abigail. Two little words.

can't sleep

He rechecked the time and tried to weigh his options. He was scheduled to take the nonstop from Miami to Milan later that night, but he knew there was also a British Airways flight to London. He could have a quick layover in the UK and postpone his meetings in

Milan until Wednesday morning. He could even get to Milan for dinner on Tuesday, he tried to rationalize. He had lots of clients in London. Lots of clients who would wonder what the hell he was doing in London when he had one of the biggest deals of the year sitting on the table in Milan.

Eliot ground his teeth together as he repressed the urge to change his flight plan. He could go a week without her. He'd go to London in a few weeks to touch base.

He tried to think of something quick and light to text back:

*sweet dreams...*

or...

*dream of me...*

or...

*rest up...*

or...

*neither can I...*

or...

*meet me in Milan...*

Definitely not *meet me in Milan*. He opted for practical:

where will u be next week & may I meet you there?

His thumb hovered over the send button for many long seconds... then he deleted the *may I meet you there...* but then it seemed too interrogatory, just *where will you be next week?* A non sequitur.

Damn it.

He spent less time drafting an IPO, for chrissake. He erased it all and stared at the blinking cursor.

am standing on a sweltering street corner in miami picturing you not falling asleep... sweet misery

He hit send, shoved his phone into his pocket, and then got into his waiting limousine. He returned to the hotel and swam laps for an hour until his arms and legs and psyche were mercifully benumbed. He showered, changed into a pair of jeans and a navy-blue T-shirt, packed his small bag, took the limo to the airport, and boarded the 6:45 p.m. Alitalia flight to Milan. Eliot was asleep before they were airborne.

# Chapter 4

MAX WAS NOT KIDDING when he said Bronte would bombard Abby with ideas, suggestions, contacts, and leads to aid in her search for a meaningful next step in her life plan. They had arrived back into the private airfield at Crawley just before midnight on Sunday, Max and his brood returning to Dunlear Castle, Abby and her mother to London, and by eleven o'clock Monday morning, Abby had received fourteen emails from her sister-in-law. She called Bronte from her mother's house in Mayfair with a laughing order to call off the cavalry.

"Bronte! You're too much!"

"So I've heard."

"Stop! This is more than enough to get me started. In fact, before I speak with anyone, I think I'm going to begin at the bank. I need to have a clear idea of my resources, and I've been woefully irresponsible in that department. I just trusted my dad and then Max and Devon to keep an eye on the big picture while I used my Coutts cash card when I needed it. Pathetic really."

"All good problems to have, Abby. Don't forget that."

"I know. I'm certainly not complaining, just trying to be clear-headed. I really appreciate all these contacts, Bron. Is there anyone in particular I should start with?" Abby wasn't sure whether or not to mention Eliot's idea to speak with the corporate communications department at Danieli-Fauchard to inquire about some of their charitable contacts. Bronte's boutique advertising agency specialized in the luxury goods market, so for all Abby knew, some of the names she'd given her were the very same ones Eliot would have suggested.

"You know, you might want to talk to Eliot Cranbrook about Melanie Grey and Stephen Knickerbocker. They're pretty heavy hitters."

"Yeah, he mentioned that he might have some ideas…"

"He did?" There was a hint of keen curiosity in Bronte's voice, but Abby chose to ignore it. "Well, not to be overly mercenary," Bronte forged ahead into the silence, "but an introductory call from a major CEO might be more, how shall we say, expeditious, than a friend-of-a-friend in New York. What else did Eliot have to say? Did you talk to him today? Is he in London? I'd love to get that little Amelia leather goods account, and he's so totally impossible and unaccommodating when I see him socially." Bronte had clearly switched gears to business mode, but caught herself. "I mean, he's fabulous, of course."

"Good lord, Bronte! You are worse than Devon with your run-on thoughts. I think Eliot's in Miami." Then a touch more seriously than she had intended, she said, "He is kind of fabulous, isn't he?"

"Oh my god, you like him!"

Thank god they were on the phone and not with each other in person or Bronte would have tortured Abby endlessly to extract every incipient emotion. "Bron! Stop! Of course I like him—"

"Oh, you stop! You know what I mean. This is too perfect. I saw you guys together at the wedding and over the past few months and all that, but, you know, you just seemed like such, I don't know, best buddies. All that arm patting and back slapping." Bronte laughed, "Hilarious! It must have been driving you crazy—all that *fraternizing*!"

"Berserk."

"Well. What do you know?" Bronte's voice was warm and kind, then serious. "He's intense in his way, isn't he?"

"Yeah, I got that. I'm not sure we're pulling into the same station."

"Why? What the hell happened?" Bronte's voice switched gears from laughing friend to protective lioness so quickly that Abby almost didn't recognize the sound of her.

Since Abby's only sister Claire was many years older and had been holed up in northern Scotland for the past twenty years, the big sister inquisition from Bronte was not entirely unwelcome. Despite Abby's newfound détente with her mother, there were obvious topics that she would never in a million years broach with her. Topics like wanting sex on the beach.

"That's the problem!" Abby laughed to break the tension. "Nothing happened. I mean, after you and Max and I were having drinks on the deck Saturday night, and then you and Max went back inside, I saw Eliot down on the beach and I went down and hung out with him for a little while, and then he walked me back to the villa and that was pretty much it."

"Mm-hmm. Pretty much it, huh?" Bronte sounded theatrically skeptical. "I'm waiting."

"Well, I mean, I wanted to kiss him… I pretty much *asked* him… oh, this is mortifying…"

"Oh no! Was it disappointing? What a nightmare? Do you think he's ambivalent? Were you not into it? Was it a turnoff because he was a guy? Do you miss Tully?"

"No!" Abby nearly shrieked, then laughed.

"Oka-a-a-ay," Bronte smiled through her voice as she let the word string out a bit.

"I mean, no." Abby tried to keep her tone light. "He wanted to, you know, whatever—this is a ridiculous conversation."

"No, it's not! It's fun! Don't you ever squeal to your girlfriends about crushes?"

"To be perfectly honest, Eliot is sort of my first… real… crush…"

"Oh, sweet Abigail. You make me feel like such a harlot. First crush… just the words. You're doomed, of course." The lioness was gone and the brass-tacks businesswoman was back.

"Well, thanks for the vote of confidence, Bron."

"You know what I mean; they don't call it a crush for nothing. Someone usually ends up crushed, you know, like a bug."

"I get it." Abby gave a small laugh, but her gut turned a bit at the very real possibility that she would be the one who needed to be scraped off the rolled-up newspaper. Or worse, that she would do that to Eliot incidentally; did she really need a boatload of emotional ballast or just a light, sexual novelty?

"You might have started a little bit closer to the shallow end, Abby. He's kind of all that and a bag of crisps, isn't he?"

"Jesus, Bronte. Are you trying to make me feel better or terrify me?"

"Right! Right. Um, do you have plans to see him anytime soon? How did you leave it in Bequia? Has he been in touch with you since Saturday night? Oh my god, you don't even have a cell phone! This is hilarious. It's like *A Connecticut Yankee in King Arthur's Court!*" Bronte was now totally amusing herself.

"Whenever you're ready to come back to this conversation, just let me know, Bron."

"Oh, but Abby, admit it! It's amusing."

"It's not totally without humor. He gave me a cell phone."

"Max!!! Abby got a cell phone—"

"Bronte! Stop! You're an infant."

"I know, but it's just so prime. You and your siblings must just wake up one morning and think, *Hmm, today I shall go forth and fall head over heels for someone completely* antipodal!"

Abby heard Max join Bronte in the background. "Please, Bron. Please don't say all that beach stuff to Max. I know you tell him everything, but please, just a little privacy on that point."

"Of course, and I don't tell him everything." Abby could envision Bronte winking at Max across the room. "Just the good parts."

"Well, none of my good parts, please."

"Since you haven't given me any, I don't think you're in danger. So did you kiss him or not?"

"Bron! I can hear Max shuffling around in the background." Abby tried to be peeved, but Bronte's silly humor was contagious. "All right, so no, we didn't kiss because… damn if I even know why. I think Eliot didn't want it to be some tawdry little sex-on-the-beach scenario and then he started joking about me living in Geneva…"

"Hmm." Bronte was taking a sip of something as she listened. "That sounds promising… I mean, I've heard his house in Geneva is fabulous. I saw it in some shelter magazine a few months ago."

Abby laughed. "I'm not moving to Geneva, Bron! He did invite me to go to Miami with him."

"Oh! How much fun! I love Miami! When are you going?"

"I said no… it was yesterday… or today… or whatever…"

"So let me get this straight. Like the hottest single guy on the planet invited you to go to Miami with you and you said no because… why?"

"I know!" Abby laughed again. "I don't know what to make of any of it—especially when I start thinking of him as the hottest single guy on the planet, so let's ignore that whole part for now, okay?"

"Okay, okay," Bronte said, then lowered her voice to a whisper, "but he is so fucking hot, isn't he?"

With her heart hammering in her chest, Abby tried to sound normal, lowering her voice to match Bronte's. "I think yes."

"You are so buttoned up, just listen to you, poor thing. Anyway, so what's next? No Miami. When will you see him?"

"I don't know. He texted me. On my little private Eliot Phone."

"Oooh, I love that! How borderline creepy!"

"I know it. But I have to admit, I think it's sort of James Bond adorable. Am I an idiot?"

"Stick with adorable. Everything about falling for someone is idiotic. Get used to it. I've never been more of an idiot than when I met your brother, right Max?"

Abby heard her brother corroborate Bronte's idiocy, but she also heard the sweet sound of a tender kiss through the receiver that Bronte must have been holding near her neck.

"Anyway, enough about me for now," Abby continued. "While you've got Max there, may I have a quick word?"

"Sure. And please call me anytime about the nonprofit contacts and that other *beach* stuff. I may have been a moron with your brother at first, but I certainly know how to come through in the finish. Don't ever be afraid to pick up the phone and give me a call. Ciao, Abby!"

"Thanks, Bron. Bye."

"Hey, Abs." Max's voice was deep and sure.

"Hey, Max. I was going to make an appointment at Coutts this week to go over my accounts and investments, and I would love it, if you're in town, if you wouldn't mind going with me?"

"Of course. It's about time. Not that I minded... minding it for you, but I'm glad you're taking a proprietary interest. It's yours after all and you should do with it what you think best. I think Dad really believed that you would do something great, something more ambitious or risky than Claire, or Devon, or I would ever do."

"Well, I don't know about that, but I won't be buying any Aston Martins, so there's that." Max and Abby laughed together at their brother Devon's extravagances.

"I was planning on coming into town on Thursday, would that work?" Max offered.

"Thanks, Max. That would be perfect. What time shall I set up the appointment? Does nine o'clock work for you or is that too early?"

"Nine o'clock is perfect. That'll give us a couple of hours to go over everything with the private bankers, and I can set up my other meetings for after lunch."

"A couple of hours? I thought it would just be… a half hour to look over a spreadsheet, or something."

"Or something. Hold on a sec." Max said something quiet and gentle to Bronte, then walked across the hall to his office. Abby heard his footsteps and the sound of the door closing and pictured Max sitting down behind their father's old desk, now his desk. "Listen, Abby, you need to prepare yourself. We all got the same five million pounds when we turned twenty-one, which was perfectly generous by any stretch of the imagination, but when father died, he split the remainder of his liquid assets equally five ways, between Mother and the four of us." Max paused. "I know you know all of this, on some level, but you were so out of it at Father's funeral and you chose not to come to the reading of the will, and, well, I get it, you were devastated. But if you're serious about taking this on, as you should be, serious, I mean, then you need to face facts: You have a substantial fortune. The five million was the very tip of the iceberg, Abby. I'm not trying to be intimidating, but you're an extremely wealthy woman. Your expenses have been laughably small—at one point, the bank actually called me and implied that Devon and I had secretly cut you out of your share, and we had to convince them that you managed to live quite happily on two thousand pounds a month, and that you preferred to reinvest all of your dividends. It wasn't as if we were reaping any benefit from your monastic lifestyle."

Abby laughed quietly, and didn't bother telling Max that she usually ended up giving away most of her monthly allowance also. Living frugally had started out as a game and had become a way of life. She enjoyed the freedom of knowing she could work on a farm or canvass for a charitable organization, that no matter what happened, she could be self-supporting. Especially when she was a teenager, she had nearly suffocated under the weight of her aversion to all that dirty money and the inherent perpetuation of the centuries-old elite patriarchy that defined her family, and by extension her country, and her world. The obvious fact that she was living proof that her father did not subscribe to the traditional ideas of primogeniture and male succession did not seem to enter her flawed adolescent reasoning. Her father was a lover of women: a lover of one woman in particular, and all women in general.

"So, give me a number, Max. What do I need to be prepared to hear?" Abby asked with trepidation.

"Your share is probably now worth around thirty million pounds. Not including the properties, of course."

Abby's voice was dry and hollow. "Of course."

"Abs?"

"Yeah?"

"Don't freak out."

"I'm not freaking out."

"Yes, you are. I can hear it in your voice."

"Okay. I am freaking out a little."

"Just take it one step at a time. See if you can make the appointment with both Roger Stanhope and Caroline Petrovich. Roger knows the whole family history, of course, but I think you'll be more comfortable with Caroline. Do you want me to make the call?"

"No, no, I got it. Thanks so much, Max. You're a good egg."

"So are you, Abby. Just put on your big-girl pants and I'll see you Thursday morning. I think we'll come into Fulham Wednesday night, so I'll pick you up at Mother's at 8:30 and then we can walk over to Coutts together. Sound good?"

"Okay."

"Okay? It's all good, Abby."

"I know. Thanks again, Max."

"Thank *you*, Abby. Bye."

The line went dead and Abby was grateful her mother chose that moment to enter the kitchen and see about heading over to

Wigmore Hall for the lunchtime concert. Abby didn't think she could stand a solitary minute contemplating the enormity of what she was about to take on.

"Ready to go, Abigail?"

"Sure, let me just run upstairs and grab my bag. I'll meet you in front in five minutes."

"Okay, dear." Sylvia put her cup of tea into the sink and then turned to watch as her blossoming youngest daughter left the room, a near-palpable mist of new beginnings trailing in her wake.

⁓

By Friday morning, Eliot was back at his desk in Geneva ready to rip someone's throat out. The negotiations in Milan were at a dismal standstill. He might as well have taken the flight through London after all, since the small family-owned company of Milanese silk manufacturers had decided they were not very interested in being bought out after all. Family squabbles had erupted the previous weekend, with half the Ramazzotti clan begging for the buyout and the other half digging their heels in and refusing to sell. And to top it off, both sides acted as if Danieli-Fauchard was breathing down their necks, when the reality was the Ramazzotti family had been the ones to initiate the whole screwed up deal.

Abigail had started texting him a couple of times each day, a delightful mix of snarky seduction (*quick question: why do my fingertips tingle when I think of you?*) and to-do list (*on my way to meet with banker... texting and walking... you have turned me into an absurd multitasker*).

He was becoming desperate to touch her. At seven in the morning on Friday, he finally picked up his phone and dialed her number.

She answered with a throaty, confused, sexy-as-hell voice. "Who's calling?"

"Very funny."

She hummed and he could picture her smiling with her eyes closed and burying her face deeper into the pillow. "I'm still asleep."

"Well, wake up. I've had enough of this not-seeing-you nonsense. Will you go out with me tonight? Dinner, that sort of thing?" He heard her rustling around and was beginning to get turned on at the idea of her naked body against all that linen. "What color are your sheets?"

"White," she said with a small laugh. "Why?"

"Just trying to picture you." He exhaled. "But as I said, I'm sick of just picturing you. Are you free this weekend?"

"Mmm. I thought it was just dinner… now you want to make it the whole weekend?"

*I'd like to make it your whole damn life*, Eliot wanted to say. "Yes. And a plane ride."

She was definitely waking up now. "A plane ride, is it? Sounds glam. I don't really do glam."

"Well, then you're in luck. Because it's all blue jeans and dirty work boots and sweatshirts where we're going."

"Really? Now I *am* interested."

"It's my grandmother's ninetieth birthday in Iowa and I want you to come with me."

"Like a family reunion? Sounds serious. I don't know, Eliot—"

"Now wait one minute. How many times have I saved your ass at dinner at your mother's or made you laugh after some endless brunch at Dunlear? You owe me!"

"Okay! Okay!" She laughed. "I guess I sort of do. Fine, I'll do it. But what if people think we're a couple?"

Eliot felt his heart stop, as if someone had punched him hard in the chest. "Well…" *Shit.* Wasn't that what he wanted people to think? "I mean, worse things could happen."

"Oh my god! You're taking me to meet your family! Are we *going steady*? How cute!"

*Oh Jesus.* "Abigail. It's me, Eliot. How old are you? I'm inviting you to spend the weekend with me as my very dear friend"—*with whom I am falling desperately in love*—"and I know you don't give a crap what other people think. Of course I love the idea of you meeting my parents because I think you're really going to hit it off, not out of some weird desire to present you to them or something."

"Touchy, touchy. Okay. Fine. Yes. I already said yes. Don't get so grumpy. I was just having a little fun with you. Where do you want to meet?"

Eliot gave her the details of the airfield where his private plane would be at four o'clock that afternoon, and Abby made a crack about how much it was going to cost her to offset her carbon footprint if she started hanging out with him on a regular basis.

Abby spent the entire day forcing herself to be cavalier. Bronte called to see if she wanted to meet up for a glass of wine that night and Abby tried to hedge.

"Sorry, can't tonight, Bron."

"Okay. So, are you coming out to Dunlear tomorrow?" She sounded distracted, like she was just checking in to kill time.

"Probably not. I've got plans." *Amateur mistake.*

Bronte's voice turned laser-focused. "Really? What kind of *plans*?"

Abby silently cursed herself for playing right into Bronte's hand. "Date plans."

"Oooh! Date plans that involve an incredibly hot multimillion-aire luxury goods magnate… or wait! Let me see… is he a billionaire yet? I can't remember…" The clicks of Googling fingertips filled the background.

"I hate you more than a little right now."

"Oh, get over yourself. You're such an easy mark. So. Are you going out with Eliot or what?"

"Yes."

"Yes? That's all I'm going to get? One measly *yes*?"

"Yes. That's all you're going to get." Abby laughed and continued jamming clothes into her backpack. She was not about to start worrying about whether five black turtlenecks and a couple of pairs of jeans were the right thing to wear with a *fashion magnate*.

"Well!" Bronte tried to sound affronted but she really just sounded pleased. "Okay." Silence. "No!" Bronte cried. "It's not okay!" She laughed at her own impatience. "Come on! Throw me a fucking bone here! Are you going to be here in London? Oh my god is he staying with you at Northrop House?"

"Oh, right! Wouldn't Mother love that? She'd be posting banns by Monday."

Abby looked around the pretty room filled with antiques and draped in pale gray Italian silk that was her home when she stayed in London. It had always seemed silly to buy her own apartment in town, but now the Mayfair mansion seemed way too small for two grown, single women to share. Whatever happened between her and Eliot, this was a wake-up call it was time for Abby to get her own place.

"That she would! Well, okay. Be secretive if you like, but please have some fun, and kiss him already. He's obviously crazy about you!"

Abigail stopped packing. "You really think so?" Her emotions were all over the place; she wanted him desperately one minute and was swamped with insecurity the next.

Bronte had sounded like she was getting distracted again, but her attention returned to Abby. "Do you want to meet up for a quick coffee? Seriously. If you're asking me if he's crazy about you, I'm not sure what other glaring facts you're missing. You get that he stares at you all the time when he thinks you're not looking, right? You get that he only listens to you when you start talking—even if he happens to be in the middle of a conversation with an ambitious advertising agent who is literally *begging* for his business—"

Abigail laughed and resumed packing, tucking the phone between her ear and shoulder. "Okay! Okay! I get a bit of that. But… why me?" Her stomach got a little wobbly when she thought about Eliot really liking her with all that drive and attention. All that emotion.

"Are you fishing for compliments? Because you're *you*, of course. You are just… oh, look, I'm not going to sit here and tell you how great you are if you're not even going to tell me where he's taking you for dinner."

"Iowa."

"What? I thought you said *Iowa*. You mean, Ee-Wah? That new Asian place over by Camden Lock? I've heard they have the best—"

"Bron! I'm going to Iowa… America."

"Oh my god." Bronte burst out laughing so hard she couldn't catch her breath. "You say it like… Papua… New Guinea… Iowa… America… Oh, Eliot is a fucking genius." She sputtered and caught her breath after laughing harder at Abby's expense.

Pulling the zipper around the oversized backpack and setting it on the floor, Abby said, "Go ahead and have your fun. He invited me to go to his grandmother's ninetieth birthday party. It's hardly a steamy seduction in Paris."

"Mm-hmm. Whatever you say, Abs." She was taking a sip of something.

"You know what, Bronte? You're a serious pain in the arse. But I love you."

"I love you too, sweetie. Have the best time. Seriously."

"I think I shall. I'll speak with you next week."

"Okay."

The phone went dead and Abby put the handset back in the cradle next to her bed. She looked around the room one more time and wondered what in the world she was doing going to Iowa, America, with her *very good friend* Eliot Cranbrook.

Abigail took the Tube to Docklands then got the Light Railway out to City Airport. She followed Eliot's directions to the private section of the terminal and caught a glimpse of him through the plate glass before he saw her. He was waiting outside and he looked like something out of an old-fashioned cologne commercial, camel hair coat billowing in the January wind, his gold-brown hair slightly tousled and shining in the reflection of the setting sun. There's no way he could have heard her through the wind and the glass and the distance, but he turned when her breath caught, and when he saw her, damn if his smile didn't burn a hole right through her center.

He pulled open the door and strode toward her across the private waiting room.

"You came." He pulled her into a hug and Abby thought she hadn't felt nearly so content since he'd deposited her back at her villa in the middle of the Caribbean nearly a week ago. He set her away from him.

"Of course I came!" She smiled up at him and shook her hair in some weird effort to shake off the intensity of his look. "You invited me and I owe you one, remember?"

His smile faded. "I hope that's not the only reason." He had one arm loosely around her shoulders and was guiding her toward the exit. He opened the door out to the tarmac and pointed to a plane with the tail fin marked EC3714.

"EC for Eliot Cranbrook?" Abby asked with a mischievous grin.

"Look, I'm still a guy. What can I say? I have an ego."

They walked up the few steps and into the luxurious interior of the private jet.

"Wow." Abigail raised her head after ducking through the oval door.

Eliot gestured toward her backpack. "May I?"

She shouldered it off and handed it to him.

"I'll put it in the back so you can get stuff out of it during the flight if you want. Okay?"

"Sure." She was still looking around at the immaculate beige leather of the seats and the wide aisle that ran down the center of the plane. There were ten seats, several of which formed a small sofa with a television near the back. Abby smoothed her hair down in an attempt to smooth her nerves. She suddenly felt very small. She'd stood in the middle of twenty-thousand-acre ranches in New Zealand and felt bigger than she felt right at that moment.

Eliot was talking to the two captains, then laughed at something one of them said and turned to Abby. "All set?"

"Yes, yes," she chirped. She never chirped. She calmed herself. "Ready. Where should I sit?"

One of the captains was shutting the cabin door while the other was in the cockpit talking into his headpiece with air traffic control. Eliot walked toward her as he took off his overcoat.

"Are you nervous? Are you afraid of flying?" He looked away for a few seconds as he reached into a narrow closet and hung up his coat then held his hand out. "You want to take your coat off?"

Abby stood there in the middle of the plane and gripped the lapels of her fake-shearling coat more tightly around her. "I don't know if this is such a good idea."

"You can keep your coat on if you want." He turned to the captain and said, "We're good to go."

He turned back and put an arm around Abby's shoulders.

"Eliot, I meant—"

"I know what you meant, Abigail. Just relax. I'm not going to bite you." Her eyes widened and he smiled a mischievous, predatory grin as he pulled them both down to the small sofa. "Unless you want me to, of course."

Something snapped and Abby felt warm and comfortable and just the right size: happy she was hanging out with Eliot. "You are so bad," she said as she gave him a small punch on the upper arm and then reached around for her lap belt and buckled it into place. "I'm sorted. And no biting, thank you."

Eliot snapped his fingers with a loud crack. "Damn. I thought that was a pretty good line."

The engines squealed to life and Eliot took his cell phone out of his pocket. He tapped in a quick message. "Just letting my parents know we'll be there in time for dinner."

"We will?"

He slipped the phone back into his pants pocket. "Yeah, we should land around 6:30 local time. We'll be out at the farm around 7:00. You ready for middle America, Lady Abigail?"

Her eyebrows drew together. "Don't call me that."

"Why not? I like it. You are a lady, after all."

"Sure, with a small *L*. But the other, the upper case *L* is just daft. I didn't do anything to deserve it. It's silly."

"Blah blah. Get over yourself, Abigail."

"You sound like Bronte!"

"Why? What does Bronte have to say about it?" The plane had taken off and was making a steep ascent that pushed Eliot's shoulder closer to Abigail's. She gave him a little shove to keep him from pushing her any more than necessary.

"Oh, the usual. Like she does with Max. Which I find hilarious. But for some reason, when she turns her whole quit-complaining-about-your-very-well-tended-lot-in-life-and-do-something-about-it laser beam on me, it doesn't seem quite so humorous."

"Did you call any people this week about getting involved in a charitable organization? What happened with your banker?"

She looked down at her hands.

"I mean, only if you want to talk about it. I don't want to pry," he added.

She wanted to grab the front of his perfectly ironed white shirt and tell him to pry her wide open. She wanted Eliot to ask her everything and just be with her on this whole I'm-starting-my-real-life-right-now journey that seemed to be upon her. "Do you have any scotch on this bucket of bolts?"

"What do you think?" Eliot tapped a button on the armrest next to him and the polished burl surface lifted up to reveal a tiny bar, about one-foot by one-foot with four glasses and two bottles of excellent scotch neatly packed like a picnic basket. "Et voilà!"

He took out the Oban and offered it with a questioning look.

"Yes, please," Abby answered.

Eliot poured her an inch and passed her the cut crystal glass. He poured one for himself, closed the top on the bar, and lifted his glass.

"Cheers, Abigail. To new beginnings."

"New beginnings," she said as she stared into his eyes and they both took a sip. Eliot had demanded they always maintain eye contact when they were having that first celebratory sip, some stupid Italian tradition that was starting to make Abby crazy. For some reason, staring at him while her lips were on the edge of a glass and his lips were on the edge of a glass made her… palpitate. She finished taking the sip and closed her eyes. The heat from the liquor (and the nearness of Eliot, probably) made her flush.

"I think I will take my coat off after all." Abby set her glass into the cup holder to her left and undid her lap belt. She took off the bulky brown coat, and Eliot took it from her and set it over the back of a nearby seat.

"You look great."

Damn him. Why did he have to comment on her appearance? She supposed she was going to have to get used to it. He seemed determined. "Thanks," she said quietly. "It's just a black turtleneck and jeans."

"Oh. Your clothes are hideous. I just meant *you* look great." He took another sip of his scotch and reached for a small remote control that was tucked into a slim recess near his seat. "Want to watch a movie?" He clicked on the television and looked over Abby's head to see what movies were loaded into the system.

"Hideous?" she asked.

Without looking at her, he said, "Of course they're hideous. You do it to torment me, without even knowing you're tormenting me. That exquisite body of yours all consumed and concealed in those layers of…" He gestured with the remote in a circular motion to indicate her general sartorial mess. "The scarves and the wraps and the—" He interrupted himself to pull at the edge of an old purple scrap of fabric she'd wrapped around her neck several times. "I don't even know what to call that."

"It's a scarf, Eliot. You know perfectly well what it is. And what would you rather see me in?"

"Nothing, of course."

"Other than nothing!" She widened her eyes to chastise him, but the flush of excitement at the prospect of Eliot seeing her in nothing was obvious to both of them.

He smiled at the little victory. "Okay." He took a small sip of scotch. "Other than *nothing*, I think I'd like to see you in…" He narrowed his eyes. "Stand up."

"What?"

"I said stand up. You heard me. This is a professional consultation. There are women who would give untold sums to have me tell them what to wear. It's what I do for a living, remember?"

"You want me to stand up like a mannequin?"

"Precisely."

She laughed and took another sip of scotch and didn't move. Eliot didn't change his expression. "You're not joking?" she asked, incredulous.

"No. I'm not joking. But if you don't want to hear it, that's fine too." He shrugged. "I'll just chalk it up to cowardice."

"That is so low. You know I'd jump out of this airplane if you handed me a parachute. How dare you accuse me of cowardice?"

He shrugged again. "You're just afraid of how beautiful you are. I get it."

Abby's heart started to pound. She was running out of excuses about why Eliot's attraction to her was based on something passing or meaningless or... excusable. Because he didn't seem to be going away. In fact, he seemed to be circling closer and closer to the truth every time he opened his mouth.

"I am not beautiful." Abigail said it quietly as she stared into the depths of her glass of scotch.

"Fine. Let's watch a movie if that's what you think."

He clicked on the volume and a vintage James Bond movie began to play on the screen, Sean Connery with his jet pack over a chateau in France.

"Fine," Abby said. But she wasn't fine. She felt like Eliot Cranbrook was peeling her skin off one layer at a time, and she wasn't sure she could stand it.

Soon after Bond got his assignment from M, Abby had finished her scotch and started to doze. When she woke up several hours later, she was curled up with her head on Eliot's thigh and his hand resting lightly on her shoulder with his thumb doing this familiar, featherlight back-and-forth motion. She sat up quickly and startled them both.

"Whoa!" Eliot moved his glass of scotch away so it didn't spill on them.

"What time is it? How long was I asleep?"

"Wow. Relax, tiger." He looked at his watch. "About five hours. We're almost there."

"Five hours? What did you put in my scotch?"

"Please. As if I'd have to drug you for you to fall asleep. You're practically narcoleptic."

"Oh dear. I'm utterly disoriented." She pulled her hair away from her face and reached into her pocket for an elastic. She coiled the unruly tangle into a big loose bun at the base of her skull. "That's better. Where's the loo?"

Eliot stared at her, all rested and fresh. "Right there at the back." He pointed a few feet from where they were sitting.

"Thanks!" She smiled and sprang from her seat. "I'll be right back."

A few minutes later, she was back and looking out the window. She could see the sparkle of tiny lights on the earth below. "This is so exciting. I've never been to the middle of America!"

"Your first flyover state?"

She nodded.

"You are priceless. So glad I can provide you with a little down-home fun."

"I didn't mean it like that. You are always trying to make me sound like the worst snob."

"No, I'm not. I'm just trying to make you see that… oh, forget it. I'm not trying to *make* you anything."

"Other than a not-so-hideous dresser."

"Look. You've always appreciated my honesty. Please don't go and get your hackles up about what is really just my job. It's what I do, Abigail. I dress women for a living. And"—he gestured around the plane as if it were exhibit A—"I'm pretty damn good at it even if I shouldn't say so myself."

"All right, all right. I get it. It's what you do and all that. So go ahead and turn me into a paper doll and tell me what you'd envision me wearing if I were ever to capitulate to such nonsense." She stood up and twirled with her index finger pointing to the top of her skull like a ballerina in a little girl's jewelry box.

"I'm not going to do this if it's some way for you to try to prove that I'm objectifying you. I think clothes are beautiful. I don't think they're nonsense."

She dropped her arms. "Very well, if you're going to turn all serious on me. What would you like? First position? Second position?" She set her feet in perfect balletic stances.

"Third position. Right foot forward." No nonsense.

Abby breathed and tried to make it sound normal, but when Eliot spoke to her like that, in that confident, deep, specific way, it did something to her, something erotic and powerful. "Okay," she said, feeling soft and pliable.

Years of ballet never really left a person. Those positions were in her muscle-memory, no matter how many years had passed since she'd actually stood at the barre. The plane was beginning its descent, so she had to adjust her position.

"Turn to your left." He used the glass of scotch to show her which way, then set it down in the cup holder next to him and stood up. He had to duck his head slightly, his six-foot-four-inch frame pushing the limits of the luxurious cabin. He began pawing her.

He put both of his large hands around her waist and Abby gasped. "I knew your waist was tiny. Look at this." His hands nearly touched when he squeezed her. "I could probably get you down to twenty inches if I corseted you."

Abigail was simultaneously terrified and delighted at the bizarre vision of Eliot "corseting" her... visions of *The Story of O* and—

"Aha. You like that idea, don't you, Abigail?" He tightened his grip even more.

"Yes," she whispered.

He let go of her waist and lifted her arms, as if she were a marionette, raising them level with her shoulders, then slightly higher, then letting them drop. He circled behind her.

"May I?" He was holding the edge of the offending purple scarf in one hand, asking if he could remove it. For some reason, Abby had never liked having her neck bared. It made her feel more naked than being in a bikini... to be clothed and bare-necked.

"Sure." She swallowed and tried not to turn it into some strip-tease in her mind, but the feeling of Eliot Cranbrook very slowly, very carefully removing that one scrap of fabric from her body was probably the sexiest thing that had ever happened to her. Her heart rate sped up; her cheeks flushed; her breasts felt heavy.

"Lovely," he whispered from behind her, once the scarf was completely removed. Since he'd made it perfectly clear that none of her clothes would ever match that description, she was left with the unsettling realization that Eliot really did think that she, Abigail Heyworth, was lovely.

"Eliot."

A single finger touched the nape of her neck, just beneath the bundle of hair that she'd casually tied up. He tugged at the stretchy material of her turtleneck to expose the top of her spine and upper back. "Right here. I am going to find a gown that draws all my atten-tion to this spot. Maybe a vintage Alexander McQueen." His thumb circled the top of her spinal cord as he contemplated his options, and she felt it ping through her like an electrical shock. He released her turtleneck and grabbed her shoulders in that old familiar way. "We're about to land. Buckle up."

He took the purple scarf and threw it in the garbage bin that was built into the wall next to the bathroom door.

"Hey! That was mine!"

He came back and sat down next to her, buckling up as the sound of the landing gear rumbled in the background. "The opera-tive word being: *was*."

Abby laughed and closed her eyes, feeling the pull of gravity and the push of jet propulsion and the nearness of Eliot as the plane touched down in Iowa, America.

# Chapter 5

"ELIOT!" HIS FATHER'S VOICE was rolling and sure, just like Eliot's, but a little scratchier from age. "Over here!"

Abby looked across the small landing area, really just a paved strip in the middle of a bunch of very windy, very barren cornfields, to see a tall man standing in front of an old silver station wagon, then waving as he walked toward them.

Eliot was hauling a black weekend bag, and Abby had her large backpack slung over one shoulder.

"Eliot! Why is she carrying her own luggage? What will she take us for?"

"Hi, Dad. This is Abigail Heyworth. Abigail, this is my father, William Cranbrook, better known as Will." His dad pulled him into a quick hug, then reached for Abby's backpack.

"Please let me carry your bag since it seems my son has been so poorly raised."

Eliot shot Abby a grin from behind his father's back.

"Oh!" Abby laughed. "It's not like he hasn't tried to carry my bag. I just won't let him. And I certainly won't let *you* carry it!" Abby reached out her hand to shake the older man's.

"You young ladies today. I wouldn't survive an hour. When someone offers to carry my bag, I simply hand it over!" All three of them laughed and made their way out of the biting wind and into the warmth of the waiting car. As Eliot had predicted, they were at his parents' house in about thirty minutes.

They pulled into the garage then walked through a narrow glassed-in passage that connected to the nineteenth-century brick house. Eliot took off his coat and then took Abby's and hung them both on the hooks near the door. The door at the other side of the small room opened, and Eliot's mother clapped her hands together and walked quickly to greet them.

She pulled Eliot into a tight hug and said, "I always miss you!" loud enough for all of them to hear. It was the strangest thing for Abigail. She felt like she was intruding on some deeply intimate moment, but she was soon to see that these spontaneous displays of love and affection were the norm for Eliot's family. They actually loved one another and wanted each other to know it. How cold her own family must appear to him. She shivered at the thought.

"Oh, look at you! You must be freezing! I wish we could've ordered better weather for your first visit!"

"Mom, this is Abigail Heyworth. Abigail, this is my mom."

"It's so nice to meet you, Mrs. Cranbrook."

"Oh! It's Penny. Please call me Penny. Now let's get you all out of the mudroom." Eliot's mother chattered and bustled and led them all into the kitchen, shutting the door and sealing the cold air behind them. She clapped her hands together again and turned to look at Abby. "So you're Abigail. Let me look at you. You're so pretty."

Abby blushed from an overwhelming slew of emotions that she couldn't even begin to untangle. This woman knew of her, wanted to know her. Eliot must have spoken of her to his mother. This woman was looking forward to having her visit, to having her in her home, with her son. To cooking food for her. It was all a bit odd and confusing.

"Thank you so much for having me on such short notice."

"Oh, please. We're so happy to finally meet you. All we've heard for the past few months is Abigail-this and Abigail-that."

Abby laughed and caught a look from Eliot. He stood with

his arms crossed, leaning against the doorjamb and looking a little sheepish—as if his mother maybe spilled the beans—then he shrugged to let her know he wasn't sorry.

"Come on in," Penny continued. "I was just finishing up the pie and I know you must want a drink—or do you want a hot bath and to go straight to bed? Are you exhausted? Eliot never gets jet lag. I don't know how he does it."

Abby turned back to Penny. "I slept the whole way. I'd love to help you with the pie, and a drink wouldn't go amiss either."

"Perfect! Eliot, drinks please."

Eliot was smiling in the doorway between the kitchen and the small office that led into the living room. "Coming right up."

Abby looked over her shoulder and smiled, and Eliot's mother fluttered her hand with an off-you-go motion. Eliot looked as if he could have stood there staring at them all night, but forced himself to turn toward the living room to make the drinks. Eventually, he joined his dad in front of the fire and the University of Iowa football game while Abby and Penny finished making dinner.

The guest room for Abby was right across the hall from Eliot's childhood room, where he still stayed whenever he came home. His parents' bedroom was on the ground floor. After the delicious dinner—roast chicken and mashed potatoes and Brussels sprouts and cherry pie that Penny had prepared and served and cleaned up as if there was nothing else in the world she would have rather been doing (because there wasn't... because Eliot was home and it was his favorite dinner and she loved to make it for him)—after all that, they headed to bed.

Penny showed Abigail to her room. Eliot's mother babbled along about how she hoped Abigail had everything she wanted and encouraged her to sleep as late as she liked. She pointed out the extra towels under the sink and the bottled water and the blanket in the closet if she needed an extra layer, until Eliot finally poked his head in the room.

"Let her go to sleep, Mom."

"Oh! Sorry. It's just so much fun having you both visit. I'm sorry, Abigail. I do tend to ramble. You sleep well." She started to leave the room then turned back quickly. "And we're casual in the morning. Just come down to breakfast in your bathrobe and we'll read the paper in the sunroom and then—"

"Mom!"

"Oh dear." She reached out and gave Abby a quick hug then gave Eliot another hug as she slipped past him before going downstairs. "Good night, you two." She called from the bottom of the stairs.

Abby called good night and thank you, then turned to look at Eliot.

"You all good?" he asked quietly, after they heard the door to his parents' room shut.

"Great. Thanks." Her voice sounded a little too loud in her ears. The old house, secluded on the prairie, was profoundly quiet now that everyone had settled in. Wind whipped around the place from every direction, but instead of making it feel isolated or dreary, it made it feel more cozy inside, safe from the elements. Intimate.

Abby was starting to feel off-kilter again, remembering all that talk of being corseted and how it felt to have this man's strong hands hold her like he'd done on the plane. Then, as if he could see those hotter thoughts bubbling up in her mind, he smiled a slow, knowing smile and shook his head.

"You sleep well, Abigail." He started to pull the door shut.

"Eliot. Wait."

He held the door open halfway and looked at her, waiting for her to continue.

"What's it going to take… I mean… I really want to…"

He widened his eyes. "Yes?"

"Why are you making this so hard for me?"

"I'm not trying to make anything hard for you. I just want

you…" His words hung there between them for a few seconds, his dark blue eyes narrowing as he looked into hers, then quickly darting to her lips and back to her eyes. "I want you to feel easy, relaxed, if we do anything." He had come closer to her and reached out to put a loose strand of hair behind her ear and let his hand linger on her neck.

*If?* Abby nearly stopped breathing altogether. Who was Eliot kidding? It was definitely *when* as far as she was concerned. He was an itch she was going to scratch. Definitely. No more *if* about it.

Her breath was short and she had to make a very concerted effort not to shut her eyes and lean into him, into that warm palm of his that was gently stroking her neck beneath the fabric of her shirt.

"I want you, Abigail, but I think you need to know what *you* want, what you're asking for." His fingers were pressing against the artery at the base of her neck, as if he was checking her pulse.

"I think…" Her voice was low and unfamiliar. "I think you are seducing me and trying to make me think it's my idea."

He let his hand fall away from her neck and she missed it immediately, with a strange spike of longing for so small a touch. "I don't know if that's exactly right," he said. "I'm certainly not trying to seduce you for some temporary fling… just to get you to say yes, if that's what you mean. But you're right: I most definitely want it to be your idea. Sleep well, Abigail. I'll see you in the morning."

She huffed a little sigh. "Okay. Sleep well, Eliot…" She almost said, *lots of love* like she automatically did when Bronte took Wolf to bed when Abby was at Dunlear. Or when she was with Devon and Sarah and they all said good night at the bottom of the big staircase… good night… lots of love.

Eliot pulled the door shut behind him and Abigail leaned her forehead against the thick oak panel and listened to the sound of his receding footsteps.

It was just a throwaway bit, that *lots of love…* that *wanting* to say it. It didn't mean *I love you* like *that*. She tapped her forehead against the wood a couple of times, hoping something illuminating would penetrate her thick skull, then turned to the bathroom and set about unpacking her toothbrush and getting ready for bed.

———

Saturday morning, Abby took Penny Cranbrook at her word and shambled downstairs in her pajamas and the thick robe that was hanging on the back of the bathroom door.

"Good morning, Abigail. I thought I heard you rustling around up there. Would you like some coffee?"

"Good morning. Yes, please." Abby sat on one of the stools next to the island in the middle of the kitchen.

Penny wore a flowery flannel bathrobe that went to the floor and a pair of thick socks that looked like they probably belonged to her husband. Abby must have been staring at the older woman's feet, spacing out as she often did when she first woke up.

"Oh! I have such cold feet… not very fashionable footwear in the morning. Eliot's dad loves to joke that I always have cold feet… except when it came to marrying him!" She handed Abby a mug of black coffee then set a small creamer and sugar bowl on the counter near where she sat.

"I have it black, thanks."

"I used to be so good about that, but I'm all cream and sugar all the time these days." Penny laughed at herself. "I spent way too many years watching every calorie so I could wear all the latest things. Now I'd rather taste cream and sugar than wear a size six."

Abby smiled and took another sip of coffee.

"Let's go sit in the sunroom. I made some zucchini muffins, and we can read the papers out there. Eliot and Will went into town to pick up some shotgun shells. They thought you might want to go pheasant hunting before we head over to Grandma Cranbrook's later this afternoon. What do you think?"

"I'd love that." Abby looked up at the gray winter sky through the slanted glass ceiling. "Is this a British conservatory? It feels wonderfully familiar."

"It is. After Eliot's dad sold his company, it was our first real extravagance."

Abigail realized she didn't have a clue about what Eliot's father did for a living. She figured it would be rude to inquire.

"Has Eliot told you about his father's business?"

Well, that answered that. Abigail smiled. "No. I mean, Sarah said that Eliot's father and her father had been business associates for many years, but I never really knew the specifics."

"Oh, that's right." Penny smiled over her mug of coffee. "Isn't it considered sort of rude in England to ask *what do you do*? What a perfect example of our cultural differences." Penny leaned forward and picked up one of the muffins, then tucked her feet up under her and got more comfortable in the large wicker chair with the big down cushions. "Here in the States, we pretty much *want* to be known for what we do, rather than who our parents were or where we came from. It's what we make of ourselves that we want to be known for. Don't you think?"

"I think you might be right. Whereas in England, I suppose it seems, well, I don't know, this will probably sound elitist or something, but people would rather be known for their ideas, not what they do for money."

Penny laughed. "Oh, you sound like Sarah's grandmother. Have you met her?"

"Yes, I've met her a couple of times. She's extraordinary."

"She is. I remember Sarah telling me how *appalled* her grandmother was that Sarah had decided to go into *trade*! Isn't it funny that there are still people who think like that? *Trade!*" Penny laughed at the sound of it.

Abby smiled but she was a bit ashamed to admit that her own mother had raised her with the same contradictory set of values. One, especially if one happened to be female, was meant to be productive but never money-grubbing, busy, but never truly obligated to an employer. It was an impossible balance to strike.

"I'm sorry, did I say something wrong, Abigail?"

"Oh, no, nothing." She looked up and saw compassion in the woman's eyes—just like Eliot's. Something sweet and concerned that made Abby want to cry. "Really nothing. Just how we all sometimes get mixed messages from our parents." Abby smiled again, trying to change the subject.

"Oh! I know all about that!"

"Really?"

"Yep. This was my parents' house." Penny gestured around her head. "I was born in this house. That's why I sound like I'm from a farm and Eliot sounds like he's from... Harvard. That boarding school bred the farm right out of him. Anyway, my people were what was known as *upstanding*. Methodists. Hardworking farmers. No nonsense. And I went and fell in love with the boy in school whose father was a truck driver. His people were from *Kentucky* no less." The way she said *Kentucky* made it sound like a plague on both their houses. Which it probably was at the time.

"So... you and Will were star-crossed lovers, then? How romantic!"

Penny took a bite of her muffin and stared at Abigail. "It sounds romantic now, when you say it like that, but we eloped and it was more like the end of *The Graduate* than anything else. So scary."

"Oh dear!" Abby brought the palm of one hand to her cheek. "That bad?"

"I know! Can you imagine? My poor mother. Bless her heart. Those few weeks were probably the worst of her life. I was her only child and my father swore he'd never speak to me again." Penny gave a quick laugh. "He was always one for blowing his top on Monday morning and then making amends by the weekend. But they were long weeks, I'll tell you what."

"My mother can hold a grudge for months. Years even. You're lucky."

Penny tipped her head to one side. "I've never met your mother, but Eliot mentioned she is… formidable."

"That's an understatement! But go back to your mother and how you worked it out."

"Oh. My father came around eventually. What else could he do? He'd raised me to be honest and trustworthy and all that, and Will was the man I loved." She shrugged as if it had all been out of her hands. "So there really wasn't any way around it. I had complete faith in Will Cranbrook. He promised me he would always love me and that he was going to take his father's one truck and turn it into a hundred trucks." Penny took a slow sip of coffee. "And that's just what he did. He started shipping for all of the department stores in the Midwest, and that's when we met Sarah's parents. And they were so sweet. Sarah's mother especially. You know how some people are just good? I remember Elizabeth James like that. I only met her a couple of times when we went to Chicago for a treat, but she was a doll. Just like Sarah. So sunny."

Abby had a slight twinge of something resembling jealousy, that Sarah had made such a good impression on Eliot's mother. Not that anything had ever developed between Eliot and Sarah other than a professional friendship, but Abby still felt like she was a bit *un-sunny* by comparison.

"Oh. That's awkward, I'm sorry—" Penny blurted.

"No," Abby interrupted, embarrassed that her twinge of something-or-other must have shown on her face. "No—"

"Silly me. I just meant that you're lucky to have Sarah as a sister now. And her mother was just all sweet and smiling, like Sarah was when I met her last year. But," Penny inhaled, then continued in a lower voice, "I never thought she was the right type of woman for Eliot."

Abigail blushed, silently damning her fair complexion for giving her up.

"Oh silly me. I'd better stop talking before I say anything else ridiculous." Penny took a sip of her coffee and tried to stay quiet. But it just wasn't her way. "*You* are the right type of woman for Eliot," she whispered, just as the back door flew open and drew their attention toward the kitchen. Penny winked at Abby as the two Cranbrook men strode into the sunroom.

Eliot's father walked straight to his wife and kissed her hello, right on the lips. She reached up one hand and placed it on his cheek as he pulled away.

"How are you this morning?" he asked, as if he really wanted to know.

Again, Abby felt like she was being exposed to something too personal, that she wasn't meant to see. She looked away, to give them privacy or something, and turned toward Eliot by accident. He was watching her watch his parents and he gave her a small sad smile, as if to say, *Now do you see why I think people are meant to be loving and kind to one another?*

"How are *you* this morning, Abigail?" he asked, echoing his father's kindness to his mother.

Abby lifted her mug. "Excellent. And you?"

"Great! Perfect day to walk the ditch. No trumpets or fancy horses and hounds here, but we still manage to bag a few birds. You up for it?"

"You know I am!" She stood up and felt all hot and bothered as Eliot watched her head toward the kitchen in the frumpy robe. "I'll just have a quick shower and we can head out."

"Okay. See you in a few." His eyes narrowed and he watched her even more closely.

"Okay." She bounded off, suddenly thrilled at the prospect of shooting a rifle at some small innocent creatures in order to blow off a little pent-up sexual frustration.

---

Later that night, the January wind whipped in behind them as Eliot opened the door to the saloon and gave Abby a little shove to hurry her along. She laughed as he pushed her into the crowded space and steered her toward the back of the bar near the pool table.

One of the guys playing pool raised his cue and called out, "Hey! Eliot! Over here."

Abby loved seeing Eliot in this world, surrounded by childhood friends who knew him as the nerdy straight-A student and track star. Of course, they knew he had gone on to make piles of money and was a successful international businessman, but he was the same person he'd always been when he was back in town. He was the same to everyone—whether he was chatting with one of his private jet pilots or the checkout girl at the Kum-and-Go.

She smiled at the memory of the Kum-and-Go. When they'd pulled into the convenience store to get gas that afternoon, Abby nearly fell out of the car laughing. "The Kum-and-Go? How can you keep a straight face?"

Eliot smiled that sweet, knowing smile that was starting to drive Abigail to sexual distraction on a minute-by-minute basis. "It's just the name of a chain of gas stations. What?" But his smile was wider and she imagined all sorts of suggestive, exciting, promising ideas crossing his mind. He was seriously going to stick to his guns about this whole making-her-profess-what-she-really-wanted nonsense, and she was beginning to think she wouldn't mind downright begging if he'd just give her a tumble already.

But she kept veering away at the last minute, seeing the intensity of something deeper in his eyes, something she just didn't think she could provide. Of course, she was tempted to risk going deeper with Eliot, but it felt like a devil's wager, the kind you accept because you are so sure you can't lose—when, in reality, you don't have the collateral to make good on your debt. It was better for both of them if she kept it light.

"Oh, nothing," Abigail said. "Kum-and-Go. Shag-and-Dash. The usual."

Eliot burst out laughing and stepped out of the car to put the gas in his dad's station wagon. This whole trip had initially seemed a little strange—joining Eliot for his grandmother's birthday in Iowa—but ultimately, Abigail had wanted to satisfy her curiosity, to see what type of world created a man like Eliot. A good man. So she'd come to the middle of America to have a look.

So far, the two of them had bagged a few pheasants (a form of shooting that was locally known as "walking the ditch") and tried on an assortment of Carhartt overalls at the local tractor store. Abigail was charmed. Now, after a four-hour meal with Eliot's parents and cousins and aunts and uncles and great aunts and uncles and the ninety-year-old birthday girl, tradition dictated that the two of them head into the tiny town near where Eliot had grown up, in order for him to have a drink at the local watering hole and reconnect with his old middle school buddies.

They continued to snake their way to the rear of the bar, Lynyrd Skynyrd cranking in the background, and several people calling, "Hey, Eliot!" or "How you doin', Eliot?"

When they got back to his friends at the pool table, one guy gave Eliot a big bear hug and then pulled away. "How are you, man?"

"Good. You?"

"Good." He smiled then turned to Abigail. "And who are you?" He reached out his hand to shake hers.

"Abigail Heyworth." She gave him a firm shake. "Nice to meet you."

"Lady Abigail Heyworth," Eliot added.

"Feck off," Abigail said, punching him on the upper arm.

"Nice to meet you too, Lady Abigail. I'm Jason Mercer." He had a great smile, kind of shy and hesitant.

"It's just Abigail. Don't listen to Eliot about any of that lady-nonsense," Abby said.

"Why not?" Eliot asked as he flagged down a waitress. "Two Buds and two shots of Jack, please." Then turning back to Jason and Abigail, he said, "She always introduces me as Eliot Cranbrook, head of Danieli-Fauchard." He turned to face Abigail. "See how it feels?"

"Okay, okay," Abby laughed. "I won't introduce you that way anymore. Just Eliot, all right?"

Jason took a sip of his beer and watched the byplay between them. "So, how long have you two been going out?"

They both froze.

"We're not going out," Abigail replied way too fast. Then she put an arm around Eliot's shoulders and gave him a collegial squeeze. "Just great friends."

Eliot smiled at Jason. "Right. Just friends."

"Yeah, right." Jason said, then chalked his cue and took his shot. The other guy playing pool had been listening to their conversation and looked up at Eliot with a smile. "How you doing, Eliot?"

"Great, Mike, how about you?"

"All good. Just in town for a couple of nights to see my mom, then back on the road."

They spent the next hour getting foxed. The Budweisers and the shots kept coming. Abby settled into the rhythm of the place, sitting on a stool next to Eliot as his old friends came and went, listening to how easy and sure he was. He *was* good. What was her problem? She wanted to be with him and he wanted to be with her.

His friend Mike was standing at Eliot's left and they were laughing about their friend from fourth grade who always used to trip when he was getting off the school bus. Abby was staring at Eliot; after a few drinks, she didn't care about the propriety or impropriety of just staring at Eliot.

Feeling her attention upon him, he turned slowly and looked right into her eyes. "What?"

"Nothing." She looked away and took a swig from the beer bottle.

"Really nothing? Or something that you *wish* was nothing?"

She took a deep breath and faced it head on. Mike was still standing there, sort of half part of the conversation, smiling at her over Eliot's shoulder. It was probably a really bad idea to dive into the relationship pool, right in this tiny Midwestern bar surrounded by a bunch of Eliot's childhood friends. On the other hand, the discussion was less likely to get out of hand with an audience. "I feel like you're trying to best me somehow, and I don't like it."

"Woooooo…" Mike gave a low sound. "She's got you there, man."

"What's that supposed to mean?" Eliot asked.

"Don't get defensive," Abigail said, leaning her shoulder into his. "It's just I get this feeling sometimes that most guys just want to be the guy who gets the girl to quit liking girls."

Mike choked on some of his beer with that one. "Dude. She's kind of right."

Abigail smiled at Mike, feeling like she had scored a point in the Exposing Eliot finals. It was a low blow, because she'd never thought that about Eliot. He'd never once made her feel like her relationship with Tully was some sort of titillating appetizer to Eliot's main course. It was a deflection; she simply didn't have the courage to admit she was an emotional coward.

Eliot narrowed his eyes at her and then took a quick look at Mike. Turning slowly back to Abigail, he asked, "What do you think? That I'm turned on by the idea of you in bed with Tully… and then being in bed with me?"

Abby smiled and lifted her chin. "What do you think, Mike?

Does it turn guys on to think of me with a woman… and then to think of me coming over to the dark side to be with a man?"

"No disrespect, but… yeah, totally."

Abigail smiled, feeling victorious again, but it was short-lived. Eliot didn't look defeated and she was starting to feel a hint of worry. He was too good a debater, always getting her to look at a problem one way, only to show her why that point of view was totally screwed up.

"See, Eliot," she pressed, "it's not as though I'm creating an unheard of scenario here."

He took a considering sip of his beer and looked her in the eye. "So, you're saying only men are turned on by that idea?"

"Well—"

"Are you saying you wouldn't be turned on by the idea of *me* having been with a guy… and then falling for you?"

Abigail felt the floor drop out from under her and her heart started to hammer frantically—both from the Eliot-with-a-guy talk and the falling-for-you talk. "Well… since that…" she stammered. "I mean, Eliot… come on! That's just… so entirely unlikely!" She tried to laugh there at the end, but her face must have flushed and Eliot saw it. And he liked it.

Mike took a sip of his beer and raised his eyebrows. He and Eliot exchanged a glance and smiled at each other. Eliot turned back to face Abigail, but it was Mike who spoke. "I wouldn't say *entirely* unlikely."

"Oh. I mean…" Abigail stumbled over her words. "It's not tit for tat…" But she was turned on by the idea. Really turned on. "Were you two ever… I mean…" Abigail blushed.

Eliot turned to Mike and smiled. "She gets tongue-tied sometimes. I think it's kind of hot."

*Shit.* Shitshitshit. Here she was feeling all I'm-gay-and-you're-not and suddenly it was looking like Eliot wasn't Mr. One Hundred Percent Heterosexual American Male after all. Damn her mother for calling her out on her reverse prejudices, because now it was endless. Abby felt like she was in a perpetual state of being hit over the head with how short-sighted and narrow-minded she really was.

Abigail burst out laughing and Eliot watched her as he took a sip of his beer. They all settled down and Abigail thought they were going to move into less perilous territory.

"So…" Abigail tried, hoping to redirect the conversation.

"So," Eliot said. "Should we do an experiment?" He turned from Mike to Abby. "Just to give you the opportunity to prove that something like that wouldn't turn you on at all."

She stared at Eliot, his sparkling eyes, his lips, then leaned a little farther forward to get a better look at Mike. From a purely aesthetic point of view, he was gorgeous: almost as tall as Eliot, lean, all sharp angles and full lips. Mike was a professional dancer and traveled all over the country; he was in perfect physical condition. Abigail had to be tipsy to even come up for it. She swallowed. "What kind of experiment?" she asked Eliot.

"How 'bout a kiss?" He moved his strong hand in the air between himself and Mike.

Just like that. Flat out.

She gulped too much beer. *Feck.* Because, *feck, yes*, she totally did want to see them kiss. When he asked it like that, she felt her insides curl into some supplicating quivering mass: *yes-yes-yes-YES*, her body screamed.

But. What did it mean? Was he toying with her? Was she toying with him? Was he trying to teach her a lesson? Were they just a bit slewed and having fun? She tried to remind herself that *fun* was her primary objective. She was going to go with fun. Fun was the opposite of that terrifying I'm-going-to-make-you-mine-forever thing she sometimes saw flash across Eliot's face when he looked at her. He didn't look deep and meaningful just now. He looked mischievous and adorable.

"Quit thinking so hard, Abigail." Eliot with his bossy man voice. And that turned her on too. "Yes or no?"

Her breasts tightened in her bra and she decided not to be a liar. "Yes." She felt her cheeks burn and looked at Eliot then at Mike. "I mean, only if you want to, of course…"

Mike's laugh was low. "Oh, no need to twist my arm."

Eliot smiled. "Let's go out back so we don't frighten old man Smithers at the end of the bar with all of this man-on-man craziness." He pulled Abigail from her stool and she stumbled a bit. He held her hand in his, lacing their fingers together and squeezing tight as they followed Mike to the back door behind the pool table and into the darker area by the restrooms.

The cold air slammed into them and made Abigail give a quick gasp. Eliot pulled her closer to his side. "You okay?"

"Yeah, I'm great." She smiled up at him, her teeth chattering. "Are you?"

His smile was all the answer she needed. Eliot set down his beer on the edge of the Dumpster and Mike did the same. The two guys looked at each other, then Eliot looked at Abigail again. "You sure you're okay with this? I don't want you to get all grossed out or anything."

She pursed her lips and narrowed her eyes at him. She was so obviously turned on by the mere idea of the two of them kissing and it was perfectly obvious. "I think I'll be able to endure it, Eliot."

Mike laughed. "I'm freezing. Let's get this show on the road."

Eliot smiled at Abigail one more time, then leaned in and kissed her lightly on the cheek, barely touching his lips to her skin. She felt like a gasping fish, the way she went after him to take more.

"Oh god." Abby's eyes slid shut as she pulled his face to hers and kissed him with a ferocity she didn't know she possessed. She pressed her hips against the side of Eliot's hard thigh. When she opened her eyes again, Eliot was breathing hard and staring at her, looking into her eyes, then at her moist lips. Then his eyes darted to her hair, then back into her eyes.

Mike chuckled as he picked up the beer he had just set down. "You two have fun being *just* friends, you hear?" And he turned back into the bar.

# Chapter 6

THEY STOOD IN THE silent, biting cold for a few seconds before Eliot spoke. "Satisfied?"

"Not even close." She kissed him again, not for a cheap thrill, but because she had to have him. And then his lips were responding to hers and he tasted of Jack Daniels and beer and Eliot. Abigail felt her legs dissolve beneath her and he pushed her up against the rough brick of the old bar and kissed her senseless. His hand was rough at the nape of her neck, grabbing a chunk of her hair and pulling her head back so he could take her mouth more forcefully.

Eventually, he kissed the edges of her lips, then along her jaw and neck until he was near her ear. His voice was warm and thick. "Don't you see? I don't care what either of us did before we met. I don't care who we were with or why. I want you, who you are right now. The woman here in my arms." He kissed her again, farther down her neck, where the fabric of her polo neck rested lightly against her collarbone. "You and these goddamned turtlenecks." He pulled the fabric down so the frigid air slid across her warm skin. A tingle of anticipatory desire trilled down her spine. Her shiver was almost convulsive. She wanted more of those hot, pressing kisses. She reached her hands around his powerful neck and urged his head back, trying to pull his lips back to hers.

"Not so bossy, miss." He pulled her hands gently away from his neck and guided them down to the front of his pants, his lips and tongue continuing their slow meandering path across her neck and ear, getting nowhere near to satisfying her need. He pushed her hands against the straining, hard proof of his desire. His cock reacted immediately to the light pressure of her hands, finally, her hands, so close to being on him. "Touch me, Abigail."

He was doing things with his tongue—sucking her, tasting her, teasing her—until she was warm and dizzy. And what had she been worrying about? It was fun. Glorious fun. She felt like she was floating.

"Abigail!" His voice was a brittle, demanding, desperate, forceful thing.

She tentatively stroked the fabric over his hard shaft, lightly outlining the shape and contour of him. She shivered at the heat that came off him, wanting more. Abby pressed harder with her fingers, wanting to feel him and see him and taste him. She wasn't going to last much longer in the freezing back alley behind the bar.

Eliot groaned into the skin of her neck and then bit the edge of her ear. She cried out and his mouth swooped down on hers again. She gasped. He kissed her tenderly at first then pulled her flush against him, wedging her hand even tighter against his erection, his hands pressed into the small of her back. A second later, he slid his hands lower, grasping the curve of her ass.

*Finally*, he thought with a moan. He pulled her closer still.

"Eliot…" Her teeth were chattering. "Please don't stop… but can we go somewhere warmer."

"I won't stop." *I'll never stop*, he wanted to add. "Let's go home to my parents' place."

"Okay."

They walked back into the bar and Abby felt like the two of them might as well have a bright neon arrow above their heads that said, *Just back from a snog.*

They got a taxi back, leaving Eliot's family wagon parked in front of the bar, rather than risk driving after all the whiskey shots and bottles of Bud. They made it as far as the living room. Eliot hoisted Abigail up by her shoulders and tossed her onto the large down sofa. His parents had gone to bed hours ago, but their room was only a few yards away.

"The light of the fireplace makes you look so beautiful, Abigail." Eliot was trying to pull off her turtleneck while he focused on her face.

"Eliot! What if your mom walks in?" But she was breathy and laughing through the hoarse whisper of her voice. She was sure he could tell she wouldn't care if every detective in Scotland Yard happened upon them.

"They're dead asleep by now," he whispered. "Don't even worry about it." He was tugging her turtleneck up over her head as he spoke, and only got as far as removing it from her arms and letting it bunch at her neck.

Beneath, she had on one of her bog-standard white cotton Marks & Spencer bras.

"Oh dear," he grumbled. "We are going lingerie shopping as soon as we get back to Europe. If you have plans for next weekend, cancel them."

Abby arched her back and could see quite clearly that, despite his critique of her smalls, Eliot certainly did not appear discouraged. "Well, Mister Bossy," she said as she wriggled around under his assessing look, "turns out, I already have plans for next weekend."

He leaned over her and started kissing his way down her chest, then unhooked the front clasp of the serviceable bra as he whispered, "Change your plans." Without looking up, he began to lavish all of his attention on her breasts.

"Oh dear god. Eliot." She felt it everywhere. Not just where he was touching her and sucking and—"Jesus, Eliot!" He scraped the edge of his teeth along her nipples and then he covered her mouth with his, before her cry of delight could escape and wake the neighborhood.

After the kiss, he pulled away slowly, panting and dragging one hand through his messed up hair, the other making slow circles on Abigail's flat belly. "I feel like I'm in high school. And not in a good way. I want you in a huge hotel suite in Paris. In a huge bed. With me. And you. And no parents sleeping within earshot. I want to do things to you... all sorts of things... with you... Abigail."

He had a raw desire about him that was exhilarating; it was still intense and emotional and laced with all the feelings that terrified Abigail, but his impatience was also naughty and hot as hell. Who would have thought upstanding Eliot Cranbrook would be the one to give *fun* a whole new meaning?

"I might be able to help you with that particular fantasy," Abby whispered.

"Really?" His hand paused, then he started to trace the edge of her jeans, fiddling with the button and the zipper without actually undoing anything, then lazily trailing back up to circle her breasts. "How so?"

"Mmmm... um..." She licked her lips and reveled in the feel of his light exploration of her sensitive skin. "I'll be in Paris next weekend. At the Plaza Athénée. Why don't we meet there?"

"Done." He seemed to consider that a very joyful turn of events. "Excellent." He smiled and stood up taller. "Up," he commanded, ordering her to lift her bottom so he could pull her into his arms and carry her up the stairs.

"How romantic!" she joked as she snaked her arms around his neck to hold on to him.

He looked down into her eyes and smiled, but she could tell he wasn't joking. "It is, isn't it?"

He took her into the guest room where she was staying, setting her gently onto the bed then closing the door carefully behind him. He crawled onto the narrow antique double bed and caged her beneath him. "This whole house was built for people half my size.

It's a nightmare. There's no way we're having sex for the first time in this shoebox. Plus, I want to hear you scream."

"Eliot!" She pretended to be taken aback by his sudden straight-forwardness. Then she smiled and said, "Well, I'm sure we can think of a few things to do until you get me into one of the soundproof rooms in Paris, don't you?"

His smile was delicious. "Maybe something like this…" He kneeled back onto his heels and the bed creaked under the strain of his bulk. He rolled his eyes at the sound. "Honestly." He undid the button and zipper of her jeans, then pulled them down around her knees. A second later, her white underwear were stretched across her knees as well. "These panties are going in the fire, just so you know."

He rubbed the length of her thighs as he stared at the apex of her legs. "Dear, dear Abigail. Aren't you a little vixen?"

She lifted her chin enough to look down at her disheveled self: bra half off, turtleneck half off, pants… half off. Her head flopped back on the pillow and she shut her eyes in a show of listless defeat. "I seem to be all at sixes and sevens, Eliot darling. What ever will you do with me?"

Then he leaned in and kissed her between her legs and taunted her with his tongue and prodded her until he once again had to cover her mouth to prevent her cries of ecstasy from rousing not just his parents, but half the neighborhood. A few seconds after her release, she was murmuring his name and falling quickly asleep.

"How typical," Eliot commented, slowly pulling off her socks and her jeans and her underwear, then her turtleneck. He stared down at her supple, perfect curves, her pale, immaculate skin. He pulled the sheets and blankets up over her, and she snuggled deeper into sleep.

"Sweet Eliot," she mumbled through her burgeoning dreams.

*I'm not going to be sweet when we get to Paris, I can tell you that,* he swore to himself and quietly let himself out of her room.

Abigail awoke Sunday morning in the bed in the guest room, naked and alone. The scent of bacon and eggs and coffee wafted up from the kitchen, and she could hear the cadences, if not the exact words, of Eliot conversing with his parents. Abby pulled on her red pajamas and the guest robe and tried to act casual.

"There you are!" Penny cried when Abby turned the corner into the kitchen.

Eliot chose that moment to take a sip of coffee, but he winked over the rim of his mug and Abby blushed up to the tips of her ears.

"I hope you're not coming down with something. You look a little flushed," Will Cranbrook observed.

"Oh. No. I'm fine!" Abby put her palms up to her face. "Just woke up, pillow against the cheeks, and all that."

"Well, just in case you're coming down with something, I'm making you a big breakfast to stick to your ribs for the trip back to England." Penny sighed. "I hate that your visits are so short, Eliot. It's not fair." She tapped the edge of the frying pan with the spatula to show her irritation.

"I'll see you in Geneva in a couple weeks, Mom. It's not like we don't get to spend time together."

"I know, but I just imagine a time when we can all spend days and days eating ribs and watching football and just, you know, relaxing and being together." She turned toward Abigail. "You know what I mean, Abigail, just being with your family on the weekends. You must all get together all the time, don't you?"

"Not always. And not all of us, no. My older sister has been living in northern Scotland for years and years, so we hardly ever see her. And my eldest brother, Max, lives at Dunlear Castle with his wife and their adorable baby. And Sarah and Devon are living in Mayfair. I stay at my mother's when I'm in town, but… we were never really the all-hang-out-on-Sunday-afternoon type of family to begin with."

"Oh. That's a shame."

"Not really. It's just… the way it is. Not bad at all, really." But Abigail knew she sounded a bit too carefree about the whole thing, because she was overcompensating for how much she wanted to spend weekends hanging out with Eliot, doing nothing at all (except ensuring that they would have their hands on one another at all times).

"I have an idea!" Penny enthused. "You should come to Geneva when we're there, Abigail! Wouldn't that be fun, Will? Wouldn't it, Eliot?"

Eliot smiled into his coffee again. "Of course it would be fun, Mom. But let's not scare Abigail with visions of our inappropriately adoring family dynamics, all right?"

"Hrmph. I don't think there is anything inappropriate about affection, Eliot. That's just silly." She wagged her spatula at him.

"I know, Mom," Eliot said. "The world is a strange and terrible place. As difficult as it is for you to grasp, I'm a thirty-eight-year-old man and I might not want to spend *all* my free time with my mother. As much as I'd love to—"

"Cut it out!" Penny laughed. "I'm not as bad as all that! Am I, Will?" Her husband lived to please her, so he wasn't about to contradict her, but his noncommittal shrug was answer enough. "Oh, no! I am *that* type of mother!" She laughed again. "Okay, fine. I won't ask Abigail to come to Geneva and I guess I won't try to convince you two to stay over a few extra days."

"Impossible. I'm sorry, Mom. It's been a wonderful weekend." He looked at Abigail with that conspiratorial look again. "But I have to get back to Milan right away. The Ramazzotti family is finally ready to come to terms and negotiate with us, and I have to be at their offices, in person, first thing tomorrow morning. And it's already nighttime there." He gave her a kiss on the cheek. "See you in a couple of weeks, okay?"

"Okay. Fine." Penny turned off the stove and set the pieces of bacon onto the paper towel on a plate. "Eat your breakfast then go get on your fancy airplane."

"Oh stop with that," Eliot said.

An hour later, Abigail and Eliot had said their good-byes and were taking off from the private landing strip on the outskirts of town. In the shower that morning, Abigail had started envisioning all sorts of consummation scenarios that involved that pristine beige leather sofa in the back of Eliot's private jet, but he wasn't having any of it.

Abigail was trying to distract him from his work as the plane was making its ascent. He had already opened up his computer and was going over some of the revised spreadsheets that his mergers and acquisitions team had sent him that morning. He smiled without looking up from the screen.

"I'm so sorry, Abigail, but I just can't be distracted right now." She was running her fingers along the edges of his sandy brown hair, where it curled ever so slightly near the turn of his collar.

She might have whimpered. "Not even a tiny distraction?"

He looked away from the computer and into her eyes, then set the laptop on the small tabletop to his right. "I would love a million tiny distractions, and I want you to be thinking of every single one and have them stockpiled for next weekend, when we can take our time…" His thumbs were caressing her cheekbones and she felt her whole body melting at his small attention. This was so potentially terrifying… how easily he turned her to mush.

"Hmmm… time… yes…" she agreed.

He kissed her gently, but his hands were firm and possessive on her cheeks. "It's already late in London, you beautiful creature. Rest on my lap and we'll be there in no time. I'm going to have to continue on to Milan. I don't want our first time together to be some rushed mile-high business."

She frowned and turned her lips to kiss the palm of his left hand.

"I know you're right. And it will be wonderful, but—first no shoe-boxes, then no mile-high club—" She huffed. "No fair."

He smiled and reluctantly let his hands come away from her face. "Oh, I'll make it fair come Friday, don't you worry."

She smiled and let him guide her into a more comfortable position, resting her cheek on his thigh and enjoying the sound of his fingers clicking on his computer and the occasional pressure of his hand on her cheek or shoulder when he paused to think. Abby fell asleep quickly and didn't wake up until they were on their way into London.

"Let me guess?" She rubbed her eyes and sat up slowly. "I slept the whole way again?"

"Yep." Eliot was putting his computer aside and helping her buckle up for landing. "Sleeping beauty." He leaned in and kissed her neck and nuzzled into her, then kissed her lips. "I've reserved a suite at the Plaza Athénée for Friday, Saturday, and Sunday nights."

"Oh, you didn't need to do that."

"Of course I did. Did you think I was going to stay in a room with you and your mother?" He smiled and played with a strand of her hair.

"No!" She gave him a playful nudge. "I already have a room. I would have thought it'd be obvious that my mother is not really the slumber party type."

"Fine. We can keep both rooms. You can use yours like a changing room, or whatever. I want a lot of room to move around. To move you around."

Her stomach lurched and her cheeks burned. "Really?"

"Yeah. Really. I've got all sorts of ideas about what we can do with each other if we set our minds to it. Three days…" He was talking low and looking at her face, touching the edge of her lip, the turn of her brow. "Three nights… I might require long stretches of time to…" His voice trailed off as his other hand cupped her breast.

Abby gasped, reveling in the way he was beginning to know her body already. "...discover what you really like... make it last... test your limits..." When he fondled her in that calculating way, she thought she might have an orgasm just from the way he concentrated all of his attention on her reaction.

"I say, Eliot. I believe you might be seriously bent. Quite the dark horse."

"I admit it. You make me think very dark thoughts." He looked suddenly clear-eyed and businesslike. "Would you prefer I was the straight arrow everyone takes me for?"

She laughed and kissed him hard. "Never."

———

Friday afternoon, Abigail texted that she and her mother had made their train and they would be arriving at the Plaza Athénée in Paris around 6:30 that night. All need for subtlety now gone, Eliot simply replied:

i'll be panting in the bar.

So here he sat with a very large, very good scotch on the too small cocktail table at his knee, in the bar of the Plaza Athénée. He was surrounded by platoons of beautiful Parisian women dressed in tight black dresses and high suede boots and the men and women with whom they smoked and drank and laughed. The precision of the modern interior design was the perfect counterpoint to the bubbling anticipation that coursed through his veins; he felt like molten fire trapped in ice. And then he felt the tentative trace of a finger along the small space of skin between the top of his collar and the edge of his hairline and all the worries of the week simply evaporated. He groaned his pleasure and had to resist the urge to grab at her wrist and pull her into his lap.

Instead, he stood up and forced his face into a cheerful mask, lifting his mouth into his best good-son smile. He simultaneously put one possessive hand around Abigail's trim waist and the other reached out to shake the perfectly manicured hand of the Dowager Duchess of Northrop. The feel of Abigail's trembling ribs beneath his firm hand made it difficult to process the words coming out of the dowager duchess's lips. He figured it was something along the lines of *nice to see you*, and Eliot opted for a similar reply.

Then again, he might have missed a word or two, what with Abigail's birdlike heart pattering frantically into his fingertips.

"Eliot?" Abigail was trying to get his attention, but the room was crowded and he was simply overcome with the relief of having her in his hold.

"Yes?" He leaned his head down to hear her better.

"My mother asked if we might go out to La Galerie des Gobelins." Her lips were dangerously close to his ear; he might have swayed into her a bit. "I think it's a touch loud and crowded in here for her."

He straightened, physically and mentally, and signaled the waiter. "Of course. What would you ladies like to drink and I'll have them bring it to us?" They sorted out their orders—Eliot didn't notice Abigail's slight swoon at the sound of his perfect French conversation with the waiter—and the three of them left the commotion and hum of the bar behind them.

Eliot was consummately at ease with women (women in their twenties or women in their nineties), so having Abigail's mother along would normally have presented a pleasant addition to the evening. As it was, he thought she was the most extraneous person he'd ever come across, and wished she would simply disappear. He filed those uncharitable feelings deep into the part of his psyche that was rapidly running out of storage space, the file marked: desires-I-repress-since-meeting-Abigail-Heyworth.

The wintry Parisian night accentuated the warmth of the hotel's interior. The quieter gallery bar where they relocated had a lovely perimeter of potted trees that diffused the sound of the other people and created a calm elegance.

"Do you mind if I remove my jacket?" Eliot asked the duchess cordially.

"Of course, you should remove your jacket, Eliot. It's quite casual here."

Eliot smiled as he pulled the lightweight blazer from his shoulders, thinking that only someone of the duchess's particular character could construe the Hôtel Plaza Athénée as *quite casual*... compared to Blenheim Palace, maybe. He turned to hang his jacket on the back of the suede Bergère chair and caught Abigail staring up at him. Eliot gave her a quick wink while his back was turned toward her mother. He would have endured medieval torture for the shy smile that he earned in reply.

Their drinks arrived within seconds and they spent a comfortable time talking about their respective travels into Paris. He had taken the 4:30 flight from Milan; they had taken the Eurostar. He had taken the liberty of making a reservation at Alain Ducasse's restaurant in the hotel. The duchess nodded her glowing approval of his choice.

Eliot started talking about plans for the next Fashion Week with the duchess, and Abigail smiled and looked away from her mother, who was veering dangerously close to fawning. She supposed she couldn't blame her; Eliot was impossibly charming. As she looked around the genteel bar area, she noticed three older people talking at the far end of the room, partially obscured by one of the elegant leafy palms. From this distance, the couple with their backs turned looked remarkably like Eliot's parents. Abigail smiled to herself, and thought a psychologist would have a field day, questioning the mental health of seeing Eliot's likeness at every possible turn.

"What are you smiling about, Abigail?" Eliot asked, reaching out to touch her thigh, letting his hand rest gently on her skirt.

She paused for a second at his caress, inhaling. "I was just thinking how those people look like your parents from far away, and then I thought how silly it is that I would think random people look like your family."

Eliot turned his head over his left shoulder to glance in the direction Abigail had been looking, then rolled his eyes and very reluctantly pulled his hand away from Abigail's precious leg. "Those are my parents."

Eliot rose from the table and turned past the adjacent potted plant to see his uncle and parents enjoying a bottle of champagne in the far corner of the bar. His mother caught his eye before her companions did and she gave a quick cry of delight.

Her eyes sparkled, dark and joyful and mischievous. *Like Eliot's*, thought Abigail. The three gregarious Americans left their table and went over to say hello to Abigail and her mother.

"How much fun!" Penny Cranbrook clapped her hands together and looked at Abigail and Sylvia as if they were all a bunch of long lost friends.

Eliot made formal introductions to the dowager duchess, who remained seated. Abigail wanted to kick her mother in the shin and tell her to get up and quit being such a slave to convention. Abigail was up and shaking hands with the lot of them, and laughed when Eliot's mother pulled her into a half-hug and whispered, "Don't you look pretty!" Abigail was unaccustomed to doting of the maternal sort, but she thought she might be able to get used to it.

"Thank you. It's so nice to see you again, Penny," Abby replied.

It turned out the Cranbrooks' companion, Jack Parnell, was an old childhood friend of theirs who had moved away from Iowa when he went off to college. He must have been in his late sixties like Will and Penny—and the duchess, come to think of it—but he lifted one of the heavy Bergère chairs with ease. He settled himself right in next to Sylvia, disarming her with his easy mix of respectful interest and joviality.

Abigail looked up at Eliot with a grateful smile. He pulled her slightly away as his father pulled up two more chairs for Eliot's mother and himself. A waiter came over with their standing bucket of iced champagne and resituated it near their new location.

"Do you think we can run off and leave them now?" Eliot's warm hand was at the small of her back and his voice was a low rumble in her ear that shot straight to her gut.

She slapped him on the upper arm. "Never say!"

Eliot's mother caught the short interplay and looked away with a small smile.

"There is no way in hell I can abandon my mother to these *strangers!*" Abigail whispered in a perfect imitation of her mother's plummy, snobbish accent on the last word. Eliot laughed quietly and Abigail felt it roll through her as he guided her back to her seat with the light touch of his palm at her back.

The six of them ended up having dinner together at Alain Ducasse, with Sylvia looking more relaxed and happy than Abigail had seen her ever since her mother had been widowed. Sylvia had Jack Parnell to her right and Will Cranbrook to her left, and she looked unexpectedly young and vivacious. Abigail mused that her mother's practiced ease in society was yet another trait they did not share. But her mother's spark of vitality this night was nothing like the typical mask she wore in recent years amid her circle of friends in London. Abigail thought, with a pang, that her mother might be simply enjoying herself for the first time in years.

Eliot was sitting to Abigail's left and Mr. Cranbrook was sitting to her right. She felt as though she were bookended between American Male Specimen the Elder and American Male Specimen the Younger. Eliot and Abigail were seated on the banquette and the other four at individual upholstered seats around the immaculate table crowded full of wineglasses, fine white linen, and sparkling silver.

The seating arrangement made it much easier for Eliot's hand to wander unnoticed along Abigail's supple thigh. She wore a simple black skirt that stopped just above her knee, and rose higher once she was seated. All Eliot could think of was how quickly and easily it might be removed.

Dinner conversation jumped from the happy coincidence of Eliot's presence in Paris ("So surprising given the importance of the negotiations in Milan," Penny Cranbrook noted with particular meaning and a glance in Abigail's direction) to the recent praise heaped upon Jack Parnell and his years of service in Paris. Abigail adored the look on her mother's face as Jack talked humbly about the work he had done over the past forty years as an expat in Paris, where he had come as a clerk right out of University of Chicago Law School on a two-year assignment with a large American firm.

Parnell had been widowed five years earlier and had three grown sons, two living in the United States and one in Paris. He had spent much of his free time championing the rights of immigrants and other disenfranchised members of French society, and his recent retirement from the law had not diminished his enthusiasm for good works.

Abigail picked up and followed bits and pieces of all the conversations winging around the table (and some from the large, noisy table behind them as well), but found it surprisingly difficult to focus when she spoke to Eliot, who was practically on her lap. After a few attempts at small talk with him, Abigail had the uncomfortable realization that she couldn't say anything to Eliot without it sounding like a seductive purr. She tried clearing her throat a couple of times, but he just smiled and shook his head, as if to say, don't even bother.

She asked him about his negotiations in Milan; they talked about the small town where the family's traditional factory had been located for centuries; Eliot invited her to come for a visit to see it. He asked her all about her meetings in London and how she was

progressing with what he dubbed her *life plan*. She bristled momentarily at the perceived slight, that he was belittling her efforts to take
charge of her (considerable) finances and set a course for herself. He
caught the subtle shift in her posture immediately.

"What is it?"

"You make it sound a trifle piddling when you say it like that."

"That certainly wasn't my intention. It's your *life* and it's your
*plan*. I wasn't trying to diminish the importance of what you're doing."

"It probably rankles because there's a hint of truth. Isn't that
always the way?"

"No."

Abigail reached for her water glass, but held it up near her face
without actually taking a drink. She lowered her voice a bit so only
he could hear. "And stop looking at me like I'm the only person in
the room."

"How else should I look at you?"

"See?" She took a sip of water and put the glass back on the
table, taking care not to let her slightly trembling hand knock into
any of the myriad other glasses. "All of this badinage is second
nature to you. I can barely concentrate with six conversations
going on simultaneously, yet you sit there and it's like you are in a
soundproof box."

He gave her a deadly smile. "I have very highly developed powers
of concentration. I tend to become immersed."

"Really?" she prompted.

"Hence the so-called meteoric rise through the luxury goods
market," he continued more casually. "My first boss thought I was
trying to usurp him, which I suppose in the end I did, but it wasn't
what I set out to do. I have an insatiable appetite for information."
He shrugged. "I probably should have been a detective." He looked
away for a moment as if he were really considering it as a possible
career change. "But I would miss all the wine and women," Eliot

added as he raised his glass in a tiny salute, holding her eyes as the stunning 1995 white Burgundy slid down his throat.

As dinner drew to a close, Abigail was starting to fret about the logistics of hiving off with Eliot without making too much of a spectacle of herself. That was quickly overtaken by her more pressing concern about what she and Eliot might actually get up to in a luxurious Parisian hotel room. Her heart set to hammering in a most disconcerting fashion. The matter of the bill was settled—Eliot had quietly given his credit card to the maître d' before they'd even been seated—and the party started to break up. The Cranbrooks were staying with Jack Parnell at his house near the Bois de Boulogne. The three of them were headed out to Normandy the following morning for a few days of sightseeing, then Eliot's parents were continuing on to Geneva to meet up with Eliot the following weekend.

Jack gave the duchess his personal card, handing it to her while making a subtle, genteel bow that lent the whole exchange an odd mix of Japanese formality and boyish tenderness.

"Stop staring, Abigail!" Eliot whispered hotly in her ear.

"I'm not!" But her gaze never left her mother and Jack. "They're adorable and I've never had the opportunity to see my mother being courted. She's got a lot of humanity to catch up on. Trust me, I'm not exaggerating."

"Anyone fancy an after-dinner drink?" Eliot offered in a louder voice. Abigail's heart sank a little at the idea that he was postponing being alone with her, until she realized he had lobbed the invitation to the noisy bar knowing full well that the older four were never going to accept, and thus all parted ways in a perfectly natural fashion.

Abigail walked her mother to the elevator bank while Eliot escorted his parents and uncle out to the street to get a cab.

# Chapter 7

"Thanks for the introductions, Eliot," Jack Parnell said with a grateful wink as he got into the cab.

Will Cranbrook shook his son's hand and said he was looking forward to spending time together the following weekend in Geneva. Eliot agreed.

Penny Cranbrook was hanging back a few steps, and Eliot knew she had something to say once the two men were safely out of earshot. Eliot turned to face her with his best what-me-worry? smile. "Yes?"

"She's very young, Eliot. Have a care."

He hugged his mother with deep affection. "I think I may already have more than a care, but I'll try. And she's not *that* young. I think she can take care of herself."

His mother smiled and put her hand on his cheek. "I'm not worried about Abigail Heyworth. Looking after *you* is my job, remember?"

"No it isn't. You're retired, *remember?*"

"Oh, Eliot."

"I'll be fine, Mom. You're good to go." He helped her into the taxi, then shut the door.

He reentered the hotel with the feeling that he had been waiting not just weeks or months, but years to be truly alone with Abigail Heyworth. Her mother must have just entered the elevator and Abigail had turned back toward the main lobby to join him, but he closed the distance and grabbed her small frame up and lifted her clear off the ground, swinging her in a quick circle. He kissed a tender part of her neck that stole the laughter from her.

He set her back down and stared into her eyes, his hands still circling her waist.

"Well, that settles that," she said with a short laugh.

"What's that?"

"Whether there would be any strange alone-with-Eliot awkwardness once everyone left." Her smile was mocking, but her silvery gray eyes held a hint of anxiety.

"Do you want that drink after all?" he asked, pulling her waist closer to his. "Just to take the edge off."

She gasped and smiled at the pressure of his hips against hers. "I seem to have lost the desire to take the edge off. I think I might like the edge on."

"Atta girl." He kept one hand on her hip and reached around to jab the elevator button with his other. "Up, up, and away we go."

There were a few seconds of silence as the elevator returned from a higher floor. Abigail whispered, "Maybe I am a little nervous after all… I don't know, Eliot…"

"Oh, no, you don't! This is not a clichéd beach in the Caribbean, or a creaking bed in Iowa. This is Paris! Lights. Lovers. Sophisticates. Surrealists. *Lovers.*" The elevator dinged a cheerful prod. "Your chariot, my lady."

Abigail let herself be led into the elevator, feeling her anxiety rising. Too much thinking. It was just Eliot, after all. But it was Eliot! She needed to think—

As the doors slid shut, Eliot pushed her hard into the corner of the empty elevator, caging her in his arms, one knee between her thighs, and began kissing her with such delicious pressure: desire, tenderness, fire, caution, invitation. The skin on the back of her arms was prickling with anticipation. His hands were everywhere, along her hips, at the underside of her breast, dipping to the back of one knee, her wrists.

"What floor are you on?" she mumbled between nips at his earlobe. He pressed the button for his floor and she belatedly realized that the elevator had not even been moving when they'd been kissing.

She had assumed… she was certain she had felt it moving… then he was kissing her again and she was responding in ways she didn't even recognize. Her tongue began to battle his. The sound of his aroused moan in response made her feel powerful, joyful. She wanted to laugh. She wanted to kiss him and laugh.

"What is so funny?" he asked, holding her cheeks in the palms of his hands. Her face was a glowing, glorious thing to behold. Her eyes were shimmering with anticipatory delight; her lips were plump and moist from kissing; her skin was flushed, hot to the touch of his thumb's light caress.

"I want to laugh from sheer joy. It's not funny in that way, I suppose"—she shook her head a bit to gather her thoughts—"but I just felt this joy sort of bubbling up and out." She reached her hands up to his face then, just wanting to feel the strength of his jaw, the texture of his slight beard. Her head was tilted to one side slightly, examining Eliot like a specimen, which to her mind, he sort of was. Male.

Eliot let his thumb trail across that plump lower lip then turned when the elevator doors dinged and opened at his floor. Her hands fell away from his face and he guided her out into the hall. He kept at least one hand on her the whole time, grabbed his room key out of his pocket, opened the door, hit the light switch, and always one firm hand was at her hip or her lower back or her ribs or her forearm.

Abigail slipped away from Eliot enough to get her bearings in the room. Warm chocolate brown velvets, earthy Provençal linens, luxurious pale gray silk curtains that pooled in a sumptuous pile at the floor in front of the three sets of French doors that led out to a small balcony. She half-walked, half-floated across the room, drawn to the brilliant lights outside the windows, sparkling like little gems reflecting in the crisp night. She opened one of the doors and stepped out onto the narrow balcony. The cold air was a welcome change from the recycled air that always made Abigail feel trapped in some sort of science experiment.

Controlled environments. Fixed results. An absence of the natural order.

She could hear Eliot's movements behind her in the room, the clink of his keys being laid down on the cool marble of one of the consoles, his jacket being laid across the back of one of the over-stuffed armchairs, the slightest sound of creaking leather from his shoes as he crossed the room toward her. Abby's eyes were closed and the city sounds and smells mingled seamlessly with the intangible but very real feeling of Eliot approaching her from behind. She started smiling a few seconds before his hands actually touched her, sensing his nearness, his scent, his power, all around her. She leaned back into his strong chest and stomach, rubbing the back of her head into him, still holding on to the black wrought iron balcony railing to steady herself, turning her cheek into the warmth of him.

He leaned in to inhale her hair then kissed the top of her head.

"I have something for you, Abigail."

She opened her eyes and saw a small package in his hands in front of her. It was about the size of a slice of bread, wrapped in simple, unadorned brown paper and a bit of tape.

"Surprisingly luxurious wrapping," she joked and looked at him with a smile over one shoulder.

"I was in Milan when I found it, you ungrateful witch, and did not have the benefit of my assistant's more practiced wrapping techniques." He kissed her hair again. "It's what's on the inside that matters, anyway. Or so I've been told."

Abigail stayed in the comfortable circle of his arms and let go of the balcony railing to take the small package from his hand. She let her fingers stroke the lines of his outstretched palm and felt the response ride through him behind her.

She shook her hair to one side and focused on carefully unwrapping the small gift. Once she'd removed the wrapping, she handed Eliot the piece of brown paper to hold while she opened the white box. Nestled inside were a pair of tiny antique gold charms: a fish and a bicycle, hanging together on a length of thin black leather. She turned in his arms and looked up at his smiling, strong, absurdly handsome face.

His hair was catching a bit of the light wind and he looked like an expectant child, eager. "Do you like them?"

"They're fabulous, Eliot. How could I not? Where did you ever find them… such an incongruous pair," she said with a sly smile from under her eyelashes.

His hands were wandering down her back and around her hips. "I was in Milan for those infuriating negotiations and decided to take a walk for a bit after lunch on Thursday and came upon this crazy old bat of a jeweler who had thousands upon thousands of charms… taxis and typewriters and storks and beer steins and whistles and stars…" He nuzzled her neck with his lips near her ear as he enumerated the vast array of silly charms, then pulled away again to face her. "And then it just sort of came to me, as it were, when I spotted the bicycle… it works by the way, the pedals actually turn the wheels, so it's not so totally useless after all"—he winked— "and the fish was just waiting in a nearby velvet tray in the midst of a hundred other charms, and its little diamond eye winked at me in the sun, just like yours. Diamond girl."

She looked closer and saw that there were in fact two tiny diamond eyes on the fish charm.

"Put it on me, please. Will you?" She handed him the length of black cord, then turned and lifted her mass of black curls up and out of his way, revealing the back of her neck.

"You are turning me into a sentimental idiot, Abigail. Just the sight of the back of your neck has me in a momentary fit of pique." He reached around her neck and let the charms hang at different lengths. "Where do you want them?" He pulled them up short like a choker and then let them fall seductively between her breasts.

"What a decision!" Her laugh was breathy at the thought of which would be more sweetly torturous: a relentless, controlling pressure snug around the base of her neck or a gentle, evocative caress along her breasts. She shivered in anticipation of either. Both.

Eliot began kissing her exposed nape while she pondered the possibilities.

"Maybe just there." Abigail sighed through her desire. "Just knot it there... wherever... for now."

Eliot pulled back to get a better look at his hands and the small cord, his fingers feeling a bit too thick as he tied it off with a simple, sturdy square knot.

"That should hold." He gave it a short tug against her skin to test it, then let one hand follow the length around to her breast. Abigail gave a little whimper of pleasure. "I'm so glad you like it," he whispered into her ear as her head nodded forward and she let her hair down.

She turned into his embrace and reached around to his back, feeling the cords of muscle that ran up the column of his spine, the turning in at his hip, letting her hands run up the front of his shirt. He bent toward her and she felt his hand slide up the soft quivering flesh of her inner thigh.

"Eliot, we're out on the balcony."

"So? I've been insanely desperate to get up this functional black skirt for the past four hours." But he swung them both around so her back was flush against the cold limestone exterior of the building, his body effectively concealing her from any pervy Peeping Toms in the buildings across the Avenue Montaigne.

His hand moved slowly, continuing farther up her legs, at moments light and coy, then strong and urgently pushing the skirt out of the way. "Ah! You went lingerie shopping without me!" His hand reached the top of her thigh-highs.

"I thought you'd appreciate them," she said softly.

"You were right." He reached up higher to her underwear, where her thigh met the side of her hip. With one delightfully menacing finger, he followed the silky lace fabric from the front, around the outside of her hip, then down the crack of her bum, and, finally, briefly stroking between her legs from behind. Then he used the same finger to slowly tug at the elastic waist of her thong and shoved the interfering fabric down around her thighs.

She tried to continue her own travels across his hard abdomen, but she was quickly overcome by the delicate motion of Eliot's fingers once he began stroking her, slowly finding her, circling her hot center then taking long, leisurely passes along the slick length of her.

"Jesus, Abigail. You're so turned on."

She looked up at him. "Uh, duh! Dinner was torture."

His other hand kept her firmly pinned to the wall, the centuries-old strength of which gave Abigail much-needed support. She was slowly melting at his touch... her legs started trembling and her hands were trying desperately to grasp... something... anything... one moment his thick golden-brown hair, the next his flexing, ropy shoulder muscles, fabric, skin, muscle, bone, then the length of his erection pushing against the placket of his trousers and into her palm.

And he just kept on.

His mouth was on hers, then on her cheek, her eyebrow, her neck, nipping at her skin. She felt selfish and adored and frantic. Her breath was becoming erratic and then Eliot did something devilish with the tip of his finger, curling it into a tender, needy place, while pushing the palm of his hand into her hard peak.

"Look at me," he demanded with a hoarse command.

Her eyes flew open as her body convulsed and shuddered and broke into pieces and rose into the Parisian night, and into the winter wind, and, ultimately, into Eliot himself. She held his eyes with her unseeing, unblinking ones, her hands clenched fiercely into the fabric at his upper arms, her breath inconsistent, the back of her throat hot and dry. She wondered vaguely if she had cried out or if his name had simply burned through her.

---

Eliot stared into her eyes. They were no longer gray, but almost entirely black, her pupils dilated and stunned. She was utterly still. He moved his hand with a knowing tug, and she convulsed around his hand and flew away again, her black eyes pinned to his, her body responding to his slightest touch.

"No more, Eliot," she whispered plaintively, licking her dry lips. "Please."

"Only because you said *please*," he said as his finger and hand pulled away from her, slowly, gently. He cupped her one last time to feel the warmth of her pleasure, then tenderly put her thong back in place and pulled her wrinkled skirt back down around her thighs.

"Thank you," she mumbled as her head leaned into his shoulder, her arms too weak to grip him any longer. She felt like a rag doll.

He swept her up easily into his arms and brought her into the subdued bedroom, pushing the door to the balcony shut with his hip. Eliot had dimmed some of the lights before joining her outside, and the room exuded a welcoming, comforting glow. She was already drowsy, nuzzling into his neck, her arms slack around his shoulders. He held her with one arm as he pulled the bed linens free with his other and laid her down on the pristine, lightly lavender-scented white linen.

She hummed a sweet, grateful purr of pleasure as her body curled into itself and she turned to one side, grabbing a big down pillow into her arms.

"Don't even think about falling asleep, Abigail."

She opened one eye and looked at him through a haze of residual pleasure. "Yes, Eliot." But the one eye closed of its own accord.

"Abigail?"

"Mm-hmm," she hummed.

"Wouldn't you be more comfortable out of those clothes of yours?"

"Mm-hmm," she hummed again, this time with a wide grin. "Shall I call a valet?"

His laugh was low and suggestive. "I think you're in luck. I am more than happy to assist. I even have something for you to sleep in."

She rolled onto her back and tried harder to snap out of her postclimax fog. "You do?"

He nodded.

"What kind of something?"

"Hold on, I'll get it."

He came back from the dressing area with a large white shopping bag.

Abigail scooted up the bed so she had her back against the headboard and her knees pulled up in front of her. "What is it?"

"Many wonderful things, I hope. I confess I haven't looked yet. I just called Carine Gilson and asked her to send over a few pieces from her spring collection."

"Collection?" Abigail croaked.

"Yes, *darling*," he mimicked. "There is couture lingerie. You'd better get used to it."

"I don't even want to ask how dear it is—"

"It was free of course. Industry courtesy and all that."

"Well, of course it was free for you! You know what I mean."

He peeked into the bag, still holding it out of her reach. "Maybe you're right. You probably don't want any of this."

"Oh fine. Just give it here." She held out her arm with an impatient flick of her fingers.

"Tsk-tsk. How do you think you're going to try on lingerie for me with all of those *practical* clothes in the way?"

"For *you*?" She smiled.

"Of course, for me," Eliot said. "Who else would they be for?"

"Well, for *me*, of course."

"Ah, but you have no interest in frilly things, remember?"

"Maybe you're converting me." She raised a challenging eyebrow.

"In that case, we start with a blank canvas. Clothes off."

"You're not joking, are you?"

"Nope." He walked toward one of the armchairs in front of the fireplace and turned on the gas flames. "There. I even made it a little warmer for you." He sat down in the big chair and set the shopping bag to his left. "Let's see what we'll start with…" He rustled around and pulled out something in a goldenrod silk and let it flow through his fingers. "Maybe this."

Abigail stared at him. She was definitely fully awake again, watching him rub that delicate fabric between his fingers and making the not-great leap to imagining how those same fingers were going to feel against the silk as it slid along her skin. "Stop that, Eliot."

"What? This?" He was rubbing the lingerie with one hand and absentmindedly stroking his erection through the fabric of his pants with the other. He held up the silk. "You want me to stop fondling your lingerie?"

She dipped her forehead into her knees and spoke into the small space. "You are shameless."

"Good god, I hope so!"

She looked up and laughed. "Okay, you win."

His face bloomed into a crooked smile. "Really?"

"Yes." She slid to the end of the bed. "Really." Her feet didn't quite touch the floor and she swung her calves back and forth. She stared into his eyes as she began unbuttoning her black silk blouse.

"Great top, by the way. Vintage Chanel?"

She nodded. "My mother's, obviously. She couldn't bear to see me in the Topshop white sweater I was going to wear."

"Bless her."

"You all are crazy, you know that, don't you? They're just clothes. Bits of fabric to cover the… bits."

"Off with the bits, Abigail. Quit stalling."

"I'm not stalling. I'm just watching you—what did you call it?"

He smiled his encouragement.

"Oh, I recall now. I'm watching you *test your limits*."

His smile broadened and he undid the top button of his pants.

"Oh dear lord. Are you really going to have a wank while I strip and try on lingerie? It's just all too much!"

He burst out laughing. "That's exactly what I'm going to do. And I might make you come a few times while we're doing it, and then I'll probably screw you senseless. Any questions?"

She quit trying to undo the stupid buttons of her mother's blouse and pulled it over her head instead. The skirt was off a few seconds later. "No questions." She stood in front of him in her (still from Marks & Spencer, but better than white cotton anyway) thong and thigh-high stockings with the matching black lace bra.

"Nice try," he said, dragging his knuckles lightly across the fabric over her breasts. "But this cheap machined lace is not what I want touching your body."

"Eliot." She stomped her small stockinged foot. "You must know how it infuriates me to hear you talk about *my* body as if it were *your* property."

"Isn't it?"

"Oh my god. You're like a caveman or something."

"Or something. Take those tacky things off and try on at least one of these pieces."

She stared at him. She'd never been the least bit modest, so standing there in her thigh-highs with her arms crossed defiantly over a few inches of black lace made her feel more like a stern teacher than a call girl. "Eliot." He wasn't really asking her to do it, he was telling her. She wasn't quite ready to deal with the fact that her body hummed and revved when he told her to do things or how wrong-right it felt to *want* to do whatever he asked.

"Abigail."

"Okay. But only because you asked nicely."

He laughed again. "I didn't ask nicely. In fact, I didn't ask at all. This isn't me courting you; this is me having my way with you. It's what you want too, isn't it?"

"Yes," she whispered.

"Then take the rest of your cheap things off and throw them in the fireplace."

"You are so evil."

"Only with you, I promise."

She looked at him as she pulled the stockings off one at a time and tossed them into the grate. They sizzled and melted and then they were gone. The G-string was up next, and finally the bra. "It's perfectly good. Seems a shame to destroy it," Abby tried.

"It goes."

She flung it into the fire like a slingshot. When she returned her attention to face Eliot, she put her fists on her hips in naked insolence. "Here I am." She used her hands to gesture from her head to her toes and then put her hands back on her hips. "So?"

"Incredible." He was assessing her again, and damn if it didn't set her heart pounding. "Come closer." He gestured with one hand. She closed the distance between them and stood before him, one leg slightly turned. He reached between her legs and let the palm of his hand ride up the inside of her thigh. She gasped when he touched her intimately, with an almost careless swipe.

"Eliot!"

"What?" He looked at her like they'd just passed in the Tube station. As if he were about to reply, *May I help you with something?*

Her libidinous body was beginning to rebel against every weak excuse her brain was trying to throw up in his path. *He's bossy. He's arrogant. He's controlling. He's crazy*, her rational mind cried. *He's going to screw you senseless*, her libido rested its case.

"So what's in the bag?"

He smiled again. "How about this?" He pulled out a small white corset with black silk ribbon carefully sewn over the stiffer lines.

"Oh my."

"Right?" He smiled. "Turn around and I'll put it on you."

She did as he said, and got a little thrill thinking about how his bossy bedroom voice did all sorts of things to her insides. She tilted her head and wondered if she had a bossy bedroom voice.

"What are you thinking?"

He cinched the strings tighter than was technically comfortable, but Abigail enjoyed the firmness of it. The stiff constriction there made everywhere else on her body that much more lush and soft, tender by comparison.

"I was thinking about your voice." She looked over her shoulder, letting her hands splay around her new smaller waist.

"Holy god, Abigail. Just stay like that for a few seconds longer. You're spectacular."

She kept her chin on her shoulder and looked at him that way, slyly. "You make me feel spectacular, Eliot."

"That's the idea."

"Well, it's quite a good idea, as ideas go."

"I agree." His eyes skittered to her derriere then back to her mischievous eyes. He let his hands trace the curves of her hips and bottom. "Simply spectacular."

Abigail's eyes slid shut at the pleasure of his touch. She would play along with all the kinky corset games in the world, as long as he kept touching her like that. "When can I be touching you?" she asked over her shoulder, her eyes still closed.

"Anytime you want to," he said.

She pivoted around and dropped to her knees between his strong legs. "I want to." She undid his zipper and pulled his pants and underwear off in one firm tug. "Oh, Eliot. Look at you." She looked up at him through long black lashes. "I've been losing sleep over this moment. Wanting and… wondering."

"Well don't waste another second on my account." He was bantering with her, but his hands were gentle and coaxing. Lightly caressing her cheek, then tenderly running along her neck. "I'm all yours."

She licked her lips and looked up at him one last time before she dipped her head and tasted him. His guttural rumbling moan of pleasure vibrated through her lips and bolted through her. After a few tentative strokes of her tongue along his length, and then taking him as deep as she could, she started to experiment, finding herself in a spectacular loop of mutual pleasure. The more she turned him on, the more turned on she became. And he was seriously turned on. Almost as soon as her lips encircled him, his fists dug into her mass of curls and held on. Like the corset, the strength of his hold bordered on pain, but it didn't hurt: it just made the pleasure that much sweeter.

"Abigail, stop!" He said it so unexpectedly and with such a grinding sound to his voice that her head flew up immediately. Eyes glassy, wet lips slack.

"Did I hurt you?"

He coughed. "Hurt? Are you kidding?" He stood up from the chair and pulled her up with him. "Bed. Now."

She laughed and wrapped her legs around his waist, tightening her strong thighs to hold on.

"Jesus, Abigail. You are seriously the whole package."

She was kissing his neck. "So are you, handsome."

He crawled up onto the bed and she clung to him like a marsupial. "Let go, I need to get this shirt off." She released her hold and fell the few inches with a throaty laugh.

"Yes! Get it off, darling." She was rubbing the palms of her hands along the exquisite material of her hand-sewn corset in anticipation of finally having all that Eliot flesh at her greedy palms' disposal. "*Now!*" she snapped.

He raised one eyebrow. "Who's feeling bossy this time?"

"It's true, you know. I've been known to be a little bossy. You going to be all right with that?"

He pulled his shirt up over his head and rose above her on the bed, straddling her legs, on his knees, finally, gloriously naked. "What do you think?"

"I imagine you can be very cooperative with the proper inducements."

"Precisely," he whispered, before leaning in to kiss her with a slow, deep thrust of his tongue that sent her body into sizzling fits.

"Undo my corset." She rolled over onto her stomach, presenting him with the laces that needed to be untied. "I have to have all my skin on you. There's just no question about it."

He chuckled that low sexy roll of his. "I love when you're certain, Abigail." He finished with the laces and Abby tossed the (probably priceless) item onto the floor.

She rolled back to face him and squealed, "Finally!" His bare chest and abdomen were wondrous: hard curves, soft hair, thick corded muscles across his stomach. Her hands were all over him, wanting to touch every fantastic inch of him. "Your skin…" She kissed his neck and shoulder. "You make me feel insatiable, Eliot."

He moaned his approval and continued kissing her neck and the turn of her shoulder.

She rubbed herself into him, wanting to feel him on her. In her. She reached for his erection and held on tight, probably tighter than was strictly necessary, but she wanted to feel it. She wanted to feel everything. "Eliot?"

He kissed her neck for a few more seconds before he leaned up onto his elbows and pinned her with those dark blue cloudy eyes of his. He did that, that thing where he didn't stop doing something delicious until he was quite finished, thank you very much. A lovely mix of taking and giving. He was generous that way. Abigail could only imagine the lengths to which he would go to make sure she was well and truly satisfied. She didn't have to imagine much longer.

"Are you ready?" he asked. The twinkling mischief of corsets and stripteases and burnt offerings had dimmed. He sounded genuinely concerned about whether or not she was prepared to go on.

"Ready? Eliot. Suffice to say I've been wanting you for quite some time, and you well know it." She held him even firmer in her grip.

# Chapter 8

THE MOMENT OF TRUTH. Or half-truth, as the case may be. Eliot had been cooking up all sorts of honorable plans to tell Abigail how much he loved her and how much he wanted their first time together to be emblematic or meaningful... or something. But now that he had her, under him, breathless, *ready*, he knew his timing was off. She was still playing. Maybe she wasn't toying with him—he was a grown-up after all, not a victim—but she certainly wasn't nearly as far down the dark hole of obsession as he was. For a while, he could channel all of his too-strong desires into lingerie and barking silly orders to get her even more turned on. For a very little while.

He made love to her—of course that's what it was to him—but he did his best to provide her with the senseless, mind-blowing fornication he'd promised. She wasn't disappointed. The two of them lay spent and breathing heavily, limbs slung over limbs, recovering from the cresting physical release. Eliot hated himself for thinking of it as less-than-everything-he-wanted, but there it was. He'd never wanted Abigail-the-Plaything.

Eliot must have passed out for a few hours then woke up with a start around 4 a.m. Eventually giving up hope of falling back to sleep, he got up and stood by the side of the bed, his hands at his hips. He wondered what in the world he was going to do with this vexing, perfect woman as he pulled the sheet more closely around her, evoking a happy sigh of relief from her unconscious self.

He took a deep fortifying breath, and finally turned toward the minibar for a glass of water. He wasn't going to be asleep anytime soon, so he picked up the book he had been reading on the short plane ride to Paris and settled himself into one of the large armchairs at the other side of the suite. The position still afforded him a clear view of the delightful prospect that was Abigail Heyworth in the midst of her angelic spray of wild black curls and a drowsy look that could only be described as pure, sensual satisfaction.

Within a few minutes, Eliot was drawn back into the postapocalyptic thriller he'd picked up at the bookstore at Malpensa. He was taken aback when he looked up at the clock and nearly two hours had passed. He was bone tired and figured he'd give sleep another try, welcoming the opportunity to rejoin Abigail in the large king-size bed. He went to the bathroom and gave his teeth a quick brush.

He turned off the reading light and left one of the curtains open so the city lights and some of the night air could come into the room. The enormous bed made it perfectly possible for Eliot to slip in without disturbing Abigail, but she was a heat-seeking missile, and within seconds of his careful slide into his side of the bed, she was reaching and stretching and touching and shimmying herself along his length until she was happily pushed right up against him.

She was still very much asleep, but she inhaled deeply and muttered his name in a delightfully erotic tone. The idea of his sleep retreated further into the realm of the impossible. Eliot felt like a tree trunk unwilling to wake the climbing vine. Ultimately, he must have fallen into something approximating sleep because when the first strands of gray morning light came weakly through the window and the sound of the street sweeper rolled through the air, he opened his eyes to see a very awake Abigail staring intently at him.

"Can we do that again?" she whispered as her fingers danced lightly down his stomach and then farther below, until she was circling him with her hand.

"I'm in love with you, Abigail."

She tried to steady her galloping heart, her hand frozen at that suddenly absurd location. "I was expecting a more honeyed seduction... lips like moist berries, eyes like liquid silver... that sort of thing... you've... well... I'm at a loss for words."

"I wasn't planning on unnerving you. To tell you the truth, it just sort of crossed my mind and I thought I'd let you know."

"Well, thanks. I guess."

"Thanks? *You guess?*"

Abigail pulled her hand out from under the covers in a matter-of-fact way and turned to face the ceiling. "You were the one who said no relationship dissection, remember?"

"That seems like a long time ago already." Eliot knew he was on very dangerous terrain and proceeded with painful slowness. "I just thought"—he paused again—"I thought it best I should give you a heads-up on the nature of... my affection... I don't think I'll be able to play at a casual affair for very long."

"I'll say. One night is traditionally considered *not very long*. Over before it's even begun, innit?" She tried to sound coquettish but it came out stilted. The air between them cracked with emptiness.

Eliot's hand dropped away from Abigail's arm, where he had been tracking up and down in a delicate continuous motion. He turned his gaze to the ceiling as well. "My mother warned me to have a care."

Abigail raised one eyebrow and turned to face his profile. "Bronte gave me the same advice about you. I think her exact words were something along the lines of, 'he's intense.'"

"How astute of her. Whereas I think my mother was implying that you would toy with me."

Abigail turned quickly away. His words stung more than if he had slapped her swiftly across the face, and her cheeks burned as if he had.

Shame.

It was an unfamiliar and profoundly unpleasant realization. She was perfectly ashamed of herself. She had every intention of toying with him. Not like she was some sort of Mata Hari who dallied with international playboys for sport, but she had certainly intended on using him in some way. Some uncomplicated, unemotional, physical way. Didn't all men fall into bed with a willing female? A quick shag for the eager beginner? Her stomach soured at her own small-mindedness.

If Abigail was perfectly honest with herself, she had to admit that from the very beginning, her feelings for Eliot had been all tangled up in her desire to satisfy what she and Tully had once jokingly referred to as *heterosity*, their shorthand for heterosexual curiosity. Or at least, Abigail had *thought* that was why she wanted to stand near Eliot and sit next to Eliot at tedious dinner parties and walk on Caribbean beaches with Eliot. He was so preternaturally male, larger than life, broad, heroic. He seemed like a perfect primer.

But somewhere in the past few months, as he helped her down from her horse, or brought her that soda on the beach, or looked at her in the restaurant that very night, she was sure she was not dealing in idle curiosity any longer. Even so, she wanted to hold tight to the possibility of something light and frivolous. Why did he have to spoil all that?

She liked the idea of a passionate, physical, uncomplicated romp with Eliot. She was not so sure she liked the idea of a big, deep, demanding well of emotion.

Rolling out of the far side of the bed, Abigail walked into the bathroom to freshen up, then put on one of the heavy beige robes hanging on the bathroom door. She crossed the bedroom without looking directly at Eliot and continued out to the balcony, hoping that a bit of fresh morning air would lend a touch of clarity to what was rapidly devolving into a murky, sentimental mess. Abigail wished she knew where her room was in relation to Eliot's; at this point, she was nearly willing to take a chance at scaling along an adjacent balcony to make her escape, rather than having to go back into Eliot's room to apologize for being a selfish tart.

She stayed out on the balcony for what felt like an eternal quarter of an hour, but there was nothing for it. She was going to have to walk back in, in order to get out.

Eliot was holding a heavy crystal glass of water loosely in his long, beautiful fingers. He had put on his rumpled pale-blue collared shirt from last night, unbuttoned, along with a pair of worn jeans. He sat in that same large comfortable chair from last night, his long legs extended and crossed at the ankle. She stared at his bare feet for a few seconds. He looked as if he might have splashed water on his face, and his hair was a damnably sexy tousled mess.

"I guess I'll go then," Abigail said hesitantly, wanting him to stop her or make her apologize or demand that she explain away whatever she had been unable to explain.

But instead he just looked at her, his face cool, hard, and shuttered. And he waited.

She was torn between wanting to crawl into his lap, into him, to give herself over to every carnal fantasy she had been harboring for the past few weeks—months really, if she were in the mood to be honest, which apparently she was not—particular textures and positions and smells and ideas that had been distracting her for days, things she wanted to do to him and for him and with him. Things that she had only just begun to discover last night.

Abigail was torn between those desires and the very real possibility that she was just using Eliot—good, true Eliot—for some sort of sexual picnic. Her face heated again and it was as if he could follow every unspoken word of every tawdry thought.

"I just figured I could be one of the girls…" She tried, and failed, to convey a semblance of levity.

His gaze clouded and she realized he was truly and utterly

furious. She had never seen him this way, and if she were not so ashamed of herself, she might have taken a moment or two to be terrified. Eliot was not a hater, but he despised a liar. In that moment, she saw herself reflected in his cold stare for the liar she was: maybe not a factual liar, but an emotional one certainly.

His voice was not one she had heard before. It was cruel. "Would you like me to *use* you, Abigail?"

The horror of it was that her first response, physical, was an unthinking, primal *yes*. Her breasts felt heavy and taut in response to his harsh words. She felt an involuntary quiver at her center. Her body simply called to his. Her body didn't care about conscience or manipulation or cruelty. Or, perhaps, one day, she would think about it long enough to realize that her body knew much more about those things than her overwrought, immature, theory-filled brain was able to concede. Manipulation? *Yes*, her body screamed, *let Eliot manipulate the hell out of you. Stop thinking, you stupid woman! Cruelty?* Her body taunted. *Yes, have Eliot show you the very limits of what you can stand, what we—body and mind, finally united—can bear.*

The farthest reaches of abasement, submission, loss of control, giving of control. Consent. *Concede, Abigail.* Her treacherous body hissed the suggestion like the last temptation.

Then she blinked away the strange lure of forbidden desires that she was trying to convince herself had to be *wrong*. But they hadn't felt wrong when Eliot touched her and ordered her about last night. She was a strong, independent, modern woman. That kind of submission and consent were the antithesis of everything she believed in, weren't they? Her nape was tingling where the knot of the black leather cord was caught in a tiny strand of hair.

Eliot watched her, watched the wheels of her thought process play across her eyes—first lit by the spark of desire and then dimmed by the leviathan pallor of fear. He saw the exact moment fear won, when she turned inexorably away from that tempestuous black sea of brutal, unreined passion they could have shared. For a few moments there, he thought he saw clear through to some dark beautiful place where she understood him and they would be free of... everything. Some place of abject truth, removed of every societal code, every gender constraint, every preconceived notion. Wild.

And then he saw her emotional retreat. She wasn't going to go there. Or, at least, she wasn't going to go there with him now, knowing he was a fool in love with her. She probably would have done any kinky thing he could think of if he'd been cool and playful, erotic and empty. Instead, the bright silver light in her diamond eyes turned to pale, gunmetal gray right there in front of him. She slipped back into a world of fear, or perhaps a healthy caution, if he was feeling generous. A world where people stayed busy, alert, moving, bustling, the better to keep their roaring passions in check.

He wanted to kill her. For a split second, less than a split second, even, he understood that often clichéd phrase *crime of passion*. It had never rung true for him, this idea that you could love someone so much that only their destruction would ease the pain of loving them. How could she be such a despicable liar? So completely dissociated from what was passing between them?

She had changed back into her black skirt and her mother's shirt, but she no longer had a bra. He'd seen to that. When his eyes raked her body—naked to him, even in clothes—her nipples tightened and protruded through the thin fabric of her black shirt. He took it as the smallest, meanest concession that her body, at least, had no need to prevaricate.

⸺

Abigail briefly considered mentioning that she despised herself more than he could ever possibly despise her, but figured it would be of little consolation to either of them. She quickly bent to pick up her shoes, then grabbed her slim purse, and walked slowly, dreadfully, to the door. She didn't bother to wipe away the stupid tear that fell down her left cheek.

She pulled the door shut and tried to catch her breath, leaning back against the cool metal. A part of her still wished he'd come after her, to swing the door open with a violent pull behind her back, to force a confession she didn't even understand.

Little pieces of the truth were already starting to coalesce, forcing themselves into her mind. At base, she didn't have the courage to admit what she really wanted.

For all her talk of independent thought and a sense of herself that hinged on an utter disregard for society's mores, she was a prisoner. The entire system had turned on her. Here she thought she was returning to some pedestrian, simplified male-female stereotype, a relationship that bore no undue scrutiny. Mainstream. The Usual.

What a hideous joke.

He would never open that door and pull her back in. She knew that after a few seconds. Not out of spite or to taunt her or to teach her a lesson, but simply because they both knew *she* was the one who had to acknowledge what she wanted... to open the door and walk in. Eyes open. Honest.

The tears were running hot and messy down her cheeks. She was quietly slobbering. She tried to count to ten, to gather the requisite self-control, the most basic courage. But she had no reserve. She tried to take a quick breath to right herself, to look at the opportunity she was about to squander.

She could not do it.

She had not made a sound. No whimper. Only silent, copious tears. But even through a thick fire door, Eliot must have been following the trajectory of her thoughts, the loss of every possibility. Her cowardice.

A brief, violent sound of shattering glass on the other side of the door sent her sprinting down the hall and—after an embarrassing visit to the front desk to ask for her own forgotten room number—back to her luxurious, lonely chamber.

———

Eliot was breathing hard after hurling the glass at the door. He heard Abigail's footsteps retreating and got up slowly to gather the larger pieces of glass and to call housekeeping to deal with the rest of the mess. He gave a short, vicious laugh at himself, marveling at the fact that certain clichés were so patently obvious that the very nature of what was meant was lost. *Nice guys finish last.*

Well, sure.

Obviously.

But to be taught such an object lesson by a flighty, airy, idiotic woman was almost more than he could stand. A piece of glass caught the edge of his left thumb and he dumped the shards into the small garbage bin in the bathroom and put the bit of bleeding flesh into his mouth to staunch it.

If all women were, if not repelled, at least bemused, by the good, true version of Eliot, he supposed he was perfectly capable of becoming a philandering, misogynistic rat bastard. He grabbed his cell phone from the desk and pulled up the TGV schedule site and made a reservation to get home to Geneva by lunchtime. It was just after six in the morning and he could easily make the eight o'clock train, allowing him plenty of time to shower and change and be out of Paris—and away from Abigail—long before she had any ridiculous notions about discussing or talking or coming to an understanding.

He needed to get home to the cool, organized comfort of his home in Geneva. Where he had what he needed.

Order.

Respect.

And he would start screwing women for the hell of it. As many models and stylists and fortune-hunters and dancers and poetesses and waitresses and heiresses as there were days in the week. And maybe he would lead a few of them on, just for sport, with ambiguous promises of delightful shared futures, and then laugh at their woeful misunderstanding of his intentions.

Silly trollops.

He doubted he could erase his feelings for Abigail, but he could certainly bury the hurt under a stack of meaningless affairs. He needed to get busy. He didn't need to spend another ounce of mental energy dissecting unfathomable ideas like why he had fallen in love with her or how it might have felt for the two of them to spend the rest of their lives mapping uncharted sexual territory.

What a debacle. He stormed into the bathroom and showered as if he were scrubbing off acid rain.

By the time he walked into the front hall of his nineteenth-century home in the Geneva enclave of Versoix, he was honest enough with himself to acknowledge he would not be sleeping with every woman he came across, and probably would not be inclined to sleep with anyone at all for quite some time. Nor did he think Abigail was an idiot; some small, sad part of him even thought of calling her to apologize for something she'd never even heard him say. To apologize for his mean thought.

All he really wanted to do was get into his pool. To wash it all away. He swam for hours, lap after lap draining any residual energy he might have left in reserve to contemplate the possibility of rapprochement with Abigail. He might not be cut out for meaningless sex with faceless strangers, but he was dead set on eradicating thoughts of meaningful sex with one woman in particular.

No apologies were in order. No future. As Abigail had so perfectly pointed out, they had barely begun.

He had nipped it in the bud.

Almost.

# Part Two

# Chapter 9

Abigail smiled as she turned from the narrow hall into the kitchen and saw her mother and Jack sharing one large bowl of café au lait between them and trading different sections of the newspaper across the battered wooden breakfast table. It had been almost a year since Abigail had seen or heard from Eliot Cranbrook, but being in Paris always brought on painful waves of longing. She stuffed the memories and tried to focus on the present.

Her mother and Jack's house in Paris was something out of a fairy tale. The fact that it was a tiny, seventeenth-century, free-standing cottage tucked into the far end of a small lane, hidden in the very heart of the Sixteenth Arrondissement, made it unique. But the residual evidence of the nearly fifty years that Jack had spent living there was what made it truly magical.

The two bedrooms upstairs had accommodated his family, but barely. His three sons shared one room and he and his Spanish wife, Nina, another. None of them had ever thought to complain of overcrowding. They lived like young adventurers in an enchanted, private world that opened up to the expanse of the Bois de Boulogne out the off-kilter back door, and onto the sophistication of the Avenue Foch out the shiny red front door.

Jack Parnell had taken the house on a dare after hearing about it from a law colleague as a rental during his first year in town, almost half a century ago. At the time, he thought he would be in Paris for a two-year stint, then he would return to Iowa to start a small law practice in his hometown. Instead, he fell in love with Paris. He fell in love with the little house down the lane. He renewed his lease year after year, constantly offering the owner inducements to sell until, after twenty years of renting, the owner was suitably satisfied that Jack had no nefarious intentions that involved altering or razing the unique property.

"Oh, Abigail, did I tell you that Eliot Cranbrook is getting married?" Sylvia looked up from the article she was reading and glanced at her beautiful, if a bit wan, daughter.

"No, Mother, you hadn't mentioned it. Who is he marrying?" Even after so much time, Abigail found it difficult to keep her voice perfectly level when she spoke about Eliot, so she tended to avoid actually using his given name aloud. The fish and the bicycle still hung low between her breasts; she had never taken them off. Whether she wore them as her own scarlet letter or a token of love—or both—she still wasn't sure.

"What's her name again, Jack? We met her in Italy last summer with Penny and Will, remember?"

Jack hummed a noncommittal response, his interest engaged elsewhere in the newspaper he was reading.

"Jack?" Sylvia prompted gently. Abigail noticed that her mother never lapsed into being short-tempered or cross with her second husband. The two of them had married within a few months of their first propitious meeting at the Hôtel Plaza Athénée.

At least it had been propitious for *someone*, Abigail often reminded herself with no small amount of self-deprecation.

"Yes, love?" Jack answered absently.

"What is the name of Eliot's fiancée again? I can't recall."

"Marisa Plataneau, I think it was. Something like that. Nice woman. French. Very accomplished." He returned his full attention to the newspaper while Abigail felt her heart fold in on itself at the thought of a most likely beautiful, nice, accomplished French woman sharing Eliot's life.

And bed.

And having Eliot's children.

*Where the hell did that come from?* she wondered, then stuffed the stray thought firmly away. But she must have sighed aloud because her mother was looking at her intently when Abigail turned from the counter with her own large cup of hot black coffee.

"What?" Abigail asked defensively, in response to her mother's inquisitive gaze.

Not looking away, Sylvia said, "Jack, darling, Abigail and I are going to pop by the boulangerie to pick up some extra baguettes for tonight."

"Mm-hmm. Good idea," he replied without looking up from the paper.

The cool January air helped jar Abigail out of her reverie, along with her mother's abrupt inquiry.

"Are you still fostering feelings for Eliot? After so much time?" Sylvia asked as they made their way along the narrow, cobbled lane that led from the small house out onto the avenue.

"It's not as if I haven't tried to get over it. I just haven't met anyone... that I like as much... since I knew Eliot..." Her voice cracked on his name and she didn't try to hide it from her mother.

"Oh, dear."

"How can I still feel so much about him when I haven't seen him or talked to him in a year? I only knew him for a few months, really. We only had sex that *one time* for goodness' sake!"

"Please, Abigail. I am trying to be modern, but there are only certain hurdles I can clear. Kindly spare me the accuracies."

"Very well. I shan't go into detail. But I only mention it because I stupidly thought I wouldn't become attached, or deeply affected, or whatever." Abigail's voice trailed off as she realized her mother had slowed to a stop and was staring at her.

"Really, Abigail? You thought you could only have deep feelings for someone if the two of you had lots of *sex*?"

The way her mother pinched the word *sex* out of her patrician mouth made it sound very small and tawdry indeed.

Abigail sickened anew. "Yes. No! Mother. Please. I obviously botched the whole thing. I don't know what I thought. I thought it would be a fling, something light and fun. I adored Eliot..." Then quieter, "Adore Eliot... but I treated him so abominably, so *cheaply*, I don't think I would want to ever see me again either if I were Eliot... I can barely live with myself, much less imagine someone else wanting to live with me. And he was so tender and sweet."

"Whatever transpired a year ago is no longer the issue. The man is on the verge of marrying another woman. *Think!*" her mother commanded. "Are you willing to sit by and watch? To just let that happen?"

Abigail smiled a poignant smile at her mother then looked across the almost painfully quintessential Parisian side street. A blond woman in stylish navy trousers and fitted black jacket walked her little son to school, the boy looking like a miniature, respectable banker escorting his lady friend; a bent older man carrying his folded newspaper tucked under one arm and his cane in the other, his perfectly cut, vintage trench coat catching the wind as he walked slowly away from them; the fishmonger replenishing the piles of crushed ice in the display bins inside his plate glass storefront window.

"I don't know. Maybe I am willing to sit by and watch," Abigail said. "I don't want to hurt him."

Sylvia Heyworth Parnell looked away from her daughter's pained expression and exhaled through her nose, silently cursing the double-edged sword of the depth of her late-in-life affection for her youngest child. Life had certainly been simpler back when she left the care and feeding, and emotional well-being, of her children to nannies and governesses. Now that Abigail was a twenty-nine-year-old adult, Sylvia had actually come to care for her so deeply, it was impossible to sit back and watch her flail. "Abigail, this is not a potential investment or philanthropic opportunity for you.

This is your *life*. Please do not turn fainthearted now. It does not suit you."

Abigail tried to turn away, but her mother's gentle hand on her cheek forced her to look her in the eye. Perhaps it was the absence of any maternal affection whatsoever for the first decades of Abigail's life, but her mother's subtle touch here on the sidewalk next to the newspaper kiosk was more than she could stand. Her eyes stung with unshed tears as she looked into her mother's eyes.

Just as Sylvia had been confused by the unfamiliar tenderness that had built gradually over the past few years, Abigail was equally befuddled. She wanted so much to rely on her mother, to simply fall into a hammock of strength, but Sylvia had been so completely unavailable for so long, it was, at base, a frightening prospect.

"Why did you have to turn into a real mother all of a sudden?" Abigail asked through a hiccup of emotion.

"I wish I knew. My life would be much simpler if I didn't seem to live in a parallel universe where I felt every triumph and catastrophe of yours as if it were my own. It's highly inconvenient."

They both laughed as Sylvia lightly patted her daughter's cheek twice and wiped away a tear with her perfectly manicured index finger. The two women stared at each other: the one tall, elegant, fair-haired, and proud, the other petite, brooding, dark, and nearly defeated, their silver-gray eyes exact mirrors of one another.

"I hate to admit it," said Sylvia, "but I believe this is a situation that calls for Bronte's version of sledgehammer subtlety." Sylvia's eyes tightened around the edges as they always did at the mention of her brash daughter-in-law. "You must simply pick up the phone and speak to Eliot, to discuss matters plainly."

"And say what, exactly? 'Oh, hi, Eliot, Abigail here. Even though I behaved abominably, and I've never had the courage to apologize in all these months, I would like you to reconsider your plans to wed the lovely—and *accomplished*—Miss Marisa

Plah-Whatever-Her-Name-Is, who probably shows you unreserved love and respect, and contemplate tossing your hat in the ring for fabulous me'? Something along those lines, Mother?"

Abigail shook out her crazy head of hair and wished her thoughts would shake right out of her head along with her unruly tresses. "I'm exasperated, Mother. I'm fine. I'm just going to walk for a bit, then I have meetings the rest of the day with the two professors from the Sorbonne about partnering with our foundation in Uganda. Don't count on me for dinner."

"Tant pis. I thought you might join us. All right then. I will see you back at the house later tonight."

"I think I'm going to go back to London tonight, after the meetings. Do you mind?"

"Oh, all right, darling." They kissed each other on both cheeks before parting.

Abigail wandered around the cold city streets, the gathering, ambivalent gray clouds a perfect embodiment of her mood; directionless and mildly disappointing, with momentary glimmers of tentative, bright sun trying to come through. She was happy on so many levels, she argued with herself. Even her mother's brief regret that she wouldn't be able to join her for dinner represented such a wonderful change from the brittle, formal nonrelationship the two had tolerated until a few years ago.

Sylvia's love affair with Jack had transformed Abigail's mother in many ways. She not only shed her former aristocratic title, but a slew of attendant responsibilities and social codes. All of the commitments and strictures that had defined her—or that had defined the person called the Duchess of Northrop—were set down like a long-carried parcel that was suddenly of no use whatsoever. She was still as opinionated and single-minded as she'd always been, but there was a new tone in her voice, a burgeoning acceptance of other people's foibles. Lately, Abigail noticed that her humor was based on empathy rather than scorn. Jack Parnell loved Sylvia in a transcendent way that went far beyond the honorific title with which she had previously identified so closely. He was helping her see the world through a joyful lens.

After Sylvia met Jack that night at the Plaza Athénée, she gradually realized that she might have a go at something—someone—for the sheer pleasure of it. Prior to that moment, Sylvia's entire life had been a prescribed adherence to convention: her socially ambitious mother had schooled her in etiquette and proper behavior; her shrewd father had ensured she knew more than her fair share of economics, politics, and trade. She was a wife in training. Her father's wealth ensured she would make a fine marriage, but even well into the twentieth century, the fact that her father was in trade was never far from her (or her more aristocratic mother's) mind.

When Sylvia met George Conrad Heyworth for the first time, he was a shy, sweet farm boy from Northrop. His pedigree was unassailable—nephew of a duke on his father's side, nephew of a king on his mother's—but back then, it had never seemed that he would one day hold one of the oldest, most prestigious titles himself. In those days, he was not in line for the dukedom. George's uncle Freddy, the sixteenth Duke of Northrop, was hale and quite reproductive. At the time Sylvia met him, George already had three female cousins and twins on the way. Surely Freddy would sire a son at some point.

On the other hand, if Freddy ended up with a gaggle of girls, George's young, virile father, Henry, would be the duke if it came to that, and even then, George's older brother Ned would take the reins from him and off it would go down that side of the family. And by then, they'd all joked, who even knew if there would be such a thing as a dukedom?

Abigail's father had grown up living the life of an innocent (albeit wealthy and educated) country bumpkin. George's parents, Grandpa Henry and Grandma Polly, had little interest in the glittering

London high life, opting instead to create their own small universe populated with eight children, myriad animals, self-produced dramatic performances, athletic competitions. George had a sister who started writing novels at the age of nine, a brother who built his first small tree house in the woods at eleven, all amid an environment that seemed to foster every form of creativity imaginable. By George's own reckoning, he was the most boring of the clan. He simply loved the land. Sylvia found him utterly charming.

She and her sister Claudia had been raised in bourgeois splendor in the small city where their father's mills prospered. Regimental precision was always the order of the day: breakfast, lunch, and dinner served at exactly the same hours; clothes and linens pressed mercilessly; menus planned weeks in advance; social schedules adhered to. Sylvia felt a pang of insecurity when she suspected the contrived aristocratic life her mother aspired to bore no resemblance whatsoever to the real aristocratic life that George Heyworth enjoyed.

The two of them had first danced at the small hunt ball in the town of Brinby. Sylvia felt an instant attraction to the dark, brooding, shy George. His older sister had dared him into asking "the ice princess" to dance. Sylvia only learned of the nickname later, to her horror. Her posture, the set of her jaw, the perfection of her blond hair—these were all things her mother had given paramount importance. It had never occurred to Sylvia that they could be sources of derision.

George might have been shy around pretty (beautiful!) girls, but he was never going to turn down a dare from his bossy, sophisticated (or so she told everyone) older sister. He was sure the willowy, fair goddess in the corner would decline his invitation in any case, so there was no chance of further ridicule. When Sylvia Parker not only accepted his tentative offer to dance, but punctuated her response with a smile that transformed her face into something else entirely— something glorious—George swore he would be grateful to his domineering sister for the rest of his days.

Their marriage had been one of mutual attraction more than respect. The characteristics that had initially drawn them to one another—his lack of polish and natural charm, her precision and grace—were the same traits that often drove them apart. They always loved one another, and their romantic life was perpetually satisfying, but the fabric of their love was rent after the unexpected chain of events that led to Great Uncle Freddy's title being passed to George's father, and then, in due course, to George (brought on by Uncle Freddy siring six daughters and Ned's death in a car accident while Henry was the seventeenth duke).

When the title fell to Abigail's father, Sylvia felt a responsibility—an almost-ingrained burden—to fulfill the role of the Duchess of Northrop admirably. George was ultimately grateful for her direction—she was socially adept in ways that baffled him—and Sylvia made his transition from tweedy eccentric to accepted member of the royal circle run far more smoothly than George could have ever managed. Unfortunately, her difficult pregnancies and lack of maternal instincts tore them apart. After Abigail's birth, an event that served as the coda to nearly fifteen consecutive years of attempted pregnancies that had resulted in five miscarriages, two stillbirths, and four healthy babies, Sylvia simply shut down.

She took her eldest daughter, Claire, and spent most of her time in London, enjoying the culture, society, and entertainments that were her due, or so her mother had drilled into her all those years ago. The genuine, profound affection George showered on his three younger children, Max, Devon, and Abigail, became one more thing the two parents did not share.

Up until George's premature death, however, Sylvia had always felt the ping of excitement when she would see him after a week's absence, when she would return to Dunlear Castle from short absences spent trotting about London and enter their private rooms, sensing his childlike eagerness to touch her, embrace her, look upon her. If it were only the two of them on earth, she sometimes mused, it might have been perfect.

On this earth, however, neither one of them were ever quite what the other had hoped. There was a world of love between them, but it seemed to Sylvia that something or other always forced them to focus their attentions elsewhere. To George, Sylvia's lack of attention to her children was heartbreaking; to Sylvia, George's lack of attention to *her* was equally heartbreaking.

Since none of those intimacies between her parents were ever really clear to Abigail—what child ever understands the nature of her parents' marriage?—having the opportunity to see her mother's emotional journey with Jack Parnell was a particular gift. An emotional sympathy had developed between mother and daughter that allowed Abigail to forgive her mother's absence during her childhood and had provided them both with a new and welcome friendship.

Abigail sighed with a mixture of gratitude and capitulation, thankful for what she had gained with her mother and resigned to what she had lost with Eliot. By the time she looked up, she realized she had crossed half the city and was close to the Sorbonne.

This meeting with two members of the anthropology department at the esteemed Parisian university was the culmination of a solid year of hard work. After her brief time with Eliot, Abigail had turned her full attention to her financial—and moral—responsibilities.

Following that first meeting with the personal bankers at Coutts—and with Max's kind, steady shoulder to lean on when necessary—Abigail had spent all her time researching everything she could about setting up her own philanthropic foundation. She learned about advantageous tax structures and sound investment strategies, and took two semesters of night classes at London Business School on trusts and estates, accounting, and corporate finance.

Occasionally, she came upon Eliot's name while she researched other organizations or the best way to go about populating a board of directors. He would have been an obvious choice to sit on her board. His personal work in the charity sector was far-reaching, as well as the corporate foundation he had set up as an arm of Danieli-Fauchard. Last summer, Bronte had pressed Abigail to contact him.

"So what if you guys didn't click in the sack? You could still be friends. Or at least professional associates. Sarah doesn't have any problem with him. He can't be all bad."

*Not click in the sack? If only.* "Bronte—"

"I mean, it's none of my fucking business why you never saw each other after last winter…" Bronte let the words hang in the air between them.

"You're right, Bron. It's none of your business."

"All right, all right. Point taken. But still—"

"I mean it. No more talk of Eliot Cranbrook being involved with the Rose and Thorn."

Putting the kibosh on conversations about Eliot had become second nature in the intervening months since they'd gone their separate ways.

Abigail met three times a week with her private banker, Caroline Petrovich from Coutts, to go over the intricacies of her finances. She often looked back, almost fondly, at her own idiotic belief that her first visit would require less than an hour and would entail reviewing a few ledger sheets. In reality, it had run over three hours and led to the happy professional relationship that Abigail and Caroline now shared.

At the end of the first three months, Abigail—with Caroline's astute advice, and lots of cheering on from Sarah and Bronte—was starting to have a clear idea of how much of her fortune she wanted to put into trust and how much she wanted to strategically give away through the creation of a well-structured foundation. She named her foundation the Rose and Thorn Foundation in memory of a distant Tudor relative who had been beheaded after specious accusations of adultery. The foundation battled the diminution of women's rights or outright destruction of women through economic and medical education. Financial independence and physical health were the best weapons she hoped to provide against centuries of oppression.

While Abigail tried to steer clear of moral or religious arguments, she often found herself writing letters to the editors of many papers. The mere suggestion that there was honor in the punishment of women for real or imagined moral turpitude was the philosophical evil against which the foundation railed. It was a battle Abigail hoped to fight with an arsenal of rational, hands-on education and aid, not unwinnable religious arguments.

She took it all very seriously and treated the entire enterprise with the same fervor and enthusiasm one would apply to starting any new business. Or digging a well.

She persevered.

She enlisted her sisters-in-law: Bronte for the PR and marketing (how should Abigail promote herself and the foundation; how would the foundation reach potential applicants), and Devon's wife, Sarah James, whose experience running her shoe company had given her a wealth of firsthand experience in start-ups and how to maintain creative and corporate enthusiasm. In addition to their credentials, both were simply women who had succeeded in pursuing their own achievements and thrived in the face of challenge.

Abigail was about to duck into Balzar for a quick lunch to kill the spare hour before going to her meeting at the Sorbonne, when her phone rang and she saw it was Sarah.

"Hey, Sar."

Sarah mumbled something dismissive to someone in her office then turned her voice back to the phone. "Hi, Abs! You're on your way into the Sorbonne, right?"

"Yes. I'm a little nervous."

"Why? You've stared down bigger dogs than these guys."

"I know. But it's always easier staring down the big guns when I am going after their dirty money, but these people are so tuned in and... if I could get them on the board... well... I am really, *really* keen. If their estimation of the work we're doing in Uganda is that it's a load of ineffectual—"

"Stop!" Sarah laughed with sisterly affection. "You are *so* your worst enemy, sweetie. It makes no difference what those dusty academics say. Of course, it would be a feather in your cap to have their name on your letterhead, to forge that alliance, but you of all people know that those women in Uganda are getting proper health care thanks to *you*."

"Not me! The group of doctors and students who are giving their—"

"Oh, Abigail! Please. How would any of those doctors or students afford the supplies and... well, it's just too boring. I'm not going to waste time praising you. You'll never have any of it, anyway. So, more to the point, what are you wearing?"

Abigail laughed way too loud and a decidedly aristocratic French woman of a certain age lifted her Gallic chin and looked away as she passed her on the uneven sidewalk. "Only you could place equal importance on the desperate lives of impoverished Ugandan women and what clothes I have on."

"That is sooooo not true," Sarah said plaintively. "You know I think the clothes are more important."

Abigail laughed even harder and leaned her shoulder against the side of a building along the Boulevard Saint-Michel across from Brasserie Balzar, since she didn't want to carry on her conversation inside. Abigail refused to answer calls in restaurants on the simple principle that she despised when other people did it, so she couldn't very well excuse the same abominable behavior in herself. She marveled that she might very well be turning into her mother after all. Her silly adherence to antiquated forms of etiquette was a constant source of humor to Sarah and Bronte, who were perfectly happy to bark entire soliloquies into their cell phones in the middle of lunch at the Wolseley.

"All right, as long as we're being honest." Abigail's laughter died down, then she pulled her cashmere muffler a little bit tighter around her neck to fend off the chill. The thought of Eliot peeling off her old rubbishy purple scarf skittered across her mind. "I'm wearing the Brora cashmere scarf you gave me for Christmas, the long-sleeved, stretchy black silk top you made me buy at Harvey Nichols, and that black thigh-length coat-sweater thing—"

"I told you you would wear that!"

"And the gray pants from Precious—"

"Great combo!"

"And my big dark green Mulberry bag—"

"You should always carry one of *my* bags, but I'll try to remain objective."

"And the most fabulous pair of little gray suede boots from some American shoe designer, Sally Jones, or something—"

"You are impossible. Well, at least you're wearing the right shoes. Go knock 'em dead, Abs. You'll do great. When do you come back to London?"

"I hadn't really decided…either tonight or tomorrow. Jack and Mother are having a few people over for dinner and want me to stay, but I'm not really in the mood. I'll probably come back on one of the early evening trains tonight. What are you and Devon up to?" Abigail added hastily, trying to speed into a cheerful segue, afraid that her "not-really-in-the-mood" might pop up on Sarah's overly keen radar.

No such luck.

"Why are you not in the mood?" Abigail heard Sarah shush someone out of her office again.

"No, I mean, I'm not in the mood to hang out with a bunch of Jack's friends…" Abigail sputtered out. Sarah knew that Abby adored Jack and everyone in his generous, intelligent circle.

"What is it, Abby? You heard about Eliot's wedding, didn't you?"

Why did her stomach still have to contract. Why? A year of trying to convince herself he was a blip. A fruitless year. "I can't really get into it right now, Sar. I have to be in full super-together mistress-of-the-universe mode for this presentation, and if my already ill-applied mascara smudges, it will ruin the effect."

"Please come home tonight; meet us at our place for a casual supper. We're all working late and then ordering a bunch of Indian food. Max and Bronte will be here—you have to come if only to make fun of Bron. She's so ridiculously enormous, and she's already called me twice to find out when you're coming home. Apparently Wolf toddles around with your picture and points and says your name."

"Aww. All right. I'll come back tonight, but I might be too knackered for dinner." Abigail took a deep breath of cold air to push all that stupid emotion back and away from the inside of her eyelids. Nothing like the undying love of a toddler to put things back into a positive light.

"You won't be too tired. Just take a cab straight from Waterloo to our place." Then Sarah started talking so fast Abigail could barely understand her: "And we'll wait for you to eat and I'm hanging up so you can't change your mind!" Click.

Abigail held the phone at arm's length and looked at it with a Mona Lisa smile—the same bittersweet smile that had dogged her all day—the one that expressed her gratitude for the love and support of all those in her small circle, while simultaneously missing... *him.*

The brasserie was quietly humming with the efficient bustle of waiters and the patter of many conversations. Parisian women never ceased to amaze her: their style seemed so inherent, impossible for a mere Briton like herself to really achieve. But Sarah James was doing her level best to make it happen. Sarah had spent several years living with her grandmother in Paris and managed to exude the same easy elegance.

Abigail finished her roquette salad, tried not to think about how many solitary meals she spent pondering Eliot, and paid the bill. She headed out into the brisk, sunny afternoon light, and checked her phone for new messages. She still thought of it as Eliot's phone, even though she'd unblocked the account and changed it into her own name over a year ago.

A couple of charms on a bit of black string and a scuffed-up cell phone. That's all she had to show for the love of her life.

What a fool.

Pushing her shoulders back and shaking herself into the present, Abigail looked to her right and left then crossed the wide avenue, setting her thoughts firmly to the pressing needs of the women of a small Ugandan village who lived every day under the weight of life-threatening disease and starvation.

After a few minutes, she reached the anthropology building with time to spare before her meeting was scheduled to begin. *Get over yourself, Abigail,* she snapped under her breath, then marched into the corridor leading to the esoteric university department.

# Chapter 10

GET OVER YOURSELF, ELIOT, he snapped under his breath.

He was not angry, exactly, but he was almost constantly annoyed. And then he became exponentially more annoyed because he had absolutely nothing whatsoever to justify his state of perpetual annoyance.

Danieli-Fauchard was making so much money, with so little effort, he was embarrassed to look at the latest profit and loss statements. It only engendered guilt for how it was possible to generate millions of dollars in income with what amounted to a half-assed effort on a good day. He knew that seventeen years of solid, disciplined—some would say obsessive—attention to every aspect of the industry was probably paying off. It still bothered him. He was starting to feel meaningless.

The small flashing green light on his office telephone's private line was blinking patiently and he knew he ought to pick it up—that he genuinely wanted to pick it up—but he just didn't feel like it. He let his secretary get it and take a message. His assistant knew better than to poke his head in the office.

Or so Eliot thought.

He raised one angry brow when the etched glass door opened and the young Swiss man he'd hired several months ago poked said head through the narrow opening like a wizened tortoise emerging from his shell. At least he had a healthy look of fear around his eyes.

"What is it, Marcel?" Eliot asked in impatient French.

"I am so sorry, but Ms. Plataneau—"

"If I'd wanted to speak to her, I would have picked up the phone. I cannot impress upon you enough that I'm not to be disturbed when I'm busy."

"I understand," the near trembling man persisted in slightly accented French, "but she is quite insistent and—"

"Marcel. Please pay very close attention to what I'm about to say," Eliot replied in razor-sharp Parisian French. "If you ever interrupt me again, for any reason, I will contact human resources and suggest you be transferred to another position in the company. I am quite insistent about this. Do you understand?"

Eliot hated the sarcasm and near cruelty that had seeped into his business demeanor in the past year or so, but he had adopted it gradually and now it was his normal affect. He might not have bedded all that many women since that stupid night at the Plaza Athénée in Paris, but he certainly had the rat bastard part down flat.

"Yes, sir. Of course, sir." Marcel had almost shut the door completely, when Eliot called out the young man's name to stop him.

Eliot spoke in English, the language in which—for some reason—he tended to be nicer. "I know she can be hard to resist." Eliot offered a slight shrug and a grimace of shared defeat instead of an apology. "I'll pick it up here."

Marcel nodded his gratitude and shut the door quickly, before his mercurial boss changed moods again.

Eliot took a deep breath and picked up the receiver. "Marisa, darling."

"Oh, Eliot. I know how you despise being interrupted when you're working, but I just couldn't resist. And please don't fire poor Marcel for disobeying you. He was just doing my bidding."

*Aren't we all*, Eliot thought involuntarily, then hated himself just a little bit. "What is it, Mar?"

"I got the grant for the research project in Tanzania!"

She was so excited and genuinely deserving that Eliot continued in his downward spiral of self-loathing. "That's so great! You totally deserve it."

"I know! Isn't it the best?"

Initially, Eliot had been drawn to Marisa's stand-alone exuberance. She loved drawing people into her orbit of interest and shared excitement. She rarely let anyone, including Eliot, quash her enthusiasm. What had at first been an appealing independence, sometimes, lately, had a whiff of blind arrogance. But Eliot chastised himself silently, she was always being blindly enthusiastic on behalf of someone or something utterly honorable or utterly deserving, so casting aspersions bordered on heresy. "Absolutely. Congratulations! Let's go out tonight and celebrate."

"Oh, I can't tonight, I'm meeting with some of the research fellows, but I'll stop by your place around ten so we can pop a bottle of champagne then, *bien*?"

"Perfect. I'll have a chilled bottle at the ready. And congratulations again. Well done."

"It is well done of me, isn't it?"

She wasn't conceited, really. She was just agreeing with him, wasn't she? "It's great, Mar. I'll see you at ten."

"Oh, and Eliot?"

"Yes?"

"Did you see the wedding announcement in the *International Herald Tribune*? It's so silly, really, but it's exciting to see it in print, isn't it?"

Eliot had tried to avoid the very real truth that his perpetual simmer of annoyance was even more pronounced since seeing their engagement listed in the *International Herald Tribune*. "I did see it. Yes." His reply wasn't a lie, at least. Marisa had already shared her enthusiasm, which was usually the object of the exercise, so she did not even notice Eliot's less than joyful response.

"I'm so glad," she added warmly, then quickly changed tone. "Sorry, Eliot, there's my other line. I have to run. Ciao!" Click.

Eliot supposed he should be grateful that the woman had no false reverence for his supposedly vaunted position in the business world. They were equals in nearly every sense of the word: intellect (keen), ambition (pronounced), and sexual drive (as and when).

While swearing off unrealistic romantic notions after parting ways with Abigail Heyworth a year ago had seemed a practical element of his own self-preservation, Eliot now realized that all such germinating decisions led, necessarily, to the propagation of certain consequences. Namely, in his case, it led to a primary relationship of the very *non*romantic variety.

On their first date, Marisa Plataneau had informed Eliot that she was the least romantic woman he would ever meet. She loved jewelry and flowers and chocolates as much as the next girl, but she had no interest whatsoever in twined souls or mystical joinings.

About six weeks after the debacle with Abigail, one of Eliot's friends from Harvard Business School put him in touch with Marisa. She had just moved to Geneva from New York to head up an NGO that focused on promoting industrial innovation in sub-Saharan Africa. She had been raised in Paris, the eldest of three children, to parents who made no secret of their expectations for their progeny: anything less than excellence was failure. Marisa attended INSEAD and then moved to the United States to pursue her interest in international relations at Johns Hopkins, where she earned her master's and doctoral degrees. She worked at the United Nations for eight years after that, biding her time until the right job presented itself. The Geneva position was the right job. As Eliot's father liked to say, "Marisa is no slouch."

Despite their obvious drive, the Plataneaus were a joyful lot, if intellectually fierce, and Eliot welcomed Marisa's brutal wit and rapier honesty. He did not miss the torment that had assailed him for months (even now, occasionally) about what exactly had gone so terribly wrong with Abigail Heyworth—about whom he had felt so terribly right. The only person to whom he had been able to confide even a watered down version of events had been his mother. He was a thirty-nine-year-old man, for chrissake. Forced to confide in his mother.

*Let it go, Eliot*, had become his constant internal mantra.

The private line started blinking again and Eliot figured it was Marisa calling with one last item she'd forgotten to mention. Then he looked at the caller ID and saw it was his mother.

"Hi, Mom."

"Hi, Eliot. Nice piece in the *Herald Tribune*."

"Thanks."

"You never did like publicity, did you?"

"Not really."

"Is that it?"

"Is what it?"

"You sound, I don't know, *ambivalent*."

"We're just getting married, we're not curing cancer. I guess a part of me feels like it's sort of ridiculous to trumpet it about as if it has any real importance."

"Eliot? What is it, dear?"

"Please stop being cryptic, Mom. What is *what*?"

"Forgetting the newspaper mention for now, why is it, do you think, that you don't think your marriage to Marisa has any real importance?"

"You're twisting my words to get me to enter into some sort of therapeutic discussion and I'm not in the mood."

"It's not a therapeutic discussion, Eliot. It used to be called a conversation. About your feelings. Which you used to have."

Eliot remained silent.

"Oh all right," Penny Cranbrook continued in her kind Midwestern drawl, "we're not going to bother with emotions, I guess. They're messy and I know you can't stand that. So, what else is new?"

Eliot smiled at how well his mother knew him and how all of that squirmy, emotional-intelligence crap drove him crazy, even if he knew it was true, and that it might even be worth giving his full attention. He just could not do it. He and Marisa were getting married and that was the end of it.

"We're getting married and that is the end of it."

"Of course. Fine. Yes. That part of the conversation is over. So, tell me what else is going on? Are you going to Paris for the shows? Do you want to meet up for lunch or dinner or will you be booked up?"

Her wholesale dismissal of his precarious emotional state was even worse than her inappropriate prying, but he opted for the shallows for now.

"I could probably squeeze in a meal. What works best for you? Will you be with Dad?"

"I don't think so. He's not as keen on short transatlantic trips these days. A month in Italy is one thing, a week in Paris, as you young people like to say, not so much."

"Where are you staying?"

"Oh, I haven't decided. Jack and Sylvia asked me to stay with them, but as charming as it is, I think I'm getting too old to bunk in."

"*Old* is one word for it." He tried to stay focused on the conversation as his mind wondered if Abigail was a frequent visitor to Paris, now that her mother lived there with Jack Parnell. Eliot had become adept at not wondering such things aloud.

"All right, then. I think I am too *spoiled* not to have room service and a large private bathroom. I opted for the George V. What about you?"

"The marketing department always prefers for me to stay at the Ritz, so I reluctantly comply."

"What a hardship."

"Very funny. All right, which day? Which meal?" Eliot called across his office to Marcel and asked him to come in with the calendar for Paris Fashion Week.

Penny knew her son was probably rescheduling someone of far greater importance but she tried to sound passably clueless. "How about Thursday, February twenty-seventh? Breakfast at Hôtel Costes?"

"Let me check."

Penny heard a bit of murmuring in French as Eliot covered the mouthpiece of the phone and shuffled his schedule with Marcel.

"Done. I'll see you then. Anything else? I've been avoiding these profit and loss statements for the past hour, and I really should deal with them once and for all."

"Nothing else, honey. I'll see you then. Love you."

"Love you too. Bye, Mom."

Marcel overheard the fond parting words as he left Eliot's office, and supposed he should be grateful that at least one person on the planet was able to elicit a ray of humanity from his otherwise robotic boss.

Later that night, Eliot heard the bolt in the door to his kitchen slide free, then Marisa swung into the room in a flurry of happy self-congratulation. Eliot was sitting at the eight-foot long, reclaimed nickel table he had found in Provence several years ago. He stretched his neck and saw the stars were visible through the ceiling of the glass conservatory. He had added the room on to the kitchen shortly after he had purchased the house in Versoix eight years ago. It reminded him of home. He had pictured a family in it, a family of his own.

The property had been uninhabited for many years, but the structural elements were sound. It was a traditional lake house, made of white plaster and exposed rough-hewn beams, with a narrow spit of lawn that led directly down to Lake Geneva. At the time, when the estate agent commented offhandedly about the abandoned indoor lap pool that had fallen into disrepair, Eliot made an immediate aggressive offer on the place.

In addition to the classical Franco-Swiss architectural elements, the previous owners had also been art collectors in the mid-twentieth century and had commissioned Philip Johnson to design a small guesthouse. It was a beautiful, meditative miniature, a study, for the architect's future work in the freestanding glass houses for which he became famous. The low, modern structure served as a private sanctuary for Eliot. For the most part, he loved living in a big house that was warm and cluttered like the one in which he had grown up, but he also needed the occasional break from the lately oppressive feeling that every physical object he looked upon held the weight and importance and power to remind him of some other part of his existence. The Johnson house provided a haven from that.

If he had not been expecting Marisa, he would have spent the night out there tonight. His mind felt crowded with little splinters of thoughts and ideas. He had always prided himself on his ability to compartmentalize all aspects of his life: work, family, friends, athletics, what have you. Every element fit neatly into the appointed quadrant of his brain. He hated to admit it, but ever since he had met Abigail Heyworth, all of the various components of who he was, or what he did, bled together in a frustrating and composite mess.

Work complications wove together with repairs that were needed on the pool. Appointments with buyers in Paris reminded him uncomfortably of Marisa's frequent desire to discuss her wedding dress. He found this type of blending annoying and disconcerting.

Eliot got up to meet her about halfway across the kitchen. She dropped her briefcase on the seat of one of the barstools near the counter and put her arms out wide in a welcoming gesture. A gesture that welcomed praise of Marisa, Eliot thought cruelly.

He took her in an embrace and congratulated her again on the great accomplishment of securing funds for the Tanzania project. He started to kiss her on the neck (since he didn't really feel like kissing her on the lips). He needn't have worried about false intimacy, he realized, as she pushed him cheerfully, but surely, away.

"Eliot, you are too sweet. But where's that champagne you promised me? I'm parched."

Eliot smiled at her brass tacks demeanor. She probably thought he smiled out of affection, but he knew it was more out of relief that he wouldn't have to feign an interest in physical contact. He was simply worn out.

"Right here, darling." He opened the glass-fronted industrial refrigerator that had been one of his few concessions to the Bohemian Bourgeoisie. Of course, any refrigerator would have kept his food and drink the proper temperature, but he wanted a restaurant-grade Traulsen, and decided he would simply live with the guilt and absurdity of spending five thousand euros to have one.

Despite his financial success, his modest upbringing made Eliot rather self-conscious about vast displays of wealth. His jet was the glaring exception to the rule. His car was old, but reliable. His house was very old, and reliably needy. Even though the house's posh location made the price exorbitant, buying and restoring it had been an act of love, not commerce.

The champagne cork popped with a satisfying *THWAP*, the hiss and breath of the bottle emerging through his fingers as he caught it. Eliot had already set out two crystal flutes on the counter and filled them with quick efficiency. He handed one to Marisa and then rested his empty hand on the cool marble counter. After a few seconds of silence, he realized she was waiting for him to toast her accomplishment. He raised his glass and gave her a silent wink. He just could not quite bring himself to say, "To you," and have to watch her preen.

She winked back and took a grateful sip of the cool, crisp liquid. "Aaah, that is heavenly, Eliot. Thank you. The meeting tonight was so boring, I thought I was going to jump out a window." She took another sip and let her eyes close a bit.

Eliot took the moment to have an objective look at his wife-to-be. He narrowed his gaze and looked at her as he would have looked at a runway model or a piece of jewelry. The parts were impeccable: the long, thick blond hair, cut with expensive precision at the middle of her back, letting everyone know she was feminine, but not frilly. Her cheekbones were severe from her mother's side of the family: high near the crest, giving her eyes an almost Inuit aspect, especially when she laughed and they lifted even more at the outside edges. Nose: perfectly straight, no-nonsense. She contended her nose was too Gallic, whatever that meant. And her mouth. Well. Eliot found it very easy to objectify her mouth. She had a full, wide mouth, that, unfortunately, she did not enjoy in the least.

"What are you looking at?"

Her tone was sharp, but her look was bordering on seductive. Eliot knew it was only bordering because Marisa never bothered with seduction. "Who has the time to bother with that?" she'd once laughed as she'd grabbed his hand in hers to haul him up into bed for a tumble.

"Your beautiful face."

Why Eliot, are you going all sentimental on me?" she asked in a rather clinical fashion, as if she were interviewing someone for the Kinsey Report.

*Quite the opposite*, he thought, but thankfully caught himself before uttering the words aloud. "Hardly sentimental, Mari. You know you're beautiful. I was just remarking on it." He raised his glass again. She was just as opposed to messy emotional discussions as he purported to be on the phone with his mother, and he could tell she appreciated his transition back into the familiar territory of friendly banter.

"Do you want to watch a movie? Have you eaten?" he asked, moving further into the happy country of practicalities.

"We did eat during the meeting, but I would love to jump in the shower and watch something with you afterward. That sounds perfect." She clinked her glass against his, passed behind him, and picked up the bottle of champagne, smiling over her shoulder as she took the whole thing with her and headed up the stairs to the bedroom and master bath.

Marisa still had her own apartment in the center of Geneva, but she kept a full wardrobe of clothes and complete selection of toiletries and personal effects at Eliot's in Versoix. After they got engaged, they had agreed that they would keep both places after they were married as well, the apartment being a great crash pad for visiting friends or after their own late nights at their respective offices in the city.

Initially he had thought she would sell her apartment and they would live together in his house, or that she would want them to buy a new house together, but she was right in her practical approach, he reminded himself. He was slipping into sentimentality again. Why would she want to go to the trouble of getting a new place to start their married life together when, between the two of them, they already owned two perfectly good residences?

Now that he thought of it, Marisa was quite fond of all things that were Perfectly Good. She was grateful in that way. If something was already Perfectly Good, why mess with it? Which, several months ago, had led to a premarital discussion of the Perfectly Good nature of their childless state. Over the past year, Eliot had become fairly certain that he had no interest in children whatsoever. Marriage was something he could get his mind around: companionship, friendship, sex, a life partner. The thought of children, on the other hand, set him into a world of worry. While he and Marisa were well matched as spouses, he doubted very much that they would see eye-to-eye as parents.

In his younger days, Eliot had entertained absurd notions of attaining his career ambitions by the time he was forty and then abandoning them altogether to devote himself to a huge family. Penny and Will Cranbrook had started early, but they'd only been able to have one child. Eliot wanted to make up for all those solitary hours of his own childhood with a large, loud, boisterous next generation of Cranbrooks.

Apparently, it was not meant to be.

After Eliot and Marisa started discussing marriage, Eliot figured the discussion of children was not far behind. He had been avoiding the topic because he had assumed Marisa would want children. It seemed likely that Marisa would welcome the idea of more Marisas. But then he was just being mean. He need not have worried. Marisa burst out laughing at the idea of being a mother.

"Eliot! You have been worrying, haven't you?" They'd been in a small French restaurant in Annecy.

"Well, not worrying really. Just wanting to discuss it."

"Look at me, Eliot. Do I look at all maternal to you?"

Eliot smiled his response. She looked like a Valkyrie, the kind who did not produce babies… the kind who ate them.

Perhaps Marisa deserved some credit. She obviously knew herself a lot better than Eliot knew himself. As a matter of fact, he was probably the most sentimental person, and certainly the most sentimental male, that he had ever come across. His mother suspected this, but he'd never confessed it to anyone else.

Eliot's parents were a ridiculously happy little unit. He had no illusions that theirs was the norm, or even replicable. Somewhere along the line, the idea of being ridiculously happy had become merely ridiculous. He and Marisa suited. That was enough.

As he stood there in his kitchen, holding the stem of the champagne flute between two fingers and listening to the shower turn off upstairs, he thought about the most satisfying moments of his life. The ridiculously happy ones. They certainly did not include corporate buyouts or share prices. They included a Parisian balcony. And a Caribbean beach. And a kiss next to a Dumpster behind a crowded bar in Iowa.

They included Abigail.

―――――

Abigail finished the meeting at the Sorbonne in about an hour. The professors did not commit to the foundation absolutely, but they were wonderfully encouraging and said they would be back in touch with her within two weeks with their final decision. Seeing it as a near-victory, Abigail decided to treat herself to a quick visit to Cadolle. The tepid reminders brought on by naff scarves and cell phones were nothing compared to the silky version of the hair shirt with which Abigail now tortured herself. In the year since she'd last seen Eliot Cranbrook, she had become a lingerie addict.

He had created a monster. And no more Marks & Spencer ticky-tacky thigh-highs from the sale bin either. Abigail had become a connoisseur. She preferred to buy her treats in Paris, sneaking off to Louise Feuillere or Carine Gilson whenever she got the chance. She wasn't above popping into Agent Provocateur or La Perla when she was home in London, but Cadolle was her particular favorite.

She walked into the shop and waved to the woman behind the fancy gold-filigreed counter.

"Bonjour, Abigail."

"Bonjour, Therese." Abigail sighed gently under her breath at the absurdity of being on a first-name basis with an haute couture corset maker. "Anything new?"

Abigail was usually in Paris every couple of weeks to visit her mother or just to get out of London and out of her head. Her French accent was still appalling, but she had a thorough vocabulary when it came to undergarments.

"Yes. We just received a new shipment. Come." The older woman led Abigail back to the rear of the shop and took a delicate, pale peach lace garter belt off the rack, holding it up for her inspection. "What do you think?"

Her fascination with lingerie was not just about Eliot. First, that would have been psychotic. Second, well, she didn't know about second, but she knew she loved how she felt when she had her practical blacks and navies and grays and serviceable wools on the outside, and something peachy and soft like this against her skin. It felt like a kindness she could give to herself, this touch of invisible elegance and beauty that no one would ever see. Okay. Maybe one day in the very remote future someone would see it and enjoy taking it off her eager body—or leaving it on and proceeding apace anyway; that would be fine too—but in the all-important present, these little pieces of feminine art gave Abigail a pleasure all their own.

"I love it. The color is sublime. Do you have a matching bra and corset?"

Therese smiled. "Of course. How could we not?" She gave a little shrug and turned. "One moment."

Abigail looked around at a few other pieces that she considered a tad ambitious. The cupless bras and black lace bondage bits were not her thing. Especially since no piece of lingerie would ever make her feel quite so deliciously bound as the feel of Eliot tightening the strings of that small white satin corset in front of the fireplace at the Plaza Athénée. Or, even better, the way he wrapped his strong fingers around her waist with that ever-increasing pressure. Somehow, black lace struck her as ersatz or grasping after the reality of his controlling hands.

She paid for the three new items and thanked Therese for her assistance. After returning to her mother's to collect her bag, Abigail made her way to Gare du Nord to catch her train.

The Eurostar pulled into London's Waterloo Station at exactly

8:17 Friday night. Abigail felt lighter the minute she stepped off the train and had her feet firmly back on British ground. Paris put her in a fug of abstracted self-analysis that bordered on depression, marriage announcements or not. The train trip back from France had been the perfect decompression chamber. She went over her meeting notes from the Sorbonne, and then uploaded them to the foundation's server for her assistant to have them properly edited and then sent out to the board in advance of their February meeting.

Abigail hopped on the Tube from Waterloo to Green Park station and was at Devon and Sarah's loft in Mayfair by 8:40. She tried to convince herself that she was only having dinner with her family, not facing a firing squad. She pressed the buzzer and went up the narrow staircase that led directly to their home, rather than the main door that led to Sarah's shoe shop. She could hear the laughter and music coming from Devon and Sarah's apartment.

Waiting at the top of the stairs, trying to collect herself, Abigail closed her eyes and took a deep breath. When Abigail opened her eyes, her sister-in-law Sarah was leaning out her front door, staring at her. "What are you doing out here, Abs?"

# Chapter 11

"JUST PREPARING, I GUESS," Abigail answered.

Sarah gave her a knowing look, half-joy, half-sadness. "Oh, Abby. Are we that overwhelming?"

As if on cue, her two brothers and her other sister-in-law burst into uproarious laughter at some (probably bawdy) joke. Bronte guffawed.

"That was unfortunate timing," said Sarah.

"It's just me." Abby said, still waiting in the foyer. "I know I'm long overdue for a family grilling. I've been coasting for too long without the four of you raking me over the coals. Is Wolf here at least?"

"Sorry, no nephew to run interference. Just the grown-ups, with their grown-up opinions and grown-up—"

Bronte swore loudly and emphatically just then.

"—enthusiasm," Sarah finished.

"No point in delaying further, I suppose."

Sarah took Abigail's small wheelie bag and opened the door wider to let her lead the way into the large open space. Her favorite people in the world all leapt up and surrounded her with hugs and offers of drinks and questions... questions... questions.

"Look! Stop!" Bronte demanded the floor, interrupting everyone. "I am so fucking pregnant I might not even make it to the end of supper, so I get to go first. Where the hell have you been? I haven't seen you in over a month. Wolf is apoplectic."

"It's been really busy at the foundation's offices. I've been—"

"Yeah, yeah. We all work, Abs."

"Be nice, Bronte." Max put his arm around his wife's shoulders and smiled at Abigail. A warm, it's-okay-whatever-it-is kind of smile.

Abigail wanted to cry.

"Come sit down," Devon said softly as he put his arm around his younger sister and led her over to the seating area in the middle of the room. "What do you want to drink? Beer or champagne? Scotch?"

"Scotch sounds lovely." Abigail sat down on the large, ornate French sofa that was one of Sarah's contributions to what they all referred to as the humanization of Devon's design aesthetic.

Sarah poured her a big welcome-home scotch and handed it to her slowly.

Max and Bronte sat close to one another on a smaller couch, Devon sat next to Abigail on the large sofa, and Sarah sat in an overstuffed armchair, her lovely legs stretched out in front of her and crossed with ladylike care at her ankles.

"Well?" Sarah prompted.

"Well, what?" Abigail took a cautious sip of the scotch, closing her eyes in pure pleasure. "Devon, you are such a star for having this great scotch on hand."

"What else would I have?"

Abigail smiled her thanks, then opted for offense rather than defense. "So what's with the family meeting? This is feeling way too confrontational. I don't even get Wolf on my team."

"Abs, this is so *not* confrontational," Bronte launched in. "We just haven't been together in weeks and it usually happens that you come out to Dunlear for the weekend or we meet up in town, and for one reason or another it just hasn't happened for a while, so here we are. So, I'll be the bitch as usual and talk about the elephant in the room. What did you think about the announcement of Eliot's marriage?"

Max rolled his eyes at his wife's blunt approach, but he also admired the affection that inspired it. They all knew how Abigail could withdraw—occasionally to other continents—in her effort to avoid too-close examinations of her feelings, especially those of the close-family variety.

"Do I even get to eat before the inquisition?"

Devon patted her leg. "You never eat before ten, so don't pretend you're all of a sudden peckish. We ordered the food about fifteen minutes ago. It'll be here in a bit. Want a crisp?"

"No, I don't want a crisp!" Abigail's voice was tight. Why did they all have to love her so much? "This is like a bad movie of the week on the telly. Is this an intervention?"

Sarah spoke gently. "Abigail, you know we're not prying. Well, maybe we are, but if we don't act, who will? Certainly not you. It has been over a year! Not like I'm keeping tabs, but it happens to coincide with our wedding anniversary, so it's difficult not to notice. We've all been through our share of…" She looked at Devon with enough love to kill him, then winked. "…delayed gratification when it comes to loving members of your family. Even for a Heyworth, you've waited long enough."

"All right. Setting aside the fact that you invited me here with false promises of spicy food and lots of Kingfisher, I will tell you." Abigail looked at each one of their nosy, affectionate expressions. "My life is filled with rewarding, fulfilling sources of happiness. Anything else seems grasping somehow. There is nothing else to tell."

All four of them started speaking at once and Abigail took a pleasant sip of her scotch. Then another.

Max pulled rank. "Quiet. I go first. This is not an inquisition, Abs, you know that. We're all so happy and proud and all that. The foundation is a huge accomplishment; your efforts over the past year have gone far beyond admirable. You've created something of deep, intrinsic value that will go on long after any of us are still bumbling around to see it. We're not talking about that and you well know it."

"But that's just it, isn't it? A year ago, you were all focused on how I needed to take myself more *seriously* and build something and create meaning and all that. Now you're acting like that was just some sort of item on my life's to-do list. It's reprehensible of you to diminish the importance of that now."

"You should have been a lawyer," Devon added with disgust, then continued with deep affection. "Abby, you and I are too much alike to mince words. You're spending more time worrying about the health and well-being of the Ugandan women's water supply than you are about your own right to happiness. I'm not saying this from a place of judgment."

Bronte leaned her head on Max's shoulder in a small, tired gesture that did more to clench Abigail's heart than any of their compassionate words ever could. Max had been a brittle mess after their father died, and now he was a source of comfort to everyone. Somehow, through his relationship with his wife, the seemingly impossible had been accomplished. A spell had been broken. Bronte caught Abigail looking at them. "What? I'm so sorry to fade. I'm full of energy one minute then bordering on collapse the next. I'm sorry. Twins are hard."

"It's not that," Abigail said. "It's just that you all seem to deserve"—she forced herself not to become overly emotional, but it was difficult—"one another's affection. I just don't know what I deserve anymore."

Sarah moved over to the couch, so Abigail was sandwiched between her and Devon. "I swore I wasn't going to get involved, but I can't stand it another minute. I know Eliot still has feelings for you—"

"What? Have you talked to him about me? You promised—"

"Of course I haven't talked to him about you! It's just so flipping obvious. He's like Mr. Bingley for chrissake: 'Are *ALL* your sisters still at home?' That sort of thing." Sarah was holding Abigail's hand, lightly rubbing the top with her other hand. "It's okay to want to talk to him, Abigail. Don't you want to be *sure?*"

"I was such a tiny blip on his radar. He spends his life with supermodels and accomplished fiancées. It's all too ridiculous. I'm ridiculous!"

Devon slapped both of his hands on his thighs. "Okay! That's enough of that then. No pity parties allowed. I was happy to go along with all this American prying-in-the-name-of-caring nonsense, but only up to a point. Which has been reached." The intercom buzzed and Max and Devon both leapt to get it.

"The food is here," Max added, as if they didn't all know that already.

Sarah spoke in a low voice so only Bronte and Abigail could hear. "They are complete frauds, you know. They are far more emotional than either of us, Bron. You Heyworths like to pretend you are all sewed up tight, but the smallest rip in your seam, and you're flooding out all over."

"Come and get it," Devon called across the room as he opened the brown bags and undid the carryout containers. Sarah had already set the table and put a stack of antique French plates on the kitchen counter.

They all piled on the food, opened up many bottles of the promised Kingfisher, and got down to the much more enjoyable—to Abigail's mind, at least—pastime of gossiping about other members of the extended Heyworth family.

Toward the end of dinner, while Max, Devon, and Abigail were dipping their spoons directly into the pints of ice cream in an act of lifelong defiance against their mother, Sarah turned to Abigail and asked, "Why don't you come to Paris with me for Fashion Week, Abs?"

"Why in the world would I do that?"

"Because it's fun and Bronte can't come in her condition."

"I could too!" Bronte protested.

"No you may not!" Max barked.

"I love it when you are all bossy." Bronte batted her eyelashes in mock obedience to her husband.

Abigail had looked in their direction and Sarah continued, "Ignore those infants, please. Come to Paris. It will be plain old fun. I'm staying in a crazily over-the-top luxurious two-bedroom suite at the Ritz, and we can just strut around at Dior and Galliano and your cousin James is going to be there, with Mowbray showing its fantastic women's line—"

"Stop!" Bronte pretended to cover her ears. "I can't listen to another word of what I'm going to miss. It's torture. These babies are not even out and they are already cramping my style!"

Everyone laughed at Bronte's false frustration. After getting pregnant with their first child, as Max liked to joke, after a wink and a smile, it had taken over a year for Bronte to get pregnant again. They were all relieved and overjoyed that it had turned out to be twin girls. Big brother Wolf was already telling everyone who would listen that the princess train was coming.

Abigail gave in to Sarah's prodding, knowing full well that some sort of accidentally-on-purpose crossing-paths with Eliot was obviously part of her well-meant plan. "All right, Sar, I'll go with you, but let's drop the pretense that there's not some Eliot component to the whole thing."

"I never pretended otherwise," Sarah answered with a snotty impersonation of an upper-crust British accent, turning her nose up and taking a sip of her beer as if it were vintage Dom Perignon. "I'm going to drive there. I'm leaving two weeks from tomorrow. I have too many clothes and shoes and what-have-you to take the train. Let's make a day of it and have a little road trip."

"Sounds great. In the meantime, I'm going home. You're all way too happy for me to spend any more time here."

"We'll give you a lift," Max chimed in as he picked up a stack of plates and brought them over to the counter next to the sink.

"Perfect."

~~~

Soon after returning from Paris *that weekend*, Abigail had set about finding her own place to live. Her mother had balked at the idea.

"But Northrop House is so big and accommodating and right there in the middle of Mayfair."

"Mother. It's just not on for me to be living with you when I'm a grown woman. I need my own place."

"I wish you would stay for my sake," Sylvia said quietly when they were finishing a game of cards one Saturday afternoon.

"Really?" Abigail was stunned.

"Yes. But I suppose it's selfish of me. I've loved having you."

"Oh, Mother. You know I've loved being here, but… how about this? We'll look for the perfect place for me to buy. If we look for one we *both* love—since we know that's not likely to happen right away—I can stay here and at least feel like I'm looking for my own place. We'll call a proper estate agent and have showings and everything."

"Oh, I love that idea."

"I'm thinking Shoreditch or Spitalfields—"

"Absolutely not."

Abby burst out laughing. "Mother! I'm the one who's going to be living there, not you."

"All right. *Please no.* Is that better?"

"Yes," Abigail replied. "Much better. And what's so horrendous about Shoreditch anyway?"

"How would I know? I've never been there. Just the sound of it. *Shore. Ditch.* No."

Abigail laughed again. "Okay. I'll make my way into darkest Shoreditch when you have a previous engagement."

"If you must. Why don't you look here in Mayfair?"

"I'll give up on Shoreditch if you give up on Mayfair."

Her mother was wonderful at games and negotiations of all types. She licked the tip of her pencil and ripped the page off the small elegant pad she'd been using to keep score of their card game. "Perfect." She used the grid of the scoring sheet to keep track of the various neighborhoods.

"I'll trade you Mayfair for Shoreditch." She wrote out the name of each of those neighborhoods in her neat hand, then struck them through with a perfectly straight line of her pencil.

They spent the next hour riffling through the *A* to *Z* together and winnowing down the selection, negotiating out the likes of Chelsea and Spitalfields, Sloane Square and Bethnal Green. Abigail was going to live wherever she liked, but she loved this idea of her mother participating in the search. It felt more ambitious somehow.

Eventually, though, Sylvia released Abigail from their bargain. As her relationship with Jack Parnell progressed and she was in London less and less often, Sylvia was forced to admit that a twenty-eight-year-old woman living alone in a six-thousand-square-foot mansion was, as Abigail had said, just not on.

A limited staff stayed on and the house was made available to everyone in the family. Wolf in particular enjoyed spending the occasional weekend there with Abigail and showing her which room would be his when he was the duke. "Duke like Papa!"

She laughed then chastised him.

"If your Mama or Papa ever hear you say that, you will be in much trouble, mister."

"Shhh! Abigail! Secret!"

More often, her little man would stay with her in Fulham, where she'd finally found the perfect home. On those nights, Abigail would swing him up in her arms and kiss him hard in the crook of his little, soft neck, then carry him down to the kitchen, where they made hot chocolate, ate ice cream out of the container, popped popcorn, and watched old episodes of *Bob the Builder*.

They usually spent the night at her house every couple of weeks, but Abigail had been so consumed with her work that a couple of months had slipped by without her realizing it.

Wolf, on the other hand, was keeping track of her absence.

When she got home from Devon's that night, she had four messages on her home answering machine from Wolf, bemoaning her absence. He always called her by her full name. *Just as Eliot had*, she thought wistfully. Wolf tried very hard to be formal, especially on the telephone, but his little baby voice was never quite as intelligible on the answering machine as it was in person.

"Abigail… This Wolf. You-shoo-be-home-now. I wanna come over. Please call." Then a fumbling pause, then, "Okay, bye."

Then, "Hi, Aunt Abigail. This Wolf, your nephew. I'm ready for sleepover, so you-shoo-call or come home so we can have sleepover, okay?" Then some fumbling with the phone, Bronte's encouraging voice in the background, then, "Mama says she miss you too. Bye."

Two more messages along the same vein took up the rest of Abigail's answering machine.

In the spring of last year, after spending a few months contemplating her options and spending some enjoyable wine-soaked afternoons traipsing all over town with her mother and a very patient estate agent, Abigail had finally purchased a small freehold mews house a few streets away from Bronte and Max in Fulham. The price had seemed outrageous at the time, especially given her scrimping nature, but after discussing the long-term benefits of owning versus renting with everyone from her banker to the chemist in Shepherd Market, she'd finally done it. An older widow had been living there, alone, for years, and it was exactly as Abigail wanted it to be.

She didn't update the kitchen, or refurbish the two small bathrooms. She loved the three tiny bedrooms upstairs with their yellowed wallpaper and ancient windows with years of chipped paint. Unfortunately, Max had demanded she have the windows replaced ("On account of security," he'd claimed, but Abigail suspected it was really because of the potential lead-filled chips of paint that might find their way into a particular little nephew's curious mouth).

Abigail had compromised, going to the trouble and expense of having all the original windows stripped and refurbished, then reinstalled in their bare wooden state.

That night, after mentally revisiting her dinner conversation at Devon and Sarah's, and the fun, chatty ride home with Max and Bronte, Abigail fell naked into her bed after tossing her clothes on the worn-out, hand-me-down chair in the corner of her small bedroom. It seemed impossible that they were the same clothes she had put on in Paris that morning. Time was starting to telescope and spread at odd angles. She reached for the charms around her neck, as she so often did when she fell asleep. Like a security blanket, she rubbed the familiar gold scales of the tiny fish, feeling the metal warm to her touch.

Feeling Eliot.

Her body was starting to crave his touch. She was naked under the old sheets that she had reclaimed before they were going to be thrown away after years of use at Dunlear. The antique linen felt like cool dry satin against her skin. Her body was becoming foreign to her, she thought absently. She didn't feel unattractive; she just felt pale. Out of use. Except when she thought of Eliot. She knew it was unhealthy, that she had built him up in her mind to embody a very unrealistic, near-perfect ideal. A nonexistent dream.

But she couldn't help it. She tried, she really did. She tried to picture erotic images that did not include Eliot, to read erotic novels that did not feature Eliot, anything to kick-start her desire: anything to help her move on from the obsession that was Eliot. But the primordial, hungry, visceral part of her, the part without a past or future or a hang-up in sight, the most basic atomic matter that defined Abigail Heyworth, before she had a name and long before she had any nicknames, knew what it yearned for.

She tried silly don't-think-of-Eliot mental games and exercises: think of beautiful, blond Tully, your lover of ten years.

Nothing.

Think of that hunky movie star who always gets loaded and throws phones at chambermaids.

Sigh.

Think of that Bond girl with the knife and the conch shell.

Ho-hum.

Think of everyone beautiful and sexy and naked and groaning and having a fantastic orgy right here on your bedroom floor.

*And? So?* her libido seemed to answer, unimpressed.

Think of Eliot.

*Yes! Do that!* her body cried. *Think of Eliot!* Think of Eliot doing all those things that he would have done, that he wanted to do, that he had only just begun doing. And she would think of Eliot. And her hands would wander. And she would have a few moments of pleasure and then almost immediately, after her breath would subside and the longed-for mindlessness of pleasure would drift away, she would remember again that she had been small and selfish and shallow all those months ago. She had been a coward.

And then there she was, alone. And sad. In her lovely bed, in her beautiful sheets, in her comforting room, in the bosom of her family, in the city that was opening its arms to her, in a world that she might actually be in a position to improve.

Yet, she was not with Eliot, so all of it felt… off. She pulled the sheets into her fists and tucked them under her chin. She would have to tell him, to his face, how wrong she had been. How scared of the truth. How much she loved him and how she understood that he had moved on, and she would try to do the same, but she didn't want either of them going to the grave with that love of hers going unspoken through eternity.

---

Eliot heard the shower turn off and stayed in the kitchen, nursing his glass of champagne. There was no way he could move forward with Marisa without at least giving her a heads-up about what was going on, maybe not about Abigail in particular, but about his ambivalence in general. She deserved that at least. She might be the least romantic woman, by her own accounting, but no woman was going to marry a man who spent all his time envisioning someone else. Or at least imagining the possibility of a very particular someone else.

Marisa had changed into a charcoal gray cashmere sweatshirt and matching loose lounge pants. Her hair was combed straight and hung damp down her back. She had the glass of champagne in one hand and the bottle in the other.

She lifted the bottle in Eliot's direction. "Would you like a refill?"

"Sure." He walked toward her and held the glass up as she filled it.

"What would you like to watch?" She had already turned back toward the living room, expecting him to follow.

"Mari." He walked behind her as he spoke. They might as well get comfortable in the living room, rather than standing around in the kitchen with all those knives at the ready.

She sat in a large, comfortable armchair, pulling her legs up under herself. *Totally self-contained*, thought Eliot, which gave him a bit of courage to say what he had to say. He sat at the edge of the sofa nearest her, looked down into his champagne glass. He twisted the thin stem once then looked up at her.

"What is it?" she asked directly. "Are you really pissed that I interrupted you at work today? I'm sorry about that. I was so excited and I know I'm so me-me-me—"

"No!" He laughed. "I mean, yes, you are me-me-me, but I kind of love that about you. I think for the first time in a while, I'm the one who is going to be me-me-me."

She took a careful sip of her champagne and looked at Eliot with a keener interest. Then she waited for him to speak.

"The thing is, Mari…" He paused to put his glass of champagne down on the coffee table then clasped his hands loosely between his knees. "I might want to postpone the wedding."

She continued to look at him, almost scientifically observing him. *Uncharacteristically patient*, thought Eliot.

As far as she could tell, he already had all the rope he needed to hang himself. She certainly wasn't going to have to provide him with any in the form of prodding speech.

Seeing that she was not going to say anything until he asked her a direct question, or even a rhetorical one, he continued ahead as best he could. Perhaps he shouldn't have fended off all of his mother's recent attempts to speak to him honestly about his emotional state; he was sorely out of practice.

"Okay." He took a deep breath, then continued. "Without going too deep into it, there was a woman I was involved with before I met you, and I thought it was resolved, or over, or what have you, and I think I might still have feelings for her and it didn't seem right to move forward"—he gestured loosely between the two of them— "you know, with us. If that was the case."

Marisa narrowed her eyes for several moments, but that was it.

On he went. "So, I will defer to your wishes. I'll do whatever you want to do. If you want to call it off altogether, if you want to postpone, if you want to talk about it, or whatever. What do you think?"

She refilled her glass of champagne with methodical precision, took a sip, and opened her mouth to speak.

Then she shut it without saying a word.

Eliot supposed he was grateful she was not prone to hysterics, but her controlled response only proved to be one more nail in the proverbial coffin. What would incite a passionate, unplanned, ill-considered response in this woman? He'd like to see that, but he was fairly certain he would never be the one to bring it on.

She collected her thoughts and started to speak, almost casually. "Here's the thing, Eliot. Why do you think you waited until it was in the newspaper, for the entire world to see, to tell me about... this..." She looked away, as if casting about for the word. "...Information? Did you forget about this woman for the past year and only now, as you are checking off your prenuptial packing list, consider that you had unfinished business in the ex-lover department?"

She was right, of course. It was not the tack he had expected, but she was right.

"Perhaps the reality of the newspaper announcement forced me to face the truth in a way that all of the planning and our hypothetical discussions had not." Eliot tried to consider this. He was a thoughtful, contemplative person by nature, and this type of off-the-cuff discussion was particularly difficult for him. In business negotiations, he was always overly informed and ready to react to every eventuality. Why had he not thought to bring the same level of preparedness to this, one of the most pressing negotiations of his life?

"Those discussions were not hypothetical to me, Eliot."

He looked into her stunning eyes and saw through to a tender heart. She was all brass tacks, but she was also a good person and it wasn't for Eliot to constantly try to compile all her bits of narcissism and self-satisfaction into a wad of unappealing characteristics that might make it, if not honorable, at least tenable to abandon her.

He wanted to put his arm around her, to comfort her, but she had chosen to sit in an isolated chair that made it impossible. She had thought they would be watching a movie at the time she sat there, but the fact remained.

"Aw, Mari, don't say it like that. You know what I meant. I feel like a total heel, not that that's your problem," he added quickly.

"But wouldn't it have been worse if I came to you after we were married and said I don't know what to do about this, well, my feelings for, well…"

"Good god, Eliot!" She was finally angry. "You don't even know what 'this' other thing is. How the hell am I supposed to respond to 'this'?" She regretted losing her temper. She always regretted losing her temper, but particularly now. "I'm sorry to raise my voice. I refuse to be the shrew whose incivility makes it easier for you to excuse yourself from this relationship. I'm sorry."

"Mari, please. You have nothing to be sorry for. I would have expected at least a little fire. And I certainly know you're not the type to enjoy unnecessary histrionics. Which was probably why I put off addressing this, either to myself or you, because…" He took a breath. "Well, because I just thought it was so long ago, and so over, it seemed, it seems still, so ridiculous to even address it… her… whatever…" Eliot looked away from Marisa's penetrating look for a moment, to catch his breath, or corral his stray thoughts. He continued with care, "But the fact that it was all so unresolved has not led to the forgetting that I'd thought time would provide."

A brief silence ensued.

"I want to move ahead with the wedding as planned."

"What?"

"You heard me," Marisa said in her businesslike tone. "I want to move ahead with the wedding. You go deal with whatever *this* is, whomever *this* is. I'm a grown up. I can handle it. We're too good for each other, Eliot. It's so easy, so right with us. We're both mildly annoying—"

He smiled, but it hurt.

"—and overly ambitious and we care about each other. I genuinely care about you, I really do. I want you to be happy. But I would much prefer it was with me, of course." She gave him a winning smile that was so perfectly Marisa—confident, optimistic—but with a new hint of longing. She wanted this wedding, perhaps more than she had been willing to let on up until now.

"I don't know, Mari—"

"Let me finish while I have the momentum." She smiled that small hopeful smile again. "But if it's not with me, then I will"—she paused in an unfamiliar, emotional way—"then I will accept reality. I deal in reality. You know that. Listen. It's only February. The wedding is not until June. It's going to be small. We will tell, or you will tell, your Danieli-Fauchard PR wolves to drop it. We've always wanted it to be an intimate, private ceremony. Let's keep it that way. No more press."

Eliot took another sip of champagne and contemplated his options. If he told her it was over, permanently and finally over, he might be throwing away a wonderful, companionable life with a beautiful, intelligent woman. A smart, accomplished woman who could actually *express* herself. He had done his part in confessing his immature worries. She had responded.

She continued, back in charge. Sure. "Think of it as a deadline of sorts. Now that I know this other… *situation*… exists for you, you can do what you need to do, meet up with her, talk to her, whatever you need to do"—Mari looked at him with a meaningful stare—"to be done with it. Once and for all."

"I've never been unfaithful to you, Mari. I am not going to start now."

"You're not betraying my trust if I'm asking you to go figure this out and deal with it. It would be one thing if you were skulking around behind my back, but now that you've been your honest, true self, how can I possibly cry foul? I'll be in Tanzania for the next three weeks. Do what you need to do, Eliot."

She moved over to the couch and sat next to him, more as a sister or a friend, sitting cross-legged on the cushion next to his. "Now let's watch a movie and just relax. I'm exhausted." She reached for the remote control and Eliot felt the anxiety of confronting Mari begin to drain away, only to be replaced by a whole new battalion of worry about confronting Abigail Heyworth.

It was only later, as he was falling asleep next to Marisa—a platonic sleep—that Eliot realized she had never once used the word *love* when describing what they had with each other. She had used all the right words: *good, true, honest, caring, meaningful...* but never the one simple word *love*. His mind was awash in what, if anything, that might portend. When he had been with Abigail, he had felt the burning, bubbling need to express that word, and look how poorly that had turned out. Maybe Marisa was right to use it sparingly, if at all. Maybe the word *love* was a simple trap, a shiny lure that made fools of everyone who misapprehended its nature.

# *Chapter 12*

Sarah's Range Rover looked like a Depression-era transport vehicle, piled high with the sum of its owner's worldly possessions. Only this was no hegira.

Or, then again, maybe Fashion Week in Paris was a pilgrimage of sorts. Vintage Louis Vuitton steamer trunks, hat boxes, and valises were stuffed into every possible square inch of the huge navy-blue SUV. The backseats had been folded down to accommodate all of the items, and Sarah and Abigail sat in the two front seats, looking like a couple of lorry drivers or transcontinental adventurers.

Devon, arms crossed in front of his chest, stood on the sidewalk in front of their building looking askance at the unlikely pair. "Are you two sure you are going to be okay?"

"What is that supposed to mean?" Sarah asked.

"Nothing. Off you go, then. I can see the headlines now: 'Freya Stark and Beryl Markham hit the road. With enough supplies to last a year.'"

"Very funny. It's Fashion Week, for goodness' sake! I need to bring *fashion*. Get it?"

"The fact that your insane attachment to luxury goods is co-opted by other insane people for a week or two, several times a year, does not make it any more logical to the rest of us. Go have your fun with all your cronies in Paris. I'll stay here and remain rational."

Abigail, unable to let that one pass, leaned across the center console toward the driver-side window and said, "Yes, you go be rational in that new Aston Martin you just bought. Sarah, ignore that man and let's get to France!"

"That car is a piece of art, a handmade—"

Sarah held up her hand to stop him. "Enough! My shoes are pieces of art. But we shall not embark on this tedious argument. Kiss me passionately and wish me well."

Devon smiled and leaned in to kiss his wife with fresh joy. Abigail looked away from the two lovers and out her window, ignoring the slight mewl of pleasure that might have been Sarah or Devon or both. She was less embarrassed than she would have ever imagined possible, since their public displays of affection were both perpetual and legendary within the family circle. Everyone had become necessarily immune.

Devon gave the roof a firm pat to send them on their way and pulled away from the car. Sarah rolled up the electric window and continued to smile her stupid postkiss smile, then turned to Abigail and her face turned serious with comedic haste.

"So."

Abigail laughed and looked back out her window as they pulled away and headed toward Berkeley Square. "So."

"Shall we dive right into the Eliot discussion or would you rather talk about a bunch of other stuff and then pretend to happen upon it in a falsely organic fashion?"

Abigail stared at her sister-in-law, who, in turn, continued to face straight forward, navigating a snarl of roundabout traffic, then quickly looking in the side and rearview mirrors to check her position.

"Well?" Sarah prodded.

"Well, I suppose we might as well dive right in. There's nothing to discuss. Honestly, Sarah, he is engaged to be married. It is so over. Whatever *it* was to begin with," she added.

"First of all, it's never over. Even if he is engaged; even if he were married, for that matter. I am not one to build upon false hopes." With that, she turned and looked at Abigail for a brief direct moment. "I've seen him over the past year, and he is *not* happy. It's obvious."

The familiar emotions battled: I hate that he is unhappy, I hate that I am unhappy, I am the cause of his unhappiness, he deserves to be happy, I think I made him happy for a bit, but then I made him so unhappy.

"Quit ruminating!" Sarah snapped.

"Okay, okay. It's hard not to, well, go over things a bit in my mind. I haven't really had anyone to bounce ideas off, as it were."

"Why not?"

"What do you mean?"

"I mean, why haven't you bounced any of these so-called ideas off of Bronte or me? You have certainly bounced off every idea imaginable when it came to starting your foundation or buying your house or even how to improve your wardrobe—I know that last cost you a treasure in pride—so why stop at Eliot?"

"You know why. Let's start with the fact that you dated him. It's simply awkward."

"Let's dispel that myth once and for all. He kissed me a couple of times on the cheek, maybe the neck, but it was gross, like a brother. Nothing, I just wasn't attracted to him like that. I had just met Devon. I couldn't think about anyone else." Sarah checked the side mirrors again in what Abigail suspected was a gesture more intended to end that line of thought than to verify any approaching vehicles.

"I'm not sure I totally buy that, but for the sake of argument, I'll move on," Abigail said. "Eliot and I were never really a couple. I mean, he came to visit Dunlear a lot when you and Devon were engaged and he was in town, and all the house parties and riding and dinners and whatever—"

"Then what?"

"Well, then after your wedding, we had a little rendezvous on the beach at Moonhole. It was not a big deal. We didn't even kiss."

"Uh-huh… and then?"

"You are a pain in the ass."

"I know! And you are my hostage in this car for at least four hours. So sit back, relax, and spill the beans. What happened after Bequia? I was totally incommunicado on my honeymoon, and this is where everything went pear-shaped, right? Go on."

"Sort of. I went to Iowa with Eliot… for his grandmother's birthday. I told you about it. Totally sweet. Sexy. Promising." She looked out the window and sighed.

"Yes. I remember. Then what?"

"Then I went to Paris with Mother."

"Of course! The famous Jack Parnell weekend. You completely wrote Eliot out of that whole story, you rat. Was he there?"

"I can't believe I'm such a liar. Yes, he was there and I begged Mother not to tell anyone after the fact. I only saw him that Friday night, and then Mother and I spent the rest of the weekend shopping and going to museums, and she was on such a girlish high from meeting Jack that I didn't see the point in spoiling her fun with my tales of woe."

"Okay. Back up. How did we get from assignation-on-the-beach and kisses-in-Iowa to tales-of-woe?"

Abigail realized she was finally and completely sick of picking and choosing what to tell, what not to tell, what was private, what was relevant. She unburdened herself completely, telling Sarah every glorious and gory detail, down to the last shard of crystal smashed against the back of Eliot's hotel room door and her cowardly scurrying back to her own suite.

Sarah whistled in a low, almost admiring tone. "Wow, I didn't know he had it in him."

"Oh, believe me, he's got it in him."

Sarah looked across the front of the car and noticed Abigail rubbing the charms together at the end of the black string around her neck. "And that's the necklace he gave you? I can't believe you've been wearing that this whole time. I must have asked you a dozen times where you got it and you were all, 'Some secondhand shop.'"

"Well, that's not a total lie. He found the charms at an estate jeweler's in Milan, so they're technically secondhand—"

"Cut it out, Abigail!" Sarah's voice tore at her. "This whole unhealthy, secretive shitty mess is over. You can either call him yourself or I will call him. But either way, you're going to sit down in a room together and figure out what the hell happened. If not for your sake, then for his, since you seem to be bent on martyrdom."

"I know you won't call him if I ask you not to. That's just too immature and stupid. I will call him. Just give me a day or two in Paris to adjust to the idea. He's obviously going to be there for work the whole time, so I don't need to call him right away."

They fell silent for a little while as they continued south toward Folkestone and the Channel Crossing car trains.

Sarah reverted to different topics of conversation when she resumed talking: plans to spend time with her aging grandmother, plans to see Jack and Sylvia, how much fun they were going to have in the big suite at the Ritz.

"It'll be like a weeklong slumber party. We can go to the shows all day then come back to the room and chill for a few hours, then go out all night!"

"If you'd told me, even a few months ago, that I'd be on my way to Paris for Fashion Week, I'd have laid odds on your sanity. I don't know what I was thinking to let you talk me into this."

"You weren't thinking—for once!—you were just going along for the ride for the hell of it. Remember? You used to live your entire life like that. When did you become such a square? Just enjoy yourself, Abs. Stop overthinking everything."

Abigail looked at her with widened eyes.

"Yes, even Eliot. Especially Eliot!" Sarah laughed. "Stop over-thinking Eliot. He's just some guy, already. I know he's all that American brawn and debonair blah-blah-blah, but, well, just let's see what transpires, shall we?"

Watching things transpire without overanalyzing was not Abigail's forte. Overthinking had become her default setting. She found herself endlessly decoding everything from the latest Hollywood take on same-sex marriage to why dry cleaners were still able to charge women more for "blouses" than they charged men for "shirts." And then she overthought how those two were quite obviously threads that wove through the same bolt of cloth—gender bias—that curtained not only her internal landscape but the entire world around her.

Abigail had been back in touch with her old girlfriend, Tully, soon after the debacle in Paris. They'd never really lost touch, but their communication had taken on a much lighter tone after they broke up. After Eliot, Abigail wanted—needed—to talk to Tully, to help analyze (Sarah would say *overthink*) the nature of what the two of them had had for all their years together. She hoped that knowledge might help her better understand what had gone so terribly wrong with Eliot.

It did.

Tully was patient and loving, and particularly kind given the fact that Abigail had been the one to cut off their relationship. Shortly after Abigail broke up with her, Tully had fallen in love with an energetic, adoring Scottish woman named Christine Cunningham, and they'd been together ever since. They frequently stayed with Abby in London, and Christine had a lovely, open way about her that let them all speak candidly about, well, everything.

The week before Abigail went to Paris with Sarah, Tully and Christine had been staying at Abigail's house and were planning on continuing on at her place while Abigail was away for the next ten days.

Christine and Tully were sitting close to one another on one sofa; Abigail had her legs crossed under her on the other. They had been trying to parse out the idea of long-term love over too many glasses of wine.

"The thing is," Abigail asked through a philosophical wine buzz, "if all of that is true, then why do people fall *out* of love?"

Tully looked at Christine, then back to Abigail. "I honestly don't think I will ever fall out of love with Christine."

Christine smiled and grabbed her hand. "I know!" Then she turned back to Abigail. "I mean, Abby, I know you've always loved Tully, but were you ever truly *in love* with her?"

Abigail nodded then shook her head, not in dismissal, but in utter cluelessness. "Yes! God, when we were first together... for years, you know that, Tul."

Tully nodded. "I do. But Abs, you don't like..." She looked away, her pale blue eyes dreamy with wine and remembering. "You don't really do *deep*... or you didn't then. Obviously Eliot wanted to go too deep... or too soon. But you can't fault him for that."

"Is that what I did to you?" Abby was almost crying.

"No, sweetie. Stop. We've been over this a million times. We were heading in different directions for ages. You did the right thing to break it off." Tully turned to Christine and smiled, then looked back at Abby. "But you want Eliot... it's so obvious. Why are you so afraid of that? Why are you afraid to admit you're in love with him?"

"Other than the fact that it's fruitless since he's about to marry someone else?" She tried to laugh it off.

Tully kept staring at her. "You're right. I'm sure he's madly in love with that lovely Marisa. I've heard through the grapevine she's been incredibly successful with those microfinance projects in Tanzania. A real go-getter."

"I hate you."

Tully raised her glass in a small toast. "That's a start."

"I don't even know what *in love* means." Abigail said on a frustrated sigh. Ever since Eliot had said it, blurted it like a fait accompli after he'd brought her to that impossible pleasure, she had felt it like a strangely painful, but not unwelcome, knife. She wanted to feel it.

She looked up at the two people seated across from her who were so patently emblematic of what she thought she couldn't understand. "I mean, I look at you two and I *see* it. But for myself, I don't know if my monkey mind will ever let me *have* it. I am in such a state of thinking and parsing and deciphering. It seems so implausible."

"Did you parse and think when Eliot made love to you? When he touched you?" Tully asked quietly.

Abigail felt the pressure behind her eyes and shook her head no.

Then Christine and Tully both smiled, and Christine said, "Well, there you have it! Problem solved."

"That's all?"

"Of course that's all, Abs," Tully said. "At some point, you just want to give yourself over to it. And not in an unthinking way, but in that blissful surrender way, like tipping backward into a pool. Free falling. Some things are *beyond* thinking."

"She's right," Christine said. "I bet when you see Eliot, you'll find you can no longer abide the passive role you've created for yourself."

Abigail laughed at the idea of herself as passive. She was painfully active. "I wish my mother could hear you call me passive. If I write one more op-ed piece to *The Guardian*, I think she'll throttle me."

They all laughed a bit, then Tully continued. "It's funny, isn't it? That you're able to put yourself out there for every disenfranchised woman on the planet, but you still aren't quite ready to put yourself out there for yourself?"

Abigail took a sip of her wine and set it back on the coffee table.

Tully continued, "Remember when you left me?" Abigail winced a little. "Sorry, that sounds accusatory, but you know what I mean. You said a few things about how I was hiding from the privilege of my upbringing, or dismissing its importance, or what have you, and I hated that. Then, after I realized the truth of it, I knew that's why I hated to hear it. I was so grateful in the end that I had a friend who could call me on that, that I could open myself to my whole self, not just the warrior or the revolutionary, but the granddaughter of the Duke of Bedford. Why did I have shame in that? I suppose you taught me to see that I needn't have."

Abigail nodded.

"But the irony is, and I think about this still, how were *you* able to give me something that you yourself did not possess? For someone so impassioned, you have become one of the most self-effacing women I know."

Abigail tried to hear the words without feeling the sting. It was not easy. She had spent so much time and effort and guts trying to build her foundation and her life, and now everyone she cared about was acting as if it all amounted to some sort of convoluted screen she had built up around herself, to hide behind.

Abigail slumped deeper into her couch. "I am erasing myself?"

"A bit," Tully said.

"Oh, Tul, I'm really frightened. I've agreed to go to Paris, with Sarah James of all people, and I know Eliot will be there and I just don't even know anymore."

"Good," Christine said. "I like the idea of you not knowing."

"Me too," Tully added.

"Well, I don't. I hate the not knowing." Abigail pouted and the other two started laughing until all three of them were in a state of lifted spirits.

———

Just after three o'clock on Saturday afternoon, the blue Range Rover pulled into the Place Vendôme, slowing in front of the Ritz. A hive of activity surrounded the car almost before it came to a complete stop. Without even realizing it, Sarah was able to command the same abject devotion from porters, valets, and bellman the world over that her mother and grandmother had always been able to elicit. She knew many Ritz employees by name, embraced two in particular, and before Abigail could get her comparatively shabby Tumi bag out of the car, the rest of Sarah's vintage luggage had been piled with architectural precision onto a shiny brass cart and wheeled effortlessly into the main lobby. The car was whisked away by a valet, never to be seen again for the following ten days.

"Isn't that so easy?" Sarah marveled, with genuine gratitude, looking around the now-empty sidewalk.

Abigail hoisted her computer bag farther up onto her shoulder and shook her head in mild amusement. "You are unbelievable."

"I can't help it if people are accommodating." Sarah winked and bent to pick up Abigail's other wheelie bag. "Now, let's go see if they upgraded us," Sarah said with adolescent excitement.

The two-bedroom suite was so ridiculously over-the-top that Abigail did not even bother to comment on it. The gold, the marble, the silks, the fringed pelmets, the ironed pillowcases. It was a study in the art of glorious overstatement. Every surface was polished, every scent was evocative. Baskets of exotic Asian fruits, arrangements of hothouse flowers.

"I can't believe Devon lets you stroll right in—unattended, unescorted—to this den of iniquity," Abigail said after they had deposited all of their bags in their respective rooms then joined up again in the shared sitting room. "Everything about this hotel, this town, is pure seduction."

"Speak for yourself, Miss Nothing-Happened-at-the-Plaza-Athénée. As far as I'm concerned, this is all work and no play for Ms. Sarah James. I can predict, almost to a farthing, my entire year's worth of sales on the tilt of a certain buyer's head when a new style goes down the runway at the Dior show. The dinners, the lunches, every casual encounter is forming, strengthening, or destroying a business relationship for me. You'll see."

"When you put it that way, I'm not sure I want to."

"Yes, you do. It's awesome. Millions of dollars in effort and potential revenue, years of styles, ideas, creative energy flying in every direction; music, art, beauty."

"So, what's on for tonight? Are you going out? I might stay in—"

"Absolutely not! No staying in. You can sleep when you're dead. You're not getting any while we're here. You are my fashion prisoner. Go take a hot bath, or cold shower, or whatever kind of revitalizing ablution suits and be ready to go in an hour and a half. I'm going to swim for a little while then change. Dinner at La Coupole, then we'll go meet up with some friends who are having drinks in Montmartre. Casual. Well, dressy for you, casual for me." Sarah turned back into her room, grabbed her swimsuit, crossed back to the door of the suite, and gave Abigail a half-wave in farewell.

Abigail marveled again at the woman her brother had married, and whom he'd dubbed the Botticellian stealth missile.

━━◦◦◦━━

Eliot was on the final two laps of a forty-five-minute swim. It still seemed to be the only thing that cleared his mind, even though the window of postnatatory clarity was getting shorter and shorter. He felt like a drug addict who needed more and more of the stuff to achieve a shorter and less satisfying result. Marisa had gone to Tanzania as planned, and he was supposedly resolving his unresolved feelings for the Other Woman. He did a flip turn and swam the final lap, concentrating on his labored breathing to the exclusion of all else. He finished in the shallow end and stood, his muscles humming, his legs vibrating with the effort of his exertion. He pulled his goggles off, then smoothed the excess water out of his hair.

"Well, if it isn't Eliot Cranbrook as I live and breathe!"

He looked up at the fetching, familiar, mischievous blond. "At your service, Ms. James." He bowed slightly, the water at his waist shifting slightly at the movement. "I figured you would be staying with your grandmother." He walked through the water toward the few steps at the corner of the shallow end and started to climb out of the pool.

"Oh, god no! Could you imagine Cendrine taking messages from André Leon Talley?" Sarah laughed, then thought about it. "On the other hand, that might be hilarious. But, no, too much going on and I need the concierge and everything here. What about you? I thought you hated the Ritz."

"It's not bad."

"Your PR department is making you stay here, aren't they?"

"Well, of course they are. Do you really see me draped in gold satin atop Carrara marble? I'd be much happier in an attic room at the Hôtel d'Angleterre, but that doesn't jibe with their idea of what I'm supposed to *project*." Eliot was drying off his lean torso and caught Sarah looking his way. "I thought you were happily married."

She blushed. "I am ecstatically married, but you are quite the specimen these days. From an objective standpoint, of course. Do you eat? Or just swim and take astronaut pills marked 'daily intake'?"

He tossed the towel over his shoulders then slipped on the hotel robe that he had worn from the dressing room, tying the knot at the waist with a firm tug. "Mostly the latter. Without the pills. Just the swimming."

"Let's remedy that! What are you doing for dinner tonight? We just got here a little while ago and I was going to meet some friends for drinks, but let's fatten you up first!" Sarah's hands were clasped together in childish delight.

"Is Devon with you? I thought he hated this stuff."

"Did I say *we*?"

"Yes. You said *we*. Who did you drag along this time?" Eliot finished collecting his room key and cell phone and turned slowly to give her his full attention.

She simply folded her arms, quirked her mouth, and widened her eyes. "Who do you think?"

His heart stopped flat for a few seconds then careened off in an arrhythmic stampede. He tried to stand still, unremarkable, unaffected, but thought she might have caught the transitory coronary. "I can't begin to imagine."

"Can you not?"

"Bronte?"

"No. As you know, an eight-months-pregnant-with-twins Bronte Talbott Heyworth does not make for a congenial traveling companion."

"Julie from your New York office?"

"She's here somewhere"—Sarah gestured loosely—"staying at the Intercontinental, running the show, as it were. But no, we aren't staying together. Here. At the Ritz." Sarah never thought she had much of a mean streak, but watching Eliot squirm was divine. All she could think was, *Abigail, this is SO not over.*

"I'm not ready to see her, Sarah."

Now she really did feel mean. "Oh, Eliot." She reached out her hand and stepped toward him; he stepped farther away and shook his head.

"It's nothing to do with you, Sarah. I have too much going on right now."

That line of defense Sarah could dispute. "Please, Eliot, we are all busy. Look at me. Do you think I have time to be showing my sister-in-law how to be a grown-up? I'm supposed to be wooing you into buying my company, not, you know, helping someone woo you!"

He looked down at the tiled pattern in the mosaic floor, then back up at Sarah. "Where are you guys going for dinner? Can I have any advantage… element of surprise? I honestly don't think I can walk into the Posen show Monday morning and see the two of you in the front row and behave naturally."

"There's the man I know and love. Strategic thinker. Element of surprise. I like it. Let's see… we will be at La Coupole tonight from ten o'clock on. Give or take. I don't want to appear too obvious."

"All right. I may or may not be able to make it."

Sarah rolled her eyes. "Whatever, Eliot! If this all works out the way I think it will, you are most definitely going to be *making it*."

"Very funny, Sarah. I'll try to be there."

"I suppose that's the most any of us can promise." She gave him a quick hug before he could slip away. "Hang in there, Eliot. It's all going to work out for the best."

"You sound like my mother."

"I'll take that as a compliment."

"So you should. Enjoy your swim, Sarah."

"Thanks, Eliot." He was nearly to the door of the changing rooms when she called after him in a sing-songy baiting tone, "See you later!"

Eliot managed to get into the men's locker room, the smell of chlorine and cleaning fluid working as a sort of modern-day smelling salts to keep him on his feet until he went to the far end of the antiseptic room, and down one short row of lockers, to collapse gratefully onto a small teak bench.

He put his head down, nearly to his knees, trying to convince himself that he was still catching his breath after a vigorous hour of exercise, rather than trying to tamp down his first full-fledged panic attack. He felt entirely out of control. The abstract feelings of loss, confusion, and disorder were not even the half of it. His physical body was an erratic, unfamiliar combination of mismatched parts. His lungs were starting to burn; his heart was palpitating in random beats, one minute a shallow, rapid flutter, the next a thudding pounding with empty pauses between hard beats; his scalp was tingling, his fingertips throbbing, his feet leaden.

He opened his eyes cautiously and saw his hands clenched onto his knees, and he forced himself to relax the muscles of his shoulders, then his arms, then slowly, each finger. He relaxed into his own breathing, trying to ride the wave of unfamiliar fear, rather than grasp after it. He felt as though he were coming up from a rough tumble in the ocean, breathless, disoriented. He relaxed further as his heartbeat returned to a normal pace, with only the occasional erratic thud, and realized, after the fact, that he must have been deathly pale as he felt the warmth of blood seeping back up his neck and cheeks.

Eliot could not tell whether he had been sitting there for ten seconds or ten minutes, but in either case, a lifetime had passed. He had often heard of people suffering from panic attacks, confusing them with heart failure, foolishly checking themselves into hospitals while clutching their chests. Or he had supposed them foolish. Eliot stood, testing the strength of his legs to hold him before pulling his full weight off the bench.

A Ritz employee, a masseur or weight trainer perhaps, turned the corner toward the area where Eliot was recovering his senses.

"Ça va? Is everything all right, Mr. Cranbrook?" the attendant asked in quiet French.

"Yes, thank you for asking." Eliot answered in French as well. At least he hadn't lost any of his basic faculties: speech, language recall, "I gave it a rough go in the pool and just realized I forgot to eat lunch this afternoon. Just a bit light-headed, I think."

"Let me bring you a bottle of water and a bit of fruit, shall I?"

"Thank you, I'd appreciate that."

Eliot watched as the trim, young man in the fitted white T-shirt and white exercise pants moved toward the other side of the room, then returned with the drink and food.

"Are you sure you are well, sir?" the man asked as he handed Eliot an apple and a bottle of Evian.

"Very well. Thank you again for your assistance."

Eliot twisted off the pale blue plastic cap and poured the contents of the bottle of water down his throat as if he had never tasted anything better in his life. He ate the apple, barely tasting it, but grateful for the sustenance, then stripped and showered. He changed back into his jeans and button-down shirt, slipped on his loafers, gathered up his phone and keys again, and said his thanks and farewell to the young man on his way out.

He rode up in the elevator in a half-conscious state, as if he were emerging from a long dream. The ping of the elevator sounded too loud, the voices of the couple next to him sounded too low, vibrating around him in a strange foreign fog. He found his way back to his room, shut the door, and then wandered across to the French windows that opened out onto the Place Vendôme.

What was it with Parisian hotels?

And balconies?

And Abigail?

He sat in a desk chair that he turned to face out the window, taking in the beautiful view as the late afternoon sun began to set over the rooftops and the cobblestones and the pediments and oriels and pilasters. Every surface exuded artistry and planning, forethought, design, beauty. The stone facade of the building across the way was capturing the last rays of the February sun, turning it to gold and bronze. The entire edifice seemed to throb with life, or the end of the life of that particular day.

Eliot felt Abigail all around him. He wasn't prone to what his father would dub spiritual mumbo jumbo, but he could tangibly sense her nearness. He still wasn't sure if he had the strength (he purposely avoided the word *courage*) to meander over to La Coupole and casually drop by their table later that night, but he knew some sort of interaction was going to happen. His eye moved to the large column in the center of the Place Vendôme, Bonaparte's likeness standing atop in eternal self-assurance.

Napoleon never worried overmuch about Josephine, he suspected, certainly not to the point of having a panic attack in the corner of a basement. The hotel phone was nearby on the elegant parquet desk. Eliot picked it up and ordered a light meal of smoked trout and mâche, and decided to treat himself to a split of the 2003 Pomerol that caught his eye as he was shutting the room service binder.

Napoleon's statue, proclaiming Bonaparte's inherent arrogance, galvanized Eliot into action. He had to take control, if not of Abigail, then at least of himself and his reactions to her. He forced himself, applied himself really, to the much-avoided process of analyzing once and for all what had transpired on that miserable night, or very early morning, really, at the Plaza Athénée last year.

His food and wine arrived, and he began to feel fortified. He took out a pen and paper and started assessing his dealings with Abigail just as he would a potential buyout. Pros. Cons. Irritants. Potential pitfalls. Intellectually, he knew the entire exercise was immature and futile. Pointless. What did spreadsheets and brainstorming have to do with messy emotions, as his mother called them? On the other hand, it was the method he was most comfortable with when assessing problems, and since he had failed miserably at dealing with Abigail in the abstract—his logic devolving into endless, circular philosophical cul de sac—he thought it worth a try to deconstruct her just as he would any other business proposition.

After he felt the mellow effects of the half bottle of wine and the healthy satisfaction of a decent meal, Eliot thought he might actually have the requisite strength to meet up with Sarah and Abigail. He was grateful for the fact he was able to think her name without succumbing to his usual worry. Resolution, one way or another, was near.

Eliot's cell phone rang and he checked the caller ID and answered. The photographer Benjamin Willard and the delectable Russian model Dina Vorobyova were in town for the week and, amidst a background of clinking glasses, loud music, and the generic hum of hundreds of chattering voices, Dina was yelling into Eliot's ear about the need for him to stop being such a corporate lackey and to get "eez ass out of eez 'otel room."

"And a fine hello to you too, Dina!" Eliot laughed into the phone.

"We're meeting up at La Coupole, darling, and you must come! We pick you up at your hotel in thirty minutes. Wear something handsome!" Then the line went dead.

Eliot stared down at his meticulous list of Abigail-related idiocy, with phrases like *reality vs. fantasy* and *passion vs. pragmatism* clouding his vision, then felt a wave of near-freedom and crumpled it up and threw it in the garbage. Whether it was the denouement of the panic attack, or the final, certain imposition of reality on his imaginary, escalating preoccupation with Abigail, a gratifying peace washed over him at the thought of actually seeing her in person.

Marisa, of all people, had been correct. The real Abigail would eradicate all of his imaginings and conjurings. The real Abigail was only human. The real Abigail was just a regular person. Surely she would be, if not small and insignificant, at least manageable in real life.

Surely.

# Chapter 13

SARAH SWEPT INTO THE hotel room, her hair concealed in an ivory-toweled turban. Abigail was sitting on one of the comfortable armchairs, reading an intense novel about a despotic village patriarch in preapartheid South Africa. The protagonist had just finished beating his daughter for her refusal to marry the man he had chosen.

"Another light read?"

"It's a beautifully written book."

"I think while we're here, you're going to have to be completely in my thrall." Sarah grabbed the offending Booker Prize winner out of her sister-in-law's hands. "Books, music, clothes. Everything. I decide. I'm pulling rank. You're here as my guest. Go get changed for dinner."

"I am changed." Abigail looked down at her black pants and long-sleeved white T-shirt. It wasn't just any T-shirt, it was one of the ludicrously expensive, clinging, slightly-off-white T-shirts that Sarah had convinced her to buy. "You told me to buy this shirt, remember?"

"Of course I did. For when you go to Portobello Road on a Saturday morning, so you don't go in sweatpants and one of your dear father's old gardening shirts. Not for dinner in Paris with glittering, glamorous famous people!"

Abigail laughed at Sarah's vehemence.

"Go ahead and laugh. You're going to need your sense of humor," Sarah said, not looking back as she went toward her bedroom to change.

"And why is that?"

Sarah had her hand on the doorknob, deciding whether or not to say anything, then spoke with considered nonchalance. "Because Eliot will be there." Her bedroom door shut in response to Abigail's frozen expression.

—∿∿—

Twenty minutes later, Sarah emerged from her room to find Abigail in exactly the same spot.

"Have you moved?"

"No."

"Well, let's get you dressed at least. Come on."

Sarah practically lifted Abigail out of the chair and kept her arm around her waist as she guided her toward the other bedroom, chattering on about meaningless things, the fabric on the desk chair, the pattern in the carpet. Then, like a big sister, she gently forced Abigail to sit at the end of the bed, then crossed the room to Abigail's closet.

"Okay, what did you bring?" Sarah said as she opened the closet door, then gasped as if she had just discovered a dead body. "What is this? You have about four tops in here? Are you crazy? Where is that Miu Miu skirt I gave you? The Carolina Herrera sweater?" Sarah shook her head in unfeigned pity. "You are a sad case, Abigail. Come with me." She guided her back through the living room and into her room, then settled Abigail back down on the end of the bed like a little girl.

It took Abigail a few moments to adjust to her surroundings. There were piles and piles of clothes, and trunks and shoes and belts and bras and scarves and every accessory imaginable. "Holy crap."

"I assure you, there is no crap in here whatsoever. This is the best of the best. The good stuff. Now let me think. The boobs are going to be a problem."

Abigail looked up in silent inquiry.

"Mine, not yours, of course." Sarah grabbed her generous rack as evidence, then put her hands on her hips. "Let me think of what I have that isn't going to fall off that maddeningly thin frame of yours."

She opened her closet and Abigail saw more clothes in that temporary space than she had owned in her entire life. "Jesus, Sarah. That's just what you brought for ten days? Or is that your whole wardrobe?"

"I know you're joking, so I won't come up for it." Sarah flicked efficiently through the hanging clothes, pausing occasionally then shaking her head in internal answer. "Here we go. Come over and let me see how this color looks against your complexion."

Abigail walked across the room and Sarah held up a Catherine Malandrino satin aubergine blouse.

Sarah tilted her head in a moment of aesthetic appraisal. "I will let you wear the jeans if you wear something really spectacular on top… and shoes of course. Otherwise, you're wearing a skirt."

"I'll wear the blouse. But isn't it too dressy? It's satin. Isn't that for black tie? Seriously."

Sarah looked at her and shook her head like an old medicine woman. "Have you learned so little, my child?"

They both burst out laughing and spent the next hour transforming Abigail from the wan, white-T-shirt-wearing third wheel to the fabulous, mysterious dark angel. Sarah did her makeup and congratulated herself on a job well done.

"There you go," she said as she turned Abigail around to face the large wall mirror behind the marble vanity in her bathroom. Sarah let her hands rest loosely on Abigail's shoulders, staring at both of their reflections.

Abigail did not recognize the beautiful woman in the mirror. Her lips were pronounced and full. Her eyes had a smudgy kohl effect that was mesmerizing. Her skin was perfectly even and glowed with the slightest glimmer of powder. "How did you do that?"

"Oh, my darling, I do that every day. I didn't want to risk giving you the full treatment for fear you'd be overwhelmed. Just a little foundation, a bit of something around the eyes, and that fabulous lipstick with the plumping whatever-it-is. I didn't want you to be too tarted up." Sarah had started putting the different eye pencils and lip pencils and magic potions back into her kit, when she felt Abigail's light touch on her upper arm.

Abigail was perilously close to weeping. Sarah scolded her, "No crying! You'll ruin the whole effect. You are gorgeous. Let's go get him." Sarah zipped up the last of her small makeup cases, and looked at Abigail with one final assessment. "Maybe just one more thing." Sarah pulled the black string around Abigail's neck.

"I don't want to take it off," Abigail pleaded.

"I don't either. I want to have it out in the open, not hiding inside your blouse. You are done hiding, Abs. Let me adjust it so it's a choker."

Abigail let her hand drop from her chest, where she had been holding the charms in place beneath the fabric. "Okay."

Sarah silently untied the knot at the base of Abigail's neck, then circled the long, well-worn, pliable piece of leather three times around Abigail's slim throat. The effect was miraculous. "Holy shit. You just went from hippie to rock star. Now let's get you some fuck-me boots."

Abigail had just taken a sip of water and almost spit it across the bathroom. "What did you just say?"

Sarah talked as she walked back into her crowded room. "You know what I mean. There you are in your demure, long-sleeved, satiny, feminine blouse, and that mischievous head of black hair. Let's have at least one thing on you that screams pure, unadulterated *sex*." Sarah was down on the floor, pulling out different boxes of shoes and dismissing them all.

"You don't think the black harem eyeliner or the dog-collar

version of my necklace might hint, just a bit, that I'm not opposed to a tumble?"

Sarah scrambled out of the closet and sat cross-legged on the floor with a largish box on her lap. "Of course those things hint at plenty, but I want you to wear a pair of shoes that don't hint. I want them to holler. Like this." Sarah had opened the box and was holding a single black suede knee-high boot between her thumb and index finger. "Now that's what I'm talking about."

"You're crazy! You are a hater of women. Those heels are a form of patriarchal torture."

Sarah smiled like Satan himself. "Just try them on, Abs. You might like them. Then what?"

"I'll try them on. You know I won't judge without evidence, but it is beyond impossible that three inches—"

"Four actually—"

"Very well, four inches, then, could possibly scream anything but misogynistic—or in your case, sadistic—pain. Give me the damn boots already." Abigail grabbed the dangling boot and sat on the floor across from Sarah.

"Here," Sarah said, "put these nylon peds on to protect your dainty little toes."

Abigail rolled her eyes, but did as she was told. "Does the boot go inside or outside the jeans?"

"Well, that depends." Sarah was back in aesthetic appraisal mode. "I'm going to need to see it both ways."

Ultimately, Abigail refused to wear the boots on the outside—with her jeans tucked in, she felt like some horse-crop-wielding dominatrix, much to Sarah's delight… then dismay when Abigail refused to oblige her.

"Okay, be that way. I never took you for such a prude!"

"I am not a prude!" Abigail protested.

"I refuse to argue, but take it from me. You are a card-carrying prude. If repression is what Eliot's into, I guess, you know, whatever rocks your boat."

"You are so evil, Sarah. Does my brother know how evil you are?"

Sarah's mouth twisted in mock innocence, and when she was about to speak, Abigail held up her hand. "Do not answer that! Ew!"

They both looked toward the window as the refracted lights of camera flashes played across the ceiling, then crossed to the French doors to see the latest commotion on the street below. They had been watching the paparazzi dogging the rich and famous for the past few hours—magazine editors, actresses, models—as they entered or exited the hotel. This time, it was a mile-high Russian supermodel and a rather old and charming looking white-haired man getting out of a stretch limousine.

Sarah murmured admiringly, "Damn. That's Dina Vorobyova and Benjamin Willard. Prepare thyself, Abigail."

"What do you mean?" All of a sudden, Abigail could feel the cool night air through the glass pane inches from her cheek. She felt the prickle of every hair on her body stand on end as Eliot emerged from the hotel lobby to stride casually across the sidewalk. The cameras flashed as he shook hands with the famous photographer, then turned to be enveloped by that damned Russian seductress. She was wearing something short and silver that seemed to be made of liquid rather than fabric.

"I can't believe Eliot is letting her wear that dress before the show." Sarah's voice was all business, calculating. "At least she's wearing the right shoes."

"Sarah, it's Eliot! Why are you analyzing that… that…"

"That supermodel? Is that the word you're searching for, Abigail?"

"I suppose."

Eliot lifted Dina up in a light embrace, her feet coming away from the sidewalk momentarily as he swung her around. The supposedly sultry vixen had thrown her arms around his neck like a happy child might do, and he was smiling at something she was whispering in his ear when he lifted his eyes and caught sight of Abigail in the window.

He continued listening to Dina's heavily accented English, probably hot in his ear, continued smiling as he lowered her gently back to the ground, continued ignoring the flashes all around them, and continued staring at Abigail. Then his smile altered, barely, his eyes sparkled with mischief, and he lifted his chin in a tiny gesture of acknowledgment and approval, just for her. That barely perceptible look made Abigail feel more beautiful, more desirable than any woman on earth.

She wasn't afraid anymore. Whether he was meant to be with the Accomplished Maritime Platypus or not, Abigail was ready to see him. "Let's go already."

"Really? Just like that? All right then." Sarah grabbed her snakeskin clutch and laced her arm through Abigail's. "Let the games begin."

---

La Coupole at ten o'clock on a Saturday night during Fashion Week was a natural phenomenon on par with the annual Pacific salmon run or the wildebeest migration in Kenya. The preening, the volume, the color, the lights. Abigail had eaten there before with her mother, usually for lunch or a light dinner after the theater, but this was something else altogether. It had never occurred to Abigail that the bright lights and tiled floors that her mother cursed for their utter absence of flattery were the ideal stage for people who welcomed inspection. It was a room full of people who had no need to actually say, "Look at me!" because it was simply impossible to look away.

"Try not to gawk, Abby." But Sarah knew it was empty advice. Gawking was the order of the night.

The maitre d' fawned admirably over Sarah, gave Abigail a brief, nearly dismissive once-over, then showed them to a table already packed with friends and business associates of Sarah's from New York and Chicago. Her business partner, Julie, stood up and shooed away a couple of excruciatingly handsome male models to make way for Sarah and Abigail to sit down.

The barely contained frenzy of waiters, busboys, and sommeliers; the adept speed with which they transported enormous steel platters of oysters, crayfish, clams, and lobster; the precise pouring of endless glasses of perfectly chilled champagne: Abigail looked around, astonished, and decided her sister-in-law was quite simply a genius. It was blissfully impossible to fumble through one's mind worrying about missed romantic chances or lost opportunities when life was blurring right there in front of you at such glorious speed.

Bright, efficient, alive.

Especially so when he was actually standing there, flanked by a supermodel and a world-renowned photographer, one beautiful strong hand holding a glass of champagne and the other reaching across the table to shake Sarah's hand, and then Sarah invited the three of them to join their table and Sarah's business partner Caroline said, "Perfect timing, we were just leaving," and more jostling and shuffling, and then Eliot was sitting two people away from her on the curved, intimate banquette. It was all breathtakingly simple. And infuriating.

How was she ever going to touch him with those infernal *people* in the way?

───

Eliot put his glass down on the table, staring at it for a few seconds longer than necessary to make sure it was stable amidst the glittering sea of plates, glasses, and silverware. He took a deep, steady breath and slowly turned to look at her full in the face.

"Hello, Abigail." He had to raise his voice slightly to be heard over the din.

"Hello… uh…" Her mouth looked suddenly dry. "…Eliot."

"Did you forget my name?"

She looked down for a second then smiled that shy, blushing smile that he'd come to think he'd imagined. He felt the blood coursing through the veins in his neck.

Abigail stared into his eyes and the noise and chaos around them seemed to fade, as if they were in some sort of tunnel. She tilted her head the smallest notch, and reached up to touch her necklace. It looked like a motion she'd performed a thousand times, touching the charms and letting the bittersweet memory of him wash over her. She smiled and nodded, a small affirmative drop of her chin.

They were surprisingly able to conduct normal conversations with the other people at the table. Abigail spoke to Benjamin Willard at length about his photographic work and eventually got around to asking him if he would ever consider visiting some of the villages in Libya and Uganda where her foundation was currently involved.

"That sounds perfectly intriguing. I've never been to either country. Tell me more about what you have going on there."

"Oh, it's hardly to do with me," Abigail deflected.

Sarah rolled her eyes across the table.

Abigail tried again. "What I mean is, the Rose and Thorn Foundation has been investing, really, in the small female-owned businesses and health centers of fourteen villages in Libya and Uganda."

Eliot took a slow sip of champagne and considered what else had been transpiring in Abigail's life, other than the slow boil of lust to match his own.

Sarah finally had had enough. "She is utterly impossible, Benjamin. In one year, Abigail's foundation has done more to improve the health and education of those women and children than any government or NGO has been able to accomplish in decades."

"It's not me, though, it's the doctors and volunteers—"

Eliot smiled as Sarah became more furious. "Do you see what

I'm dealing with? Eliot, you smile, but she is positively self-defeating. It is so boring!"

Benjamin Willard looked from the blond, confident Sarah James to the dark, self-conscious Abigail Heyworth and blurted out, "How many of you are there?"

"I beg your pardon?" Abigail asked.

"I mean, how many of this genus *Heyworthus Femina* roam the earth? Mothers, daughters, wives? I want to see you all in one room, preferably while I have my favorite camera and lots of time."

Abigail looked embarrassed and Sarah looked ecstatic, practically trilling her enthusiasm. "Oh! That would be so fabulous! Can you imagine if we did it now, with Bronte pregnant out to here? She'd kill us. But with two more genus *Heyworthus Femina* on the way, it does seem a shame to rush. And then there's the long-lost sister, Claire, recently sprung from her life sentence in northern Scotland and loving New York. And Aunt Claudia! Oh my, she's not technically a Heyworth, but she is formidable."

"I am at your disposal." Benjamin nodded his head, first toward Sarah, then, with a bit more intensity, to Abigail.

"You are too kind," said Abigail.

Dina leaned in front of Benjamin Willard to get a better look at Abigail. "You look so familiar." She turned to Eliot and then to Willard. "Don't you think?"

Willard smiled and looked at Eliot, then back at Abigail. "I believe she bears a striking resemblance to all the models in the Danieli-Fauchard runway shows this season."

Snapping her fingers, Dina said, "That's exactly it! Don't you see it, Eliot? You are making them all wear those crazy black wigs and all that kohl eyeliner, and you could have just hired this lovely woman to do your modeling for you."

Abigail stared at Eliot and he stared back, eventually giving her a small smile. He turned to Dina. "I'd love to get Abigail to model for me, but she once told me she is not beautiful, so what could I do?"

Dina wheeled on Abigail, eyes wide. "You said what? Do you not have a mirror?"

Abigail laughed at the Russian woman's vehemence, then replied, "I do now." She looked to Eliot and dipped her chin again.

Her shyness was the last straw. Eliot glanced at no one in particular and nearly growled, "Will you all excuse us for a moment?"

Dina and Willard looked up, surprised that the usually blasé Eliot looked so adamant. He stood up to let everyone scoot out of the large round booth, until Abigail was finally free of the banquette and standing next to him.

"Come with me."

She smiled and trailed behind him as he headed toward the crowded bar area, eventually leading them to a more secluded section down a hall, near the public phones and the restrooms. He stood in front of her, staring, taking her in.

She said, "You have been a figment for so long, I think I forgot the real you."

She reached for him and grabbed his wrist in a casual way, thinking she was merely illustrating her point—that she'd forgotten the physical reality of Eliot Cranbrook, her old friend—but it became a burning touch in an instant. He moved his other hand to cover hers, almost like he was holding her in place.

Touching her hand at that moment was the most pleasure he could ever hope for. He felt resolved. "I still feel it. Do you?"

"All the time. Especially at night."

"I think we need to leave."

"We just got here."

"Exactly. I don't want to waste another minute."

"Neither do I," Abigail laughed through the words, "but I'm starving and I want to wait for my dinner."

"Give me a little something, just to tide me over." He pulled her closer to him, his grip tightening on hers. He reached his hand up to her face and stopped just shy of actually touching her.

She could feel the heat emanating from his palm, and her eyes shut in liquid anticipation. "Please touch me, Eliot," she whispered.

"I don't know how."

Her eyes flew open to meet his. "Of course you do."

"I mean, I have dreamt and planned for this moment so many times in my imagination." He was leaning in close to her ear, whispering hotly. "Sometimes I am tender and slow; other times I am rough and demanding; and now that I have you here, really here, I—"

Abigail wrenched her hand free of his, threw her arms around his neck, and pulled his face to hers, relieving him of the need to decide. She kissed him with abandoned desperation, moaning into his mouth, grasping handfuls of his hair in her eager fingers; after a split second's hesitation, Eliot was all over her. The restaurant noises and lights faded into a low, distant murmur.

His hands moved to her waist, her ribs, the underside of her breasts, and his knee moved between her legs as one hand moved to steady her balance at her lower back. She pulled at the front of his shirt, yanking out the fabric where he had tucked it in at his waist, her lips never leaving his. When her hand finally went flat against the warm, muscled texture of his stomach, skin to skin, she felt some ancient, lost cog of her psychic machine slip seamlessly into place.

Peace.

Love.

"I love you, Eliot," she said between quick kisses. "I love you so much. I was so afraid." Her lips moved away from his mouth to his neck, the soft lobe of his ear, the tender skin at his temple. "Oh, god, how I've missed you." She was about to plant another kiss on his lips when he shook her roughly away, just a few inches, but enough to jar her.

"What?" she asked.

"What are you saying?"

"I'm saying what I was too insecure or too immature or too scared to say last year. You frightened me, Eliot. You were so... ardent."

"Say it again. Now. While you are looking in my eyes."

She blinked away the passion and spoke, as a vow. "I, Abigail Heyworth, love you, Eliot Cranbrook."

He stared at her and all the vile anger and months of confusion washed away. "And I you, Abigail. I think I've loved you from the moment you walked into the drawing room at Dunlear, like a flashing wild Medusa, come in from the storm." He traced the line of her jaw and the column of her neck, letting his finger pause at the black strings coiled around the base. "You've always been mine, Abigail, haven't you?" He put his index finger between the cord and her neck, watching, transfixed, as it tightened and pulled at her tender flesh. "I don't know why I didn't have the courage to demand you admit it. I was too easy on you. From the very first, I wanted to own you  "

She tilted her head back to feel the necklace grow even more taut, and bit her lower lip at the raw pleasure of it.

"It's all so obvious now, isn't it?" he whispered into her ear, then bit at the velveteen flesh around her earring. She wanted to drop to her knees and take him into her mouth right there on the century-old white mosaic tile. She wanted to adore him in every possible way. Every physical way. To give him every possible gift of pleasure.

"Oh, Eliot. I want you so much right now. I don't know if I can go back into the restaurant after all."

He pulled back a pace and tucked his shirt back into his pants. "Come on, it will be fun. Let's go drink champagne and eat oysters and marvel at all the beautiful people."

"Now it will be fun, eh? I think I see how this is going to go."

She shook her hair and looked down to make sure Sarah's silk blouse wasn't too obviously disheveled.

"You look perfect."

She looked up quickly to see him drinking her in. "You had better not look at me like that when we get back in the restaurant…"

"Or what?" he asked.

"Or I might just slither under the table and start doing all the things I've been reliving for the past long, long year."

He pulled her hand in his and started back toward the restaurant. "Pray tell."

"It's a rather long and comprehensive list."

"I love lists," he said, then gestured for her to precede him into the large main room. "After you, *my lady*."

She winked over her shoulder at the old volley… about being his… and about being a lady. She winked because now it was all true.

When they were reseated at the table, they ignored Sarah's pressing glances and endless leading questions for the rest of the evening. They laughed and chatted with an ever-changing stream of models and writers and photographers, while Eliot's hand never lost contact with her body, whether trailing idly along her thigh, catching her hand under the table, or slipping one arm loosely, possessively behind her shoulders.

Near midnight, she turned to Eliot, thinking he was still engaged in another conversation with Dina, but he was silently watching her. She gave him a questioning look then asked, "Have you had enough *fun* yet?"

"Have you had enough to eat? You're going to need your strength." His dark blue eyes sparkled, the sapphire irises nearly aglow.

"See?" she whispered. "Now that's the look that's going to put me under the table."

"We're out of here," he growled so only she could hear, then he lifted his chin toward Sarah. "You can pick up the tab. Just add it to the already outrageous amount you think Danieli-Fauchard should cough up to acquire Sarah James Shoes."

"Value for money, Eliot. Value for money. Have fun, you two. I won't wait up, Abigail."

Abigail groaned in embarrassment, but she knew Sarah was only trying to keep everything light. Abigail said her good-byes to Benjamin and Dina, and kissed Sarah on both cheeks. Abigail ducked into the taxi and just missed seeing her cousin, James Mowbray, enter the restaurant.

―∿∿―

As the taxi sped down Boulevard Raspail, Abigail climbed across Eliot's lap, straddling him. She took his face firmly in her hands, almost as if she were chastising him. "Where have you been?"

"I've been right here." He grabbed her narrow hips. "Right here," he murmured as he began kissing her, pulling her more firmly against his lap. "Where have *you* been?"

She was kissing his neck—"Here"— then kissing his lips—"and here"—then just below his ear—"and often here." Then she undid one button of his shirt and kissed the strong, warm flesh over his heart. "And always, always here." She let her tongue slide over his nipple and felt his response in her lap and on her lips. "Oh, I've missed you terribly, Eliot. I'm so sorry for all the time I wasted."

His head had fallen back onto the headrest of the taxi as he enjoyed her eager attention, but her apology brought him back to his senses. "No more of that. We were both foolish." He took both of her hands in his and kissed the palm of each, then brought one of her hands back to his chest so she could feel the pounding of his heart. "You do this to me. Only you, Abigail."

Her eyes faltered as she thought it was only her… and his fiancée.

He caught her change immediately. "What is it? We can't afford any more senseless misunderstandings. Tell me."

"It just popped into my mind. I'm not trying to be difficult or self-defeating or whatever. But, only... only me... and your fiancée?"

"Oh god," he muttered as he turned to look out at the passing streetlights. "Mari."

"Ugh, she even has a cute nickname," Abigail said as she rolled off his lap and settled into the seat next to him.

"This was all her idea."

"What?!"

"Not this." He gestured with a quick dismissive flick at his opened shirt and her mussed hair. "I mean, I told her last week that I wanted to postpone or cancel the wedding—"

"You did?" Abigail was momentarily thrilled that she wasn't entirely to blame for destroying poor Marisa's dreams. It was easier to think of her as Poor Marisa now that Abigail had won. She could afford to remember that her name was Plataneau and not Platypus, now that she was in a position to pity her.

"Yes, I did." He smiled, but it was tinged with sadness. "And she told me she didn't want to call it off, but that she just thought I needed to get you out of my system."

"She knows about me?" Abigail was mortified. She felt like a home wrecker. "You left her for me?"

"Well, I guess, I mean." He paused to choose his words. "Yes. I left her to make sure. About you."

"I still feel like a rotter. If it hadn't been for me, you two—"

"No. There wouldn't have been a *you two*. This was never about you personally, but I told her that I had been involved with someone before I met her and that my feelings were... unresolved."

"Are they?"

"Are they what?"

"Are your feelings unresolved?"

"How can you even ask that?" He was instantly angry. "Stop that. Of course they're not unresolved. When you put your hand on my arm earlier tonight—no, when I saw you in the window at the Ritz—the first thought I had wasn't even a thought, it was pure conviction. Finally! At last! Complete resolution."

It made her so happy to hear how his determination mirrored hers; it was profoundly gratifying. But the guilt about Poor Marisa made her look at her clasped hands in her lap rather than let Eliot see her gloating pleasure.

"You like the sound of that, don't you? Get back here." He grabbed her back onto his lap.

"I do like the sound of words like *resolution*"—she reached her cool hand back on to the warm skin of his chest—"and *conviction*"—she trailed the thumb of her other hand over his bottom lip—"coming out of your mouth in reference to your feelings for me." Her thumb dipped into the silky warmth of his mouth. "I have been living in a hellish half-life of irresolute confusion for so long." She gave her hips a provocative twist. "Hard certainty feels really good for a change."

# Chapter 14

WHEREAS A YEAR AGO, Abigail had worried and fretted about everything from her mother knowing she might not be sleeping in her own room to the night porter at the Plaza Athénée suspecting she was a hooker, at this point, she wouldn't have cared if Eliot had dragged her across the soaring marble and gilt lobby with a prehistoric club in one hand and a clump of her hair in the other. He walked quickly toward the elevator, her hand in his; she stumbled and laughed a couple of times as the four-inch heels of Sarah's boots combined with her giddy excitement to transform her into an uncoordinated, spastic schoolgirl.

"I never thought of you as a giggler."

"I am not giggling. That was a sexy, throaty laugh."

He tugged her along with more urgency. "It was definitely a giggle."

Just then, the tip of her boot caught the edge of one of the thick Oriental runners that covered the marble floor on the way to the elevator banks. Eliot pulled more firmly on the hand he was holding and reached under her other arm to steady her, then took her into a perfectly orchestrated embrace. "Am I going to have to carry you across the lobby?" he whispered as he nuzzled deeper into her thick, dark hair.

"I wouldn't mind if you did."

Baited, Eliot whipped her up into the cradle of his arms for the final ten strides to the elevator bank. Abigail shrieked, then quaked with silent laughter. She buried her face into the warm, clean scent of his neck and chest, as much to hide her face as to simply relish the careless, public intimacy that she had been hiding from the world, from herself, for so long.

Once inside the elevator, he pushed the button for his floor then lowered Abigail's tight, small frame along the full length of his front. He closed his eyes and appreciated the textures as they passed along his palms and fingertips, the fitted denim on her legs, the smooth silk of her blouse, the inviting heat of the skin of her neck. She was hugging him around his waist, her cheek resting against his heart.

He moved a piece of her hair aside to get a better look at her cheek. "I forgot you were so petite. You had become so huge in my mind. You are really just a wisp of a thing."

"And you are just exactly as formidable and delicious as I remembered. I kept thinking," she spoke into the fabric of his shirt, "that when I saw you in real life, it would dispel all of my crazy fantasies—"

"Ah, yes, the crazy fantasies—"

"Because, let's face it, I thought, no one could possibly live up to the crazy fantasies. And that would be the end of it. The reality of you would surely prove a disappointment." She looked up at him with a mixture of tenderness and mischief. She trailed her hand along the placket over his zipper, savoring the feel of him, hard, in her palm. "More fool me."

Eliot closed his eyes and groaned his appreciation. The elevator doors opened on his floor and brought them both back to some semblance of the present. They held hands and didn't speak as they walked down the plush carpet of the corridor. Abigail's heart was starting to hammer again. She had thought the initial palpitations at La Coupole might have been some sort of one-off shock effect, but apparently tachycardia was to be a regular component of her life with Eliot.

An involuntary smile of incandescent joy spread over her face. *Her life with Eliot.*

He was holding the door open to his room. "What are you smiling about, beauty?"

"I was just remarking to myself that we might need to have an attendant cardiologist because my heart seems to pound when I'm around you. And then I thought, oh well, that will just be part of *my life with Eliot.* And then I thought, that has a very nice ring to it. My. Life. With. Eliot."

Eliot shut the door with more force then he'd intended, causing it to startle them both when it struck the jamb. He grabbed Abigail with all the drive and power he'd been holding at bay— on the beach in Bequia, on his parents' couch in Iowa—and that he'd only just begun to hint at a year ago in this very city.

He pulled her shirt off in a whisk of motion and stopped, stunned, at the sight of her lacy bra.

"My, my. What have we here?"

She flushed from her chest, right up her neck to her burning cheeks.

"Have you been lingerie shopping without me again?" His finger slipped under the delicate lace and the edge of the cup, then along the satin ribbon that trailed over her shoulders.

She nodded and hummed, unable to speak amid the crashing waves brought on by his touch.

"Lovely. Perfectly lovely. I've never seen anything like it."

"I had it made," she whispered. "It was appallingly expensive."

Eliot laughed. "Turn around. I want to see it. I want to see you in it."

She moaned again and gave in to all the pleasure that welled up inside her when Eliot wanted to look at her like that.

"Exquisite. You are exquisite, Abigail."

The bra came off a few seconds later. He bent his head to her breast and kissed one exposed tip, barely touching his lips against the tender, sensitive nipple. He licked a gentle circle around the hard nub, then grazed it between his teeth, in a near painful repetitive abrading.

Abigail hadn't caught her breath since they were walking down the hall. She was holding one hand in his, and her other had a desperate grip on his thick, wavy hair. She groaned his name as she rode the intense sensations. He lowered himself to his knees to better contend with removing the provocative suede boots that Sarah had insisted she wear.

"That woman is an agent of evil," he grumbled as his fingers fought with the tiny button closures that ran up the inside of Abigail's calf.

"I think she has some distorted vision of patient lovers when she creates them," Abigail spoke on her exhale.

Eliot took a deep breath to refocus his efforts. He got the boots off with persistence, then nearly tore off Abigail's jeans and—exquisite, lovely, matching—underwear. He was kneeling back on his heels, fully clothed, in front of her perfectly naked body.

He grabbed her hips and looked up into her eyes. "I adore you, Abigail." He leaned into her lower stomach and kissed the tender skin just above her thatch of hair. He dipped his tongue into her navel, then kissed his way gently down. His hands held her pinned against the wall in the small entryway of his suite. The lights were dim, except for a lamp somewhere in the main living room farther inside.

His hot breath teased her mercilessly. The closer he got to her throbbing center, the slower he went. Inhaling her scent, nuzzling into the skin, licking at the tender flesh of her upper thigh. He kept zeroing in and then meandering farther away. She began to whimper with desire. She felt the moisture of her own eagerness begin to slip down the inside of her thigh. "Please, Eliot," she whispered.

He shoved her legs wider apart and thrust his tongue into her, feeling the beginning of her climax after only a few seconds. He nipped at her, licked and delved until she was crying out for him, holding his head in a rough grip as he held her, his arms wrapped around the back of her waist for support. He kept slipping his tongue across her slick flesh, causing her orgasm to go on and on, taking her far beyond anything she could fathom.

Beyond herself.

Quaking in his arms, she finally collapsed over his broad, strong shoulders, softly crying his name in low, begging, repetitive pleas.

He finally gave her one last gentle stroke of his tongue and rested his cheek against her moist, beautiful center. He inhaled, to catch his breath and to take her in, to consume her through all of his senses. His own desire was making him so hard against his pants that he wasn't sure he could stand up easily, but Abigail's first sweet surrender was enough incentive for him to get them both into the large waiting bed in the other room.

He carried her in a fireman's hold over his right shoulder, her limp arms hanging down his back. He pulled back the covers at one side of the bed and set her down with a careful slowness. Her eyes fluttered open momentarily and she smiled at him as he looked down at her. She moved one hand up to her own face, having a momentary desire to shield herself from the strength of his love, then thought better of it and flung her arm wide across the nearby pillow. She closed her eyes and arched her back up toward him, stretching, offering, welcoming him to her body. When she reopened her eyes, he had taken all his clothes off except his close-fitting boxers. He was running his thumb around the elastic waist. Abigail felt that all of her senses were so heightened, she could actually hear the slight friction of the small hairs on his lower stomach as he scratched past them in that maddeningly leisurely gesture. She found it delightfully arousing and crawled, catlike, onto all fours and looked up at him. "Do you need help with those?"

"Why yes. I think I do," he said as he let his hands move away and hang at his side.

She scooted up closer to the edge of the bed and rose up on her knees. He was still far taller, but it was a perfect angle to see him in all his masculine glory. His erection was straining against the soft pale blue cotton, and Abigail let her thoughts fly away and her body took over.

She was going to devour him. Finally. No more parsing. No more gender politics. No more worry. It was simply the person she loved the most in the world and she was going to show him that love in every possible manifestation of desire. Devotion.

She bent her head, rested her hands at his hips, and nipped at the fabric over his cock. He began stroking the smooth skin of her bare back, his fingers lightly tracing her spine, as she let her curiosity and her love take shape. She reached her hands around to the hard muscles of his backside, her hands going up under the fabric at the top of his thighs. The transition from the fine rasp of hair on his legs to the supple curve of his ass set Abigail's heart thudding again, and she must have released an involuntary hum of pleasure.

"Aaah, the humming…" Eliot whispered, as if he had just discovered a well in the midst of a days-long journey across the desert. He let his own hands mirror what she was doing to him, stretching his palms to conform to the roundness of her hips and bottom, letting his thumb venture tantalizingly close to the tender, pink flesh between the cheeks of her ass.

"That"—Abigail's voice was strained and hoarse—"is the limit." She ripped off his underwear as if it were the most offensive, despicable thing on earth.

Eliot worried for a second that Abigail had been uncomfortable that he was touching her in such a provocative fashion, until she made quick work of taking him fully into her mouth and letting her own hand reach around him to grip and pull and dip into his. His head flew back in the sheer pleasure of feeling, his thoughts a mixture of half-formed phrases including words like: *Beauty. Love. Joy. Abigail.*

He looked down as her head moved in time with the rhythm of her mouth and tongue. He ran his right hand through her gorgeous black hair, his left hand remaining on her lower back. Right before he was about to lose it, he wrenched her head back with a quick tug of her hair and she smiled up at him, licking her lips, savoring the feel of him there, her gray eyes nearly black with pleasure, blinking lovingly up at him.

"I am so happy, Eliot. I never knew I could be this happy."

He stared at her in simple wonder. "I will make you so happy, Abigail." He tossed her flat on her back in a light, careless motion, then straddled her hips and knelt over her, stretching her arms taut above her head. "I will do anything, everything, to see this expression on your face, every day, all day." He reached across to the drawer in the bedside table and she took the opportunity to lick his nipple as he leaned in close and stretched to get the condom.

"Good god, Abigail. You are better than anything." He stayed stretching over her as she continued to lick and scrape at his nipple until it was a small, hard nub in her mouth.

He hissed as he forced himself to exhale, leaning back between her thighs, on his heels, to tear the packet and put the condom on. When he finished, he looked up and saw her eyes on him. "Are you ready for me, Abigail?"

"Oh, Eliot." A single tear slid out of one eye, and she turned her head as if to hide it from him.

He grabbed her jaw with gentle force, making her look directly at him. "Tell me you want me now, Abigail."

She shut her eyes for a moment, as if she could somehow contain or manage the riptide of emotion. When she opened her eyes, more tears slid down her temple. "I have always wanted you, Eliot," her voice cracked, "but never more than right now. In this moment, you are... everything."

His eyes never left hers as his hand moved from her face to

make a slow trail up the length of her sinuous arm. He stretched himself along the length of her, imagining that he could feel every molecular connection, every atom of their shared experience. Everywhere they touched created new, combined matter. He was no longer Eliot; she was no longer Abigail. They were something new and glorious together.

He kissed her slowly on the lips, his tongue a tentative flicker across her lower lip. "It is now, Abigail. Okay?"

She nodded.

"Tell me." His voice was low and hot in her ear. "I want to hear your beautiful, lilting voice as I come to you. I have never felt this close to anyone."

"Please, yes, my beautiful Eliot, yes—" She gasped as he thrust full into her in one fluid motion of powerful joining.

He watched as her pupils dilated, adjusting to the reality, the physical reality of his body melding with hers. At first, he held himself perfectly still, as much as his body raged against pausing for any reason. Soon his blood would demand satisfaction, but for a few moments—seconds or minutes, he didn't know—he would freeze this moment in time: the first moment of their life wholly together.

He made an exact mental picture of how her irises glowed silver, edging the deep, telling black of her pupils; how her thick black eyelashes were perfectly still. The slow flick of her tongue at the corner of her mouth that presaged a quick intake of breath, as if she was quite literally making space in her soul to accommodate him, to welcome him into her being.

"I love you, Abigail," he said. "It's so perfectly obvious now, isn't it?"

Another tear slipped down her cheek and she smiled a small grateful smile. He started to pull away, only to begin the rhythm their bodies demanded, but a flash of beautiful, desperate longing blinked across Abigail's face.

"Please don't move. It's so perfect."

"It will only get better. I promise." He moved slightly to show her, gently pulling away then tilting his hips to touch her exactly where they both knew she needed to be touched.

She felt the initial tightness begin to fade.

"That's it," he said, urging her on. "Just relax into me."

And she did.

She let him drive her body like he would drive a machine. He guided her pleasure, leading her, until she was meeting his every parry and thrust, arching her hard, narrow hips into his, throwing her head back in a state of abandon that she never could have imagined (even in any of those crazy fantasies). He had her strung so tight, she thought she would break. His lips and teeth and a slight roughness from the new growth of his beard set her breasts ablaze. Her nipples felt like they were connected to her core—every quick kiss or long pull he gave them sent her deeper, tighter, further into this realm of striking pleasure.

Every part of her took him, made him her own. She rose to meet him again and again.

When she felt she could no longer postpone the culmination of their shared joy, the final consummation of all the waiting and wanting, she lifted her hips to his, as a demand and a gift, offering herself to him, taking, giving. Then she simply tipped over the edge of the world, annihilated, lost to everything but him. Her voice, a distant, foreign shriek, became woven together with his guttural roar of triumph, an ancient, deeply familiar cry.

Not very long after, *too soon, really,* thought Abigail, he was pulling away from her and making shuffling noises with the condom and the tissues from the bedside table. She turned on her side and put her hands flat between her cheek and the pillow, and simply marveled at the corded strength of his back. She thought she could while away the rest of her life watching that play of muscle and skin a few inches from her face.

He must have thought she had dozed off because his eyes widened in surprise when he turned back to see her perfectly awake and staring in his direction.

"Oh, you're still awake."

"Quite."

He stared at her eyes, seeing the familiar mischief returning; he looked forward to the next time he could bring her to that place of black and silver magic.

"Why are you staring so intently at my eyes?" she asked.

"Because they are delightfully revealing."

"Tell me how."

"In the mood to be flattered, are you?"

She warmed to his touch as his hand moved languidly along the curve of her hip, blinking slowly to encourage him. "Mm-hmmm."

"Well, when you are all business, like when I first came over to the table at the restaurant tonight, and you didn't know if I was going to fall at your feet or fail to acknowledge you at all, they were cool, opaque, steely gray. Your pupils were tiny pinpricks. No access." His hand continued soothing her body as his words soothed her soul. "Then, when I took a bit of what I wanted in the hall by the *toilettes*, or you gave or whatever—I want to address that giving and taking business in a minute—but at that moment, the slow molten silver of your eyes started to shimmer." His hand reached up to trace the delicate peak of her eyebrow. "Then, when you were on your knees, on the bed, taking me with your lips and tongue and—"

She buried her face in the pillow, embarrassed by his retelling. Had she been so eager?

He pulled her face back where it had been, the two of them inches apart, simply talking. "It was the most beautiful sight. Please don't ever turn it into anything else. You were so beautiful and you were so happy and making me so happy, and you were like a wild seductress, a sorceress, with black, knowing eyes, eyes that knew pleasure, that knew *my* pleasure—and yours, I think—to the very depths of our souls." He touched a piece of her hair and rubbed it between his index finger and thumb, just as he had done on the beach in Bequia. "And then, when we came together, I felt I could see everything, the whole galaxy, multiple universes, there in your silver eyes."

He kissed each of her eyelids in silent affirmation.

They stayed there, inches from one another, for many hours. Abigail got up to go to the bathroom, or to get a bottle of water, but they spent the rest of that night simply lying next to one another within the soft, cool perimeter of their private world. Sometimes they spoke at length about trivial things—foods they adored, their opposing views on naps, places they wanted to visit—other times, they talked about profundities—children, commitment, family. Yes. Yes. And yes.

When the morning sun began to impart a promising, evocative light, Abigail, who must have been dozing, got up to go to the bathroom and to pull a juice from the minibar. When she came back to stand at the foot of the bed, Eliot was sitting up, the sheets pulled loosely to his waist, covering his firm legs and, Abigail thought with a touch of greed, all the good parts.

"Why are you covered?" Abigail asked. "I don't like you covered," she added with a petulant look.

"I was just wondering, why didn't you ever tell me you were a virgin, you know, last year when we got together?"

She kept still, standing at the end of the bed, holding the compact green glass bottle of French peach juice in both hands, as if the cool container anchored her to the spot.

"You were a virgin." Not a question.

"No, I wasn't."

"Abigail, please. After everything, just be honest. Why would you hide that?"

"I wasn't hiding anything!" She was suddenly angry. "It's such a preposterous construct. I was in a sexually *complete* relationship with someone for over a decade. It's patently ridiculous to act as if I was somehow *unsullied.*" She said the last word as if it were poison on her lips.

"That's not what this is about."

"Really, Eliot? You might want to check with your centuries—millennia!—of patriarchy and get back to me on that. You think it's not about my purity? The very word is loaded with misdirection and false meaning: *virginity.* Think about it!"

Eliot smiled and got out of bed as her ire escalated. He came up behind her. She couldn't possibly stay mad at him—if she ever was to begin with—when his warm, strong body rubbed up against her back, his hands circling around her in a safe hold. She sighed and leaned back into him on reflex. He was near; ergo, she bent toward him, like a plant to the sun.

"Oh, Abigail. You're such an idiot."

Her eyes were placidly closed as she relaxed into his immovable strength. "Thanks for the heads-up."

"Of course I don't give a crap about any of that other virginity bullshit—purity, preservation, what have you—but I might have proceeded at a slightly more well-considered pace if you'd just let me know. I reamed you, for goodness' sake. I practically nailed you to the goddamned bed."

She smiled as she felt her stomach roll at the pleasant prospect of being impaled by Eliot. Skewered by lust. *Love*, she corrected. She wanted him to do everything to her: to have his way with her, to attack her, to ravish her, to slam his being into hers.

"You are so naughty," he whispered in her ear as she tilted her neck and smiled even more broadly, eyes still closed. "You want me to take you like that, don't you?" He bit and licked his way down her warm neck.

"I would very much rather you didn't make me admit it." Her prim voice was the epitome of upper-crust patrician formality. "But yes."

Eliot burst into uncontrollable peals of laughter and tightened his embrace around her upper arms. Opening herself up to every possible permutation of their love, every possible ramification, standing there in his arms, holding the small bottle of juice, it was almost more intimate than their actual lovemaking.

Abigail's knee-jerk anger to his questioning her virginity stemmed entirely from her misconception that he valued that idea or gave it false importance for reasons that would have appalled her. "I'm sorry, Eliot. I seem to be the one who is constantly selling you short."

He kept nipping at her neck and ear. "You don't need to apologize." He sucked at the tender skin below her ear and then at the base of her neck, then said, "I've had an entire year to come to terms with the fact that you are a bigoted, narrow-minded misandrist."

She pulled out of his arms and turned to glare at him. "Take that back. I am the most open-minded person you'll ever meet." Abigail set the bottle of juice down on a nearby end table and folded her arms across her bare chest, feeling—suddenly—a touch defensive and very naked.

Eliot had no compunction about his nudity, strolling over to a large sofa and sitting down as if he were sporting his best Italian suit, one foot set casually across the opposite knee.

"I won't take back the truth, Abigail." He looked at the back of his hand vaguely.

At least she was partially concealed from the waist down by one of the side chairs that separated the seating area from the sleeping area. She wanted to go to the closet and throw on one of the plush hotel robes, some flimsy defense, but it seemed like that would be admitting defeat.

"Eliot! It's me, Abigail! How can you possibly accuse me of being a bigot?"

"You have a heart of gold for every underdog, Abigail. But the rest of us, well, we are simply guilty."

She huffed a small, dismissive breath. What he said was too absurd to countermand. Wasn't it?

"That just can't be true!" She was adamant, but there was the slightest hint of uncertainty. She wanted Eliot to absolve her.

"Abigail, just face it and let's move on. You were the one—granted, I probably appeared quite accommodating—who assumed I would shag you and call it a day. You were the one, minutes ago, who assumed I craved knowledge of your pristine hymen as some medieval badge of your worthiness or some shit. I have never pigeonholed you. Well, almost never. And you seem perfectly content to lump me together with every outdated Cro-Magnon chauvinist archetype. Admit it. Or don't." Then he shrugged, implying that the truth was self-evident and her admission or denial did nothing to alter it.

She bit her lower lip, hard, in a painful attempt to fend off the truth. It was just too ugly, especially after such a glorious, beautiful night. Why would he be so cavalier about what a despicable person she was? After all that? All the soft conversation and lovemaking?

She gave a bark of a laugh as the painful tears started to throb at the back of her eyes, then slid down her cheeks. "I suppose, now that we are properly entwined and you can see clear through me, I'd better give myself over to the fact that I've become what is commonly known as a crier." She swiped at a stray tear before it became verifiable weeping.

Eliot was rubbing the pale gray silk brocade of the seat cushion next to him. At first, it had been an absentminded tactile gesture, but when he caught Abigail's eye, he sort of patted and stroked the seat cushion in an inviting circular motion. "Come."

Whether it was the commanding timbre of his voice, the double entendre, or the inviting look in his eye, Abigail looked up through wet lashes and felt the tension and heat of her physical response. She wanted him again. Her arms dropped away from their protective, defiant position across her chest. She wanted Eliot to see all of her as she walked toward him, as she came to him. She crossed the few yards between them, then stood, naked and willing, before him. "Where do you want me?"

He sat staring at her as if she were a runway model he was considering for the shows later in the week. Bloodstock. A possible investment. Her eyes were at once stormy and submissive as he continued to contemplate her, to objectify her. He leaned forward and trailed the edge of one fingernail from the base of her neck to the warm, moist mound between her legs. The light touch left her scorched. Eliot let the pressure linger, taunting her, and watched her eyes flutter in pleasure then return to some attempt of steely resolve.

"Give in, Abigail." There was nothing diplomatic about the way Eliot spoke to her. He was all business. Taking her in hand. His finger tarried at the needy little bud, then slid farther back. "You want me to do everything to you, don't you?"

Her body quaked in agreement, but her mind was half a step behind, one foot stuck in a quagmire of rhetoric and theory. What did it mean that she wanted to submit every cell in her body to the loving care of this man? She wanted that. He wanted to give her that. Why was she *still* looking for reasons for that to be *wrong*?

His finger began a merciless slide, back and forth, from front to back, toying with her, tempting her, bringing her to a new desperation. Not just physical. It felt moral, ethical, beyond anything she could have anticipated or imagined.

He wanted to take every last bit of her.

And she wanted to give it.

She reached up to her breasts and palmed their weight in her hands, holding her nipples between her thumbs and fingers, mirroring Eliot's lazy tempo between her legs. She rolled the needy tips in the same back-and-forth motion. Eliot's breath hitched.

She would give him every ounce of her being.

And then take every piece of him in her turn.

"Yes," was all she said.

# Chapter 15

ABIGAIL FELT LIKE THAT dead gilt Bond girl in *Goldfinger*. She was splayed listlessly across the huge bed, spread eagle on her stomach, shamelessly nude, one arm hanging off the side, her mess of black hair flung across the pillow and partially concealing her face.

Eliot came out of the bathroom and stopped to take in the erotic tableau. "Jesus, Abigail," he whispered. He stalked around the bed to get a better look at her slack-jawed expression of bliss, carefully moving aside a lock of her hair to better see her face. She was in her netherworld: a place that Eliot now adored, the half-sleeping-half-waking zone she collapsed into after her most powerful orgasms. Her body fully sated, warm, and flushed. Her lips slightly parted. Her tongue making the occasional, lazy reminiscent foray to the corner of her mouth. Her eyelids were closed, but pulsing as if the visions of pleasure and satisfaction were replaying there behind the tender skin.

He smiled to himself as he contemplated the never-ending vortex of pleasure the two of them could devolve into. When he saw her like this, he wanted her more vehemently than ever. And so it began again, her gentle denouement serving only to ignite him anew.

Eliot breathed a small sigh of displeasure; the cycle had to be broken just now. Eliot had a full day of meetings and preparations for the various Danieli-Fauchard clothing labels that were showing this week. Of course, his brand managers and salespeople and marketing people were in charge of everything, but his presence was expected everywhere, especially with the major buyers from the high-end department stores and the top editors from London, New York, Paris, Milan, and Tokyo.

Marcel might have been a bit of a pup when it came to dealing with Eliot's demanding fiancée (Eliot stuffed the attendant guilt that spiraled up as he thought of Marisa), but his Swiss assistant was a genius when it came to scheduling. All Helvetican clockwork comparisons aside, Marcel had put together seven days of perfectly orchestrated breakfasts, morning meetings, lunches, afternoon meetings, cocktails, dinners—not to mention allowing for Eliot's presence at all the requisite fashion shows.

Eliot picked up his phone and checked his schedule for the day, then looked across at Abigail's tempting body. He had already showered, he might have time for a quick—

He shook himself of that foolishness and walked determinedly to the hotel closet with his neat selection of clothes. Since it was still the weekend, he opted for a clean pair of Fauchard blue jeans, a checked shirt from his shirtmaker in Rome, and a cashmere sweater from Ramazzotti. Something about finally closing that deal put his mind back to his first time with Abigail in Paris. Maybe she was right. Maybe it had been too soon then, too raw. The timing between them was off.

But now.

He sat down to check a few emails on his laptop then turned the desk chair so he could enjoy the view of Abigail's ass, still slightly raised how he had left her. Finally forcing himself to look away, he methodically laced up his favorite worn-in brown calfskin brogues. Eliot set his feet down when he was done, placed his hands on his knees, and inhaled deeply.

He had to go.

He got up and crossed back to stand over Abigail. "Hey, beautiful.

Wake up." He caressed her cheek, then pushed her disobedient hair back out of the way so he could enjoy one last unimpeded view of her gorgeous face.

"Mmmmm."

"I agree, but I have to go."

"Mmmm, Eliot…"

"Well, yes, it is." He was dragging his index finger across her bottom lip, loving the feel of the satin edge, loving the memory of everywhere her mouth had touched him. He groaned and pulled his finger away as she tried to suck it into her mouth. "You are quite demanding."

She opened her eyes slowly to look at him, her lids heavy with sleep and luxury. "And you are so good at meeting them." She rolled onto her back, eyes closed again, and stretched out her entire body, arms extended toward the headboard, legs fully tensed and feet in full point.

She was pulled as taut as an archer's bow.

It was a physical, methodical gesture that she probably did every morning, but in that moment, Eliot had never seen anything more soul-satisfying. He reached his hand out, as if in a dream, and let his palm rest on her flattened stomach.

Her eyes flew open and she laughed at his touch.

"I am going to be so groggy today," she croaked.

"Unfortunately, I cannot be groggy with you. I have more meetings in the next seven days than I have had in the past month. Our timing, as usual, is not the best."

His hand stayed on her stomach as he sat down on the edge of the bed. "I'm afraid to get any closer to you or I won't have the willpower to resist. Give me a kiss and wish me well and get the hotel to move all your things up to this room. Here's an extra key for you." He gestured toward the bedside table where the Ritz key card sat next to a glass of water. "What else?"

"You are stupendous. Marvelous. I can't think of enough words. I adore you." She leaned up on one arm and flung the other around his neck, pulling him in for a quick kiss. "I shan't keep you. Go be your powerful, captain-of-industry self and just think of me every now and then."

"Ha! If only it were now and then, perhaps I'd be moderately productive this week. As it is, I will be so distracted by the thought of you, the vision of you, as you looked when I came out of the bathroom just now—legs akimbo, arms flung out—I will be half-present at best. But present I must be. So kiss me one more time then release me."

She leaned up again and kissed him gently on the lips, then on his neck, inhaling deeply, to take in the smell of him. "Just to tide me over," she added, mimicking his words of the night before.

Eliot pulled his hand away from the warm silky skin of her abdomen and stood up reluctantly. "I am literally scheduled for every minute of every day. Do you want to come to any of the shows, or any of the cocktail parties or dinners? Some of them might be fun."

She tilted her head a bit in consideration. "You know, I kind of like the idea of being your secret love slave, sequestered here in the room, available." She winked at him. "But if you want me to trail after you on a satin leash, I'm happy to do that too."

"You are so *not* what people think you are, by the way. Incorrigible."

She laughed with seductive, mischievous humor. "It only matters that I'm everything *you* think I am."

"Absolutely. All right, then, stay here and be my kept woman for the rest of your stay. I'll return like the conquering hero every night to claim my favor." He pulled on a lightweight khaki-colored coat and put his slim wallet, phone, and room key into the pockets. "Be good." He winked and was gone.

Abigail wasn't sure if she had been asleep for minutes or hours when the phone started ringing. She ignored it. It was still Eliot's room after all. The last thing she needed was Poor Marisa calling from Africa to fine-tune wedding arrangements. Unfortunately, it didn't stop ringing. It would pause for a few seconds then resume another lengthy, repetitive chorus of infernal ringing. During one of the brief pauses, she picked up the phone and called down to the front desk.

"Bonjour."

"Uh, hello. I was just, um, visiting Mr. Cranbrook's room and the phone seems to be malfunctioning. Is there something wrong?"

The poor Frenchman cleared his throat and began carefully, "Excuse me, but ah, the Miss Sarah James was trying to reach, the guest of Mr. Cranbrook—"

An audible scuffle of the phone being wrenched from the appalled concierge and then Sarah: "What is Eliot's room number, Abby? Your cell phone is going straight to voice mail. This is ridiculous!"

Abigail tried not to laugh as she told her the number and put the phone back in the cradle. She looked around the room with fresh, practical eyes and made a clumsy, quick attempt to do away with at least the most egregious evidence of the past few hours: a condom wrapper that was peeking out from the edge of the bedskirt, and her silky underthings hanging half-off the edge of a side chair. The rest of her clothes she put in a neat-ish pile in the bathroom, and then she grabbed one of the enormous Turkish bathrobes out of the closet. She went back to the bed to yank the comforter atop the tangled sheets, in a feeble effort to cover the scene of the crime. As the duvet settled, a slight puff of air came to Abigail that was entirely Eliot. She closed her eyes to savor the small evocative moment, then tried to fortify herself when her sister-in-law's insistent tap-tap-tap sounded through the door.

Abigail must have looked like exactly what she was: a well-used lover.

Sarah stood, stunned, staring at her through the opened door-jamb. "Who are you?"

"Very funny. Are you planning on coming in or simply judging me from the corridor?"

"I haven't decided," Sarah folded her arms. "Is it all sex-foggy in there?"

"What did you just say?" Abigail laughed and covered her mouth to hide her embarrassment. "Just don't go near the bed and I think you'll be fine." Abigail opened the door wider and pulled Sarah into the room.

Sarah looked into the bathroom and then around the perimeter of the entire room, as if someone might jump out from behind a sofa or curtain at any moment.

"Sarah, Eliot left ages ago—"

"I know, I saw him at the shows this morning. I wish I had remembered to ask him his room number so I wouldn't have had to go through all that phone ringing business with the concierge. When I got back to our room and there wasn't a note or anything, I assumed you were still here… languishing."

Abigail smiled. "Quite."

"I'm trying so hard to be, you know, gracious, and not ask for sordid details, but you look so damned happy, I think you have to give me a tiny morsel. Was he fabulous?"

Abigail blushed and felt a range of strange, unexpected emotions. She didn't want to talk about Eliot, on the one hand, and diminish the importance of what had passed between them. Idle gossip might trivialize her profound experience.

But.

What they had shared, or created, or discovered last night was so incandescent, so intensely life-affirming, that Abigail felt it welling up and exuding out of every pore. She didn't even need to say anything, her physical being simply shone.

She looked up tentatively at Sarah through sleepy dark lashes.

Sarah took an involuntary breath. "Oh. My. As good as all that?"

Abigail smiled another conspiratorial grin and nodded her silent answer. She felt the skin on her neck prick and realized that she was not just conspiring with Sarah; she wanted to conspire with the whole human race. Her joy felt infinite and peaceful.

Sarah inhaled slowly and tightened her eyes. "Well. That about says it, doesn't it? Do you want to move your stuff up here or just have the hotel do it?"

"Would you mind? I mean, if I stayed here in Eliot's room? I know you were into the whole girls-week-out and all that."

"You're such an idiot. Of course I would rather you stay with Eliot, but I couldn't very well come out and say that when I invited you, now could I?"

"You're such a duplicitous scoundrel... what is the female equivalent of a scoundrel? Witch?"

"Never say so! I'm a loving, guiding hand... gently directing you toward your happy fate."

"That's one way of describing it. Did you really just bump into Eliot yesterday at the pool?"

"I swear. I never called him about you or said a word. That was all divine intervention."

With how divine Abigail felt, she half believed her.

"Anyway, what are you up to the rest of the day?" Abigail tried to shake out her hair and shake off the residual glow of Eliot's touch. Her entire body felt like it was humming everywhere he had kissed her, which was, well, everywhere.

"I suppose I could accompany you," Sarah said, "and your salacious mind around town. Shall we go see your mother and Jack for tea or dinner? I already have plans to see my grandmother later tomorrow. What are you in the mood for?"

Abigail flushed again.

"Change back into your clothes, you harlot. Come pack up your stuff and have the porter bring it here, then we can go out for a gorgeous late lunch. You have almost slept away one of the most beautiful winter days on record. Let's get you out into the bright beautiful world so you can shine your light."

———

A week later, Marisa Plataneau was perturbed. The three-week trip to Tanzania had been a success, obviously. The school project had broken ground, the local officials were working surprisingly well with the aid workers. But she was ready for it to be over. She wasn't prissy when it came to staying in malaria-infested jungles or in Southeast Asian lean-tos with roaches the size of her laptop, but getting stuck in the Frankfurt airport for a six-hour layover when she was so close to home was simply too much. Everyone had their limits, and the Lufthansa frequent-flyer lounge after six hours was apparently hers.

She reset her expression to let the frustration drain slightly, then continued, "Yes, you have told me that the missing part is being installed. But that was already happening four hours ago. Perhaps I might simply retrieve my luggage and be on my way?"

"That is not possible. The luggage must remain in the hold of the plane. We cannot pick and choose from the luggage. If you would like to take a train back to Geneva, then you may do so, but without your luggage."

"That is not possible," Marisa parroted, then gave a mirror image of the small, thin line of a smile that Saskia-the-Berlin-Wall had recently presented to her. "I can't leave without my luggage."

"Then that is your choice," she said, then returned to typing what Marisa was certain were meaningless keystrokes.

What? Was this woman a nursery school disciplinarian? Her choice?

Marisa turned away from the yellow counter in disgust and returned to her seat in the corner of the lounge. The smell of strong, stale coffee permeated the lounge and made her want to gag. She opened her boring book and tried to pass the time.

"May I sit here?" A male voice inquired.

Mari looked up. *Hmmm. What do you know? Tall. Lean. Inquisitive gray eyes with long black lashes. Nice accent.* "Sure. Go ahead," she answered, letting her eyes skid away from the sharp turn of his jaw, then looked at her bare left hand with a twinge of... something. She never wore her engagement ring when she traveled to war-torn, third-world destinations. Not only because of the threat of theft, but also because the harsh disparity between her wealth and their poverty did not need to be brought into such glaring relief. It seemed disgusting somehow. Now that she was back in Europe, however, she felt kind of bare without it.

Whatever. This handsome young man to her left was just sitting in a spare seat, not hitting on her.

She certainly wouldn't hit on her, if she were him. She looked down at her scuffed Doc Martens, khaki safari pants, long-sleeved fitted black T-shirt and shook her head. She looked like an ill-used car mechanic.

"Everything all right?" he asked.

She tried to place his accent... plummy, upper-crust, British.

"Well, I was raised not to be a complainer, but I am, if not complaining, on the verge of being very, very peeved."

And then he smiled a fabulous, spontaneous, velvety ooh-la-la smile and burst out laughing.

Marisa had never been prone to butterflies or flutterings of any sort, so she grabbed at her stomach, thinking that the fourth double espresso might not have been such a good idea. But when that rolling laugh came to an abrupt end, so did her stomach's response to the putative caffeine overdose.

"You have a very nice laugh," she said without thinking.

He was still holding his copy of the *Financial Times* opened wide in front of most of his torso, looking at her curiously over the top. Then he folded the paper, letting one finger rest in the section to hold his place.

"Have we met before?"

"I don't think so." Marisa felt a brief wave of cool suspicion. Maybe he *was* just hitting on her.

"Sorry, did that sound like I was hitting on you?"

"A bit."

"Shall I go back to reading my paper?"

"No!" Marisa answered with far too much eagerness. "I mean, no. I have been sitting here for six hours, with the dust of sub-Saharan Africa still gritting in the seams of my pants, and I have not had a pleasant word in that entire time. If I have to speak to Saskia the Lufthansa taskmistress one more time, I'm not sure both of us will come out alive."

He folded his *Financial Times* neatly and put it down on the small built-in table that separated the two of them. He reached out his hand and introduced himself. "James Mowbray, pleasure to meet you. No one should have to suffer through the Lufthansa lounge alone."

She reached her bare, unadorned hand out to shake his, and, after a quick up and down motion, she was quite reluctant to let go. He wasn't holding on to her exactly, but he certainly wasn't letting go either. She looked down at his hand then up to his face and smiled. *I'm engaged,* she almost blurted out, then was relieved she hadn't, then she was guilty she was relieved.

She pulled her hand back into her lap and resisted the urge to smooth her hair. It was probably as worn and frayed as the rest of her, but that didn't seem to be the least bit disappointing to one James Mowbray.

After all of her years in the United States, Marisa's accent sounded almost entirely American. She had never been able to fully master the very round *r*, but Eliot said it was a sexy touch and not to try too hard to rid herself of it.

Eliot. Her fiancé.

She was alone and bored in a foreign airport, nothing more. And as much as she had tried to be understanding about Eliot's recent cold feet, that was not exactly the type of conversation even the most confident woman wanted to hear mere months before saying, "I do." Marisa's eyebrows pinched together at the thought.

"And you are?" James prompted.

She realized she had not introduced herself in reply. A small, secret part of her thought of giving him a fake name and suggesting they check into one of the nearby airport hotels. His eyes were an insanely gorgeous shade of gray, and his shoulders... well, she would definitely have something to hold on to, if it came to that.

"I am Marisa Plataneau. It is quite a pleasure to meet you."

"Are you French?"

"I am. But I've spent most of my adult life in the United States and Switzerland. What about you? Oxford or Cambridge?"

"Aaah, you wound me, Miss Plataneau. It is *Miss*, is it not?"

*Isn't he the thorough one?* she thought. "Yes, at the moment."

"As long as it is yes, I don't want to know about the moment." He smiled innocently, then added, "Shall we go for dinner?"

Marisa laughed and James felt something old and broken in his gut come springing to life. And that was just after a dinner invitation.

"Which of the fabulous restaurants in the Frankfurt airport shall we grace with our presence? Or shall we be really bold and take a taxi into town? I am obviously dressed for five-star dining at Main Tower." She ran her hands down her black T-shirt as if she were a baker brushing off the day's flour.

James found the gesture utterly distracting. Her hands were careless and familiar, dismissive of her beautiful curves. Her figure, despite her self-deprecating remarks about sub-Saharan dust and too-casual T-shirts, was superb. The black cotton top clung to her firm, full breasts and trim, flat waist. Her pants hung low and did nothing to conceal the endless, fit legs that seemed to stretch forever across the hideous yellow nylon carpet, languidly crossed at the ankle.

She supposed he was visually corroborating her less-than-satisfactory appearance, letting his gaze trail down the dusty length of her.

Then he looked up and nodded his head with a small, "Obviously."

She turned away to hide her pleasure. She wanted this man to approve of her. More than that, she wanted him to see her clear through. Past the long, cool, straight blond hair and icy blue eyes, to the warm, hungry woman beneath. With Eliot, especially lately, she always felt like she was trying too hard. She often felt she had to be "on" when they were together. Cheerful. Optimistic. Confident.

Whereas.

Whereas, James didn't seem to be in the market for cheerful, optimistic, or confident. He seemed, funnily enough, to be in the market for a travel-weary, unprimped castaway.

"Ouf," she exhaled the quintessentially French syllable, then asked, "Was that a compliment?"

"Why yes. I believe it was. You are just like a breath of fresh air." He held her gaze and she felt a wave of slowly awakening—then rather demanding—attraction. Her breasts felt unaccountably heavy and she quickly crossed her legs, as if he might see the small muscles at her core tensing in response to his unwavering look.

Crossed legs or not, he saw. He saw everything. A few minutes earlier, she had hoped that this man would see clear through to her core, and it seemed that wish had been very rapidly granted.

The anonymity of the frequent-flyers' lounge in the Frankfurt airport, so recently scorned, was ideal for whatever it was that was brewing between them. All of the other travelers were lost in their isolationist, environment-dismissing activities: reading books, listening to music on small headphones, playing games on handheld devices, working on laptop computers.

James and Marisa might as well have been invisible.

She'd always thought she was far too verbal to believe in nonverbal communication, but James Mowbray was connecting with her, without a word.

She usually balked at any kind of public display of affection, thinking it smacked of too-happy-by-half, but when James reached across the small divide that separated them, she leaned in with hungry gratitude. He cupped her cheek in his warm palm and she closed her eyes and let her head rest there, tilting just slightly into his steady hold.

"Lovely," he whispered.

She didn't know if it was a term of endearment or an adjective, but it sounded quite delectable coming out of his mouth. His thumb began to slowly caress her cheekbone and she feared she might crawl out of her seat and into his lap. She simply didn't care. She didn't care who his parents were, what he did for a living, where he lived, or with whom. She didn't care if he was rich or poor, smart or addled. She just wanted to fall into his waiting hand.

She was bone tired. She had been traveling for days. That was all it was. She wasn't really falling for a man she'd just laid eyes on, right here in a departure lounge.

Her eyes flew open. James let his hand come away slowly, his thumb happening across her lower lip as he did. They sat there, beholding one another.

Marisa's multilingual upbringing had been a blessing and a curse. She loved the formal perfection of French; she loved the emotion and vitality of Italian; she loved the quick, biting honesty of English. But she often found herself searching for just the right word in every language, and not finding it, left adrift in a sea of cultures and imprecise words.

At this moment, though, she felt she had it.

Behold.

It was ancient, spiritual, demanding, formal, compelling. She didn't want to look away. Nor did he. They beheld one another.

Marisa finally breathed a deep, long inhale and looked down at her hands resting loosely in her lap. This was one of those moments in life. One of the defining moments. Maybe her life would now be rained upon by such moments, maybe she had turned a corner of cosmic happiness. A flood of charming, interesting people would now cross her path. But what if this was not the beginning of a steady stream, but a single precious drop?

"I am engaged to be married," she said slowly, not looking up.

"Oh." James silently cursed his ineloquence.

"Yes. Oh." She looked up that time and her eyes were guarded. "That probably doesn't matter much to you—"

"It does matter."

"That is, we just met in passing, just now, for an instant. Right?"

James tried to weigh her words. Did she love her fiancé? Was she merely tired and strung out and alone in a soulless airport, seeking a comrade?

His body thought not. He could practically hear the hum of her desire. What passed through the palm of his hand when he felt her cheek was not simple friendship. The tremor on her lips when his thumb grazed the chapped tender skin there was not platonic.

He wanted to take her hands in his, but he sensed she wanted to be intellectually soothed first. Then, maybe, physically. "I don't go in for any of that fate business—"

"Phew!" Marisa interrupted. "Me neither. Total, what is the phrase?" She snapped her fingers, eyes alight. "Claptrap."

The whole finger-snapping, word-searching animation made James even more certain he was not going to let this moment pass. He held up one hand slightly, to stall her. "That said… I don't think we should simply pretend it is nothing whatsoever. The two of us meeting, that is."

Marisa's mouth felt like dust. "Go on," she said.

"Well, and stop me if I am being presumptuous…" James smiled that crazy, deadly smile again and Marisa wanted to tell him to presume the night away. He continued in a businesslike tone, "What we might benefit from is a simple battery of tests. You seem like the scientific sort. Evidence, that sort of thing."

"Very true. I am a lover of rational thought." But her throat caught for a nanosecond on the word *lover* and she felt it hanging there in the space between them.

James forced his thoughts back into order and proceeded apace. "I suggest a kiss—"

"I don't know about that." Her hand flew up to her lips, at first to cover them from his seductive look, and then to steal a quick touch, a gentle foretelling of what his lips might feel like against hers. She forced the treacherous hand back into her lap. "It feels duplicitous, no?"

James looked up for a second when a flight to London was called out over the loudspeaker, then let his eyes lock on hers. "Does it? What would be the greater deception? Lying to him? Or to yourself?"

She knew what he was asking before he finished the thought. Marisa's pants were feeling too warm and too tight, but she forced herself not to squirm in the nondescript airport chair. Her exhale was a hiss between her teeth. "Maybe that would lay it to rest. As they say."

Perhaps she was right, that a quick kiss would be the end of it, but James thought not. "Come with me." He didn't reach for her hand or look back, he just got up and headed for the small alcove across the private lounge where coffee and light snacks had been set up for the elite travelers. James assumed, correctly, that she would follow of her own accord.

He had his back to the wall, and stood immediately to the left of the entrance to the partially concealed room. Marisa had been a few paces behind him, and he grabbed her hand when she crossed into the small space a few seconds behind him.

"Just a kiss. Okay?"

"Okay. Just a kiss," James agreed.

Then Marisa stood up on her toes to bring her mouth closer to his, one hand still held in his encouraging grip. She stopped, her lips scant inches from his, and licked her own in a moment of tentative anticipation. Suddenly, Marisa was unable to resist the urge to taste his lips in exactly the same way: after sweeping her tongue over her own lips, she held his gaze, inches from hers, and let the very tip of her tongue trace the full, beautiful curve of his mouth. His contracting pupils and a low moan were her reward.

"Was that the just-a-kiss?" James whispered, his hot breath touching her lips.

"No. That was just a taste," she said.

"So… do I get a taste and a kiss too?"

She nodded very slowly, her heart and stomach beating a crazy rhythm that had nothing to do with those espressos.

# Chapter 16

THE FOLLOWING WEEK AND a half in Paris floated by in a dream. In the mornings, Abigail worked from their hotel room, rewriting a funding proposal she had been focusing on for the past two months. Eliot offered to help in any way he could, reading over the revisions each night and making suggestions that were always helpful without being needlessly particular. She also heard from the professors at the Sorbonne, letting her know they had reviewed her presentation and they were pleased to announce they would join the board of the Rose and Thorn. She put together plans to meet them for lunch on Thursday.

That morning, Eliot asked what time she was going to be free after lunch.

"I'm not sure. We're set to meet at one o'clock and I don't want them to feel rushed or anything. Why? What do you have in mind?"

He was tying his tie in the bathroom mirror behind her while she brushed her teeth. He had a negotiation that morning with a group of French investors and was looking particularly sharp. "A little surprise for you. For me, really." He smiled at her reflection. "But I think you'll like it too."

She finished wiping her mouth with the hand towel and turned away from the sink to face him. "You are looking quite the corporate raider this morning." She tugged on his perfectly knotted tie to pull him down for a quick kiss.

"Mmm," he hummed, then pulled away slightly. "Do I get more kisses when I'm looking predatory?"

She smiled and shrugged. "Maybe. It's kind of working for me. Do you get dressed like this every day in Geneva?"

His face turned slightly more serious. "Why don't you come and find out for yourself?"

She tipped her forehead into his chest and inhaled. "We're going to have to sort that out, aren't we? Little things like where we're going to live? And you not being engaged to someone else by the time I get there?"

He put his finger under her chin. "Yes. But it's all good, okay? It's all going to work out."

"Okay."

"I have a sneaking suspicion you're going to love my house." He traced the angle of her cheekbone, then trailed his finger down her neck. "It would suit you."

She loved the way he touched her while he spoke to her, as if his touch was part of the conversation, punctuating his words. "Everything about you suits me," she said. "Why should your fabulous house be any different?"

He smiled. "Precisely." He walked out of the bathroom and pulled on his suit jacket, shooting his cuffs and smoothing his lapels. "So call me when you get out of your lunch and I'll pick you up at… where are you having lunch?"

"Soufflot. Do you know it?"

"I think so. Up near the Panthéon?"

"Yes."

"Okay. Call when you finish."

"Okay. So…"

He raised an eyebrow and smiled.

"Are you going to give me a hint?"

He narrowed his eyes and looked at her from head to toe. "Wear your best lingerie." With that, he gave her a peck on the cheek and left.

Nearly three hours into lunch, Abigail was trying to stay focused, she really was, but the two anthropology professors were settling into their second coffees and more cigarettes than she'd seen since Humphrey Bogart worked at Rick's. Her eyes were watering and she had to clasp her hands in her lap to keep from swiping her hand in front of her face to push away the smoke.

Finally, the older of the two looked at his watch and widened his eyes. "Alors! I didn't realize it was almost four o'clock. I'm so sorry to cut our lunch short, but we have a department meeting in thirty minutes."

Abigail used all the restraint in the world to keep from laughing in his face at the idea of cutting a three-hour lunch *short*. But she managed it. The waiter finally came with his portable credit card machine, *like an extra lifeboat on the* Titanic, thought Abigail. She whipped out her credit card and smiled at the two men. They had been utterly charming, thrilled about the prospect of working with her and having research trips that would take them to Uganda and Libya, but Eliot's words about her *best lingerie* were starting to clang distractingly through her mind.

"It's been such a pleasure, gentleman," said Abigail. All three of them stood up from the table and walked out to the curb to say their good-byes. "I cannot thank you enough for your confidence in the foundation. It's been such a pleasure to spend time with you both. I'll call you next week about—"

"Abigail, is that you?"

Her head swung around and there was Eliot, all glamorous and fabulous, sporting his mirrored sunglasses that reflected the neoclassical buildings and his perfectly cut five-thousand-euro suit. He came up to the three of them and leaned down and kissed her neck. Right there in front of everyone.

The two professors smiled, a little taken aback. Abigail was tongue-tied. Eliot extended his hand and introduced himself in his perfect French. Abigail stared as he impressed the two professors, accomplishing in thirty seconds what had taken Abigail weeks of phone calls and meetings, and one endless, smoky lunch. After a few minutes, the three men were laughing about something in French and Abigail was beginning to get peeved. Eliot sensed it immediately, drawing her back into the conversation and into him, draping his arm around her waist.

"I'm so sorry. It was rude to launch into French. How did the meeting go?" He looked at Abigail and then back to the two men.

She supposed she should feel grateful that staying mad at Eliot was impossible. She looked at the professors. "I think it went well, don't you?"

They nodded enthusiastically and bid their farewells, walking back to their department meeting.

"What did you say to them? And I did not call you yet. Have you been hiding behind a streetlamp or something? I feel like you are my own personal version of *The Red Balloon*."

He squeezed her more tightly and led them in the opposite direction from the professors. "I missed you." He leaned into her neck and did that half-kiss-half-inhale thing he'd been perfecting all week. "And it's such a beautiful, crisp afternoon, I thought we might walk to your surprise."

"Oh, Eliot. You're so impossibly good. Of course I've been distracted the entire lunch thinking about my *best lingerie*, because there's quite a lot of it to choose from." She pulled him closer to her side, reaching her hand around his back. "I wasn't exactly sure which you would think was the *best*."

They were strolling toward the Luxembourg Gardens, then Eliot led her down a narrow street that curved away from the main avenue. They came to a narrow building that looked like the crooked house on the crooked lane. Eliot smiled that mischievous boy smile and pushed one of the unmarked buttons by the entry. They were quickly buzzed in. The entryway was ill-lit and unkempt. They walked up a narrow circular staircase that felt as though it might pull away from the cracking plaster wall if they decided to jump up and down on it.

"Eliot. Where are you taking me? There's delightfully wicked and then there's illegal."

He smiled over his shoulder as he dragged her up the last few steps to the top floor. There was music coming through the thick oak door that had been left slightly ajar for them to enter. Eliot rapped on the old wood once and then pushed it open. The space was dilapidated and gorgeous. The rough beams of the ancient building's sagging roof were exposed, roof tiles and partially shuttered windows let in slanting beams of the Parisian winter sun.

Photography lamps were set up in different areas of the room and a man was looking over some images on a makeshift table in the far corner. Benjamin Willard turned around when he heard the two of them come in.

"There you are." He smiled as he approached them. When he crossed the room, he extended his hand. "How are you, Abigail?"

"Good, thanks. How are you?" She shook his hand and looked around for the model and stylists. "Where's Dina?"

Ben looked at Eliot. "You haven't told her yet?"

"Told me what?"

Sarah came flying out from another room to the left of the front door. "Are they here yet? I don't have all—"

"Sarah! What are you doing here?"

"Oh, Eliot. You didn't tell her, did you?" Sarah was holding two different shoes aloft, as if she was on her way back to the room to ask someone's opinion. Abigail glanced briefly at the shoes, which she could only describe as sadomasochistic thigh-high… things.

"Tell me what? What is going on?"

Eliot leaned in and kissed her neck.

"Eliot, sack it!" Abigail had had enough surprises for one week. "Is this a photo shoot or not?"

"Yes." He crossed his arms in front of his chest and stared at her.

She felt the blood drain out from her face and started to back up. "If you think I'm going to prance around in my underwear—" The heel of her shoe caught on one of the loose floorboards and she would have fallen flat on her back if Eliot hadn't reached out to grab hold of her.

"I've got you," he whispered into her ear, holding her tight and hard against him.

She reached her arms around his waist and spoke into his chest. "I don't think I like surprises."

He laughed and kissed her forehead. "Abigail?"

She looked up at him. "Yes?"

"I don't want you to parade in your underwear."

She exhaled. "Oh. Well, okay good. So there's that."

He smiled again. "I found the dress… the imaginary dress that I've pictured you in all these months of our separation. And with Ben here and Sarah willing to help, and this building that I've always loved even though it's a wreck… because aren't we all a wreck?"

Abigail had stopped breathing. "Yes."

"So, for me, would you let Ben take a few pictures of you in the dress?"

"I'll feel ridiculous. I'm not photogenic, I swear. I'm not being overly modest." She loosened her hold around his back, but he held her tighter.

"The pictures are for me, not for you. If you don't like them, you don't have to look at them."

"Oh, Eliot." She rested her cheek against the lapel of his soft suit. "How can I deny you anything?"

He kissed her full on the mouth, hot and open.

*All this kissing in front of everyone all of a sudden!* thought Abigail, before she couldn't think anymore.

She gasped when he pulled away, his eyes sparkling. "Thank you." He kissed her again, but it was a quick buss.

"My, my. You're welcome. Maybe I should have said yes sooner. That was quite a kiss."

He leaned in near her ear and whispered, "I love you, Abigail."

"I love you too, Eliot."

They stood like that for a few more seconds.

"Great!" Sarah barked. "Now that we've reestablished for the nine hundredth time this week that you two love each other, could we please get a move on the photos. I *have* to be back at the hotel at seven o'clock."

Abigail took a deep breath and Eliot released her. "Okay, I'm ready, Sar. Where are the clothes?"

"This way, come on. No dawdling."

She followed Sarah to a small garret off the main room and saw the dress. It was breathtaking. Abigail covered her mouth in shock. "Is that even a dress?"

"Of course it's a dress. Only the most beautiful dress I've ever seen."

"What's it made of?" Abigail reached for the diaphanous layers of fabric then pulled her hand away, afraid she was going to stain it or ruin it.

"This is so wrong." Sarah stomped her foot. "I can't believe *you* are going to end up with someone who gives you vintage Dior gowns and I ended up with someone…"

Abigail folded her arms and raised an eyebrow to hear how Sarah was going to describe Devon. "Someone?"

"Oh, fine. Devon's perfect, but he might be a tiny bit perfecter if he knew the first thing about fashion. Honestly! He doesn't even care!" Sarah sounded genuinely despondent.

"There, there, Sarah. We can't have everything."

"Oh cut it out! Let's get you into this incredible piece of art, shall we?"

"Okay." Abigail took a deep breath. "I guess I need to undress, then?"

"Yes. Abigail. You need to get undressed. What is your problem? You are usually so immodest. What's come over you?"

"Oh, I don't know. Let's just do this."

"Try to be a tad enthusiastic, for my sake." Sarah lovingly unzipped the pale gray beaded gown from the mannequin. "It's so fantastic."

Abigail undressed and watched as Sarah carefully finished removing the dress and held it up for her to step into. "Oh my god! Does he buy you haute couture lingerie too?" Sarah pulled the dress closer to her chest and away from Abigail's reach, staring at Abby's fancy underclothes.

Standing in her *best lingerie* in front of Sarah had never been part of Abigail's plan. Now that she had removed her navy-blue wool skirt and white turtleneck sweater that she'd been wearing for the meeting with the professors, she was back to looking like a harlot. Abigail put her hands on her hips (which happened to be sporting a gorgeous pale lavender lace garter belt). "I buy my own lingerie."

"I don't believe it! You are a closet lingerie whore? Oh my god. Wait until I tell Bronte."

Abigail shook her head. "You are so juvenile. Give me the damn dress."

"There, there." She extended the dress and continued talking as Abby stepped in, trying to be extra careful not to crush the hem or get caught on the delicate lining. "All of this falling-in-love-with-Eliot-business has really got you going, huh?"

"You could say that." Abby smiled as Sarah lifted the dress into place.

"The bra's got to come off."

Abby looked down.

"Strapless," Sarah elaborated.

Abigail took the bra off and set it on top of her skirt and turtle-neck, which she'd laid on the rough floorboards.

Sarah stared at the tag on the bra. "Are you kidding me? Did Louise Feuillère make that bra for you?"

Giving a guilty shrug, Abigail said, "Well, Eliot did tell me to wear my *best lingerie*."

"I sort of hate you right now. Turn around and let me zip this up." Sarah sighed with frustration. "I mean, of course the 1947 gown in a size negative four fits you perfectly. I wouldn't be able to get one boob in here."

Abby looked over her shoulder at her gorgeous blond sister-in-law. "False modesty doesn't suit you, Sarah."

"Oh, fine. I'll do, but this is…" She finished clasping the tiny hook and eye at the top of the zipper, then turned Abby to face her. "This is something else altogether. Really smashing, Abs."

"So, what do I do? Just walk out there and do whatever Benjamin tells me to do?"

"Let me put a touch of makeup on you first… I know Eliot wants you all sooty-eyed and crazy-looking like all his models at the shows yesterday. Why didn't you come to the Danieli-Fauchard show, by the way?" Sarah applied makeup and waited for Abigail to reply.

"I don't really want to be seen with him until everything is taken care of with his, you know…" Her voice trailed off.

"Oh, god. I keep forgetting he's married."

"Sarah!"

"Engaged, whatever. Sorry." She was distracted, putting on some of her magical foundation and lightly powdering Abigail's skin. "Now for those diamond eyes of yours." Keeping her eyes closed, Abby felt the light pressure and soft texture of Sarah's fingertip as she smudged the makeup to her satisfaction. "Okay. You're all set. I think. Let me look at you."

Abigail opened her eyes. Luckily, there weren't any mirrors around so she didn't need to obsess about how ridiculous she must look in some crazy vintage ball gown in the middle of some ramshackle, falling-down building.

"Lipstick!" Sarah cried. "Come here." She pulled two gold cylinders from her bag. "These will be perfect. Dark, bloody red—"

"Sarah—"

"Don't talk or I'll mess up, and this stuff stays on for*ever*. They were not kidding about that six-hour promise. I mean, seriously, you can do *anything* with this lipstick on."

"You are seriously perverted."

"Sure. You keep telling yourself that, Abs. You're not the least bit perverted."

Abigail burst out laughing. "All right, all right. Let's go."

"Shoes!"

"No. I'm sorry, that's where I draw the line. I refuse."

Sarah narrowed her eyes, deciding whether or not to wage war on her sister-in-law for shoe heresy, then her face bloomed into a smile. "Now that I know about the lingerie situation, I'll let you off the hook this once."

Shaking her head, Abigail turned and left the small dressing area.

"So? How do I look?"

Eliot was standing with his arms crossed, his back slightly turned to where Abigail was. Benjamin Willard saw her first and started snapping photographs immediately. Eliot was speechless.

"I know!" Abigail laughed. "I was speechless too when I saw it. Isn't it incredible?" She did a pirouette then turned slightly right and left, enjoying the movement of the layers and layers of lace as they floated around her hips and legs. She really did feel like a princess.

Eliot walked toward her in silence, her heart pounding harder and harder as he got closer and closer. She vaguely remembered the sound of the camera clicking-clicking-clicking while Eliot pulled her into his arms and twirled her around the abandoned space, and their laughter and joy as she flew into his arms. The music surrounded them. Her bare feet were a few inches off the ground one moment, then they were dancing the next, or he would stop to kiss her neck or dip her back to kiss her chest while her head lolled back and stretched until the crown of her head nearly touched the floor.

He battered her with all those too-strong words like *magnificent* and *splendid* and *perfect* and *miraculous*. At one point she felt tears, and he kissed those too, and they danced like that for what felt like hours but was really just fifteen or twenty minutes.

"Oh my god, Eliot." She breathed into him, feeling winded, not so much from the physical activity as the crashing waves of all that love.

"I'll try not to kill you with it."

"Okay. Love me in doses until I'm truly addicted and I've built up my tolerance."

He smiled and kissed her one last time. "How did you like your first photo shoot?"

She laughed, ringing clear, turning to look at Benjamin Willard, and said, "Oh, is that what that was?"

He smiled and replied, "I'm not sure what to call it, but I think I captured it on film."

"Thank you for that," Abby added. "So now I just walk out of here in this priceless gown?"

"If you like, but I'm afraid you'll be furious with me if you ever find out how much it's worth. Probably better to put it back on the mannequin and I can have the museum people come retrieve it."

Abby gulped. "The museum people?"

"Don't ask. Trust me on this one. You do not want to know."

She turned and walked toward the changing area, where Sarah was watching her, and muttered, "I have fallen in love with a crazy person."

"Haven't we all," Sarah agreed as she began to help with the zipper and removing the dress from Abigail's flushed body.

———

Abigail spent the last few days in museums and parks, sometimes alone in cafés or, a few times, with her mother or Sarah. But for the most part, she meandered through the city as if it, too, was her lover. Eliot called her a *flaneuse*, whatever that meant. She wandered down small cobbled streets, and sighed at their ancient intimacy. She visited crowded tourist spots like Notre Dame and trailed her hand along the cool medieval stones and inhaled the evocative scent of incense and small memorial candles. She sat on benches alongside large, crowded avenues and watched normal people stroll or rush by, carrying bags or ambling alone, holding hands or chirping into a cell phone.

Normal people.

She no longer felt like a normal person. She felt like a new species altogether. She felt like she and Eliot had emigrated to another country. She spent the nights in his arms or taking him into hers, his every nocturnal whisper binding her tighter and tighter to him. She spent her days reliving the exquisite delight of each gentle or fierce touch.

By the time she got back to London Sunday night and faced the prospect of spending the night alone in her own bed, the whole idea of Eliot not being there was quite unacceptable. She picked up her phone and dialed his cell.

Before he had a chance to say hello, she snapped, "How is it that I am staring at an empty bed right now?"

"I told you to move to Geneva a year ago. I have no idea what you're doing in that dismal, gray city. I seem to recall some discussion about real life and responsibilities... something vague and meaningless like that."

Abigail smiled into the phone and flopped down onto her bed. If she closed her eyes, the sound of his voice was a pretty good approximation of his touch. He had spent the past week talking softly into her ear while touching her body, and the voice and the touch were permanently imprinted on to her. Into her.

"You are humming, my dear. Is this going to turn into some perverted phone sex?"

"Did someone say *perverted*?" Abigail asked optimistically. Her hand reached for her breast before she had time to even give it a thought. She bit down on her lower lip, closing her eyes and tugging at her nipple, just as Eliot had done earlier that morning when she screamed through the peak of another glorious orgasm.

"What are you doing, damn it?" His voice was adamant. "This is cruel. I'm standing in the middle of the Malpensa Airport. You're going to get me arrested."

"Just talk to me. You know." She moaned involuntarily as she continued to tease her nipples and think of his tongue on her. "Like normal."

"Abigail," he growled.

"Yes, just like that, like you need to…" She gasped at the memory from yesterday when he had taken her from behind. "…Like you need to have me right now…"

"Stop it this instant!"

An elderly Italian woman who was waiting for her luggage looked up at his rude tone and shook her head in disgust. She obviously thought he was a despicable, controlling man. What a travesty of the truth: Abigail controlled his every waking moment.

Abigail's breathing was starting to fracture. She switched her phone to speaker and set it on the pillow next to her. "Eliot," she whispered into the phone, "it's Pavlovian, darling. You come to me at night. It's just how it is. I can't help thinking of you now." Her back arched to force her moist center more firmly into her own palm, and she whimpered her pleasure. "I'm sorry to be so selfish, but please talk to me," she begged.

His angry breathing was crackling through the ether. He sighed then. "Oh, all right, let me move off to a quiet corner at least. But you are asking a lot and I plan to be properly compensated at a later date." She could hear the background noises changing and then he must have settled himself. "Tell me where you are. Where are your hands?" he demanded.

"I'm on my bed and I have one hand, you know, and the other at my breast."

"Okay. First of all, there can be none of this *you-know* business. I want to hear exactly where your hands are and what your fingers are doing." His voice rasped against her, like a brutal, knowing touch.

"Mmmmm, Eliot, keep talking like that. Your voice is so damned sexy." She let her finger dip into her slick folds, and cupped one heavy breast. "One finger just slid into my wet... pussy, the other"—she twisted her nipple methodically while pressing into her needy breast—"mmmm, the other is toying with my nipple... like you did... like I want you to... I need more hands..."

"Oh. Good. God. I don't think I can do this. Seriously, Abigail, I'm going to get put in jail for lewd and lascivious behavior in a public place. I'm so hard for you right now." He could hear her breathing accelerating in that familiar way, toward her release. "Do you like that idea? Of my hard cock wanting to be inside you so badly that I am going to have to go into a fucking public bathroom stall and pull it out?"

"Yes..." Her breathing was a mix of whimpers and desperate, encouraging inhales.

"And I'm going to take a few long, hard pulls with my hand—" Her sharp intake of breath told him that was exactly the idea. He was still whispering into the phone, one hand covering his mouth to ensure no one else could hear him. "And I am going to think of your taut, hard, willing body taking me… taking me everywhere, Abigail. Now. Come for me now, Abigail."

She screamed his name into the empty bedroom, into the red flash behind her eyelids, into him: he was so close, right there, in her mind. "Oh, dear god. Eliot," she panted out the words.

He sat in the corner of the airport and softly cursed every possible, vile deprecation he could think of. "I'm glad one of us is satisfied," he bit out. "You need to get your ass to Geneva. Right. Now. Or I need to move there. I don't care which, but we need to deal with this immediately. I'm not going to be alone and harder than a brick—did I mention how alone I am?—for any longer than absolutely necessary. Decide where you want to live and let's be done with it, Abigail."

Click.

Abigail's lolling head stared at the small phone, propped on the pillow by her head like a little hotel mint. He was right, of course, but she still didn't want to think about the realities of all that. She groaned at the prospect of real life encroaching on her small, private dream life with Eliot. He was going to have to extricate himself from his engagement. Abigail was going to have to decide whether staying in London was truly important. He was willing to throw it all over for her. His company. The beautiful house in Versoix he had described in loving detail. She tried to fight him on those points, claiming he didn't know what he was saying or hadn't thought it all the way through.

But he looked more angry and intractable at those moments than ever. Their conversation on the last night in their room at the Ritz had been one of many that week that always ended at the same impasse.

"I have had a lifetime to contemplate what I am and am not willing to do or not do, and a year on top of that where you're concerned, Lady Abigail Heyworth. I am not going to settle. I want you.

Unequivocally. All of you. All the time. I don't care for those British ideas of absentee spouses—"

"That's not fair! Bronte and Max are not absentee spouses—"

"Exactly. They live together. In the same country, in the same city, in the same bed! We have already squandered entire lifetimes *not* being together. I'm done with that."

"I suppose you're going to want to get married and all that."

"I don't give a crap about that and you know it. You're mine. I'm yours. Nothing will change that." He was looking out the window at the Place Vendôme, quiet and glistening in the middle of the night. He turned back to face her where she was sitting cross-legged on the bed with the sheets pulled up loosely onto her lap. "Nothing." He stalked, naked, as usual, back to the bed and sat in front of her. "This is totally unconditional for me, Abigail. I don't know why. It's not like me to be so completely unanalytical, but I have no desire to parse it any further. I spent the last year trying to figure out what went wrong, and you know why it was such a mind bender? Because *nothing* was wrong. It was always right between us, but we were too"—he waved his hand in her general direction—"something... to see it. You were scared. I was demanding. I don't know. After a while, though, I think people start to recognize when life presents them with a truly unique opportunity. I think I knew it the minute I saw you. What we have is indisputable. Immoveable."

Abigail was trying to distract herself from the power of his words. The truth of them always made her want to wince a little, as from a too-hot coal fire in the old-fashioned grate at Dunlear. "I know. I know it's all true, but it's just so—"

"Abigail!" He didn't raise his voice often, other than to roar his carnal satisfaction, so when he did, Abigail started.

"Yes?"

"Look at me."

She kept her gaze down. "I don't need to look at you to know you're right. I feel kind of weak when I look at you." He put his finger under her chin, and with a gentle urging, brought her face to face with him. Her eyes were shimmering with unshed tears and her lips were twisted into a lopsided smile. "See?" she croaked.

"Oh, Abigail. It's all too much, isn't it?"

She hated feeling like a little girl, but something about broken engagements and moving across continents made her feel entirely *small*.

"It will all turn out right," she hiccuped and wiped at a stray tear. "I know that's true, here"—she put her hand on his heart— "but everything out there?" She tossed her head toward the large windows overlooking the Place Vendôme. "It feels tricky and loaded with obstacles and trials."

"Abigail—"

"No, wait, because I think this is legitimate. It's not just that I feel like a home wrecker"—she knew it was tired ground, they'd argued that point past death—"but more that I don't want to look back a few years from now and feel like we were swept up in this part of everything. I love feeling swept up." She gestured between the two of them and let her hand return to his warm chest, loving the feel of his constant, reliable heart pounding beneath her touch. "Swept up here, this way, but all of the realities of where we will live and how we will live, I need to own all of that."

Eliot rolled his eyes. "I don't even know what that means. My mother says crap like that all the time, about *owning* this or that, and it makes me feel like a friggin' caveman that I have no clue what that really means."

She brought her hand up to his cheek for a moment then let it rest back on his chest. "You know exactly what I mean. I want to go through all of it together. To decide together. Not feel thrust along by circumstance… or you."

"I'll thrust you along." He winked, then tried to give the

situation the serious attention she wanted. "That's all fine in theory, but the reality is that someone has to at least initiate the plan. Let it be you. I'd welcome that. But the sad, immature truth is that I'm simply overcome with eagerness. I don't think any decision at this point could possibly be construed as rash, after all the hand-wringing that's preceded it."

She released a long exhale. "You're right. I think I'm just being a coward and wanting to crawl under the bed until you sort everything out with Marisa... what if she fights for you? I would. I will!"

"That's more like it." He kissed her and nipped at her soft bottom lip. "Please leave all that to me. If it helps assuage your conscience, you were first. For whatever that's worth. She can't win, and I doubt she even wants to. I mean, after the initial shock of not having her plan executed," he pinched the words out, "I think she's honest enough to know it's all for the best... for her most of all."

Abigail gave him a cynical look.

"Well, maybe not *most* of all, but, at least, on some level, it's got to be better for her to be free than to be with someone whose heart is firmly held by another." He looked down at Abigail's hand resting on his chest to make his point.

She leaned in to kiss his chest, loving the feel of his heart beating on her lips, the feel of his chest hair against her wandering fingertips. She pulled away slightly, still looking up at him. "Your heart really is mine, after all, isn't it?" Her lips were moist and full from their endless lovemaking of the past week. Her eyes were shining with hunger and satisfaction and anticipation and simple love.

Eliot tried to win the ongoing battle within him: to stare forever into those willing eyes, savoring the timeless beauty of her skin, the straight perfection of her nose, the high arch of her brow, or to dive at her and take and give everything her look promised and demanded. He looked his fill, then he took her hard and thoroughly, with an animal ferocity she had encouraged him to honor over the past days.

Sharing that demanding, primal part of him always brought Abigail to the highest reaches of her own satisfaction.

She relived the sweet aftermath of those powerful moments again and again as her body lay there in London, alone and empty. He was right, as usual. Being apart was simply not tenable.

# Chapter 17

ELIOT HAD MEETINGS IN Milan for the two days after he left Paris. Marisa had had very limited access to reliable communication while she'd been in Tanzania, so he had not expected to hear from her for the weeks she was away, but he was surprised he'd only had one quick text that morning letting him know she was back in Geneva.

He took a deep breath and dialed her cell. It was early Monday morning and she sounded like she was already deep in work mode.

"Hey, Eliot. How are you?"

"Good. How was your trip?"

"Great," she answered a bit too enthusiastically, thinking foolishly of that kiss in Frankfurt, then reminding herself that Eliot was asking about Africa. "They broke ground on the hospital. It was really something to be there for that. Thanks for asking."

Eliot was surprised at the mellow, grateful tone of her voice. She sounded oddly relaxed. "So, I'll be back in Geneva tomorrow night. Are you free for dinner?"

She swiveled in her office chair to take in the priapic spray of the fountain in the middle of Lake Geneva. The early morning sun was clear and pristine. *Fresh start* popped into her mind. "Yes. I don't have anything booked. Where do you want me to meet you?" *Please don't say your place*, she thought as soon as she'd asked him to decide. She was afraid he had recommitted himself to their wedding, and she was no longer sure she wanted to recommit. She needed to think a bit more about James before she gave up on Eliot, certainly, but she didn't want to be lulled into the comfortable routine of their life together—the subtle ease of Eliot's beautiful home and how easily they got on there—and let that affect her decision.

Eliot tried to tease out some meaning from the strange tone that kept creeping into Marisa's voice: cautious, but certainly not fearful. "Let's just go for beer and fondue," he suggested, "if you don't mind. I've had enough fancy French food to last me a year. Unless you're craving sushi or something?"

"No. Fondue sounds fine. I'll see you tomorrow night at Soleil at seven. Sound good?"

"Great, see you then."

"Okay, I've got to hop, Eliot. I'll see you then."

Then the phone went dead. Eliot held his quiet cell phone in the palm of his hand and stared at it as if it were a curious Etruscan artifact. What in the world was that about? No outpouring of detailed successes from Africa? No (justifiable) interrogation about the status of his unresolved feelings for the anonymous other woman? What the hell? Was she going to act as if their discussion of three weeks ago had never transpired?

---

Marisa looked at her desk and decided to drown herself in the backlog of work that had piled up in her absence. After two hours, she had slogged through most of her emails, dealing with those she could, delegating where possible, and setting aside the others for closer replies later in the week. She was just starting to open her paper mail when the phone on her desk rang.

"Marisa Plataneau." Her tone was bitter: she was grimacing at a letter from a foundation in New York that was declining a recent grant application.

"As bad as all that?" The British lilt was unmistakable.

Marisa dropped the piece of paper she was holding and watched as it floated down onto her desk. A flash of sizzling joy crackled through her. "Just got a lot better."

"Are you still engaged?"

"Last time I checked, yes."

"Are you free this weekend?"

"How did you get my number?"

"Your luggage tag."

She laughed at his tone, as if it was perfectly right and just that he would do so.

"Hi, James."

"Hi, Marisa."

She turned to look out at the lake again. The golden midday sun shone on the dark blue surface. Two small craft were braving the brisk, Alpine wind, their sails perfect white triangular silhouettes.

"So? Are you free this weekend?" His voice was even more intoxicating on the telephone, if that was possible. His low rolling timbre had been heady in person; now it was downright erotic.

"I don't know James. I mean—"

"Hear me out. Obviously, I have my own crass, selfish interests clouding my powers of analysis, but listen. I'm not saying you should throw over the future Mister Plataneau for me, but I'm not sure this guy you are with now is the right guy."

"You don't even know him. Or me, for that matter."

"I don't know him, and I don't care to. But you... now there's the interesting part of all this. You just don't seem, I don't know, fully committed."

Marisa corralled her thoughts as best she could, weighing the strong desire to be completely honest with James against the fact that he was a veritable stranger. This newfound, compelling urge to expose herself to him won out. "Here's the thing, and I kind of hate you a little bit for it, but you are absolutely correct. I don't feel comfortable going into the details—he is still my fiancé after all, and he is, on every level, a very good man, and I am a good woman, I suppose." James hummed his agreement as she continued. "But whether or not he and I are good together? I wonder. And then, well, I do not think these are the thoughts that an engaged woman is supposed to be entertaining."

James was sitting on the edge of his desk in the mahogany, wood-paneled office that his father, and generations of Mowbrays before him, had occupied. He felt her bending slightly toward him, like a palm tree in a gentle leeward breeze. "I can't say I envy your position, but since you already seem to be questioning the… viability… of the whole enterprise, perhaps you'd enjoy a weekend in the country to, you know, unwind."

"What country might that be?"

"England. The English countryside. Perhaps you've heard of it? I'm heading out to my cousin's for a house party, for the weekend, and he told me to bring a date. And I want you." He paused. "As my date, I mean."

"James." She said his name matter-of-factly, simply to hear it and feel it on her lips.

"Marisa."

She closed her eyes and felt the caress of her name on his lips. And then decided that she had as much right to second thoughts as Eliot and threw caution to the very blustery Swiss wind. "Yes. My answer's yes. I can probably get to London by suppertime on Friday… I might even be able to schedule some meetings for Friday there during the day."

James tried to think of something more eloquent than *thank you, God*, but nothing came to mind so he stayed silent.

"James?"

"Yes."

"Well, what do you think?"

"I think... I think I am feeling very lucky and can't quite get past that at the moment."

Marisa felt herself respond to the heat of his voice and his enthusiasm. "Oh. I thought maybe you were just toying with me, you know, to see if I would say yes."

"Why would you think that?" He sounded irritated.

"I don't know. I am not well-versed in the art of planning secret weekends."

"It's not secret as far as I'm concerned. I'm bringing you to a house filled to the rafters with prying relatives. Prepare yourself."

"Well, maybe it's not right, then. I feel a bit treacherous."

"Oh, please don't change your mind now. I mean, I suppose we could check into a hotel somewhere, but that feels even more clandestine and guilty somehow. And I don't want to feel the least bit guilty. You will have your own room. It's rather a castle."

"What do you mean it's *rather* a castle? Is it a castle?"

"Well, it is. Yes."

"I think I need to know a bit more about you, Mr. James Moh-Bree."

James loved the slight hint of French on that last syllable. "What would you like to know?"

"Just a few basic facts. What do you do for a living? Any family to speak of? Ex-wives? Children? That sort of thing."

"I am thirty-six years old."

"So am I."

"Never married."

"Neither am I. Yet."

"No children. Yet."

Marisa felt a ping of excitement that she'd never felt before, with Eliot or anyone else. The idea of participating in the creation of James Mowbray's children made her feel a little light-headed. "I don't have any children either," she added. "Yet."

"I work for my family's clothing business, a British men's clothing business that I'm attempting to wrest out of the dark ages and into the twenty-first century. I have four sisters and live in London. Does that suffice?"

Marisa felt suddenly deflated. What was it with her and men who worked in textiles? He most certainly knew, or knew of, Eliot. It was impossible. She remained quiet.

"What is it?" James asked.

"*Ouf.* It is just... well... you probably know my fiancé because he's in a similar business and I think it all feels a bit too close to home. I don't know, James. I—"

"Do you want to tell me who he is? I don't want to cause you any trouble. Maybe you're right."

That wasn't what she wanted to hear at all. She felt let down and a bit lost that he had given in so easily.

"But," he added carefully, "I don't think you are."

Maybe if she avoided Eliot for the rest of the week, she could spend the weekend with James and chalk him up as a prewedding fling. Over and out, as Eliot liked to say. It seemed terribly conniving, but Eliot had really been the one to set this whole ball in motion in the first place by making his own hesitation known. She exhaled. "All right, you are probably going to Google it anyway, so I might as well tell you. He's Eliot Cranbrook... of Danieli-Fauchard."

James was gutted. Eliot wasn't just a good man, he was one of the best. James had met him at Devon's wedding last year and they had spoken many times at fashion awards ceremonies and other industry events. He had seen him from afar at several of the shows in Paris only last week. "Huh."

"Yeah," Marisa said. "Huh."

"I kind of wish you hadn't told me."

"I know. I kind of wish I didn't have to. But that's why I need to be, if not clandestine, at least a bit discreet. I am so not a romantic, James, truly. But whatever sprang to life between us at the airport yesterday… it feels real to me. Does that make any sense?"

"Perfect sense," he replied gently.

"So. What do you think?"

"I think you should still come to Dunlear with me and we will have a great weekend, and it's none of anyone's business who you are or what you are doing there. Max invited me and I invited you, and that's the end of it. The only thing is, I think one of my cousins' wives is a pretty good friend of Eliot's. It's Sarah James, you know, the shoes? Anyway, it's her brother-in-law who's hosting the party. Max Heyworth is his name and he's one of my oldest, closest friends."

"I don't know, James. If it gets back to Eliot—"

"Would that really be so bad?"

She was silenced into contemplating the truth of what he said.

"Look, Marisa, I'm not saying he should be the brunt of gossip or anything, but the more I talk to you, the more I feel like I might be the way out you have been looking for. Just tell him."

"Jesus. It's like I am riding along thinking, *Yes, yes, yes*, and then you say something like that and I stop short, and think, *No!* Tell him what, exactly? That after he and I have been dating, living together, and planning to marry over the course of the past year, that suddenly I have met someone—precisely *one* day ago—and am now having second thoughts. It's ludicrous. I am notoriously rational. My father is a philosophy professor. I have never lacked conviction!"

James burst out laughing and then Marisa started laughing too. They both simmered down. Then James continued with his gradual assault. "Here's the thing, Marisa. I want to parade you around on my arm and laugh at a big table of friends with my hand resting on your leg beneath the tablecloth and, well, you can imagine quite well what I want to do after that, but you will have your own room and it's not an orgy or anything. Just come as my guest and meet my friends and see parts of my life other than those few hours spent on layovers in Frankfurt. *Please*."

She suspected she would have followed him into a burning building when he asked like that, his voice kind, but laced with something dark and compelling. "Very well. I must be losing my mind, but I feel like I've been such an obedient, driven thing for so many years and now I just want this bit for myself and everyone else can take their suicidal French rationalists and stick them somewhere."

James started laughing again, joyfully. "Fabulous. If you are able to come into London on Friday for meetings, that would be ideal. We can drive out to Dunlear that afternoon. Otherwise, if you come in that night, try to get a flight into Gatwick. That's the closest airport."

"I'm really going to do this?"

"Yes. Thank god, yes. Here, take my details and I'll be back in touch in a day or two to confirm you got everything settled." James gave her his phone and email contacts and told her again how much he was looking forward to seeing her at the end of the week.

---

Eliot didn't know if he was more grateful or frustrated that Marisa had avoided him all week. She basically blew him off that first night, calling him late in the afternoon and saying she was swamped with a backlog of work from being away for three weeks. He didn't doubt it. His own office was in a wild flurry of post–Fashion Week activity, following up on huge orders for the coming season.

She said she was staying at her flat in town that night and would probably spend the rest of the week there as well, seeing as she'd be working late for a few nights to come.

It wasn't unusual for them to touch base with brief texts or phone calls for days at a time, but even Eliot was beginning to rile at her continued dismissal. By Thursday morning, he was more than irritated. He wanted to move on with his life and he was tired of trying to do the right thing. He called her office number because she was more likely to answer.

"Hey, Eliot. I'm really busy, what's up?"

"Hi, Mari. I know it's been a crazy week for both of us, but I really want to see you in person… to talk everything over."

"Look, Eliot. You came to me a few weeks ago and basically jilted me—"

"Hey!"

"Or almost jilted me, or whatever, and I just don't want to hear it right now!" Her tone was escalating and she breathed in to get it back to a normal level. "I certainly don't want to have this conversation on the phone any more than you do, but I'm not willing to meet you in person right now. I know I'm being selfish, but I think it's my turn. Don't you agree?"

Eliot felt the verbal slap keenly. Obviously he could just tell her over the phone that it was 100 percent and completely over between them, but it felt crude and awkward. Inadequate. She didn't deserve it, but his patience had run thin. "I suppose I deserve that, but—"

"No *buts*, Eliot. I don't care if you are going to break up with me or get down on the floor and prostrate yourself to me—I don't want to know—I just want a few days to think about how I feel and what I want, for me and me alone, not as it relates to you. I am going away for a few days. Trust me. No matter how it turns out, I need this. I will meet you at six o'clock on Monday night at your place. I promise. It may seem irrational to you, but after all this time, I don't think one more weekend is asking too much. Just grant me that, okay? Please do not call me again between now and Monday, all right?"

Jesus. Whatever Eliot had been expecting, it wasn't this. Abigail was already justifiably concerned that he hadn't broken it off with Marisa at the first possible opportunity. If he waited out the whole weekend, she might be furious. On the other hand, it just wasn't in him to deny Marisa this small concession, to contemplate and prepare, whether to reject him or accept him. "Fine. I will see you on Monday."

"Thank you, Eliot."

"Bye, Mari."

Eliot hung up the phone and wanted to talk to Abigail, but dreaded telling her he had been put off again. He inhaled and dialed her number.

"Hey, handsome," she answered.

"Hey, to you too."

"Did you tell her?"

"Well, it's the weirdest thing—"

"Let me guess. She's too busy to meet with you in person and you don't want to break up with her over the phone?"

"That pretty much sums it up. It's just for a few more days, love, I promise. I know you understand… don't you?"

"I wish I was more melodramatic and demanding, but yes, I do understand. She obviously senses what's coming and needs a few days to pull herself together, and I kind of respect her for it. When are you going to see her?"

"Monday night."

"So then come to London, you fool. Come tonight! Come now!"

"Good god, Abigail. You have no idea how good that sounds. I might as well put in my resignation for how much I am able to concentrate. I let my mother take the jet back to Iowa. You're reducing me to flying commercial. I'll be on the afternoon flight into Heathrow. It lands around six thirty your time. I'll take the train into town and see you at your place around seven thirty. Sound good?"

"Oh, Eliot. That will be heavenly. You. My place. Seven thirty. I'll be waiting. Do you want me to pick up something for dinner or do you want to go out?"

"Order in. I'm not letting you out of bed for at least twenty-four hours."

"Sounds divine. I'll stock up on supplies. Oh, I almost forgot. Bronte is going stir crazy so Max invited a bunch of us out to Dunlear to entertain her. Mostly family and close friends, James Mowbray, and some others. Want to go?"

"Whatever you like. As long as the bed is large and the walls are thick."

"Check. And check. I think it would be fun and Bronte will kill me if you're in town again and she doesn't get to see you."

"All right, love. See you tonight. If anything changes, I'll let you know."

"Eliot, I love you."

"I love you too, darling. See you soon."

He hung up the phone and set it aside to the left of his desk blotter. Then he forced himself to give his full attention to the stack of paperwork on his desk, buzzing for his assistant Marcel to come in and go through the huge pile along with him. They broke briefly for lunch and continued until four o'clock.

Eliot was relieved that he was still capable of focusing. After his time of carnal abandon in Paris, he had worried whether his brain would still be able to function with any real acuity when he returned to work. When he looked up at the time, Eliot realized he hadn't given himself enough leeway to return to his house in Versoix to pack a bag. He was mildly concerned, then just shrugged it off and decided he would make do with his briefcase. He could pick up everything he needed in London, and he wasn't about to risk missing his flight.

"That's it for me, Marcel." Eliot nearly sang as he got up from his desk, "I'm going to London for the weekend."

Marcel looked askance at the unfamiliar—cheerful—person who had taken the place of his boss. "Now? Do you want me to call you a car?"

"Yes, I'm leaving right now. No car. My flight leaves in a little over an hour. I think it'll be faster if I hop on the train to the airport. I should make it."

"Very well, sir. Do you want me to set up any meetings while you are there?"

"No. I'm taking the day off. If anything of real importance comes up, just call me on my cell. But you can probably handle everything." Eliot gave Marcel an encouraging pat on the shoulder and strode out of the office and on toward the elevators, swinging his briefcase without a second glance back.

Marcel shook his head in confused wonder and muttered something about going from inadequate phone screener to deputized CEO in a matter of weeks.

---

Abigail was giddy. Everything about Paris had been otherworldly and dreamlike. The hotel room with its sumptuous fabrics and gold and marble. Their schedule of days spent apart in simmering anticipation and nights spent in heated, joyful reunion. But Eliot's impending visit felt like the beginning of their real life together. No room service, no glamorous views out over the Place Vendôme. Abigail had a momentary panic that Eliot would feel like a too-large giant when he entered her *Alice in Wonderland* home. It was intimate and small, packed with tender reminders of family and friends, postcards resting against books on the shelves on either side of the fireplace, a pinecone that Wolf had given her on a walk at Dunlear, a program from a particularly passionate Wagner concert at Wigmore Hall. A shell from Bequia.

For someone who had spent the first few decades of her life shucking off any connection to the past, she looked around her little home and realized she had turned into a pack rat. She loved the silver porringer her mother had given her. She loved the eight-by-ten black-and-white photo of Bronte, Sarah, and Abigail laughing so hard their eyes were squinting and their backs were hunched over a table at Le Caprice.

She put the huge vase of hothouse flowers down on the rough wood of the coffee table and put Regina Spektor on the stereo. She stood stock-still in the middle of her living room and felt the frightening, then soul-satisfying realization that she was building a life for herself.

Eliot's urgent double-knock scared her senseless, then had her running the few yards to pull open the door. The winter rain was pounding all around and behind him and he looked so damn good standing in her doorway with his perfectly functional black umbrella with the bamboo handle in one hand and his briefcase in the other.

Her beautiful man.

She leapt up onto him like she was climbing a tree, throwing her legs around his waist and her hands around his gorgeous neck, kissing his jaw, licking the rain off his cheek. He tossed his bag onto the floor inside the doorway and pulled her closer, with his one free hand cupping her bottom. He fumbled inelegantly as he turned to get the two of them through the doorway while trying to pull the opened umbrella in behind him. He kicked the door closed and threw the open, sopping umbrella on the living room floor and brought that freed-up hand to the other side of her ass.

"Where's your bed?" he growled.

"Up," she whispered between hungry nips at his ear, his lower lip, the tendon on his neck.

He carried her up the stairs as if she were weightless. "Right or left?"

"Left…"

He brought them into Abigail's bedroom, which she had filled with about a hundred votive candles. He tossed her down on the bed and pulled off his overcoat, then his blazer, and started unbuttoning his shirt as he kicked off his shoes with his heels. Abigail was lying on her bed, reveling in the sight of him.

"You look so fine. I mean, really, really good," she said softly.

He smiled and undid his pants, his erection springing free, and he felt himself harden further at the responsive glimmer of desire that flashed in her silver eyes. "This isn't going to be pretty, Abigail."

"I hope not." She smiled as she pulled her practical brown corduroy skirt up from her argyle thigh-high socks and revealed herself, completely bare, except for a new, sexy-as-hell garter belt in a sheer nude lace, which she had picked up at Fleur that afternoon in honor of Eliot's arrival. She bent her knees slightly apart and tilted her hips in invitation.

"Holy hell."

"A little welcome present."

He pushed her knees up to her shoulders and kissed her at the very warm, very moist center of her being. She screamed and begged him to make her come right then. He licked and sucked and bit at her until he felt the quivering beginning of her orgasm, then pulled himself up and away and thrust into her, to the very hilt, feeling his taut balls slap against her as her orgasm clenched around him, deeper, harder, as he kissed her lips and neck and felt the fire of her breath against his skin as she keened his name in a final, joyful cry, and he met her there.

His release was a silent, powerful, profound binding.

They were fused together.

"Always," he whispered. "It will always be like this for us, Abigail."

She had tears of joy rolling silently down her temple into her hair. "I know," she choked out. "I finally know."

He kissed her tears, wanting to taste and know every ounce of her. He felt the familiar dissipation of her control, her gradual slipping away toward postcoital oblivion. "Stay with me a few minutes more, love."

"You are with me now more than ever, Eliot." Her voice was barely audible. "When I reach this place of joy, of ecstasy, of freedom, you are the only one with me." She stretched her neck to reach her lips near his ear, then continued in a tiny voice, "I am not retreating from you—I am joining you there." Her head sank back slowly into the pillow and her eyes slid closed as she smiled and drifted on the cool air of rapture.

Eliot leaned his forehead into hers, closed his eyes, and felt a deeper intimacy than he would have ever thought possible. He pulled a light blanket over them and repositioned his body into a snug cocoon around hers. The two of them dozed off, finding each other in that place of shared freedom.

# Chapter 18

MARISA COULDN'T RESIST DOING a little research about the castle where she and James would be spending the weekend. She looked it up online Thursday night and got a feel for the scale (massive) and scope (vast) of the buildings and surrounding gardens and parklands. She saw photos of James's cousin, the current duke, Max Heyworth, and his American wife, Bronte Talbott, and other shots of Devon Heyworth and his wife, Sarah James, the one who knew Eliot, and a few pictures of the younger sister, Abigail Heyworth, who, Marisa realized, was the same Abigail Heyworth she had started to hear about in her own circle of foundations and funders of African aid projects. Perhaps Abigail would be at the house party over the weekend and Marisa could further justify this crazy escapade by securing some additional funding for the school in Tanzania.

She had managed to schedule two appointments in London, which made her feel a tiny bit less guilty about lying so categorically to Eliot. She was on a business trip, after all. She wasn't entirely without honor.

She took a 6 a.m. flight out of Geneva Friday morning, which gave her plenty of time to make a ten o'clock meeting near Victoria Station and a one o'clock meeting in Marylebone. She hoped that last one would be over in an hour or so and she could meet James at his office in Mayfair immediately after.

He had called her each morning and each night of the past week to wish her a simple good day and a simple good night. He never pressed or brought up Eliot, or the heat that had passed between them in Frankfurt; he proffered a consistent, supportive friendship.

Sure, she could try to believe that, she chided herself. Her one o'clock meeting had finished in just under an hour, and she was riding in a taxi from Marylebone High Street toward Oxford Street, making her way inexorably toward Mayfair to meet James at his office. Her attempts at controlling her excitement with lame rationalizations about James-the-supportive-friend were futile. She tried a different tack and began immersing herself in the very real possibility that, upon seeing her, he would kiss her as passionately and heedlessly as he had in the Lufthansa lounge. She hoped that if she could anticipate a tidal wave of passion, perhaps she could prepare herself for it.

Foolish, foolish woman.

All that did was make her squirm and feel like the opaque black tights under her practical black suit were entirely too warm and annoyingly confining. And while the James-as-supportive-friend theory might have been a blatant prevarication, it did not lead to the unfamiliar pulls of sexual tension that always accompanied even the most glancing contemplation of the James-as-passionate-lover hypothesis.

The taxi was feeling close and overheated, so Marisa rolled down the window slightly, welcoming the brisk, wet air that signaled the very beginning or the very end of winter rain. She took a deep breath through her nose and then looked down at her purse and pulled out her compact. She smirked with a not-much-I-can-do-about-it-now look then pulled out a small brush and gave her hair a few quick pulls. It was straight and it was blond, that was about all she could manage at the moment. Her face was a bit flushed from the cool air (and those other thoughts, no doubt), so she didn't bother putting on any powder or blush. She added a bit of lip gloss to her bottom lip, then put everything back into her large black Fauchard bag. A gift from Eliot. Ugh.

She should have switched to her black Longchamp purse, but it hadn't occurred to her until she was already on her way to the airport at five that morning. Too late now. She was fastening the closure when the driver tapped on the dividing plastic and said, "Here you are," in a far too normal voice.

Didn't he know she was about to open his taxi door and step out onto a very large, very deep metaphorical lake that had only the thinnest treacherous layer of ice to support her? She breathed again, paid the driver through the glass, put her purse over one shoulder, and hefted her weekend bag out onto the sidewalk with her other hand.

Marisa wasn't sure what she had imagined, but the Mowbray store was so quintessentially British, so quintessentially male. The enormous mahogany doors had gleaming brass handles, and the panes of glass on the upper portion were so crystal clear, they looked as if they were cleaned hourly. The four full-story picture windows on either side of the entrance were designed with formal but stylish flair. Large black-and-white photographs provided a grainy, classical background to offset the rich colors and immaculate cuts of the men's clothes. The mannequins were antique, and the linen that covered them looked tea-stained with age.

Marisa let her stare rise slowly up the solid, formidable facade and felt defeated.

This was all a terrible idea.

She was not a frivolous woman. She was not inclined to larks and mischief. And her aversion to such trifles was a characteristic that she liked about herself. She respected who she was and how she acted. And now she had traveled halfway across Europe to meet up with a virtual stranger.

What had she been thinking?

She turned to see if she might still be able to catch the taxi that had just deposited her on this precarious sidewalk and watched, deflated, as it pulled quickly away into traffic.

"There she is now!"

James.

Her chest tightened in a split second of fear, then an unavoidable spilling warmth spread from her solar plexus out to the tingling tips of her fingers and toes.

James.

"Abigail, let me introduce you to my new friend—"

"Mary Moreau," Marisa interrupted quickly, reaching out her hand to shake Abigail's.

James looked at her askance, then tightened his eyes and deferred to the deception. For now. "Mary..." he said slowly, "this is my cousin Abigail Heyworth. Abigail, this is... *Mary.*"

Abigail looked from one to the other and felt a sweet recognition of the tender affection that she had recently rediscovered with Eliot. It looked as though James might have finally found someone he could tolerate for longer than his typical five minutes.

More than tolerate.

Marisa pressed on with forced ease. "Abigail, it's a pleasure. I was hoping I might get to see you while I am here. I work for an aid agency that's working in Tanzania and really admire everything you're doing with the Rose and Thorn Foundation."

Abigail turned to James with real concern. "Why didn't you tell me about Mary? We have so much in common. Have you been hiding her from all of us?" She turned back to Marisa with a wide, genuine smile. "He's notoriously secretive, you know. All sorts of internecine goings on. Watch out!" But Abigail's complicit wink was all encouragement, despite her supposed warning.

James looked down at his perfectly polished shoes and shrugged his shoulders. Marisa thought he was the most engaging man she had ever seen. It was strangely hard for her to look away from him. Even if he never wanted to see her again after this weekend, she decided in that moment, she was going to enjoy as much of him as she possibly could.

She must have been staring like a fish-eyed idiot because Abigail looked from James to Marisa and back to James again then burst out laughing. "You two are pretty bad. I thought I was pretty bad, but you two are…" She smiled and shook her head.

James looked at Marisa and didn't even care if Abigail could see how obviously glad he was to see his *new friend*.

Abigail straightened her back and tried to reposition the eight Mowbray bags she was lugging, then gave the parcels a guilty look. "I have a friend in from out of town and he arrived on my doorstep without any of his personal possessions. A few essentials." Abigail lifted the bags in evidence. "Fetch me a taxi, James, so I can leave and the two of you can greet one another properly."

The taxi pulled up and James helped load the shopping bags.

"And we will see you at Dunlear tonight?" Abigail asked with an inquiring eyebrow.

James nodded to confirm that both of them would be there.

"Great to meet you, Mary," Abigail said, then turned and settled herself into the cab as James shut the door and the black vehicle pulled away.

"She's quite nice," Marisa tried.

"Yes, she is… *Mary*. Let me take your bag." James reached for the heavy weekend bag that she had set on the sidewalk between them.

"What do you have in here? We're just going to a friend's house for the weekend, not to meet the queen."

Marisa looked at him cynically. "Really? I Googled your so-called-friend's house and I thought I might pack a little bit more than my long-sleeved black T-shirt and my Carhartts."

"Touché. And by the way, I liked that T-shirt very much." He smiled, then pulled the door to the store wide open. "Come on in." As they walked through the main floor, James held her substantial valise over his right shoulder as if it were as light as a shirt from the dry cleaner, then he reached for her, resting his palm against the small of her back. "I can't wait to hear more about you… *Mary*."

She opened her mouth to speak and he shook his head to stop her, then added quietly, "Let's get up to my office and you can tell me all about your split personality."

She smiled despite herself as she took in the wonderful smells of leather and wool and old wood and a hint of beeswax from the floors. Masculine scents of sandalwood, bay rum, and pine floated through the centuries-old store. She saw racks of perfectly hung suits, a section of country tweeds, a shoe area in the far corner to the right, and a manned elevator, complete with a perfectly polished brass cage directly in front of them. James didn't release his hand from her back until they were in his office and he had shut the door behind him and tossed her bag on the very old and very comfortable-looking leather Chesterfield sofa along the wall to her left. A fire burned in the small grate.

"Wow. Some office."

He remained standing with his back against the door and watched as she dropped her handbag on the sofa and continued to walk around the room, his space. She picked up the occasional paperweight or photograph. "Is this you?"

"Probably." He wasn't going to look away from the way her skirt hugged her perfect hips long enough to pay attention to the frame she was holding.

"James! You are not even looking at me."

"I beg to differ." He met her eyes and she flushed, then looked quickly away and put the picture back on his desk. She continued to the other side of the office, where floor-to-ceiling bookcases were filled with nearly three centuries of hand-bound chestnut leather ledgers, dating back to a time when the Mowbray wool had to be carted across Scotland and England behind a team of horses.

She let the pads of her fingertips trail along the tooled ridges of their bindings. James felt his mouth go dry as those delicate fingers tripped mindlessly across those lucky books.

She came back to where she'd begun, standing a few feet in front of him in the center of his domain, trying to keep calm as her heart pounded amid the warring artillery of fear and desire. "So."

"So," he said, "why is your name now Mary?"

Marisa felt a little disappointed that he hadn't showered her in kisses by now, then shook her head and reminded herself she had advanced degrees from prestigious universities and shouldn't be having pattering thoughts about showers of any kind, much less those of the kissing variety.

"Ugh. It's so stupid, I suppose." She turned half away so she was looking at the fire, then pulled her perfectly straight blond hair in front of her left shoulder in an impatient gesture that, James noted, had the added benefit of revealing a lovely kissable spot at the nape of her neck. "I just didn't want to have to explain myself to anyone. Our wedding announcement was in the *International Herald Tribune* about a month ago and just now with Abigail… I mean, she and I are in the same industry. I've admired her work over the past year. Not to mention her mother is married to a close family friend of Eliot's, for goodness' sake. I even met Jack and your aunt Sylvia on holiday in Italy last summer. It's all too close."

"Aunt Sylvia is not going to be there this weekend, I can assure you of that. And your *engagement* announcement," he rephrased her words with pointed meaning, "probably passed by most casual readers."

"From what I've heard, Bronte Talbott is not most casual readers; she is a marketing and PR fanatic. She probably knows every wedding announcement ever made about every employee of Danieli-Fauchard. Not to mention Sarah James."

James shrugged again.

Marisa continued, "You know she'll probably end up there this weekend too. I'm sorry. It seems silly now, but in that moment when you introduced me to Abigail Heyworth, I had this spontaneous dread

of saying my real name and having her ask, 'The Marisa Plataneau?'"
She was still staring at the low fire when she felt the sudden touch of
his lips at the nape of her neck. She swooned. Or she imagined that's
what it must have been, because she'd never really believed that such
a thing was possible.

"I've changed my mind..." he whispered provocatively.

She stiffened, then softened into him when he nibbled at her
exposed earlobe and said, "I don't care if your name is Mary or
Gertrude or Sam or Bill." He kissed his way down her bare neck as
he recounted a lengthy list of progressively ridiculous names. Then
he turned her so she was forced to look him straight in the eyes. With
her no-nonsense three-inch black heels, they were exactly the same
height. He held her chin in his right hand, then added, "As long as
you know, I like Marisa the very best." And then he began to kiss her
with a gentle, demanding passion that made her forget any name she
had ever possessed.

She was still holding the bulk of her hair in the clench of her
right hand, as if it might fall off her head if she did not keep it in
place. Her other hand flew up and fisted around a piece of his shirt
fabric at his chest to hold herself steady.

After he had kissed her to the point of throwing her into a mael-
strom of confused lust, he trailed the tip of his tongue around the
perimeter of her full lips, just as she had done to him in Frankfurt.

"Welcome to London," he said formally and guided her to the
sofa and settled her into a sitting position. She felt boneless. "Have a
seat for a little while and I'll wrap up what I was working on, then we
can head out to West Sussex," he said as he walked back toward his
large mahogany desk in front of the wall of windows that overlooked
Sackville Street.

She was staring across the room at his amazing form, his broad
shoulders beneath the striped broadcloth, his strong thighs in the
moleskin jeans. Marisa wasn't sure she'd ever wanted a man like

this... like she wanted food. She was hungry for James Mowbray. She couldn't string two thoughts together. *How was he able to kiss like that and then speak in complete sentences*, she wondered with abstracted academic interest.

He sat behind his desk then smiled at her stunned silence. "I think you are going to like it here."

She let herself fall back, mouth slightly open, into the well-worn leather of the sofa and let out a nonsensical, "Huh."

They spent the next two hours in a businesslike silence that was punctuated by distracted looks and a few irrepressible sighs of silly joy on Marisa's part. James had more loose ends to tie up at work than he'd originally thought, but Marisa was happy to go over her notes from her meetings earlier in the day and clean out her emails. She kicked off her shoes and sat on the sofa with her laptop, a position that afforded her a spectacular view of James at his helm. It was a surprisingly comfortable arrangement.

---

Bronte was in the particularly foul mood that only someone in the late stages of a multiple-birth pregnancy could appreciate. She was swollen everywhere. The skin around her ankles and wrists was so stretched, she questioned whether or not those parts still contained bones. On the other hand, since she hadn't actually *seen* her ankles in weeks, the bone discrepancy was moot as far as those joints were concerned.

Everyone was being overarchingly accommodating and protective. At first it was adorable, especially her husband's sexy remonstrances about how she needed to be particularly still while he took care of her, you know, there. But after a while, even that became annoying... her body repelled the slightest touch, as if her muscles were starting to reserve every bit of energy for the coming onslaught. All of her husband's fussing and caring made her want to slap him, and not in a spanky, fun sort of way. She needed a distraction from her confinement, because—despite the archaic sound of it—that's exactly what it was: confining.

Of all the prenatal visits she'd attended, of course Max randomly decided to join her on the one in which the doctor told her in strict tones that she must "take it *very* easy" for the final three weeks.

Bronte's idea of taking it easy was diametrically opposed to her husband's. She would have cut back to half-days at the office, or maybe three days a week instead of five. She wasn't paralyzed, after all, she was just an enormous waddling beast.

"Surprise!" Max said far too cheerfully as he entered their bedroom with a beautiful breakfast tray in his hands.

Bronte groaned as she tried to heave her cetacean mass into a more upright position. "These two angels better love me so profoundly and infinitely."

"Now, Bron. Don't go blaming the girls. They can certainly hear you at this point."

"Hear that!" She patted her huge belly with firm authority. "Love your mother!"

"Careful!"

"Jesus, Max. It's my bloated beast of a body. Trust me to know how hard I can whack it, all right?"

"Did you just say *whack* and *hard* in the same sentence?"

In the absence of actual sex, Max's sense of humor had disintegrated into something akin to a twelve-year-old boy who just found the word *fuck* in the dictionary.

Bronte smiled and waved him toward her. "Get over here. What delights have you brought me?"

Despite all her complaints about gaining seventy-four pounds during the course of her pregnancy—"*five stone*" *sounds so much nicer, dear*, her mother-in-law had kindly suggested—Bronte had no intention of curbing her eating habits. She looked appreciatively at the fresh baked oat-nut bread, the glistening honey still in the comb, and the rashers of bacon. "You are truly the most wonderful man alive. You know that, right?"

He winked and settled the tray onto the middle of the bed (since it no longer fit across the expanse of Bronte's stomach).

"So. I have a surprise for you."

"Is it measured in carats?"

"No. That's for when the babies come out. Shipping and handling and all that. This is more of a distracting surprise."

She took her first sip of coffee, the only prenatal nutritional battle she was not willing to lose. Max watched skeptically as she drank the potential poison. "And stop ruining the loveliest part of my day—my first sip of coffee—with that whingeing look of disparagement. Tell me more about my surprise."

"Very well. We're having a house party this weekend."

"That's hilarious," she replied, deadpan.

"I'm not joking."

"Because I look so beautiful and so capable of organizing food and sleeping arrangements and a shooting party for twenty of your nearest friends?"

"I've already made all the arrangements, and it's only ten of us, not twenty. And it's just family and Willa and David, who might as well be family, so just try not to be so controlling."

"I am *not* controlling!"

Max rolled his eyes. "Fine. You're not controlling. I meant to say, try to forget your physical unease and enjoy yourself for a couple of days. I gave everyone very strict instructions to plan on being hilarious and diverting when in your presence."

"So I will just sit here in bed and they will parade before me? Jester!" She snapped her fingers in mocking regal command. "Amuse me!"

He took the fingers she had just snapped and brought them to his lips. "I know you have been bored to tears—I've been here for the

crying jags, remember?—so let's just have some fun. It's fine with me
if you stay in bed and we bring the dining room table to the edge of
the duvet, or if you want to be carried downstairs on a palanquin—"

She reveled in the feel of his lips and the warm air of his breath
against her fingertips, then felt the girls begin their morning battle
for the nonexistent space in her womb.

"They know your touch already," she said softly. Bronte pulled
the covers down to the top of her thighs and pulled the light cotton
nightdress up under her breasts, revealing her obscenely large stomach.

Max's eyes sparkled in joy. For as much as Bronte would be very
happy if she could never look upon her distended, veiny abdomen
again, Max found it endlessly fascinating. He began rubbing the flat
of his left hand along the smooth skin. The babies were jockeying
for position and he could feel the hard elbow or knee of one as it
protruded through Bronte's flesh. He looked up to his wife's face
to share his pleasure and laughed when he saw she was drinking her
coffee and looking out the window, as if he—or they—were not
even in the room.

"What?" she asked.

"You are so beautiful."

"Yeah, right. For a whale."

"No, I mean it. Look at you. This gorgeous, fecund, bountiful—"

"The thing is, Max, I feel like I have turned into some sort of
alien host. I don't even feel like myself. I'm tired." She put the coffee
cup down on the bedside table and felt the press of tears behind her
eyes. "Fuck, and now more crying."

Max took the tray off the bed and then resituated himself alongside the length of her body. He cradled her head in his arms. "It's
okay, darling. It's just a few more days." He kissed away her tears and
she sighed into him.

"I know. And it will be fun to have everyone here this weekend.
Thank you for arranging it. I'm sorry I was churlish. Am churlish."

"You can be as churlish as you like. Oh, and in addition to the usual suspects, I think Abigail is bringing Eliot and James has some secret new bird he's going to take out of hiding."

"Maybe I can be so pitiable that Eliot gives me the Fauchard fragrance account once and for all."

Max laughed and then began kissing her neck. "You are an ambitious beast."

"I told you I was a beast. Look at me." She gestured dismissively toward the still-exposed flesh of her belly.

Max continued kissing her, slowly. "I am looking at you."

"Mmmm." Bronte tilted her neck and closed her eyes. "That feels surprisingly delightful."

Max spent the rest of Friday morning and much of the afternoon in bed with his wife, loving the body she was no longer able to appreciate, cajoling her into a world of sparkling pleasure with the power of his own tender adoration. She ended up in quite a good mood by the time all of her entertaining guests started to arrive.

# Chapter 19

ELIOT AND ABIGAIL PULLED in around five o'clock that afternoon and Max greeted them at the large, arched front door. Abigail looked flushed and alert; Eliot looked satisfied and confident. Max shook his head and tried not to picture the two of them pulled off to the side of the road for a quick shag before arriving at the ancestral home.

"How are you two doing?"

They both smiled the same idiotic smile.

"Very well, I take it?"

They nodded stupidly and walked past him into the dimly lit central hall of Dunlear Castle. Abigail dropped her weekend bag down onto the floor unceremoniously and turned back around to look at Eliot and Max standing in silhouette against the last red remnants of the fast-setting winter sun.

"Where is Wolf? I miss my boyfriend!"

Eliot clutched his hand to his chest, wounded.

"What can I say?" Abigail asked rhetorically. "He was my first, my last, my everything." She shrugged as if Eliot would have to deal with the realities of her abiding affection for her nephew or suffer the consequences.

"Aunt Abigail!" Wolf's earnest tenor sounded much older than the typical two-year-old as he nearly flew over the cranberry red–carpeted stone steps.

She held her arms wide and Wolf dove into her welcoming embrace. "Where have you been?" she asked.

He pushed himself away from her hold, his hands resting seriously against her shoulders. "Me? Here." He frowned. "Waiting for princesses." He raised his eyes heavenward, as if his sisters were due to arrive from the clouds above, or merely from his mother's bedroom. Either way, it was entirely tedious.

"I see. Is it completely boring?" Abigail asked seriously.

"Well," he thought aloud, "not always... but mostly. Mama's cranky and Papa tries to make her laugh, but she no wants to laugh, because the princesses are taking over her big fat body. But—" He looked across the entryway in his father's direction, where Max was shaking his head to ward off any mention of fat bodies. "We still love Mama very much. Even though she's *very* cranky. And large."

"Of course we do, darling." Abigail kissed him on the cheek and set him down to stand on the floor, but made sure to keep his hand in hers. Wolf looked up into Abigail's eyes then peered around her hips to give Eliot a thorough once-over. "Is he coming to our sleepover?" His voice was slightly lower than it had been, but still utterly diplomatic.

"Oh, dear. Yes..."

Wolf's little lips firmed and his brow creased to fend off his tears. "He's too big for the bed."

"What about... what if just the two of us go up now and watch a movie in bed and eat popcorn and fall asleep? Wouldn't that be nice?"

"Yes," he agreed softly.

"And you remember Eliot."

"Hello, Eliot."

"Hello, Wolf. Take care of Abigail, okay?"

That cleared up Wolf's expression right away. "Yes, sir. Come on, Aunt Abigail." He tugged her toward the stairs and she began babbling about how much fun the two of them were going to have, then he started to explain about his new Thomas train and Abigail looked over her shoulder and winked at Eliot to let him know he would always play second fiddle to a toddler.

Abigail and Wolf spent the early evening curled up in front of the TV, snuggled together on the enormous bed in the palatial pale green guest suite, gorging on fruit leather and popcorn and hot chocolate and watching a variety of charming alien creatures attempt to befriend humans in order to prevent world domination by the megalomaniacal villain.

By seven o'clock, Abigail heard the telltale cadence of Wolf's steady, sleepy breathing, and thought dazedly that she might have fallen into a light sleep herself. She pulled her arm gently out from beneath his neck and looked up to see Eliot standing at the side of the bed.

She smiled stupidly, like she always did when she caught Eliot's eye, especially when one or both of them happened to be in a reclining position.

"Hi," she whispered, so as not to wake the little boy next to her.

Eliot bent his finger in a quiet, inviting gesture.

Abigail slid off the bed and followed him into the enormous bathroom.

He leaned down to turn on the hot water full blast, then added some cold, to fill the huge claw-foot tub in the middle of the vast white marble room. Eliot approached Abigail slowly, with an unmistakable look of purpose. He began peeling off her shirt and undershirt, then unbuttoned her blue jeans and slid them, together with her underwear, down her legs.

All in perfect silence.

He stood, like a valet, fully clothed in front of her pale, smooth, naked body. He trailed his hands idly down the curves of her hips and thighs, then lightly back up along her forearms and shoulders.

Abigail closed her eyes and tried to absorb how absolutely right it felt to be stepping into a hot bath, in the home she'd grown up in, while her lover—her mate—touched her skin in gentle affection.

"Oh, Eliot," she whispered. "We're going to be so happy, aren't we? I'm so happy with you." She let her forehead move forward to rest against the warm cashmere over his heart. "I love you so much."

"Get in the bath, love."

Eliot had never considered himself the type of man who would enjoy doting on a woman to this extent, but he found himself entirely and positively committed to satisfying Abigail's every whim. She was so damned grateful, he rationalized.

Every sigh.

Every whimper.

Her pleasure was so absolute and so pleasantly contingent on Eliot, never cloying, just infinitely appreciative. It was never that her shoulders needed a good rubbing; it was that she loved it when Eliot touched her shoulders. She did not simply need a bath; she adored that Eliot drew the hot water, then helped her slip into it.

"You make everything lovely, Eliot," she said, reinforcing the validity of his thoughts.

He was slowly cleaning her shoulders with a soapy washcloth as her head lolled back against the curved white cast iron rim of the tub and he stared into her eyes. "So do you, Abigail."

She smiled that grateful smile, let her eyes slowly shut, and looked forward to a long weekend of family and friends. And Eliot.

He was both, she realized. Friend. Family.

And far more than both put together.

―⁓―

Max got up from the sofa when he heard the rumble of another car pulling into the forecourt. Devon and Sarah had arrived shortly after Abigail and Eliot and were still upstairs. Bronte had suggested a late nine o'clock supper, so everyone would have time to relax and change before coming down for drinks at eight.

James Mowbray shared Devon's affinity for expensive cars with engines that were better suited for sprints on the autobahn than trips down narrow lanes in the English countryside. So Max was mildly surprised to see he had chosen his comparatively mild Audi A8 on his first road trip with his new mystery date. Max wondered if he should rib him for trying to appear more mild-mannered than he really was. Then a delightful, if formal, blond peered out the passenger side window. Max stepped forward a few strides to pull the car door open for her.

"Aaaah, the lovely mysterious houseguest arrives!" Max reached out his hand in gallant fashion to assist her exit from the low leather seat.

Her appearance seemed austere at first glance, then, in response to Max's chivalry perhaps, her face broke into a spectacular smile that transformed the air around her. By that time, James had stepped out of his side of the car and walked around to where the other two were standing. Marisa's hand rested lightly in Max's. James removed her hand from Max's loose hold with a not entirely jovial, "I'll take that."

Marisa turned the power of her happiness back toward James and that seemed to set matters to rights.

Max wheeled on his cousin with a particularly cutting look, the infamous Heyworth eyebrow raised. "Shall I no longer offer assistance to ladies as they exit a vehicle, then? Without incurring your wrath?"

Then Marisa laughed and brought the back of James's hand up to her mouth for a quick kiss and bubbled, "Oh! This is going to be so much fun." She looked at James with a bit of the devil in her eyes, then turned back to Max. "Thank you very much for including me. I know it was on short notice and guests of guests and all that. I'm very much looking forward to it."

Max just shook his head and wondered how he had managed to put together an entire house party of lovesick idiots. At least the desired effect of amusing Bronte would be very easily achieved. He looked toward the long gravel drive that led out through the park and saw another car coming in.

"Aaah, that must be Willa and David." Max turned to James so Marisa couldn't quite hear. "I trust they, at least, are past the annoying first blush of new love." Then back to the lovely mystery guest: "And welcome to Dunlear, Miss…"

James spoke formally as he introduced them. "This is Mary Moreau. Mary, please allow me to present His Grace, Maxwell Blah-Blah-Blah Heyworth, the Duke of Northrop."

Max bowed with extreme formality, then looked over James's shoulders at the approaching headlights of the next guests. "Just for that, James, I think I might have Jeremy announce you when you enter the drawing room this evening. Drinks at eight, by the way. I am sure the lovely Miss Moreau would be delighted to hear the full extent of your titles and holdings. Perhaps I shall leave a copy of *Debrett's* on her bedside table for some enjoyable late-night reading." Max patted his cousin lightly on the shoulder and started to wave at his other friends. "You are in the scarlet guest rooms on the second floor to the left at the top of the stairs. Jeremy will show you in."

The aforementioned Jeremy Paulson stood nearby, having silently emerged from the house to assist with their luggage and to see them situated in the right rooms.

James, never letting go of Marisa's hand, introduced her to Jeremy. "I suppose we're all going to have to sing for our supper this weekend, eh, Jeremy?" After decades of visiting Dunlear Castle, James Mowbray was as familiar with the staff and inner workings there as any member of the immediate family. Jeremy Paulson would never say anything to compromise the integrity of his position as head houseman, but the tiniest raise of his eyebrows spoke volumes.

"Lady Bronte must be delightfully eager to welcome the new babes," James offered.

"Quite eager, sir."

James broke out laughing as the unflappable, devoted servant was clearly pressed to the end of his rope. The brewing tension that always accompanied the days and weeks before labor and delivery was surely reaching a rolling boil.

Marisa looked up at James and squeezed his hand in hers. She looked happy, but there was a touch of anxiety about her eyes.

"What is it?" he asked.

"Oh, nothing. I'm very pleased to be here. It's just… I feel ridiculous having you introduce me with that silly fake name. I shall confess all at drinks this evening. It all seems quite unimportant now."

"It does?" James knew the pace of his feelings. The escalation of what he felt for this woman was completely irrational, but he hoped her desire for absolute honesty meant what he suspected.

She looked at him meaningfully, then down toward the gravel at her feet. "James."

He leaned in to kiss her neck. "Yes."

She pulled away slightly, to keep her train of thought. Jeremy was making his way into the house with their bags, but Marisa held James in place, there in the forecourt, for a moment longer. "I think I've known for some time that my engagement was… well… not ideal, perhaps… but he was… is… a perfectly good man, an excellent one, really, and it seemed greedy somehow to hold out for something… someone… better… but I seem to have found… just that."

James tried to remain steady, letting that glorious bit of news wash right over him. "I want to kiss you very thoroughly, but I fear this might not be the place or time."

Marisa's smile bloomed at his easy understanding and quick reciprocity.

He turned toward the loud threesome that was nearly upon them. Willa and David Osborne were barking jokes and ribald comments with Max about colonics that were more pleasant than the motorway on a Friday night, when they stopped short and James made his introductions.

Willa clapped her hands in front of her copious chest in a show of her quintessential ebullience. "Aren't you a refreshing burst of sunshine on the arm of James Mowbray!"

Marisa's expression felt like sunshine, and she realized that there was not a touch of embarrassment to it. She was quite pleased to be there on the arm of James Mowbray. She looked from Willa into James's eyes to let him know.

James turned to Willa. "She is quite... refreshing, that is."

They all smiled and resumed talking as they headed through the enormous front door and on into the main hallway. James and Marisa pulled slightly ahead to catch up with the patiently waiting Jeremy, and held hands as they followed him up the stairs.

Max, Willa, and David hung back and Max gave his old friends a conspiratorial eye roll. "It seems to be in the water."

---

Abigail got dressed quietly and headed back toward the bathroom to blow her hair dry as Wolf still slept and Eliot read a novel in front of the fire in their room. She trailed her hand lightly across his broad shoulders as she passed from the dressing room to the bathroom and back again. He reached up absently to acknowledge her touch, then he kept reading as she continued on her way.

The domestic comfort of their intimacy was one of the most joyful discoveries for Abigail. The sexual fireworks were, well, pyrotechnic. But this simple melding of their daily rhythms was more profound at times. The past twenty-four hours at her house, then driving out of town, and now here, felt so perfectly balanced. She finished drying her hair, then went back into the bedroom, slipped on a pair of black ballet slippers, and walked over to the fire.

"Shall we go down?" she whispered.

Wolf was sound asleep in their big bed.

Eliot put his paperback down on the mahogany drum table next to the chair he was sitting in, then stood up and stretched his arms over his head. Abigail reached her slim arms around his waist and pressed her cheek against the vibrating tension of the extended muscles across his chest. He brought his arms down around her waist, so they nearly doubled back around to the sides of her hips.

"Are you nervous?" he asked.

She looked up, surprised. "No. Why would I be?"

"I don't know. We are really a couple now. I am having anti-quated notions of asking the duke for your hand in marriage. That sort of thing."

"Oh, Eliot. You wouldn't!" She was still whispering in deference to the sleeping child, but it was a rising whisper.

"Let's not argue in front of the child." He loosened his arms from around her waist and pulled her hand into his. They left the room quietly and stepped into the wide carpeted hall. "Why wouldn't I?" he asked in a low voice, now that they were out of the boy's earshot.

"Because it is patently absurd. I don't need Max's approval to get married. I might need the queen's, but that's another matter altogether." She tried to laugh it off.

Max was having none of it. "That's not what I meant, and you know it."

"Enlighten me."

"I meant, I want everything about us to be valid, official, open to scrutiny. Pure."

"You are such a mystery to me sometimes, Eliot. On the one hand, you are this passionate, freethinking lover, and on the other, you use words like *scrutiny* and *valid* with no hint of irony."

He smiled and shrugged to let her know it was all true.

"I'm yours," she gave in simply. "Do with me what you will."

She kissed the palm of his hand, giving it a tiny lick that sent a hot surge of desire shooting through him.

"Don't do that, you devil." He pulled his hand back as if it had been scorched.

Abigail's smile was all innocence as they held hands and made their way, together, down the wide front stairs and across the main hall into the drawing room to meet up with the others for a cocktail.

# Chapter 20

DEVON AND SARAH WERE sitting in a snug corner of one of the dark green velvet sofas in front of the large fireplace in the main living room. Bronte was beached at the opposite end.

James was standing in front of the fireplace, having just taken a drink from Max, who was just then making a place for himself next to Bronte.

Marisa was having an animated conversation with Willa that seemed to put James's forward tendencies into question. Before getting his glass to his lips, James laughed and added, "Marisa is totally exaggerating!"

Sarah looked up quickly and said, "Wait, is Mary a nickname?" Then turned to clarify with the lady in question.

Bronte felt the slight buzz of tension and put her hand on Max's arm to stave off his conversation. "What was that?"

James looked apologetically at Marisa, then shrugged his shoulders. "I'm sorry. Do you want to tell them or shall I?"

"Ooooh," Bronte said as she rubbed her palms together, "a proper drawing room drama! Tell! Tell!" Then to the ensuing silence. "Someone!"

Sarah looked from James to Marisa and back to James. "Well, one of you needs to say something apparently."

Marisa spoke first. "It all seems quite silly now, but we all have a mutual acquaintance and I didn't want to, well, for it to get back to him that I was here. You know. With James."

Sarah seemed to sense the gravity of what was about to happen before anyone else did. Her back stiffened and she leaned forward to put her drink down on the coffee table. Devon continued to smile his happy, ignorant smile as he enjoyed rubbing her now-accessible lower back. She flicked his hand away in absentminded irritation, needing to give her full attention to what was about to explode in messy clumps all over the perfectly innocent walls of the Dunlear drawing room.

"What is—" Devon tried quietly.

"Shhhh!" she snapped at him without looking.

"Go on," Bronte prodded kindly.

"Well," Marisa looked to James for support and his kind eyes offered plenty. She took a deep breath. "So, basically, it's just… my real name is Marisa Plataneau—"

Abigail stood frozen in the doorway, Eliot coming behind her.

Bronte looked over to Sarah and asked idly, "Why does that name ring a bell?"

James put his glass down on the mantle and looked across the room at Eliot Cranbrook and asked Max, "What the hell is he doing here?"

Willa Osborne took a careful sip of her vodka and watched the entire scene as if she had a front row seat at the Wimbledon men's finals. David looked at Devon to see if there was anything to be done and Devon merely shrugged his shoulders in response, still sulking at his wife's dismissal of his roving hand.

Max stood up to see Abigail and Eliot standing like statues at the entrance to the room. "Well, are you going to come in or not?"

Bronte spoke again, in Sarah's general direction, but to anyone who might be able to answer. "Why is James mad at Eliot?"

Marisa was sitting on the club fender in front of the fireplace and choked on her sip of wine. James knelt in front of her to see if she was all right and asked all sorts of murmured versions of whether or not she wanted to leave or what else he could do. She was shaking her head quietly.

Bronte snapped her fingers. "That's Eliot's fiancée's name!"

Max looked from Abigail to Eliot to Bronte to Marisa to James and back to Bronte. "I think you may be right, Bron."

Bronte started laughing, quietly at first, then with such hysterical convulsions that her husband was momentarily concerned for her sanity. "Oh, Max," she squeezed out, "you always have to get everyone's name at least when you put together a party!" She continued laughing uncontrollably. "I mean, it's like Oscar Wilde, for fuck's sake. Ow!"

For a few moments, he thought she was grabbing her stomach in peals of laughter, then he realized her face had gone from mirth to misery. She looked up at him with a quick, intimate plea. "Oh, Max, of all the times. I was finally starting to have some fun." She squeezed her eyes shut and bit down on her lower lip. The first contraction passed and she looked up to see nine concerned faces in a perfect semicircle around her, Max on one knee in front of her.

He started barking out orders almost immediately. "Devon, start timing her contractions, please. Sarah, call Dr. Armitage and ask him if it's best to move her to the local hospital in Bognor Regis or if we should take the chance of getting her to St. Mary's in London. Abigail, go tell Jeremy that he should bring the Range Rover around front and be sure it has the bags in the back. He knows which ones. And maybe a couple of pillows and blankets just in case Armitage says we can make the trip into London."

Bronte tried to ignore the next contraction—she refused to believe they could be coming on this strong this quickly—but her strained, pale face and the telltale lip-biting gave her away.

"Was that another one?" Devon asked.

She didn't say anything.

Max looked at Devon and then at Bronte. "Well, was it?!" he cried.

She nodded and a single tear came down her right cheek.

Sarah came back from the phone in the front hall, where she had finished speaking to the doctor that she and Bronte shared. "Dr. Armitage says not to worry. The contractions probably won't come again for a few hours. She's just beginning, so—"

"When did he say the contractions would be too close together to move her?" Max asked.

"Not for hours or even days. They'd need to be within three minutes—"

"Was that another one?" Devon asked again, smiling because he felt like he was getting the hang of seeing the signs cross over Bronte's face, and that gave him some sense of accomplishment. Scientific method and all that.

She nodded.

"Very accurate little things already, aren't they!" Devon crowed, tapping his watch in admiration. "Three minutes exactly. Both times. Let's see what happens next, shall we?"

Bronte bared her teeth at Devon and a low rumble escaped her lips.

"Did you just growl at me?" he asked, affronted.

She tried to lean forward to hit him, but her stomach was so huge and the residual pain from the contraction so fresh that she just looked like a tick stuck on its back.

Sarah intervened. "Devon! Keep your eye on the timing and no more jokes. It's not a spectator sport, for goodness' sake."

Devon looked a bit crestfallen for having failed at his duties, but he reset his digital watch to zero again as the pain faded from Bronte's eyes.

Jeremy came to the door to let Max know the car was ready and he'd be happy to drive them if Max would prefer to ride in the back with Her Grace. Abigail came in behind him and made her way quietly to Eliot's side, where he seemed to still be in a state of shock at the presence of Marisa Plataneau right here in the Dunlear drawing room.

Bronte screamed out this time, no longer willing or able to repress the guttural response to the bone-crushing pain. "Max!"

He waved Jeremy off and returned to kneel in front of Bronte. "I'm here, darling. I think the girls are eager and we're going to do it here, okay?" Max looked at Devon for confirmation.

Devon, chastised, simply said, "Two minutes, forty seconds." He clicked the side buttons on the watch to reset the timer to zero when Bronte sagged back into the sofa.

"Bron, let's get you upstairs to the bed. You'll feel much more comfortable. Dev and I can carry you."

She had her eyes closed and her complexion looked gray. "It's a complicated birth, Max. Get a doctor to attend, please."

Sarah caught Max's look and nodded, then left the room to call Dr. Armitage again to let him know the turn of events and ask him how best to proceed. By the time Sarah returned to the living room, Devon and Max had carted Bronte upstairs, with Willa trailing behind for moral support. That left Marisa and James, Eliot and Abigail, and David Osborne all staring at one another in silent confusion.

Sarah looked around the room and caught Abigail's eye.

"Everything okay in here?"

Abigail snapped back to reality and stood up. "We're all set. I'll make sure everyone has a fresh drink. No worries. You do whatever needs doing and we'll all"—she looked around the motley guests—"be just fine. Please tell the cook to hold supper until whenever you think best."

"Okay," Sarah said. "I'll run upstairs to let Max know the doctor from Bognor Regis is on his way, and Dr. Armitage is coming out from London as quickly as possible. I'll also make a pass through the kitchens to let the cook know that dinner will need to be somewhat delayed."

After Sarah explained what was happening to the cook, the young kitchen maid muttered something to her superior. Upon receiving a gentle shove from the head cook, the woman stepped forward. "Miss Sarah?"

"Yes, Pam?"

"Well, I wanted to let you know I am a midwife and a doula. If you think Lady Bronte might welcome it"—she looked back at the cook, who gave her an encouraging lift of her chin—"I'd be happy to assist or—"

"Ah! You blessed woman. Come with me, this instant!"

"If I may? There are a few oils and things I might be able to bring along to help her relax."

"Of course. And something for Max wouldn't go amiss either."

The capable young woman grabbed a breadbasket and put in some dried lavender, some hempseed oil, some other herbs and small bottles that Sarah didn't recognize, and a stack of freshly pressed white cotton kitchen towels. Then she ducked into the pantry and came out with an unopened bottle of very old scotch. "For the duke," Pam said with a smile.

"Off we go then," said Sarah, gesturing with an open arm to move the girl along.

---

The physician from Bognor Regis happened to be attending a sick child in nearby Binsted. When he received the call from the hospital that he was needed at Dunlear, he was in attendance within fifteen minutes. Between his somber, traditional, no-nonsense organization, and sweet Pam's gentle ministrations to ease the tension in Bronte's back and legs, the whole scene in the ducal suite took on the aspect of a perfectly orchestrated play.

Bronte labored for another three hours, ample time for Dr. Armitage to make the trip from London, in possession of the neonatal oxygen tanks and other specialized equipment that might be required. In any event, nothing was needed to assist in the births.

Little Lady Sylvia arrived first, just before midnight, with an almost instantaneous demanding shriek that made an exhausted Bronte smile at how apt her chosen name already proved to be.

Bronte had assumed the two babes would slide out one after the other, like peas shelled from a fresh summer pod, but the doctor said it was not uncommon for hours, or in some extreme cases, even days to pass between the delivery of one twin and the next. Pam cleaned tiny Sylvia quickly and efficiently, wrapped her in tight, clean linen, and then handed her back to Bronte to nurse. Max crawled up on the bed alongside the two of them and watched as Sylvia's glassy but strangely probing eyes gazed first at Bronte, blinked slowly closed, then opened again to look at Max. She looked at him with a fierce curiosity, then her tiny lips began to purse and a wave of hungry fury flashed across her features.

"You'd better feed her, I think," Max whispered.

"You think?" Bronte laughed softly. She adjusted her breast to get the newborn situated for what she supposed would be days of fidgeting, fine-tuning, and micromanaging until they found the proper latch, as it had been with Wolf.

"Ow!" Bronte yelped, startling the baby and setting off a new wave of shrieking.

Pam walked quickly to the side of the bed. "May I?"

Bronte nodded.

"You need to let her know who's in charge, Lady Bronte, or she'll pick up bad habits right from the start."

Bronte looked at the lovely Pam as if she were an angel sent from heaven.

Pam smiled and treated Bronte's breast as if it were a loaf she were preparing in the kitchen. "Here, let me…" She brought baby Sylvia's squalling, open mouth to the nipple at an odd angle, then shoved the babe onto Bronte's breast with firm authority. Bronte looked down in surprised relief. Baby Sylvia was suckling with hearty satisfaction and there was no pain other than the residual sting of the original bite.

"Thank you, Pam," Bronte said, then looked back at the beautiful little baby and felt the familiar tears. "She's already a demanding little thing, isn't she?" Bronte whispered to Max.

He kissed Bronte's neck, then moved lower to kiss Sylvia's downy forehead. The baby's eyes flickered behind closed lids, acknowledging the soft attention. "She certainly is. I can't imagine where she gets it."

After the babe had taken her fill, and the first burst of new life was being overtaken by the subsequent exhaustion of her ordeal, Sylvia dozed happily off to sleep in her mother's arms, her tiny mouth agape like a little drunken sailor.

Bronte carefully handed the swaddled infant to her husband and sighed in exhausted pleasure. "I love you, Max."

As if on cue, Bronte's body went into labor again, this time producing a docile lamb after forty minutes of near-painless pushing and controlled breathing. Little Catherine was a tender, quiet morsel from the moment she emerged. Her eyes were serious and probing like her sister's had been, but they held a sweet curiosity as opposed to that regal insistence that Sylvia would possess for the rest of her days.

---

Downstairs, the strained interactions between Abigail, Eliot, James, and Marisa were slowly progressing beyond the initial wave of stunned confusion.

After Abigail had refilled all their glasses, Devon and Sarah returned with Willa and they all continued to stare at each other.

Eliot recovered his powers of speech first.

"Marisa, I think you and I should go speak privately—"

"I think that's a stupid idea—" James barked.

Marisa patted the fine nap of James's moleskin trousers and

looked up into his eyes with a tender affection that, Eliot remarked silently to himself, she'd never given to him. James scowled at Eliot and, then by association, at Abigail.

"What are you looking at me for?"

"You might have mentioned you were buying bags of clothes for *Eliot Cranbrook* when you came to the store today."

"I didn't lie to anyone about my name," Abigail retorted.

"Abigail!" It was Devon this time.

Abigail folded her arms across her chest. "Fine. I'll shut up."

Sarah stood up and offered to show Eliot and Marisa to a small den across the hall. Eliot gave Abigail a comforting squeeze on the shoulder and got up to leave the room. Marisa followed him slowly out and across the hall into the other room.

Abigail stared at James, her foot kicking in mild irritation, then crooked a tiny smile at the absurdity of it all. "Mary?"

"I thought you said you were going to shut up, Abby?" But James smiled a little bit too, because as awkward and raw as all of this felt right at this moment, he now realized that Marisa was well and truly free. Her only lingering hesitation had been tied up into something approximating guilt at abandoning the perfectly marriageable Eliot, but even *that* she had come to terms with. If they could all be honest, they might still have a perfectly good weekend ahead of them.

*Much more than just a weekend*, James thought.

Sarah came back into the living room and looked from Abigail to James, then across to Willa and David, then down toward Devon, who was sitting on the couch to her left.

Devon looked up at her with a wry look. "I am so relieved you and I never had any misunderstandings like this, aren't you, darling?"

Abigail started laughing, then James tried to stay angry and failed. Willa almost snorted her vodka out of her glass and grabbed at her husband's shirtsleeve to prevent herself from falling off the couch in a fit of hysterical laughter.

By the time Eliot and Marisa came back into the living room, the other six were laughing and talking as if nothing unusual had transpired. Eliot cleared his throat to let them know they were back in the room.

They all came to a stunned silence, as if on cue, and then Devon failed to repress a laugh and the rest of them disintegrated into uncontrollable laughter again. Eliot looked at Marisa and said, "Perhaps it is unwise to mix with this crew, but I fear it is too late to turn back now."

Abigail hopped up from her seat and crossed the long Aubusson carpet to take one of Eliot's hands between both of hers. After a few seconds, she let go with her right hand and reached across to Marisa. "I'm Abigail Heyworth. Nice to meet you, Marisa."

Marisa looked down at Abigail's small, firm hand for a second, then smiled and shook it. "Marisa Plataneau. The pleasure is all mine."

Devon stood up and turned to face them as he took Sarah's hand in his. "Now that all of the proper introductions have been made, shall we go in to dinner?"

David stood up and stretched his neck and shoulders as if he had just spent two hours sitting through a very boring Swedish film. "Finally." He yawned. "I'm starved."

The eight of them went into the dining room and enjoyed a very long, intoxicating meal. Hours later, when Max burst into the room to announce the arrival of Sylvia, imagining he would be met with a group of silent, hand-wringing brooders, he had to shout in order to make himself heard.

"What the hell?"

Sarah was wearing Devon's shirt, which, apparently, Devon no longer thought he required. Marisa was draped across James's lap with one hand around his neck, the other mysteriously absent below the tablecloth, and his tongue tracing the edge of her ear. Willa and Eliot were dancing their own uncoordinated version of the tango to the too-loud flamenco music, and David and Abigail were vehemently agreeing with one another about the absolute necessity of wearing socks with certain loafers.

"I know!" Abigail yelled to be heard. "The last thing I want to see is some man's pale bony—god-forbid hairy—ankle!"

Devon spotted Max first. "Hey Max! Where've you been? Dinner was delicious."

"I have been in the company of my wife as she labored to deliver my second child. Baby Sylvia was born healthy and hale in case anyone was wondering, but don't let me interrupt you." He was trying to be the picture of ducal chastisement, but it just came out as peevish and they all broke down into riotous laughter again.

"To Sylvia!"

"To Sylvia!"

"More champagne!" Devon called out to no one in particular.

Sarah poured a healthy measure of the Dom Perignon into a nearby glass of scotch after emptying the previous contents into the floral centerpiece. "Hereyougomax," she slurred as she handed him the thick-cut crystal lowball.

"Aren't you the picture of elegance, Sarah?"

She looked down at the pale blue shirt that hit her at the knees, and her bare feet beyond. "Why yes. Yes, I am," she agreed then skipped back to kiss Devon on the cheek.

Devon looked at his older brother and raised his glass. "Let us know when the next one comes down the pike, old man!"

Max chugged the champagne in a few quick pulls, then let the glass come down onto the centuries-old dining table with a solid clap of authority. "Apparently, I have gone to the trouble and worry of bringing children into this world, only to see them forced to ally themselves with a tribe of *infants*!" He stormed out of the room, pleased with the resulting stunned silence, then walked quicker as he heard the ensuing coughs bubble up into loud, unrestrained laughter.

When he returned an hour later, with news of Lady Catherine's safe arrival, everything in the dining room was much as he had left it.

Devon looked up. "That was fast! Did she pop out another one?"

"Yes, Devon. Bronte just popped out another one." Max turned to leave, exhausted and irritated.

Abigail ran up behind him and caught the back of his shirt. "Don't go, Max. Please. Come, celebrate with us. Bronte must be passed out by now—or you wouldn't have left her, of course."

Max looked at Abigail, finally happy in her own skin, then up to Eliot, who was sitting at the dining room table with his hand resting on the back of the chair where she had been sitting, as if he were protecting her space even in her short absence. James sat in one of the deep window seats with Marisa sound asleep in his lap, her body curled up next to him and her head resting on one thigh.

Max felt his shoulders settle and put one arm around Abigail's small frame. "All right, Abs. I think I will. It's all a bit much to process. Pour me something old and brown, please."

"Will do." She gave him a mock salute and went to the sideboard to fix him a celebratory scotch.

⁓

Abigail went to make drinks and tried to take in everything that had happened in the past few weeks. She was actually standing in what she still thought of as her parents' dining room, pouring her brother a congratulatory scotch to celebrate the births of his second and third children. The man she loved was splayed out across one of the dining room chairs, waiting for her, watching her; her other brother was besotted with his wife as the two of them mooned over one another at the far end of the table, Sarah in a mortifying state of half-dressed disarray.

And her cousin, James.

He was in a stupor of affection over his newfound Marisa. Whether the two of them would expire in a brief flame of passion or build upon this strange beginning, Abigail was not certain.

She dropped the ice cubes into a clean glass and chose a particularly delicious scotch in honor of babies Sylvia and Catherine. She smiled at the idea of Wolf playing big brother upon awaking tomorrow—this—morning. Abigail watched as the clear, caramel liquid drained into the waiting crystal and tried to honor her brother in this brief moment of service. She put the top back on the bottle of scotch then set the bottle back into place at the back of the aged mahogany sideboard that had served as the bar at Dunlear Castle for decades.

Abigail turned back toward Max, feeling the weight of her own glass and his in each of her hands, reminded of that warm night in Bequia a year ago. She walked with renewed purpose to stand next to him, then handed over the solid glass. "Here you are, Max. To new beginnings, eh?"

He looked at her with an exhausted but penetrating expression. "Well put, my lovely little sister. To new beginnings. May yours lead to many years of connubial bliss. May mine lead to… patience."

She smiled at his sweet toast and took a sip of her drink as he did the same.

"Let's go sit in the living room, shall we?" Max offered.

James looked up from his happy occupation of tracing the edge of Marisa's jawline with his thumb. "I think we'll head up to our rooms. But thanks for everything… and thanks again, Max. I'm sorry for the confusion  or the upset… or whatever. I'll see you in the morning." He moved Marisa gently off his thigh then swung her up into his arms. "I think it's best not to wake her, don't you?"

Max just smiled and raised his glass to James with the same pleased wishes, "To new beginnings."

"Just so," said James.

Sarah and Devon were equally spent, nearly falling off the edge of their chairs in the fast approaching posthilarity slumber.

"Take your wife to bed, Devon," Max ordered. "And you too, Osborne. Get Willa upstairs already. You will all be miserable in the morning. I suppose that is some consolation for your lack of propriety."

Willa and David weaved out of the room, their path leading in the general direction of the stairs, although their journey was marked by the occasional collision with the odd side table.

Eliot stood up to join Abigail and Max as the three of them walked toward the living room.

"Let's go into the den, shall we?" said Abigail. "So much more cozy." She smiled over her shoulder to catch Eliot's eye.

As they settled themselves into the smaller room, Eliot and Abigail curled up on the sofa and Max collapsed into the deep leather armchair.

Abigail began to question Max about Bronte's ordeal. "So, how was the delivery?"

"As Bronte would say, a fucking bloody mess." He tried to smile through the reenactment of his wife's notoriously crude manner of speech, but it wasn't enough to conceal the real worry that had plagued him for the past five hours.

Eliot squeezed Abigail's shoulder in what she suspected was some anticipatory show of husbandly camaraderie for her future childbearing.

"What are they like?" Abigail asked quietly. She had always been able to hold her liquor as well as the next longshoreman, and she felt a mellow quiet settle in upon the three of them as the antique mantel clock ticked toward two in the morning. She loved the protective feel of Eliot's arm around her shoulders—it was the future. And she loved the knowing glance of her brother's skeptical brow as he observed them—the very comforting past.

"You mean the babies?" Max asked.

Abigail nodded as she took a small sip of her drink.

"Already inclined to express their unique personalities. Sylvia was screaming her demands before the umbilical cord was cut, and Catherine waited until her big sister was fed and in bed before making her quiet, gentle entrance into the world. And once she arrived, Catherine was perfectly happy to look and listen until the world provided her with its bounty. Their time in the womb has probably defined them for life. Sylvia will devour. Catherine will abide."

A bright log broke, and the small fire crackled in the grate across the intimate wood-paneled room.

"I'm sorry again for all the mayhem, Max." Eliot's voice was low. "I hope our little scene wasn't to blame for the early onset of Bronte's labor."

Max waved his glass out in front of him to dismiss what Eliot had said. "Look. They were going to come. Especially Sylvia. I can almost believe that she was waiting until as many people as possible would be inconvenienced by her arrival before she decided to make her entrance. There's nothing any of us could have done or not done to alter that. But I appreciate the sentiment. Especially after all that insanity in the dining room."

Eliot dipped his head in a small apology, then spoke. "So, Max. While I've got you here in the postpartum lull, as it were, do you mind if I marry Abigail?"

Max held his glass a few inches from his mouth, paused in the midaction of taking a sip, then slowly lowered it back down, holding it in two hands at his lap. "Are you asking for her hand?"

"Yes. I think I am."

Abigail looked at Eliot as if he had lost his mind, then turned to Max and begged him with her eyes. She shook her head in a tiny no.

Max looked at her then at Eliot. "I suppose as head of this bizarre assortment of people otherwise known as a family, it should fall to me to make such life-altering decisions, but I could no more weigh in on the suitability of Abigail's spouse than I could perform a frontal lobotomy on a rhino. You are utterly and completely on your own, Eliot. Why you would ever want to dive into a gene pool of this— shall we say, eclectic?—scope… is beyond me, so I'm hard-pressed to accept or deny your suit. The mere fact that you remain interested after all you've seen of our putative mental health means that you're either very brave or very deranged. In either case, welcome." Max lifted his glass again, then brought it to his lips for the longed-for sip. After the warmth of the liquor reached his stomach, Max opened his eyes again. "On the other hand, I suppose it's worth finding out if you love her. Do you love Abigail, Eliot?"

Abigail's heart skipped the proverbial beat when Eliot paused to consider his reply.

"You know, Max. I'm not sure I do."

Max's eyes narrowed and Abigail stiffened in his arms. Eliot leaned in to kiss the warm exposed flesh of her neck then continued talking. "*Love* seems a small, mean little word sometimes, don't you think?"

Max shook the ice in his glass and thought of the woman in the bed upstairs who had just delivered his two children. "It is. Quite."

"It's a meager syllable to embody the full satisfaction of a man's soul. The final arrival at an end that could never be considered because of its seeming impossibility. I think I'd survive, walk the earth, whatever, without Abigail, but I don't think I would *live*. Does that make sense? Does that mean I *love* her?"

Abigail was grateful she was already on the couch because the lower half of her body was weak and useless. She burrowed her face into Eliot's chest and wished she could crawl up the face of him.

Max smiled again. "Yes. I think that's a rough approximation. Add in a dollop of stomach-flipping terror and the occasional loss of sanity and I think you're well on your way to a perfectly apt defini- tion of *love*."

# About the Author

Megan Mulry writes sexy, stylish, romantic fiction. *A Royal Pain*, Max and Bronte's story, was chosen as an NPR Best Book of 2012. She graduated from Northwestern University and then worked in publishing, including positions at *The New Yorker* and *Boston Magazine*. After moving to London, Mulry worked in finance and attended London Business School. She has traveled extensively in Asia, India, Europe, and Africa and now lives with her husband and children in Florida. You can visit her website at www.meganmulry.com or find her procrastinating on Twitter.

# If the Shoe Fits

## Megan Mulry

### The only thing worse than being in the spotlight is being kept in the dark...

With paparazzi nipping at his heels, Devon Heyworth, rakish brother of the Duke of Northrop, spends his whole life hiding his intelligence and flaunting his playboy persona. Fast cars and faster women give the tabloids plenty to talk about.

American entrepreneur Sarah James is singularly unimpressed with "The Earl" when she meets him at a wedding. But she's made quite an impression on him. When he pursues her all the way across the pond, he discovers that Miss James has no intention of being won over by glitz and glamour—she's got real issues to deal with, and the last thing she needs is larger-than-life royalty mucking about in her business...

### Praise for *A Royal Pain*:

"A romantic, fantastic, enchanting treat... Don't miss *A Royal Pain*!" —*Eloisa James,* New York Times *bestselling author of* The Ugly Duchess

"Megan Mulry is a must-read author. Highly recommended." —*Jennifer Probst,* New York Times *bestselling author of* The Marriage Mistake

### For more Megan Mulry books, visit:

www.sourcebooks.com

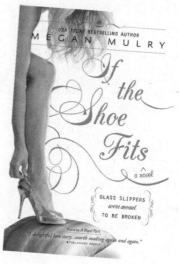